MURDER AT
THE RITZ

JIM ELDRIDGE

Allison & Busby Limited
11 Wardour Mews
London W1F 8AN
allisonandbusby.com

First published in Great Britain by Allison & Busby in 2021.

A CIP catalogue record for this book is available from
the British Library.

First Edition

ISBN 978-0-7490-2513-7

Typeset in 11/16 pt Adobe Garamond Pro by
Allison & Busby Ltd.

The paper used for this Allison & Busby publication
has been produced from trees that have been legally sourced
from well-managed and credibly certified forests.

Printed and bound by
CPI Group (UK) Ltd, Croydon, CR0 4YY

Once again, for Lynne,
without whom there'd be nothing

CHAPTER ONE

Tuesday 20th August 1940, London. 7.30 a.m.

The Hon. Edgar Walter Septimus Saxe-Coburg – better known to his colleagues at Scotland Yard as Detective Chief Inspector Coburg – pulled up in his Bentley outside the small terraced house of his sergeant, Ted Lampson, in Purchese Street, Somers Town. Lampson, a stocky, muscular man in his early thirties with a boxer's face, a bent nose and one ear flattened, was standing on the pavement with his ten-year-old son, Terry. The boy was looking up beyond the silver barrage balloons that hung in the sky over London, tethered to the ground by their steel cables, staring at the air battle going on in the sky as two Spitfires attacked a German bomber.

Lampson hurried over to the car, a concerned look on his face.

'What's up, guv'nor?' he asked. 'I was just leaving to get the bus to the Yard.'

'Which is why I called,' said Coburg, getting out of the

car. 'Change of plan. We've got to go to the Ritz.'

Coburg was in his early forties, taller than his sergeant and dressed with more elegance – the sign of a good tailor. A streak of white ran from front to back at one side of his thick dark hair, the result of an old war wound.

Lampson's face lit up into a smile. 'For breakfast?'

'You'll be lucky,' said Coburg. 'You ought to get a phone put in, then I could have called you.'

'Can't afford one, guv,' said Lampson. He turned towards his son and shouted, 'You got your gas mask, Terry?'

Terry opened his jacket to show the gas mask in its holder dangling from around his neck.

Coburg gestured towards Terry, his turn now to look concerned. 'You sure he should be standing there?' he asked. 'He should be at the shelter.'

'I was just making sure he went,' said Lampson.

'Not well enough,' commented Coburg.

'That's a Dornier!' shouted Terry excitedly. 'A Do 17. It carries over 2,000 pounds of bombs.'

As they looked up, one of the Spitfires let burst a tracer of bullets that ripped into one of the German bomber's two engines, which suddenly poured smoke, first grey then black, and flames could be seen licking at the plane's wing.

'It's going down!' yelled Terry delightedly.

'For God's sake, get in the car!' barked Coburg, pulling open the rear door.

As Lampson pushed his son into the rear of the car, Coburg asked: 'Where's the nearest shelter?'

A woman had appeared from the house next door.

'What's going on?' she demanded. 'What's that posh car doing outside my house?'

'It's an air raid, Mrs Smith,' said Lampson. 'Didn't you hear the sirens?'

Mrs Smith looked at them, uncomprehending, then announced: 'I haven't got my hearing aid.'

With that she started to return to the house, but Coburg stopped her and steered her back towards the car.

'It's an air raid!' he shouted.

He ushered her into the rear of the car next to Terry, pushed the door shut and slid behind the steering wheel, as Lampson got into the passenger seat.

'Where's the nearest shelter?' Coburg asked again.

'Maples depository, Pancras Road,' said Lampson. 'Just round the corner.'

Coburg looked out of his window and saw the German bomber, now engulfed in flames, hurtling down towards the ground.

'It's going to hit somewhere over the Caledonian Road,' said Lampson.

'If it's still got its bomb load on it's going to make a hell of a hole when it does,' said Coburg. 'I'm not taking a chance on another coming down before we get you to the shelter.'

He accelerated, taking care not to run into the pedestrians who were heading for the shelter on foot.

'I've never bin in a Bentley before,' said Terry. 'You must have a lot of money, Mr Coburg.'

'Don't be cheeky, Terry,' his father snapped at him.

'I shouldn't have left my hearing aid behind,' said Mrs Smith. 'I won't be able to cope without it.'

'I'll look after you, Mrs Smith,' Terry shouted to her.

Coburg pulled the car to a halt outside Maples large

furniture depository, whose basement was doubling as an air-raid shelter. People were still hurrying in, guided by uniformed air raid wardens.

'Get in there quick!' said Lampson. 'And look out for your gran and grandad! They'll be looking after you.'

Terry opened the door and slid out of the car, then helped Mrs Smith out. Coburg waited until he was sure the pair had entered the depository before setting off again.

'You should have sent Terry away like the other evacuees,' said Coburg.

'I did,' said Lampson. 'He went off with all the others, his name on a brown cardboard label pinned to his coat, but I brought him back two months later. The place he was staying in was rotten. The people treated him cruel, like an unpaid slave. I wasn't having that.'

'It's still dangerous him being in London,' insisted Coburg. 'Haven't you got family somewhere outside London you can send him to?'

'No,' said Lampson. 'We're all Londoners. I've got an uncle and aunt in Ramsgate, but they're too old to handle Terry. I've also got a cousin in Kent, but as he lives near Biggin Hill that's not a good idea at the moment.'

True, thought Coburg. The airfields of Kent were being bombed on a regular basis. It was a rarity that a German plane came as far as London, as that one had this morning. All the intelligence suggested that Hitler's orders were to put the airfields out of action and destroy the RAF so that he could invade from the sea. Perhaps the pilot overshot his target.

'I was thinking of joining the Local Defence Volunteers,' said Lampson.

"It's called the Home Guard now, Ted,' said Coburg. 'Churchill renamed it. Anyway, I'd have thought you had enough to do already. You've got your job, and also your son to take care of.'

'My mum and dad keep a good eye on Terry,' said Lampson. 'They do it during the day.'

'Which is why he needs you when you're not at work.'

'Other blokes do it,' countered Lampson.

'Most of them are retired people. Former soldiers with time on their hands.'

'Not all,' said Lampson. 'My neighbour was talking to me about the Somers Town Home Guard. He's a plumber and he's in it, and he's married with five kids. He goes to all the sessions, the practices and meetings and that.'

'With five kids he's possibly glad to get out of the house,' commented Coburg.

'Yeh, but I feel I ought to be doing something for the war effort,' said Lampson. 'I tried to join up but they wouldn't take me because of the fact that my wife had died, so I was Terry's only parent.'

'Those are the rules,' said Coburg. 'And quite right, in my opinion. Every child should have at least one parent living. What would it do for Terry if you went off in the army and got yourself killed?'

'You can get killed here,' insisted Lampson. 'Fire-watching. I know of two blokes who became volunteer firemen and were killed when the building collapsed on them.' He looked accusingly at Coburg as he added: 'And I don't know why you're so against me serving, guv. You volunteered in the last lot.'

'I did. And I got shot.' Then he added, in a more

conciliatory tone: 'Not that that would have stopped me. The difference was that I wasn't married, I had no children depending on me. We're all doing our bit in different ways. Like now, we've got a dead body to take care of.'

'It's not the same, though, is it? If the Germans invade, we need men to stop them. And not just on the beaches, but in towns and cities. They reckon they'll come down by parachute in their thousands.'

'Yes, I agree, I think that's likely,' said Coburg. 'And if it happens, I'll be there too, with a gun and whatever else is to hand to defend us. At the moment, my faith is in the RAF blowing German bombers out of the sky and shooting down their fighter planes. So long as those boys can keep the Luftwaffe at bay, I believe Hitler will hold his invasion fleet back.'

'His fleet's all ready around Calais,' said Lampson. 'Hundreds of ships and thousands of soldiers. My uncle in Ramsgate says you can see 'em through a telescope.'

Coburg shook his head. 'It's twenty-five miles of choppy sea across the Channel, at risk from attacks by the air and our navy when they get close to the Kent coast. The Germans are methodical. I know, I fought them for nearly a year in the first lot. They don't rush in unless they're sure of victory. Hitler will put everything into trying to destroy the RAF, as he's doing now, before he unleashes his invasion fleet.' He gestured upwards with one hand. 'Those are the guys who need our support. The ones in their Hurricanes and Spitfires riding shotgun on our behalf. At the moment they're our first – and only – line of defence.'

CHAPTER TWO

Coburg led the way as he and Lampson passed through the main doors into the luxurious marble-floor foyer of the Ritz Hotel, then made for the long, curving glass-topped desk to the right. George Criticos, the hall porter, stood there resplendent in his dark blue frock coat adorned at the collar and cuffs with gold braid, the living embodiment of the elegance that was the Ritz from his pomaded dark hair down to his highly polished patent leather shoes.

'Mr Edgar!' greeted George with a broad smile. 'Good to see you again!'

'Good morning, George,' said Coburg, shaking the man's hand. 'This is my Sergeant, Ted Lampson.'

'Mr Lampson. A pleasure. Any colleague of Mr Edgar's is very welcome here.'

'Did our uniformed officer arrive? I phoned the local station to ask them to send someone.'

'He did indeed. A constable. He's guarding the door of the suite where the body was found.'

'Has the doctor been?'

'He's upstairs, examining the body. Dr Matthews.'

Thank God for that, thought Coburg. Rob Matthews was very competent and easy to get on with, not like some of his colleagues. Dr Alexander Stewart was one of Coburg's particular bête noires, an elderly Scot who seemed to have a loathing for all things that weren't Edinburgh. Coburg had often wondered why Dr Stewart didn't return to his favourite city if he detested everywhere else so much, but when he'd made discreet enquiries he discovered that the people of Edinburgh, at least the medical authorities, considered Stewart to be an arrogant and bullying pain in the rectum. He'd left the city in high dudgeon in protest at what he considered their insolent attitude towards him and decided to inflict himself on London.

'In whose suite was the body found?'

'One of the suites belonging to King Zog of Albania and his party.'

'*One* of the suites?' queried Coburg.

'The royal family has taken over the whole of the third floor,' explained George. 'They are a large party. As well as King Zog and his wife, Queen Géraldine, and their baby son, Prince Leka, there are the King's six sisters, three nephews and two nieces, along with a twenty-strong retinue of advisers, courtiers and bodyguards.'

'In whose actual suite was the body found?'

'One of the courtiers. He isn't there at the moment, nor, so I'm told, was he there during the incident. It was one of the maids who discovered the body when she went in to clean. She found a man who'd had his throat cut lying on the floor, and her screams brought some of the hotel staff.'

'Does anyone know who the dead man was?'

George shook his head. 'Everyone claims they have no idea who he is, or what he was doing in the suite. The manager ordered everything to be left as it was until the police arrived. He asked for you particularly.' Then he added, in low tones: 'He will be most grateful if the body can be removed as soon as possible. It seems the carpet will need to be replaced, and that needs to be arranged as a matter of urgency.'

'Thank you, George. We'll see what we can do to speed things up.'

As Coburg and Lampson headed for the lift, the sergeant grumbled: 'Replace a carpet! Why don't they just clean it?'

'This is the Ritz, Ted. Make do and mend isn't for them or their clientele. They expect only the best, and they're prepared to pay for it.'

'Huh! How the other half live!' Lampson commented sourly.

The uniformed constable on guard outside the suite saluted as Coburg and Lampson approached, and handed the key to the chief inspector.

'No one's tried to come in, sir,' he told them.

'Thank you, Constable,' said Coburg.

They let themselves into the suite, which was the epitome of opulence. The only jarring note to the otherwise perfect decor was the body of a young man, dressed in what appeared to be an elegant dark suit, sprawled on his back on the carpeted floor, one arm flung out. He was of medium height, thin, deathly pale, clean-shaven, his longish dark brown hair curling just over his ears. Dr Rob Matthews, a man in his early thirties was kneeling beside the body and looked up at Coburg and Lampson.

'Bit of a messy one,' he commented.

The carpet area around the dead man's neck and shoulders bore a large bloodstain, with more splashes visible all around.

'That's quite a spread,' said Coburg. 'Must've hit an artery.' He turned to Lampson and asked: 'Still think it can be easily cleaned?'

'No,' Lampson admitted. 'It'll always be seen. Maybe next time they'll put down a carpet that's better suited. A crimson one.'

Dr Matthews got to his feet. 'Well, there's not much more for me to do here,' he said, putting his equipment into his case. 'I've arranged for him to be taken to University College Hospital, so can I leave you to phone them to send an ambulance for him when you've finished?'

'No problem,' said Coburg. 'Time of death?'

'From the blood clots, the state of rigor, I'd think some time during the early hours of this morning. I'll know more when I get him to the morgue. Just to let you know, I won't be starting work on him until later this afternoon. I've got a busy schedule of patients to deal with today, living ones who I hope to keep in that condition.' He headed for the door with a wave of farewell. 'I'll leave this one to you.'

Once the doctor had left, Coburg stood examining the scene, particularly the large bloodstain.

'Four different sets of footprints,' he said. 'Two types

of boots, two of shoes. Assuming one is the doctor's and the maid didn't come this far, that means three men were involved.'

He moved nearer to the body, to the side away from the area of blood, knelt down and began to examine the dead man, while Lampson took out a notepad and pencil ready to jot down any salient facts his boss spotted.

'Age: mid-twenties, is my guess,' said Coburg. He turned back the lapel of the man's jacket. 'Burman's,' he said. 'Theatrical tailors.' He looked at the man's shoes. 'The shoes don't match the suit. That's smart and cut to perfection. His shoes are clean, but look at the soles. They've been re-soled and look like it needs to be done again.'

'So, dressed up to look like money, but piss-poor.'

Coburg went through the man's pockets looking for a wallet or some form of identification.

'Nothing to show who he was.'

'Reckon someone took his wallet? A robbery?'

'Judging by the fact his shoes needed repairing, I doubt if there was much money in it. No, it was taken to stop us finding out who he is.' He bent down and studied the man's face, gently running a fingertip around his ears and eyes before putting his finger to his nose.

'Traces of make-up around his eyes and ears.'

'An actor of some kind?' suggested Lampson. 'That would fit with the suit being from a theatrical tailor.'

'Possibly,' said Coburg. 'Or it could have something to do with the Pink Sink.'

'What's the Pink Sink?' asked Lampson.

'It's a club for homosexuals in the Ritz's basement,' said Coburg.

Lampson looked discomfited. 'And the hotel allows it?' he asked, indignantly. 'It's against the law!'

'The activity may be illegal, but it's a private club on private premises.'

'So?' demanded Lampson. 'Two clubs in Soho were shut down last month for that sort of thing.'

'True, but I expect those two clubs didn't have the same kind of influential people among their clientele,' said Coburg. 'The Pink Sink is the haunt of some very high-ranking military types, not to mention MPs and top civil servants, as well as lesser ranks and waiters and such.'

'Disgusting!' snorted Lampson. 'They ought to arrest 'em all.'

'If they did that, half the military top brass and a quarter of the Cabinet would be in jail,' said Coburg.

'How come you know so much about it?' asked Lampson suspiciously.

'Before the war, I had friends for whom the Ritz was their home from home. Not the Pink Sink, rather the Palm Court and the Rivoli bar, which is where the straights gather, but I learnt what went on. You never know when it might come in useful.'

Lampson nodded. 'Like now. So d'you reckon this dead bloke was one?'

'It's possible,' said Coburg. 'But if so, the question is, what was he doing in one of the Albanian royal family's suites?'

'He could be Albanian,' said Lampson.

'He could indeed. We'll get a photograph of him and pass it around the King's retinue, see if anyone recognises him. In the meantime, let's go and have a word with George.'

'The hall porter?' asked Lampson. 'What will he know?'

'Everything,' said Coburg with a smile. 'He's much more than just your regular hall porter. He's been here as long as I've been coming here. He's known affectionately as George of the Ritz across four continents. He's trusted by everyone, the guests as well as the hotel management. Royalty, millionaire businessmen, politicians – they all know and trust him. And there's nothing that goes on in this hotel he isn't aware of.'

Returning to the lobby, Coburg telephoned Scotland Yard asking for a photographer to be sent to take some photos of the dead man. 'And as soon as you can,' urged Coburg. 'Send Duncan Rudd if he's free.' He replaced the receiver and turned to the hall porter.

'Once we get some pictures of him we'll be able to move the body and return your hotel to you, George,' Coburg told him. 'As soon as the photographer arrives, can you put a call through to University College Hospital and ask them to send an ambulance to pick up the body? Quote Dr Matthews' name. They'll know the drill.'

'Will do,' said George.

'Thank you,' said Coburg. 'One last thing. What can you tell us about King Zog and his retinue?'

George shot a wary and inquisitive look towards Lampson, to which Coburg said: 'I assure you, George, Ted is the perfect image of confidentiality. I'd trust him with my life.'

Reassured, George nodded, then told them: 'As you probably know, King Zog is the dethroned King of Albania. He and his family fled their home country last

19

year in the spring just a day before Mussolini's troops invaded. They've journeyed throughout Europe and ended up in Paris, managing to escape to London just before the Germans invaded. I believe they were helped to flee by a British Intelligence officer, Commander Fleming.'

'Ian Fleming?'

George nodded. 'They learnt that Mussolini's troops were about to invade their country. But the risk to them wasn't just from the Italians. King Zog had been the target of assassination attempts on many occasions.'

'Who by?'

'The political opposition in Albania. Also a group calling itself the Bashkimi Kombëtar, anti-Zog activists living in Austria. There was one attempt in which Zog was shot twice, but survived.'

'Amazing!' muttered Lampson.

'And now? I note he's got quite a large number of bodyguards with him here.'

'He has, but he's also able to take care of himself. I hear that he killed some of those who plotted against his life.'

'You mean he had his bodyguards kill them?' pressed Coburg.

'In some cases, but I believe he took care of some of his would-be killers personally.'

'He sounds like a dangerous man.'

'Not really, just a man defending himself.'

'So long as he doesn't try it in this country,' said Coburg.

George then leant forward and added in a conspiratorial tone: 'The most interesting aspect is it's said that he brought two million in gold bullion and American dollars with him, reportedly taken from the Albanian National

Bank. It's kept in strong boxes in his suite, and every now and then the King's sister takes some to a bank and changes it into sterling.'

'Two million,' said Coburg. 'There's a motive for murder. It would help if I looked at your guest list, just in case any known names leap out.'

'Of course,' said George. 'I expected that and made a copy for you.'

He took some handwritten pages from his desk and handed them to Coburg, who ran his eye quickly over them.

'It looks as if you're full,' he commented. 'Every room and suite occupied, so the war doesn't seem to be affecting you.'

George shook his head sadly. 'Not as far as clients arriving, but it's a disaster from a staff point of view. It was bad enough when all our German and Austrian staff were arrested and taken away, but now, since Mussolini declared war on England, all our Italian staff have been interned as well. Waiters, chefs, so many Italians worked here. And the irony is that most of them are anti-fascists who fled Italy to escape from Mussolini and his thugs. Just like so many of the Germans we employed were refugees from the Nazis. And now they're all locked up in prison camps.'

'Hopefully the authorities will get that sorted out soon,' said Coburg.

'If there's any chance of you having word . . .' said George.

'I doubt if the powers that be will listen to me,' said Coburg. 'I'm just a lowly policeman.'

'A detective chief inspector, with some important connections,' murmured George, appeal in his voice.

21

Coburg smiled. 'Not as important as many wish. But I'll certainly mention it to one or two people who might be able to push things along.'

'Thank you.'

CHAPTER THREE

As they made their way back up to the third floor in the lift, Lampson ventured his view: 'I reckon you hit the nail on the head, guv. The murder is connected with the money this King Zog's got stashed. I know people who'd kill someone for a fiver, so the chance of a pop at two million – it's got to be the motive.'

'The question is: was this man killed trying to steal it or trying to stop it being stolen?' mused Coburg.

'Trying to nick it,' said Lampson firmly. 'If he got done by the thieves he'd be part of the King's crowd, so someone would know who he is.' He gave a thoughtful frown. 'Unless they're lying. Covering up.'

'Yes, I wondered that,' said Coburg. 'In Eastern Europe things are often handled with discretion to avoid scandal.'

'Leaving a dead body lying around doesn't show much discretion,' commented Lampson.

'Perhaps they went out to make arrangements to dispose of the body when the maid stumbled upon him and raised the alarm.'

'It's all a bit iffy, guv,' said Lampson doubtfully.

'Yes, it is,' agreed Coburg.

The lift stopped, and they returned to the door of the suite and the waiting constable.

'A photographer's on his way, Constable,' Coburg informed him. 'Once he's done his work the body will be removed and then you'll be free to return to your duties.'

'Thank you, sir. My sergeant will be relieved about that. We're short-handed today.'

'The war makes demands on us all,' commented Coburg sagely.

Back inside the suite, Lampson looked again at the blood and commented: 'One thing's for sure, he was definitely killed here, not somewhere else and then dumped in this suite.'

'But are the King and his retinue involved?' mused Coburg. 'Or is it nothing to do with them at all?'

Out of the blue, Lampson asked: 'Who's this bloke Ian Fleming? When that George said to you about him, it struck me you knew him.'

'In a way,' said Coburg. 'We were at the same school, Eton, but not at the same time. He's nine years younger than me. But our paths crossed infrequently at social functions from time to time.'

'What's he like? George said he helped smuggle the King and his mob out of France, and while the Germans were there. He must have guts.'

Coburg nodded. 'Oh yes, he's got guts all right.'

24

'You don't sound like you like him much,' said Lampson.

'Oh, I do. He's very likeable, in an arrogant way. I just think he's dangerous. He takes risks.'

'It's war. People take risks in war. You did in the last one, guv, from what I've heard.' He paused, then added carefully, watching his inspector the whole time to check that he wasn't overstepping the mark: 'They say you got shot nearly to bits while leading a charge against a German machine-gun post just a week before the Armistice.'

'Hardly shot to bits, Ted. And I survived. Many didn't. And that wasn't so much taking a risk as following orders. There was a job to be done. Fleming takes risks just for the hell of it.'

'But he got the King and everyone else out.'

'Yes, that can't be denied,' said Coburg. 'If I see him again, I'll compliment him.'

There was a knock on the door. Lampson opened it and Duncan Rudd entered, carrying a large camera. He grinned at the detectives.

'Here we are again, Chief Inspector. Another dead body.' He looked down at the spread-eagled man with a frown of disapproval. 'Someone's made a right mess of that carpet!'

'They have indeed, Duncan,' said Coburg. 'I'm glad you were available. Well, I think the sergeant and I have seen enough. Can you get me the photos as soon as you can? An ambulance should be on its way from UCH to remove the corpse, but if they arrive before you're finished, don't let them rush you. You know what some of these ambulance crews can be like, all urgency and speed. In this case, there's no need for it. He's dead.'

'Trust me, I'll make sure I get some good pictures,' Rudd assured him.

Coburg nodded, then he and Lampson left the photographer to his work, with Coburg giving the constable a last word. 'You've done a good job today,' he complimented him. 'You can tell your sergeant I said so.'

As they left the Ritz and headed for where they'd parked the Bentley, Coburg asked casually: 'D'you fancy taking the wheel back to the Yard, Ted? Give the old girl a spin.'

Lampson's face lit up with delight, as Coburg expected it would. Lampson was a demon with cars, having been a trainee mechanic before he joined the police, and Coburg knew he would love a car of his own, but his wages as a detective sergeant didn't extend to it. Coburg was only able to get away with driving the Bentley because he'd managed to persuade the top brass at Scotland Yard to designate it as an official police car, but he knew that couldn't last for much longer. Questions were already being asked, and jealous frowns directed at him whenever he pulled up at Scotland Yard in it.

'Thanks, guv.' Lampson smiled as he slid behind the steering wheel and started the engine. Coburg made himself comfortable on the passenger seat.

'Take the opportunity while it lasts,' said Coburg. 'I calculate another week if we're lucky and then the old dear will have to go into a garage for the duration, and we'll be driving around in an official police car.'

'Killjoys,' grumbled Lampson. 'It'll be a dreadful waste to have this beauty sitting idle in a garage.'

'Rules are rules, Ted,' said Lampson. 'And we of all people have to be seen to keep them. We've had a good run for our money.'

Coburg loved driving the car, especially as petrol rationing had driven most private cars off the road, making London virtually a traffic-free zone except for official vehicles, but his decision to let Lampson drive them back to Scotland Yard wasn't entirely altruistic. His sergeant's mention of the injuries he'd received right at the end of the First World War had brought the whole thing back to him and he was worried that those memories might impede his driving. At times, when he did think about it, too often he drifted off and was back there again, twenty-two years ago at the Sambre–Oise canal.

When he thought about it now, it was ludicrous. Nineteen years old and a captain in the army, by virtue of the Officers Training Corps at Eton. Giving orders to men in their twenties and thirties, any one of whom had more experience of the war than him, who'd only been in France since January 1918. But he'd done his part, luckily only suffering minor injuries, until that final battle of the Sambre–Oise Canal. 4th November 1918. One week before the Armistice and the end of the war. They'd been told they had the enemy on the run, and that may well have been the case, but at Sambre–Oise the Germans had put up a fierce resistance as they fought to prevent the Allies getting to the canal, let alone across it. For years afterwards he'd often wake at night, drenched in sweat as he relived that attack.

It had been Coburg who'd blown his whistle to signal the assault at dawn, before being the first to ascend the wooden ladder out of the deep, muddy trench where they'd spent the night. Ahead of them was the German defensive line on the other side of the canal, their target, but first they had to cross open fields to get there.

Tacka-tacka-tacka-tacka! The German machine guns opened fire and bullets tore into Coburg's unit. Some of the men either side of him stumbled and fell, but he kept going, urging the others on, ducking low, weaving from side to side, firing all the time. Bullets thudded into the earth at his feet, others sailing past him, so close that one tore at the sleeve of his uniform.

Coburg fired back and kept running. The canal was in sight now and he made for the lock, but the Germans had put a machine gun inside the lockhouse and the rapid machine-gun fire was tearing into their advance, more soldiers falling the nearer they got to the canal. He needed to put that machine gun out of action.

He dropped down to the ground, laying flat, using what he could as cover, a small bush, before getting to his feet and running, zigzagging, firing the whole time. Around him men were collapsing, chunks of flesh coming off them, spattering blood, and suddenly there was a crash against his chest and he felt as if he'd been ripped open. He fell, sinking down, and his last thought was: *This is how I die . . .*

He was told he was in the medical tent for two days, with the expectation that he wouldn't make it. But he did, coming round to a smell of blood and vomit and disinfectant and screams of pain.

'You were lucky,' said the doctor who examined him. 'The bullets hit you on the right side of your chest, taking out the lung. If you'd been hit on the left side you'd be dead, heart riddled like a colander. But that's the wonder of the human body. We've got two of lots of different organs and at a pinch we can survive with just one. But the heart and brain, they're different. Only one of each, and get a bullet through that and it's almost certain goodbye.'

And so he'd lost a lung, which was why he'd been turned down for active service this time around. 'You're forty years old with one lung. You can't be risked. You're worth more doing what you do here in Blighty, keeping law and order on the Home Front. That's vital to the war effort.'

Twenty-two years ago, and sometimes it seemed like it was only yesterday. The war to end war, they'd called it. It was estimated that at least eighteen million soldiers had died, and they said that such a catastrophically high death rate – a whole generation virtually wiped out – would ensure such a war would never happen again. Yet here they were again, and against the same enemy: Germany.

On their return to Scotland Yard, Coburg delegated Lampson to go to the office they shared to check for any messages, while he reported on the events of the morning to his immediate superior, Superintendent Allison. Like Coburg, Edward Allison had served in the First World War, in his case surviving the carnage of Gallipoli. Half a million Allied troops fighting against half a million Turkish, with each side suffering huge casualties before the bloody conclusion and the evacuation of the defeated and weary Allied forces from the beaches of the peninsula. As briefly as he could, Coburg related the salient details of the hotel murder to the superintendent: the anonymous dead man in the King's suite and the rumours of the valuables kept there.

'Two million in gold bullion and cash,' said Allison. 'A motive for murder.'

'Indeed,' said Coburg. 'And I agree it seems the most likely. But there are other things going on at the Ritz at this moment, any of which could result in someone being killed. For one thing, there's a cocktail bar in the Ritz's basement, known as the Pink Sink. It's where politicians and senior civil servants make homosexual assignations with military personnel, as well as some of the hotel staff. So, the threat of blackmail is a possibility. And blackmailers also often end up dead.'

'And there's no clue as to the dead man's identity, or why he was found in the King's suite?' asked Allison.

'I'm afraid not,' said Coburg.

Allison frowned. 'I suspect this may be one of those cases where we spend an awful lot of time on it and come up with nothing,' he said. 'Particularly as it involves the King of Albania, who I understand to be a very private person and I assume will not like too many questions asked, especially if these reports about the fortune hidden in his rooms are true. There is also the likelihood that the Foreign Office will be involved, not to mention MI5. Plus, the business about this Pink Sink establishment. This could get very messy, Coburg. Political intrigue can be very dangerous, especially when there's a war on.'

'Yes, sir. What do you suggest our course of action should be?'

'We have a dead man and no one knows who he is. No one's reported him missing. He could well be an alien. By all accounts King Zog's retinue are keen for the matter to be closed.'

'So, you think we should call the case closed?'

'No, no, just . . . put it to one side. Perhaps things will turn up.'

Coburg was just about to leave the office and return to catch up with Lampson when Allison stopped him.

'There's, ah . . . one more thing, Chief Inspector,' said the superintendent, and the hesitancy of his tone gave Coburg a warning that something unpleasant was about to follow.

'Sir?' he asked, doing his best to stop his apprehension from showing. What was it? Bad news, for sure. Had something happened to his brother, Charles, in the POW camp? Had he attempted to escape? It would be the sort of thing he'd try and get himself killed doing it.

'Your Bentley,' said Allison awkwardly.

'Sir?' queried Coburg again.

'There have been questions,' said Allison, unable to look Coburg in the eye. 'In the House. Apparently there was an article about you in the *Daily Worker*. I don't know if you saw it?'

'No, sir. I rarely have time to read the papers and so far I haven't included the *Daily Worker*.'

'The article doesn't name you, but it mentions a high-born aristocrat working as a chief inspector in the police force who's allowed to drive his own luxury Bentley around while ordinary people are barred from running a private car.'

'It was agreed my car would serve as a police vehicle, sir, thereby freeing up police cars for use.'

'Yes, that was the agreement, but it seems the assistant commissioner was hauled before a committee of MPs and grilled about the matter as a result of one of them seeing the article.'

'I understand, sir. The Bentley goes into a garage and stays under wraps.' Then Coburg asked: 'Out of curiosity, sir, do you happen to know which particular MP raised the issue with the AC?'

'If you're thinking that it was the result of the article in the *Daily Worker*, it must have been a Labour MP, then I can assure you that wasn't the case.' he hesitated, then said: 'I believe it was the Right Honourable Wister Gormley.'

Yes, thought Coburg. Gormley, who'd smashed his own cars up, the Rolls and the Bentley, both times while drunk, and who'd appealed to Coburg to take care of the charge of dangerous driving, saying, 'After all, we were at school together.' Coburg had refused, insisting the law applied to everyone. So this was Gormley's revenge. Which was hardly a surprise. Wister Gormley had been a rat when they were at school, and he was still a rat.

'Thank you, sir. You can tell the AC I'll have the Bentley garaged and arrange for a car from the pool for myself and Sergeant Lampson.'

Lampson's reaction when he told him about the Bentley was exactly as Coburg had thought it would be: sour and bitter.

'Things are in short supply, Ted,' Coburg reminded him. 'That's why we've got rationing. And petrol for private cars was the first thing to go.'

'Some people get away with it,' he grumbled. 'Look at those rich types motoring around in Daimlers and I don't know what.'

'Official business, I expect,' sighed Coburg.

'Official business, my arse!' snorted Lampson. 'Everyone's got a ration book with a limit on how much they can buy. Half a pound of bacon a week, a pound of sugar, a shilling's worth of meat, half a pound of butter, if you can afford it. Me and Terry use margarine instead. All right it don't taste as good, they say it's made from whale oil, and it's true it's got a bit of a fishy taste, but we can get twelve ounces for a coupon instead of only half a pound of butter.' He snorted angrily. 'But I bet you them MPs and lords and ladies don't have the same restrictions!' Then he looked at Coburg and added awkwardly: 'Begging your pardon, guv, I didn't mean you when I talked about lords and ladies.'

'I am not a lord, Ted. My brother is a duke, but that's because our father was, and I assure you I have a ration book the same as everyone else. And I stick to it.'

'You may, but I bet not all the top nobs do. They keep their good cars.'

'I expect you're right,' agreed Coburg, used to his sergeant venting his feelings about the unfairness of society. 'But the bottom line is the Bentley goes in the garage. I'll let you select the best car from the pool, otherwise we'll be scrabbling for the leftovers every time we need a car and end up with the one with flat tyres and a dodgy gear box. I'll sign the requisition. If you like, you can keep it at your place, if you don't mind picking me up in the mornings.'

Lampson shook his head. 'Not a good idea, guv. Somers Town is all right for me, but I wouldn't park a car there. Not overnight. Not even a police car.'

'Yes, I take your point. All right. Sort one out and once it's here we'll do a two-car run and put the Bentley in dock. By the way, it looks as if the dead man at the Ritz is going to be put on the backburner. The super thinks the fact we don't know who he is and royalty and the intelligence services might be involved could be a complication we don't need. He also thinks there's not a lot of chance of us solving the case.'

'That's not much of a vote of confidence,' grunted Lampson.

'No, but with a war on, I'm sure there'll be plenty to keep us busy.'

The phone rang, and Lampson picked it up. 'Detective Chief Inspector Coburg's office.' A frown passed across his face, then he said: 'Yes, sir. He's here. One moment and I'll put you on to him.'

He put his hand over the receiver and whispered to Coburg: 'It's the secretary to King Zog. A Count Ahmed. He has a message from the King.'

Coburg took the phone. 'Detective Chief Inspector Coburg speaking.'

'Chief Inspector, this is Count Idjbil Ahmed, private secretary to His Majesty, King Zog of Albania. We understand that you were at the Ritz today investigating the dead man found in one of the suites.'

'Yes, Count Ahmed, that is correct,' said Coburg, wondering where all this was leading.

'His Royal Majesty, King Zog, would like to invite you to meet him to discuss the situation. Would one-thirty be convenient?'

Coburg looked at the clock, which showed twelve-thirty.

'One-thirty will be excellent,' he said. 'Tell His Majesty I look forward to meeting him.'

He hung up the phone and grinned at Lampson.

'I think we might be back on the case.'

CHAPTER FOUR

King Zog sat in a high-backed armchair so ornately decorated that Coburg wondered if the Ritz had managed to find a replica of the Albanian throne for their royal guest. One of the King's bodyguards stood just behind the gilded chair and slightly to one side, his grim face fixed on Coburg. Another bodyguard stood by the door to the suite, one hand poised over the inside of his bulky jacket, where Coburg assumed he kept a pistol.

The King was tall and slim with a pencil-thin moustache, giving the impression of a matinee film idol, made more so by the elegant way he smoked his cigarette. He regarded Coburg guardedly, obviously curious about this detective chief inspector.

'I am told that you are a member of the British royal family,' said Zog.

Coburg weighed up how to answer. The suggestion that he

might be connected to the House of Windsor was obviously the reason the King had invited him, royal to royal. Even though Coburg had learnt from a discreet phone call that, for all the regal trappings, Zog was a self-proclaimed king, having declared himself the first monarch of Albania after the country's independence from the Ottoman Empire. But being royal, and associating with other royals, was obviously of great importance to him. Aware of that, Coburg was sure that to contradict Zog could result in a curt dismissal, and Coburg was curious to find out more from the King that might lead to information about the dead man.

'Distantly related,' he said.

'And yet you work as a policeman.'

'I'm the third son,' explained Coburg. 'My eldest brother, Magnus, inherited the family title and estates when our father died.'

'You have the same name as the British royal family before they changed their name to Windsor during the last war. Saxe-Coburg.'

'They were Saxe-Coburg-Gotha,' said Coburg politely. 'As I say, related, but at the same time, distant.'

'You are a third son,' mused Zog. 'Your other brother?'

'Charles. He was taken prisoner at Dunkirk and is currently in a prisoner-of-war camp in Germany.'

'The war, it has made exiles of us all,' said Zog. He looked directly at Coburg. 'Have you ascertained any information about the dead man who was found in our rooms?'

'Not yet, Your Majesty,' said Coburg. 'We are still investigating.'

'I wish to know who he was, and why he was here,' said Zog. 'I have many enemies and need to discover if his presence indicates a plot against me here in England. Not so much for me, but I'm concerned for the safety of my family. My infant son, Leka. Queen Géraldine. My sisters, who are very dear to me.'

'Of course, Your Majesty,' said Coburg. 'I wonder if you could tell me who occupies the suite where the dead man was found?'

'Why?' asked the King warily.

'In order to get to the bottom of what happened,' replied Coburg. 'You ask me to find out who the dead man was. It would help me find the answer to that if I could discover why he was in that particular suite.'

'My personal secretary, Count Ahmed.'

'The person who telephoned to invite me here. Then at least we have been introduced. Could I talk to the Count?'

'He is not here at the moment,' said Zog. 'He is . . . away. I will get him to telephone you when he returns.'

Zog stood up. *So, our audience is at an end*, thought Coburg. He also rose to his feet.

'Thank you, Your Majesty,' he said. 'I look forward to talking to Count Ahmed.'

Ted Lampson sat at his desk in Coburg's office and studied the notes he'd made about the case. Not that there was much to put down on paper. Dead man, unknown, throat cut. Possible motive: two million in gold bullion and foreign notes. It was a queer one and no mistake. Whatever had happened, none of the money or gold had been taken. At least, as far as they knew. Maybe that was what this King Zog wanted to talk to the guv'nor about. Maybe someone had nicked it, or part of it, but the King wanted that kept secret. Nothing was straightforward when royalty was involved, and Lampson had learnt that from earlier cases, when the guv'nor and he had investigated some goings on at Buckingham Palace. They'd asked for Coburg in particular, the same as they'd done at the Ritz. 'It's cos of his royal connections,' one of his mates in the uniformed division had told him. 'Saxe-Coburg. He's one of their own.'

But the guv'nor never came across as being different. There were no airs and graces about him. Yes, he talked posh, but then he came from a posh family and he'd been to a posh school. The poshest. But he didn't lord it over people. He treated everyone the same. That was one of the reasons why Lampson liked working with him. He was straight as a die, honest and fair. You couldn't ask more from a boss. Like this business of the car. Offering Lampson the chance to keep it at his place. He couldn't think of another boss who'd do that. Not that Lampson would. As he'd said to Coburg, that'd be asking for trouble. Any car left on the street overnight in Somers Town, by morning the wheels would be gone and anything else that could be lifted. The only cars that were left untouched were those belonging to the local gangsters.

Anyway, Lampson had selected a good one from the pool, and to make sure no one else took it, he'd written a note in large letters – Reserved for Chief Inspector Coburg – and left it on the windscreen. It wouldn't be the same as the Bentley, but he felt sure the guv'nor would be fine with it.

Lampson often dreaded the thought that one day Coburg might leave and he'd be assigned to one of the complete tossers in the building. The ones who acted as if they were special, even though they weren't.

If that happened, I'd leave, Lampson told himself determinedly. *I'd rather go back to being on the beat in uniform.*

There was a knock at the door. At Lampson's call of 'Come in!', Duncan Rudd entered bearing a large manila envelope.

'The photos,' he said. 'I've just printed three for you at the moment. Paper's in short supply. How many will you want?'

'Three'll do for now,' said Lampson. 'The guv'nor's seeing the King at the moment. We'll know if we need more when he gets back.'

'The King?' said Rudd, impressed. 'Where? Buckingham Palace?'

'Not our king,' snorted Lampson. 'The one at the Ritz where the dead body was found. King Zog.'

'King Zog,' said Rudd with a smile. 'Sounds like someone from the comic books. Like Ming the Merciless in *Flash Gordon*.'

CHAPTER FIVE

Coburg had just left the lift and was heading across the reception area towards the swing doors of the Ritz entrance, when a woman's voice called out brightly: 'Edgar!'

Coburg stopped and turned, smiling at the sound of a voice he recognised. A young woman in her late twenties, petite, blonde and very beautiful, was coming towards him. Rosa Weeks: jazz pianist and singer with a list of riotous anecdotes, all of which would hold an audience enthralled. And not just an audience, reflected Coburg, as she held her face up for a kiss.

A full kiss or a peck on the cheek? wondered Coburg. It had been a long time since they'd last been together and he didn't want her to think he was so arrogant to claim ownership of her. Rosa dealt with that by kissing him firmly on the lips, then leant back in his arms and smiled up at him.

Coburg beamed happily. 'Rosa! It must be . . .'

'A long time.' Rosa smiled. 'You never called.'

'I did, but the message I got was you were away on tour. Paris, Berlin, Amsterdam.'

'Yes, although those hot spots have rather dried up for me lately. So, what are you doing here? A guest or the day job?'

'Official. We're looking into an incident.'

'The dead guy in one of King Zog's suites?'

'You know about it?'

'Baby, everybody knows about it.'

'So, you're staying here?'

She shook her head. 'Too rich for me. No, I'm doing a cabaret spot here in the Rivoli Bar.'

'Which night?'

'Every night for the next two weeks. Which is why I'm here, checking that no one's run off with the piano.'

Coburg chuckled. 'Now that would be some heist to pull off.'

'You'd be surprised some of the things that disappear. I hear that four guys turned up at the Detour Club in Wardour Street and said they'd been asked to take the piano away for restringing. And, believe it or not, they were allowed to carry it out of the place.'

'Never to be seen again?'

'You got it.' Then her face clouded and, worried, she asked him in a lowered voice: 'How long do you think we have before the Germans invade?'

'Why would I know?' asked Coburg.

'Because you were a soldier. You know how things are.'

'No one knows,' said Coburg. 'There are lots of rumours going around . . .'

'You're telling me,' she said.

'But at the moment the RAF are keeping the Luftwaffe at bay. And while that's happening the Germans won't invade.'

'There's talk the RAF won't be able to hold them off for much longer. Every day I expect bombs to rain down on us. You can see their planes even from London.'

'You can also see the RAF fighters dealing with them. And, by all accounts, it's the airfields in Kent and Sussex that are their main targets, not London.'

'So these air raid warnings that keep happening . . .'

'So far, that's all they've been. Warnings. Granted, the docks in the East End have been hit, but not the actual city.'

'So you think we're safe.'

'For the moment,' said Coburg. 'It certainly won't stop me coming to see you tonight. What time do you go on?'

'Half past eight. Gone are the days of the eleven o'clock show, everything's strictly curfew.'

'I'll be there,' said Coburg.

'And afterwards?' she asked.

Coburg smiled. 'Yes,' he said.

'I'll look forward to it,' she said with a grin. 'Like I said, it's been a long time.'

She pulled his head down to hers, kissed him again, then gave him a wink, a chuckle and headed towards the stairs.

Coburg could still feel himself smiling as he entered Scotland Yard and mounted the stairs to his office. Rosa Weeks! It had to be two years since he'd last seen her. And here she was, back in London. *I am so glad the Ritz asked for me*, he thought gratefully.

Lampson was studying the three photographs of the dead man.

'I see Duncan's been,' said Coburg.

'Yes,' said Lampson. 'The question is: what do we do with 'em?'

Coburg pointed at one of the images, a head and shoulders shot. 'Get Duncan to run off some more copies of this and hawk it around, Ted. See if anyone recognises him.'

'So we're back on the case?' asked Lampson.

'We are. You could say it's by royal command.'

'King Zog?'

'The very same.'

'What was he like?'

'Arrogant. Snobbish. He tries to cultivate the image of a film matinee idol.'

'But he's going to co-operate?'

'I'm not sure,' said Coburg thoughtfully. 'You'd think so, from what he said about needing to know who the dead man was. But, at the same time, I get the impression he doesn't want us poking around too much. It's my guess that if we started asking questions, we'd discover that, conveniently, very few of his entourage will be able to speak English, only Albanian.'

'We know one of 'em does. The bloke who phoned you.'

'Count Ahmed, and it was his suite the dead body was found in. The King says he's away at the moment. I've asked for him to get in touch with me, but I don't know how much useful information I'll get out of him.' Coburg picked up one of the two remaining photographs of the dead man. 'This might be the thing that gets people opening up. I'll head back to the Ritz and show it around while I'm there.'

'Want me to come with you, guv?'

Coburg did his best to hold back a smile as he replied: 'No, thanks, Ted. I shall be taking this to the Pink Sink and seeing if anyone recognises him, and your frowns of obvious disapproval may make the punters there clam up.'

Lampson scowled. 'Bloody deviants.'

'It takes all sorts to make a world, Ted.'

'Right, guv. Oh, I got us a car.'

Coburg gave a sigh. 'Ah well. It had to happen.'

'D'you want to take it now?'

Coburg shook his head. 'I think I'll hang on to the Bentley for the rest of the day, and we'll do the changeover later, if that's all right with you?' He grinned. 'You take it when you go and see Duncan. Test it out.'

The Lower Bar at the Ritz was almost empty when Coburg walked in, just a few men, mostly of an older generation, to judge by their hair and their outfits which harked back to the 1920s. The younger set would arrive later, many in uniform, often with adornments such as a flower affixed to a buttonhole.

Coburg made for the bar, where the barman was wiping glasses.

'Hello, Mr Coburg,' the man greeted him. 'We don't often see you in the lower depths. What brings you here?'

Coburg took the photo of the dead man and laid it on the bar.

'Trying to identify this man,' he said.

The bartender studied the photo, then shook his head.

'Sorry, Mr Coburg. Never seen him. But I've heard about him right enough.'

'Then you know who he is?' asked Coburg, suddenly feeling hopeful.

The man shook his head again.

'I'm guessing he's the bloke who was found dead upstairs because everyone's talking about it, and this bloke looks dead. But as to who he is . . .' He shrugged. 'No idea. And nor has anyone else, by all accounts.'

'My God, Coburg, it *is* you!' barked a voice behind them.

Coburg turned and found himself looking at the obviously drunk figure of Guy Burgess.

'I never thought you'd end up here.' Burgess smirked. 'Half of Eton, yes, but I always assumed you were on the other team, like that dreadful womanising lecher Fleming.' Then his eyes narrowed as he asked suspiciously. 'Or is this you in your Lily Law role, come to strongarm the buggers and march us off to jail?'

'Rest assured, Burgess, I am here in my official capacity, but nothing to do with you or any of the clientele. I just had a question or two for the staff.'

Burgess turned his attention to the barman.

'Careful,' he warned. 'The old school tie isn't what it seems to be with Coburg here.' He turned to Coburg. 'Anyway, shouldn't you be out defending us against the Hun? You were military in the First World War, I'd have thought you'd have been shooting down these German bombers who are giving us such a pounding.'

'I was in the army, not the air force,' said Coburg. 'And the Selection Board deemed me not to be suitable due to my reserved occupation, injuries received during the first lot and my age. What's your excuse?'

'Special Operations,' muttered Burgess. 'Someone needs to be around to defend the capital when the Hun finally get here. The RAF can't resist the Luftwaffe for ever. They've got about a thousand bombers to unleash on us and in the last week alone, they've put most of our airfields in Kent and Sussex out of action. Hundreds dead. Towns and villages bombed. Two weeks, that's what the experts give us. Two weeks and the RAF will be destroyed, opening the way for the invasion.'

'You're very well informed,' commented Coburg, his tone bland.

Burgess tapped the side of his nose conspiratorially. 'Like I said, Special Operations.'

Coburg lifted the photograph of the dead man off the bar and held it out to Burgess.

'Perhaps you might recognise this man?' he asked.

Burgess took the photo and studied it. At last, he said: 'He looks dead.'

'He is,' said Coburg.

'Not very attractive, is he?'

'Being dead does that to some people,' replied Coburg.

Burgess sniffed. 'He doesn't look like he was ever attractive.' He handed the photo back to Coburg. 'Sorry, no.'

As Coburg walked into the marble-floored reception area at Scotland Yard, he was hailed by the sergeant on duty at the desk. 'There's a gentleman waiting to see you, Chief Inspector. Sir Vincent Blessington from the Foreign Office, he says. He arrived about twenty minutes ago. I told him you were out and suggested he leave a number and that you'd phone him when you got back, but he said he was happy to wait.'

'Sergeant Lampson not back yet?'

'No, sir. Otherwise I'd have let him know about the visitor.'

'Yes, of course. Where is this Blessington fellow?'

'He's over there. In the brown overcoat and carrying a briefcase.'

'Thank you, Sergeant.'

Coburg turned and saw amongst the people sitting waiting on the benches the man from the Foreign Office. Even sitting down, there was something that marked him out from the rest: his stiff-backed military posture, the expensive clothes, the bowler hat resting on his knees. The others waiting on the benches were a motley crew, some obvious ruffians, a few lawyers, women wrapped in thick coats. Coburg strode over to the diplomat.

'Sir Vincent Blessington?' he enquired, and held out his hand. 'I'm Chief Inspector Coburg. I'm sorry to have kept you waiting. Please, let's go to my office.'

Blessington got to his feet, shook Coburg's hand, then followed the chief inspector to the wide stone staircase and up to the first floor. Neither man spoke, and for once Coburg wasn't able to read anything from his visitor's face. Was this a friendly visit or a warning to back off? he wondered. Once they were safely in Coburg's office, Blessington seemed to relax, taking the chair to which Coburg gestured him.

'Bit of a mess at the Ritz,' Blessington said with a rueful frown.

So, we get right to it, thought Coburg. He asked: 'Do I assume you have an interest in the King?'

'A foreign monarch setting up court here in London is always of interest to the Foreign Office.'

'Is this a gentle warning not to tread on the Foreign Office's toes?' asked Coburg.

'Oh no,' said Blessington. 'Rather the opposite. The official line with regard to Albania is that we keep them at arm's length at the moment.'

'But unofficially?'

'Let's just say we're more interested in the King once the war is over. There are going to be major changes in Europe when this is through, and especially in Eastern Europe. Albania may be just a tiny country, but it's right in the heart of what could well be a communist bloc, if the Russians have their way.'

'The Russians aren't in the war,' Coburg pointed out. 'They have a non-participation treaty with the Nazis.'

'Which means they can move in any direction. At this moment Stalin doesn't want to fight a war because he intends to expand Russian influence and take over whatever parts of Europe the Germans will let him have. But that could well change when the Germans feel the Russians are becoming too large, creating their own empire of military influence right on their northern border.'

'So, you want to keep in with the King while at the same time being seen to be not too strongly on his side?'

'Just until we see how things turn out with Albania. The King isn't the only player in the game there. I understand you met with him in his suite.'

'Yes,' said Coburg. 'He wants us to find out who the dead man is, and why he was there.'

'From what I can gather, the people at the Ritz, including the various kings and queens in exile, seem to view you as "one of us", as they call it. The name and title, I suppose.

Saxe-Coburg.' He looked quizzically at Coburg. 'The royal family used to be Saxe-Coburgs before they changed their name to Windsor.'

'Saxe-Coburg-*Gotha*,' corrected Coburg.

'Still, it's close,' said Blessington. 'Close enough to suggest there might be a connection. At least, that's what the gossip is.'

'Most of the older families of Europe are related in some part,' said Coburg. 'And I won't deny it can be useful in gaining entry to places that can be difficult.'

'Yes, that's what we thought. So, we'd quite like it if you can keep us in the picture with anything you come across.'

'If the Foreign Office is involved, do you think the dead man might have been an alien, part of a foreign conspiracy against the King?'

'That may turn out to be the case,' said Blessington. He stood up, taking a card from his pocket as he did so, passing it to Coburg. 'My contact phone number at the Foreign Office, if anything of interest turns up. My home telephone number is written on the back, in case something important happens and you can't get hold of me at the FO.'

Coburg took the card and shook Blessington's hand.

'Do you want me to see you out?' he asked.

'No, I think I can find my way,' said Blessington genially. 'I've been here before.'

Coburg sat at his desk and examined the visiting card Blessington had left him, with the number of his extension at the Foreign Office added to the switchboard number. He flipped it over to the diplomat's home phone number, which had a Maida Vale code. So, someone with an expensive address and a knighthood, not just a run-of-the-mill government emissary.

There was a knock at his door. Possibly Sir Vincent had forgotten something, guessed Coburg, and he called: 'Come in!'

The door opened and the bulky figure of James Hibbert, a senior inspector at MI5, entered.

'Coburg,' he grunted sourly.

Coburg gestured him to the chair opposite his, reflecting that he'd only met Hibbert on a few occasions, and on each the MI5 man had looked sour and aggressive. Bad digestion, Coburg decided.

Coburg smiled. 'This is a coincidence. I'm guessing you're here about a certain incident at the Ritz. And I've just said goodbye to a visitor from the Foreign Office.'

'Yes, all right, Coburg, no need for the jokes.'

'So, were your people following Sir Vincent or me?'

'Not necessary. We have our contacts. When we got tipped that Blessington was here asking for you, we knew what was up.'

'So, you waited until he left?'

'It wouldn't have been clever for me to come in while he was here, would it?' snapped Hibbert.

'Don't you want to know what he said?'

'No. I'm more interested in what you were doing meeting with King Zog and what he said to you. It was our impression the police investigation into the dead man in his suite was being put on ice, so to speak.'

'Yes, it was. Until the King himself said he wanted our investigation to continue.'

'Did he say why?'

'He said he has many enemies, and he wants to know if this dead man was part of an attempt on his life.'

'He's had a few of those.'

'I get the impression he'd rather like it if there weren't any while he was in England. He's concerned for his family's safety.'

'Not to mention two million in gold and cash,' said Hibbert bitterly.

'Have they asked for extra protection for it?' asked Coburg.

'No,' grunted Hibbert. 'But we're keeping an eye on it anyway.'

'How?'

'Through Special Branch. Every now and then one of the King's sisters, usually Princess Senije, goes to the local branch of the Westminster Bank, where she exchanges foreign currencies for sterling. She's always accompanied by a posse of bodyguards, but Special Branch aren't taking any chances. By all accounts, each trip involves thousands of pounds being brought back to their suite. That much cash on the streets is an open invitation to robbery.'

'How do Special Branch know when the princess is doing a bank run? One of your people at the Ritz sets off the alarm, I suppose.'

'Exactly. It's not something that can easily be kept secret when the princess, accompanied by a small army of armed men carrying bulging satchels, leaves the hotel. Everyone knows where they're going, and everyone knows what they're carrying is foreign currency.'

'So, it will only be worth attacking them on the way back, when it's been changed into sterling.'

'Correct. Which gives time for Special Branch to have their people waiting outside the bank.'

'Surely the King's people must be aware they're being watched.'

'I'm sure they are, but so far there have been no official complaints from the King or his family. Possibly they're glad of the added protection. After all, Special Branch are more likely to spot London criminals lurking in the area.'

'But not foreign criminals.'

'They have a good idea of who's who.'

'By the way, I ran into one of your people today at the Lower Bar at the Ritz.'

'Oh?'

'Guy Burgess.'

Hibbert shook his head. 'Not one of ours.'

'Oh? I heard a rumour he was doing some work for you, in addition to his BBC stuff.'

Hibbert hesitated, then said: 'Six.'

MI6, realised Coburg.

Hibbert got up and shot a warning look at the chief inspector.

'You're treading on dangerous ground with this one, Coburg. It's not just one of your everyday robberies.'

'Do you know who the dead man is?' asked Coburg.

'No,' said Hibbert.

'And you wouldn't tell me if you did.' Coburg smiled, getting to his feet.

'Need to know,' grunted Hibbert.

The door opened and Ted Lampson appeared, holding a large manila envelope. He stopped when he saw Hibbert.

'Sorry, sir,' he apologised to Coburg. 'I didn't realise you had a visitor.'

'That's all right, Mr Hibbert is just going.'

'You should still have knocked anyway,' Hibbert rebuked the sergeant sharply. 'We could have been talking about something important.'

'I keep no secrets from Sergeant Lampson,' retorted Coburg. 'We are a team.'

'Huh!' snorted Hibbert, and left.

Lampson put the envelope down on Coburg's desk. 'The photos, sir. Sorry it took me so long but Duncan's a bit of a pain at insisting on doing everything right.'

'I'm glad he is,' said Coburg. 'Photographs that don't show our man properly won't be much use.' He opened the envelope and examine the photos inside. 'Excellent,' he said. 'How was the car?'

'It's a runner,' said Lampson. 'It'll do.' He gestured at the door. 'Who was that bloke just now? Old sourpuss.'

'Inspector Hibbert from MI5. He was expressing an interest in the body at the Ritz and warning us off. Interestingly, I've had a visit from Sir Vincent Blessington, someone senior at the Foreign Office, who's also interested in what happened at the hotel.'

'Also warning us off?'

'No, but he wants to be kept informed, unofficially.'

'So, it's politics,' said Lampson unhappily. 'There's always trouble when it's politics.'

'At this moment, Ted, with a war on, nearly everything is politics,' sighed Coburg.

CHAPTER SIX

George Criticos was at his hall porter's station when Coburg entered that evening.

'Mr Coburg!' The man greeted him with a welcoming smile.

'Good evening, George.'

'Business or social this evening?' he asked.

'Social,' said Coburg. 'I've reserved a table in the Rivoli Bar.'

'Ah, Miss Rosa Weeks!' the porter beamed. 'A superb performer. The guests have been raving about her. Would you like a table near her?'

'No, thank you, George. We're old friends and I don't want my presence to put her off. Not that I feel it would, she's too professional for that, but . . .'

George nodded. 'I understand. A table about halfway back.'

'That would be perfect. And, from a business perspective, is Count Ahmed back? He was supposed to telephone me to arrange for us to meet, but I haven't heard from him.'

'I'm afraid not,' replied George. 'I believe he's out on some business for the King.'

'Do you know what sort of business? And who it's with?'

George gave him a knowing smile. 'I'm afraid not. But I'll do my best to find out.' He summoned a uniformed porter waiting nearby. 'Take Mr Coburg to the Rivoli,' he said. 'Table twelve.'

Coburg followed the porter and was soon settled at his table. He checked the room over as it began to fill up. The tables had been set out in a series of circles, most of them occupied by couples, just a few with a single customer like Coburg. In the centre of the circle of tables was a white grand piano, ready for the cabaret. The lights on the audience began to go down and the those shining on the piano increased to a golden halo, into which stepped Rosa, looking stunning in a long white evening dress.

She bowed and smiled at the audience in appreciation of their applause at her entrance, then sat at the piano and straightaway went into Hoagy Carmichael's 'Stardust'. Coburg sat and let her voice, her fingers gently caressing the keyboard, and the mood of the song wash over him. It was beautiful. The song was beautiful, she was beautiful, her voice and the way the piano seemed to be just an extension of her, were beautiful.

The audience sat rapt, then erupted into loud applause as the song ended.

'Thank you,' said Rosa, acknowledging their appreciative reaction with a gentle smile. 'Now, staying with the great Mr Carmichael . . .' And then she launched into 'Georgia on my Mind', and Coburg thought he'd never heard the song sound so good.

Rosa then followed with more standards, pieces by the Gershwins, Irving Berlin and the clever subversive lyrics of Cole Porter's 'Let's Do It', before segueing into 'Night and Day', and then a medley of songs made famous by Ella Fitzgerald.

All too soon the performance was over. As Rosa gathered up her sheaves of music, Coburg made his way to the piano and was delighted to see Rosa's face light up at his approach.

'I knew you were here! I saw you, hiding.'

'I wasn't hiding, I just didn't want to put you off,' said Coburg. 'Shall we go?'

'We shall,' said Rosa. 'Have you still got your flat in Hampstead?'

'I have.'

'Good. My place is too crowded. I'm sharing with two other girls and it's chaos. Or we could stay here. I'm sure George could accommodate us.'

'I'm sure he could as well, but I'd prefer to keep things here on a professional footing. I don't want to put George on the spot.'

'So, Hampstead it is. I'll just get my coat.'

'Don't forget your gas mask,' Coburg reminded her.

She laughed. 'No problem. It's with my coat. I never go anywhere without it.'

'Have you worn it yet?' asked Coburg.

'Only the first time I got it, just to test it out.' Her nose wrinkled in distaste. 'That stink of rubber is dreadful.'

'You could always spray it with a nice scent,' suggested Coburg.

'I tried that,' said Rosa. 'It just stank even worse. Wait for me in reception.'

As Coburg and Rosa left the bar, they were watched by a heavily built middle-aged man wearing a tuxedo, sitting at a table on his own at the back of the room.

I guess that's DCI Coburg, he thought to himself. *And with the girl. Interesting. Very interesting.*

As Coburg walked into the main reception hall, George signalled him over.

'I've made enquiries and it seems that Count Ahmed is out of town, in the country.'

'Do we know where in the country?' asked Coburg.

'Alas, no. But if I do hear, I'll let you know.' He smiled as he saw Rosa approaching. 'Ah, here is the delightful Miss Weeks.'

Rosa, slipping her arm through Coburg's, smiled at the hall porter and said: 'See you tomorrow, George.'

They strolled out of the hotel and along Piccadilly to where Coburg had left the police car. As he unlocked it and opened the passenger door for her, Rosa looked at it in surprised amusement.

'What happened to the Bentley?' she asked.

'Impounded as part of the war effort. So, this is my new chariot. What do you think?'

'Stylish.' Rosa smiled. 'Yes, I like it. Do we get to play with the bell and the blue lights?'

'No lights except the dipped headlights,' said Coburg. 'Blackout rules, remember.'

'Spoilsport,' she said. She leant across and kissed him. 'But I hope you'll make it up to me when we get to your place.'

* * *

Coburg's flat was on the ground floor of a small block in Hampstead, not far from the Heath. Rosa looked around the flat while Coburg poured their drinks. He handed a glass to Rosa, who took a sip and then beamed at him. 'Irish whiskey!'

'I remembered it was your favourite,' said Coburg.

'After two years? I'm impressed.'

'A Scot who prefers Irish is bound to be memorable,' said Coburg. 'And, of course, you're very impressive.'

He took a drink, then put his glass down and wrapped his arms around her. 'I've missed you.'

She gave a sceptical laugh. 'I bet!'

'It's true,' said Coburg. 'You're a hard act for anyone to follow.'

Rosa put her glass down. 'With smooth-talking flattery like that,' she said softly, 'the whiskey can wait.'

It was two hours later that Coburg rose from the bed to fetch the two waiting glasses of whiskey for them.

'Great sex, great whiskey,' she murmured. 'I could get used to this.'

'So could I,' admitted Coburg, getting back into the bed and putting an arm around her, pulling her close so she could nestle in to him.

'What went wrong?' she asked. 'Why did we stop seeing one another?'

'You were busy going all over the world, touring, and I was always seemed to be on some case or other.'

'Yet we're here now.'

'Yes, we are, thankfully,' said Coburg. 'But I guess that you'll be off somewhere again before too long.'

'Not like before,' she said. 'Not with a war on. I've got some bookings coming up, but they're all inland.'

'Where are they?'

'This week and next at the Ritz, then Ciro's the week after.'

'In Piccadilly?'

'The very same.'

'Well, that's good, you'll still be in London.'

'And after that I'm booked for five nights in Glasgow. Then Birmingham and Coventry.'

'So, we'd better take advantage of the fact you'll be in London for now,' said Coburg.

'Especially as I hope you'll be spending some time at the Ritz working on this case,' said Rosa. 'It would make a rare change for our work schedules to coincide.'

'Indeed,' said Coburg. 'Let's start tomorrow. How about I take you to lunch?'

'Where?'

'The Ritz, of course.'

'On the house?'

'No, my treat. I don't like taking advantage.'

'Unlike many of your colleagues who exist on free lunches and handouts.'

'That's them; this is my way.'

She smiled at him. 'You're a bit of a puritan on the quiet, aren't you?'

He put his glass down on the bedside table, took hers from her and placed it next to his.

'Not completely,' he said. Then he kissed her and let his hand move gently down her body.

CHAPTER SEVEN

Wednesday 21st August

The next morning, Coburg drove Rosa to the house at the back of Oxford Street she shared with two other women, then headed for Scotland Yard, where Lampson was waiting in the rear courtyard for him.

'It's not the Bentley, guv,' sighed Lampson wistfully as Coburg pulled to a halt.

'Maybe not, but it drives well enough,' said Coburg. 'And I thought we'd share driving duties. Can't have you forgetting how to handle a car.'

Lampson grinned. 'Suits me!' he said.

'In that case,' said Coburg, and he shifted across to the passenger seat so that Lampson could get behind the wheel.

'Where to?' asked Lampson.

'I thought we'd make the mortuary at UCH our first stop,' said Coburg. 'The post-mortem should have been done so we might get some useful information. It'll also give us a chance to examine the body properly for any clues that might help us identify what he did for a living. Blisters on the hands and feet. Any old scars.'

'Sounds like a plan,' said Lampson.

The streets were clearer of traffic than usual, the petrol rations taking their toll, and it wasn't long before they arrived, where Lampson pulled the car into the side of Gower Street outside the old red-brick building that housed University College Hospital.

They walked into the building and down the stairs to the mortuary department, where they were met by an attendant in a long white coat, pushing an empty trolley along a corridor.

'Police,' said Coburg, flashing his warrant card. 'We've come to look at the body that was brought in from the Ritz yesterday.'

'Gone,' said the man.

He was about to continue pushing his trolley when Coburg stopped him.

'What do you mean, gone?' he asked.

The man looked at him morosely, like a man beaten down by life.

'Like I said, he's gone. Your blokes came and took him away yesterday.'

Coburg frowned. 'I'm sorry, Mr . . . er . . .'

'Eric Nugent. Mortuary orderly.'

'When you say "our" blokes? Who were they, exactly?'

'MI5, according to the warrant cards they showed me,' said the man.

'MI5 officers don't have warrant cards,' said Coburg. 'It's a secret organisation. Or, at least, it's supposed to be.'

'Well, they showed me them,' said Nugent.

'What time was this?'

'About four. I know that because I was about to go on my break when they arrived.'

'What did they look like? And how many of them were there?'

'Four,' said the man. 'Though only one spoke.' He paused, then added: 'To be honest, they looked foreign. Though the one who did the talking spoke English well. Quite posh-sounding, in fact.'

'When you say they looked foreign, what sort of foreign?'

Nugent shrugged. 'I dunno. Maybe Greek. Mind, I'm only saying that cos we've got Greeks in the street where I live, and they looked a bit like them.'

'Did you see what they transported him in? Ambulance? Van?'

Nugent shook his head. 'No, I never went up with 'em. Not my job. I stayed here.'

'What did they take the body in?'

'A big, long bag. You know, a body bag.'

Coburg scowled as he and Lampson made their way back upstairs.

'Unbelievable!' he growled. 'There's a war on and all these signs up about watching out for suspicious strangers, but four foreigners come marching in and take away a dead body, and no one questions them.'

'They had warrant cards,' pointed out Lampson.

'Faked,' grunted Coburg. Then he stopped. 'Or maybe not. Listen, Ted, I'm going to leave you here to ask questions, including getting hold of the post-mortem report. Check to see if anyone locally saw four men carrying a body in a bag out of here yesterday about four o'clock. If they did, what vehicle did they use, and which direction did it go in. The usual things.'

'Right, guv,' said Lampson. 'Where are you off to?'

'I'm going to check with MI5.'

'But you said it couldn't be them because of the business of the warrant cards.'

'MI5 are perfectly capable of doing a double-bluff. Real MI5 pretending to be fake MI5 men to cover their tracks. I'll see you back at the Yard.'

One positive thing about being at the wheel of an official police car was that the barriers at Wormwood Scrubs were raised as Coburg arrived. He still had to produce his warrant card, but the whole procedure passed quicker than if he'd been driving the Bentley. He was directed to the area of the car park reserved for MI5. Inside the old Victorian building he showed his warrant card at reception and asked for Inspector Hibbert. Hibbert appeared a few moments later and shot a sour look at Coburg.

'I hope you've got news for me,' he said, though his expression suggested he didn't think whatever news Coburg would be bringing would be good news.

'I have,' said Coburg.

'In that case you'd better come to my office,' said Hibbert. He shot a look of suspicion towards the receptionist and muttered to Coburg as they walked away: 'Walls have ears.'

'They also make ice cream,' said Coburg innocently.

'Very funny,' said Hibbert, unamused. 'That receptionist, for example. I'd never seen her before today. Who's to say who she is?'

'A German spy?' asked Coburg.

'The trouble is, since the war, we've been taking on so many new staff in order to cope, I don't know where they're coming from. It's why we had to move here. Too many people coming in, more than the old building at Thames House could cope with.'

They arrived at Hibbert's office and Coburg followed him in.

'Right, what's the news?' he asked. 'Have you identified him yet? The dead man?'

'No, and our task has now been made more difficult. Someone walked off with the body from UCH.'

Hibbert stared at Coburg, shocked. 'What? Who?'

'According to the mortuary attendant it was MI5.'

'What!' exploded Hibbert. 'Of all the bloody nerve!'

'Are you saying it wasn't?'

'Of course it wasn't!'

'The mortuary attendant said they had MI5 warrant cards.'

'We don't have bloody warrant cards!'

'That's what I told him. According to him the men who took the body away looked foreign. Possibly Greek.'

'Greek?' queried Hibbert. 'Albanian, I bet you! This is connected to all that money and gold bullion in King Zog's suite.'

'Yes, the same thought struck me,' said Coburg.

'Who is this mortuary attendant? Did you bring him in for questioning?'

'No. We questioned him at the hospital. There was no need for us to bring him in for further interrogation at this stage.'

'Well, I will! What's his name?'

'Eric Nugent.'

'Right, I'll have him picked up.'

'There is one thing,' said Coburg. 'As I assume you've been keeping an eye on King Zog and his retinue, do you have a picture of Count Idjbil Ahmed, the King's personal secretary?'

'Why?' asked Hibbert warily.

'According to Nugent, only one of the four men who took the body away spoke English, but the one who did spoke it very well. I've only spoken to the Count on the telephone, but his English is excellent.'

'Pity we can't touch him.' Hibbert scowled. 'Diplomatic immunity.'

'But if you have a picture of him we can show Nugent, and if Nugent identifies him . . .'

'Yes, well, we haven't,' grunted Hibbert.

'I'm surprised,' said Coburg. 'I'd have thought you'd have got quite a gallery of the whole party, from the King downwards.'

'We've got some,' admitted Hibbert. 'The King, obviously, and his sisters, along with most of their bodyguards, although we've still got to put names to most of them. But Count Ahmed seems to have been able to avoid having his picture taken.'

'What about his passport? There'll be a picture in that.'

'Like I said, diplomatic immunity. We can't just take it off him without a very good reason otherwise we'll have a diplomatic incident on our hands.'

'What about Ian Fleming? He's one of yours, isn't he? I heard he was the one who smuggled the King and his party out of France. He must have had access to the passports.'

Hibbert shook his head. 'Naval Intelligence.'

'Why did Naval Intelligence carry out that operation?' asked Coburg. 'Surely it would have come under the Secret Intelligence Service.'

'I'm not saying it was done by them,' said Hibbert. 'To be honest, I'm never sure who Fleming's working for. Himself, most of the time, I think.' He looked at Coburg. 'Anyway, you could always ask him direct. You went to school with him, and it seems that's how these things are done, the old school tie.'

'I was at the same school, but some years before him.'

'Does that matter? I thought if you'd been to Eton you had a whole network at your beck and call.'

The tone of bitter resentment in Hibbert's voice prompted Coburg to comment: 'I expect it's that way with most schools. The old boy network.'

'Maybe it is for Eton and Harrow and the like, but I went to a secondary school in Surbiton, which produced mainly carpenters and plumbers,' grunted Hibbert.

'Which I imagine is more useful than being able to conjugate Latin verbs,' said Coburg ruefully. He held out his hand. 'Well, thanks for the information. If I get anything new, I'll pass it on.'

CHAPTER EIGHT

Coburg decided his next point of call should be Sir Vincent Blessington at the Foreign Office to check if he had a picture of Count Ahmed, but he realised the time was disappearing, and he had a date with Rosa he wanted to keep. Instead, he returned to his office and phoned Sir Vincent but was told he was out. He got the same message when he tried Blessington's home number. Coburg left a message at both places asking for Sir Vincent to call him when he returned. He was just hanging up the phone when Ted Lampson appeared.

'I found someone working in a building on the other side of the road who saw the men come out, put the body in a hearse and drive off.'

'A hearse? So, a local funeral director must be involved.'

'Exactly, and the one who does all the funerals in the area is Leverton's. So, I went to see them and it turns out they had one of their hearses nicked.'

'When was it taken?'

'Lunchtime yesterday. But when they arrived for work this morning, there it was parked round the corner from their place. And it was sparkling clean.'

'Getting rid of any evidence.'

'Exactly. I asked around the shops near to Leverton's to see if anyone saw it being taken, or put back, but no one saw anything.'

'It suggests local knowledge: they knew where to get hold of a hearse at short notice,' mused Coburg.

'Not necessarily,' said Lampson. 'Maybe they were looking for anything they could put a body in.'

'Yes, I expect you're right,' sighed Coburg.

There was a knock at the door, which opened and a short, stiff-backed man with a military bearing entered.

'DCI Coburg,' he said. 'Gerald Atkinson, MI6. Reception told me you were in.'

'I'm just about to go out,' said Coburg. 'I have an appointment. If you'd had the courtesy to get them to ring me, I'd have been able to let you know and save you the trouble of coming upstairs.'

'This won't take a moment,' said Atkinson. He looked at Lampson and said: 'Would you give us the room, Sergeant?'

Lampson looked quizzically at Coburg, who glared at the MI6 man.

'Anything you have to say to me, my sergeant can hear,' he said.

'This is a matter of national security,' retorted Atkinson crisply. 'You've got the necessary clearance, Chief Inspector, your sergeant hasn't.'

Coburg bridled. 'Now look here—' he began.

69

'It's all right, sir,' said Lampson. 'I've got things I need to do.'

With that, Lampson picked up some papers from the desk and left. Coburg regarded the MI6 man coldly.

'This is an outrage,' he said. 'What's so secret that my sergeant can't be privy to it?'

'We hear you're involved in this business with King Zog.'

'At the King's request,' said Coburg. 'And my sergeant is fully involved in the investigation.'

'Do be careful,' said Atkinson. 'There are sensitive issues at stake.'

'So I've already been told by the Foreign Office and MI5,' said Coburg. 'What's your involvement?'

'Protecting the security of the country, as always,' said Atkinson.

'In that case, can I suggest you do a better job of it,' said Coburg.

Atkinson glared at him. 'What the hell do you mean by that?' he snapped angrily.

'I ran into one of your agents in the Lower Bar at the Ritz the other day, the Pink Sink. Guy Burgess.'

'How do you know he's anything to do with us?' demanded Atkinson.

'Because he's a drunk, and when he gets drunk he's a blabbermouth.'

'He told you he was with Six?' asked Atkinson challengingly.

'No, but he didn't need to,' said Coburg. 'He's either MI5 or MI6, and Five told me he wasn't one of theirs.'

'How do you know so much about Burgess? Have you been keeping tabs on him for some reason?'

'No need, he keeps putting himself in situations that bring attention to him. He and I went to the same school, albeit some years apart, and consequently we both know some of the same people, and plenty of them have tales of Burgess's loose mouth. Don't you vet people as security risks before you take them on? When I saw him he was drunk as a lord in the middle of the afternoon, and I guess blatantly looking for trade and making no bones about it. You don't think that makes him a target ripe for blackmail by a foreign power?'

'Of course we vet,' said Atkinson. 'But with some people there's no need. Their background and social status are enough to qualify them. Burgess is highly recommended.'

'By whom?'

'Well, having been at Eton, for one thing. And then the crowd he ran with at Trinity. Philby. Blunt. All good chaps. Reliable.'

'The fact that he's a declared communist doesn't worry you?'

'*Was* a communist,' stressed Atkinson. 'A temporary youthful indiscretion.'

'He joined the Communist Party while he was at Cambridge,' said Coburg. 'He made a great thing about supporting a communist revolution in this country. He made visits to Russia in support of the Soviets. You don't think that raises concerned about where his true political allegiance lies?'

'I'd be more concerned if he'd been an advocate for Hitler, in the way that many of your old school chums have been. We're at war with Germany, we're not at war with Russia.'

'Technically, we are,' pointed out Coburg. 'Russia and Germany have signed a pact. They're allies. So, if Germany is our enemy, so is Russia.'

'It's a non-aggression pact,' countered Atkinson. 'They won't attack each other. And there's no reason why Russia should attack us.'

'To support it's ally, Germany,' persisted Coburg.

'I'm not getting into this with you,' retorted Atkinson petulantly. 'It's just politics, that's all. I'm here because I want to know what you know.'

'We know that a dead man was found in a suite at the Ritz belonging to a member of King Zog's retinue. His throat had been cut. We have no idea who he is. The body was taken to University College Hospital, from where it was stolen by four men claiming to be officers of MI5. I've checked with Five and they say they had nothing to do with removing the body. We believe the body was transported from UCH in a hearse stolen from Leverton's, a local funeral directors. It was my sergeant who discovered this. If you'd allowed him to stay you could have been informed of this by him direct.'

Atkinson regarded Coburg with an icy stare. 'And?' he demanded.

'And?' queried Coburg. 'That's it. There is no more. I suggest you talk to Five or the Foreign Office if you want more. Or the Ritz. Or Leverton's. Or the mortuary attendant at University College Hospital. Although I expect they'll just tell you the same as I have.

'There are two things you can do that might help to move this case along. Do you have a photograph of Count Ahmed, King Zog's personal secretary? And you can answer this: was Ian Fleming of Naval Intelligence working for Six when he smuggled the King and his family out of France?'

'Who told you that?' demanded Atkinson.

'It seems to be common knowledge,' said Coburg.

'Amongst whom?' asked Atkinson.

'Everyone,' said Coburg. 'Have a word with your man Burgess, for example.'

'I told you, he's not our man,' snapped Atkinson.

'Yes, so you did,' said Coburg.

'Well, if that's all, I'll leave you to your appointment,' said Atkinson curtly, and he made for the door.

'You haven't said if you've got a photograph of Count Ahmed,' said Coburg.

'No,' snapped Atkinson.

'No, you haven't said; or no, you haven't got one?' asked Coburg.

'Both,' said Atkinson. And he left.

There was a brief pause, then the door opened, and Lampson returned.

'I was hanging about down the corridor, waiting for him to leave,' he said. 'I didn't like him.'

'No, neither did I,' said Coburg.

'What did he want?'

'The same as all the others. We have the Foreign Office wanting us to keep the investigation going and keep them informed of whatever we uncover; MI5, who want us to just go through the motions and in reality back off and not get in their way; and MI6, who have also warned us to tread carefully and not make waves.'

'Why did MI5 and MI6 feel the need to come and say the same thing separately?' asked Lampson. 'Surely just one of them could have done it. They're both secret service.'

'But deadly rivals. They both want to be the top of the secret league. It's a bit like that between Arsenal and Spurs.'

'Nothing can be as deep as that, sir,' said Lampson with a scowl. 'Those bastards at Highbury can't be trusted in any way.'

'Of course, you're a Spurs fan.'

'Like my father before me, and his father before that. And there's none in north London can say the same about Arsenal. *Woolwich* Arsenal. That's where they came from. South-east London.'

'People move around,' said Coburg benignly. 'Look at the Irish. They move to England and say they're English.'

'Not in football, sir,' said Lampson sharply. 'A Spurs fan is a Spurs fan, wherever they are.' He looked at the clock. 'Before that MI6 chap arrived, you were talking about an appointment.'

'Yes, and I'm on my way there now.'

'Anything I should know about?'

'No.' Coburg smiled. 'Just that I'm meeting someone at the Ritz.'

'Someone special?'

'I think so. So, you keep the car.'

'Me?'

'If you go out it'll be because you're on official business. Mine is personal. I'll get a taxi.'

Lampson shook his head. 'Taxis ain't easy to find right now. If I've got the car, then I'm taking you to the Ritz. Can't have you being late.'

'Thank you, Ted. I appreciate that.' As they walked along the corridor, Coburg added: 'One last thing. You might get a phone call from Sir Vincent Blessington from the Foreign Office. If you do, ask him if he's got a picture of Count Ahmed he can let us have.'

'And if he has?'

'Take it to UCH and show it to the mortuary attendant. Ask him if he was one of the four men who took the body.'

CHAPTER NINE

After Coburg had left the car, Lampson stayed by the kerb, just in case whoever it was he was meeting wasn't around. It had to be a woman. The guv'nor should have told that MI6 bloke he didn't have time right now, to piss off and call back later. That's what Lampson would have done. But then, Lampson wasn't Coburg. Lampson hoped the woman, whoever she was, had hung around. Not many women would wait if their bloke was late. But then, this was lunch at the Ritz, and worth hanging around for.

As he watched, a young blonde woman bounced down the steps from the entrance of the Ritz, a big smile on her face, and threw herself at Coburg, who wrapped her in a hug, and the pair walked into the hotel hand in hand. So, all good, then. He was glad the guv'nor had some female company. Sometimes he worried that the DCI let himself get too caught up in the job. You needed more, which is why Lampson had Ruth, a neighbour who lived two streets away. A widow who brightened his life up when he needed it. Great company. The only drawback was that his parents didn't like her. *Well, tough luck on them*, thought Lampson. He put the car in gear and headed back to the Yard.

Rosa forked a piece of beef into her mouth and looked at Coburg with an expression of delight mixed with awe.

'This is delicious!' she sighed. 'No, it's better than that. It is . . . a supreme piece of artistic culinary genius.'

Coburg smiled. 'It's the Ritz. The chef has a reputation to keep up.'

'Even in wartime, with all the restrictions? Rationing?'

'Rationing doesn't apply to restaurants,' Coburg reminded her.

'Well, it seems to apply to the places I eat,' said Rosa.

'Surely you have some meals here if you're part of the entertainment,' said Coburg.

'Snacks,' said Rosa. 'Great snacks, for sure. But nothing like this!' She added in a wistful tone: 'D'you think we can do this more often?'

'No problem,' said Coburg. 'I think I'm going to be coming back for the next few days, maybe weeks, until we solve the case.'

'How's that going? No ideas?'

'We won't have any ideas until we can find out who he was. Which has just been made a bit more difficult because . . .' He mentally kicked himself, then stopped and gave her an apologetic smile and said: 'Sorry.'

'What do you mean, sorry?' she asked, puzzled.

'I've already said too much. It's a police matter. You're a civilian. Forget I spoke.'

She looked at him, irritated. 'No,' she said. 'I'm not just a civilian.' She lowered her voice at hissed at him: 'I'm the woman you were in bed with just a few hours ago. Or have you forgotten?'

'No,' he said awkwardly. 'The point is I'm an officer of the law and I really shouldn't discuss the case with—'

'A potential victim?' she demanded.

He stared at her, puzzled. 'What do you mean, a potential victim?'

'A man's been murdered in this hotel. I am going to be here every day this week and next. Who's to say this killer isn't stalking this place even now, deciding who's going to be his next victim?'

'I don't think that's likely,' said Coburg. 'The dead man was found in a royal suite—'

'Even more dangerous,' said Rosa. 'If he can get in there he can get into my dressing room here.'

Coburg groaned.

'Look, just tell me what you were going to say and I'll stop,' said Rosa. 'You cannot say half a sentence like: something's been made a bit more difficult because . . . And then stop. It's not fair. And it's not as if you don't know me. And I'm not just talking about . . . you know . . .'

'Yes, all right,' said Coburg, embarrassedly looking around.

'We've known each other a long time. You know I'm not the kind who goes blabbing.'

'Yes, but—'

Rosa gave him an amused look, one eyebrow raised.

Coburg sighed, defeated. 'OK,' he said. 'If you promise to keep it to yourself and not say anything.'

'I promise.'

'All right.' He looked around to make sure he couldn't be overheard before lowering his voice and whispering: '. . . someone stole his body from the mortuary.'

'No!' said Rosa, stunned.

'So, all we've got left of him is a few photographs.' He gave another sigh of defeat and added: 'Having told you this, I might as well go the whole hog. But I'm only doing this because you might have bumped into him since you've been here. We'll be showing his image to everyone who works here at the hotel.' With that, he pulled out a photograph from his pocket and passed it to her.

Rosa studied it thoughtfully.

'You're not going to believe this—' she began.

Coburg stared at her. 'You're not going to tell me you've seen him?'

'Yes, but not at the Ritz. I'm sure he was with Julie, one of the girls I share with, at a party we had at our house.' She gave him a rueful smile. 'It's wartime, which seems to bring out the party instincts in some people.'

'Have fun today because tomorrow we die,' said Coburg.

'Something like that,' agreed Rosa. She looked at the image again. 'Yes, I'm more sure than ever it's the same man.'

'Where is Julie at the moment?' asked Coburg.

'At the house, I expect. She's a dancer appearing in some nightclub, so she never gets in until it's almost dawn. Then she sleeps most of the day.'

'In that case, I don't want to rush your meal, but the sooner I get to talk to her, the better.'

Rosa looked at him. 'No dessert?' she asked, disappointed.

'Rosa, I promise you, if your friend is able to give us a name for this man, I shall buy you dessert every day for the rest of the week.'

She gave him a wicked grin of triumph. 'Now aren't you glad you told me?'

Lampson picked up the ringing telephone. 'DCI Coburg's telephone.'

'Is DCI Coburg there?' asked a man's rather plummy voice.

'I'm afraid not. This is his sergeant, DS Lampson. Can I take a message for him?'

'This is Sir Vincent Blessington. DCI Coburg left messages asking me to call him.'

'Ah, yes, Sir Vincent. He hoped you might call. He was wondering if you had a photograph of King Zog's private secretary, Count Ahmed.'

'Did he say why?'

'I believe he just wants to check something. The DCI hasn't been able to make contact with the Count, and I think he wanted to know what he looked like.'

'Yes, well, if you'll hold on a moment I'll check in the file,' said Blessington.

There was a clunk as the receiver was put down, and then the sound of papers being sifted through before it was picked up again.

'Actually, we have,' said Blessington. 'It's not a very good one, I'm afraid. It's a copy taken from his original entry documents.'

'I'm sure it will be perfect,' said Lampson. 'DCI Coburg

wondered, if you had one, if you could send it over to us by messenger.'

'It's urgent, is it?' asked Blessington.

'We are trying to get to the bottom of this case,' said Lampson in his politest voice, 'and DCI Coburg feels this picture may play a vital part.'

'Understood,' said Blessington. 'I'll have a copy made and get a messenger to bring it over.'

The red-headed young woman sat at the kitchen table in her dressing gown and stared incredulously at the photograph that Coburg had given to her.

'My God, it's Joe!' she said.

'Joe?' asked Coburg.

He and Rosa were sitting on the other side of the table, watching as Julie Stafford put the photograph aside and took a cigarette from her packet, her fingers trembling.

'I can't believe he's dead!' said Julie. 'How?'

'He was found in a suite at the Ritz being used by the King of Albania,' said Coburg. 'I'm sorry to tell you this way, but his throat had been cut.'

'What was he doing at the Ritz, and in some king's suite?' asked Julie. Having lit her cigarette, she took up the photograph again, looking at it with an expression of bewilderment.

'That's what we're trying to find out,' said Coburg gently.

Julie looked at Rosa. 'He's from the police?' she asked.

'Detective Chief Inspector Coburg,' he answered.

Julie looked at him warily.

'You can call me Edgar,' said Coburg. 'After all, you're a friend of Rosa's, and she and I are old friends.'

Julie looked at Rosa. 'Is this for real?' she asked.

'I'm afraid it is,' said Rosa.

'What we're trying to find out is who he is, where he lived and what he did,' said Coburg. 'You said his name was Joe.'

'Joe Williams,' said Julie. 'Though he goes – went – by the stage name of Antonio. He said it sounded more Argentinian.'

'Why Argentinian?'

'He's a tango dancer. He does – did – an act at El Torero, a club near Waterloo Station.' She shook her head and looked suddenly distressed. 'God, I can't believe it! It's not as if I was mad on him. We only went out a couple of times. I thought he was fun, which is why when we had a party I invited him along. But there was nothing serious between us.' Suddenly she began to cry. 'But there could have been. I mean, in a war you expect people to die. Bombs drop, buildings collapse. That's the way it is. But you don't expect someone to have their throat cut, especially in a place like the Ritz.'

CHAPTER TEN

Lampson stood in the mortuary at University College Hospital and watched Eric Nugent as he focused intently on the photograph of Count Ahmed. Finally, the mortuary attendant asked: 'Who is he?'

'We don't know,' lied Lampson. 'The question for you is: was he one of the men who took the body from the mortuary yesterday?'

Nugent shook his head as he handed the photograph back to Lampson.

'No,' he said. 'Nothing like any of 'em.'

We're getting nowhere, thought Lampson miserably as he re-entered Scotland Yard and headed up the stairs to the office. *We're never going to find out who the dead man is.*

Coburg was on the phone when Lampson walked into the office. Coburg finished his conversation and hung up as Lampson dropped the photograph on the desk.

'Your mate at the Foreign Office came up trumps,' he said. 'Unfortunately, Nugent says he wasn't one of the crowd who took the body away.'

Coburg gave him a broad grin. 'Luckily, we have a lead,' he said. 'According to someone I met our dead man is a certain Joe Williams, who, under the name of Antonio, was a tango dancer at El Torero near Waterloo Station. I was on the phone to the club just now making sure they're open at this hour. They are, and we're on our way to talk to the manager, a Mr Stavros Higgins.'

'Stavros Higgins?' echoed Lampson incredulously. 'What sort of name is that?'

'If it's real, I expect he's half-Greek, half-English,' said Coburg. 'On the other hand, it could be an adopted name for professional reasons.'

In the car, Coburg filled in Lampson on Julie. 'She shares a house with the jazz singer Rosa Weeks, who's the lady I was meeting for lunch.'

'Oh, so it was a lady, eh?'

Coburg chuckled. 'Come on, Ted, you know it was. You hung around after you dropped me off, and you saw us.'

'I wasn't being nosy!' protested Lampson. 'I was worried you might have been late and she might have left. In which case, you'd have needed a lift, that was all.'

'Your interest in my welfare is appreciated,' said Coburg.

'So, are we going to pass this info about Joe Williams on to all those others who are interested? You know, MI5, MI6, the Foreign Office . . .'

'After we've checked it out ourselves. Now we've got

something concrete to look into, I don't want things being messed up with everyone else getting involved.'

El Torero was a small low-ceilinged room in a basement beneath a parade of shops opposite the station. The decor was predominantly red: the lights had red shades over them, the walls were painted red and were decorated with paintings of bulls and bullfighters. A long bar ran the length of one wall with a variety of bottles on display behind it. Small tables with stubs of candles in jars on them were cramped around a space where the artistes performed. Next to it was a small stage for the musicians. At this time of day the only people inside were the manager and a barman stacking up glasses in readiness for the evening, along with Coburg and Lampson. Stavros Higgins did, indeed, look partly Greek, but his accent was pure London. He looked at the photo of the dead man in the same bewildered manner as Julie had.

'Yeh, it's Joe all right,' he said. 'But what was he doing at the Ritz? And in a suite belonging to a king, you say?'

'That's what we're trying to find out,' said Coburg. 'Did he ever mention the Ritz to you in any way? Or people who might have worked there, or been staying there?'

Higgins shook his head. 'No,' he said. 'But then, I'd have been surprised if he had. The Ritz was way out of Joe's league.'

'Where did he live?'

'Just round the corner from here. I'll give you his address.'

'What about friends of his? People at the club? Ones he danced with, say.'

'He only had one partner, Alice, and it was purely professional. She's the wife of the bandleader, see, and if Joe had tried anything on with her he'd have been spitting out teeth. Bert's a tempestuous type.'

'Bert?'

'Bert Watkins. Good bloke, but he's got a bit of a temper on him when he gets riled.'

'Did he ever get riled with Joe?'

Higgins shook his head. 'No. Joe did everything right, kept in time to the music, didn't try it on with Alice.'

'So, who might have killed him?'

Higgins shrugged helplessly. 'I've got no idea. And as he got killed at the Ritz, I can't see it was anything to do with working at the club.'

'Still, we'll need a list of the club's employees. Names and addresses. Bar staff, waiters, cleaners, musicians – everyone Williams would have had contact with.'

'Why?'

'To talk to them. One of them might be able to throw some light on what happened.'

'They won't,' insisted Higgins.

'Yes, well, we'll be the judge of that. So, if you'll let us have the list . . .'

'I'm not sure if I can do that,' said Higgins. 'Don't I need to get their permission first?'

'No,' said Coburg. 'This is a murder enquiry so everything else is superseded.'

Higgins looked at him sourly, obviously very reluctant to comply.

'I don't know,' he said.

Coburg shrugged. 'Of course, if that's difficult, I can

always send people to do it for you. They can go through your books and make the list for me. The thing is, because everyone's short-staffed, with a war on, I expect they'll be people from lots of different places drafted in to do it. You know, the Foreign Office, the Tax Office, Customs, who might be interested in some of the bottles in your storeroom—'

'Yes, all right,' said Higgins with a scowl. 'When you do want this list?'

'Now.'

'It'll take me a while.'

'We'll wait,' said Coburg.

It took Higgins half an hour, but finally, reluctantly, he appeared from his office with two sheets of paper.

'Thank you,' said Coburg.

He and Lampson took the list to a small cafe set amongst the parade of shops and ordered refreshments: coffee for Coburg and tea for Lampson.

'They say it won't be long before coffee can't be got,' said Lampson. 'I've already heard tales of people grinding up acorns to make their own.'

'I can imagine few things more disgusting,' said Coburg sagely. 'But I'm sure we'll get used to it. We got used to eating almost anything during the last war, especially in the trenches.'

'I heard you ate rats,' said Lampson.

'Not me, particularly,' replied Coburg. 'Although I know some did. Mind you, some of the rats in the trenches were the size of dogs, so they had a bit of meat on them.'

He took one page of Higgins's list and passed the other to Lampson.

'See if there's anyone we recognise,' he said.

They studied their respective lists, while sipping their drinks.

'There's a name here I know,' said Lampson. 'Billy Thackeray, a waiter. If it's the same Billy Thackeray, I grew up with him.'

'In Somers Town?'

Lampson nodded. 'Then he moved. Well, he had to while he still had his arms and legs.'

'A bad boy?'

'Indeed. A slimy burglar who specialised in robbing old people. And in his own locality. When word got out what he was up to he scarpered pretty quick.'

'How long ago?'

'Years. He was seventeen then. Word was he went south of the river. He'd be safe there. No one from the north of the Thames ever goes south if they can help it. It's a foreign country.'

'What's even more interesting is this,' said Coburg. He pointed to the addresses. 'He and Joe Williams lived in the same house.'

'So, shall we go and see him?'

'I think before we do, it might help to have a word with Barry Moss, the station sergeant at Waterloo nick. If this Billy Thackeray is still a bad lad, then Barry will know about him. And he might be able to tell us about Joe Williams.'

Nick Phelps, the barman at the Blue Cat club, looked up in surprise as Julie Stafford walked in and sat at the bar. At this time of day the club was empty except for the cleaners, and Nick, who virtually lived at the club.

'You're in early today,' said Nick. 'You ain't due on for hours.'

Julie sighed. 'I didn't feel like being at home. The other girls are out just now, and the house has that empty feel. I wanted to come somewhere with company, and company I don't have to pretend with.'

Nick grinned. 'That'll be me. Drink?'

'Gin,' said Julie.

Nick poured her a gin and slid the glass across the bar to her.

'You look down. What's happened?'

'A friend of mine has just died,' sighed Julie unhappily. 'Been killed.'

'Oh no. The war?'

Julie shook her head. 'Do you remember Antonio? I bought him in here a few weeks ago.'

'Sorry, no,' said Nick.

'He's a tango dancer, works at the El Torero.'

'What is he, Spanish?'

'No, his real name's Joe. Anyway, I heard that he's dead. He was killed in a suite of some foreign king at the Ritz.' She hesitated, then gave a shudder as she added: 'Someone cut his throat.'

Nick stared at her, stunned. 'Murdered?'

'That's what the police told me.' She shook her head, bewildered. 'What was he doing at a place like the Ritz in the first place?'

'It's a mystery,' agreed Nick. 'Who is this king?'

'King?' asked Julie, puzzled.

'The one in whose place he was found.'

'I can't remember. It's a funny sort of name. But the

copper who gave me the news said he's the King of Albania.' She frowned. 'Where's Albania?'

'No idea,' said Nick. He pointed at Julie's glass as she emptied it and put it back on the bar. 'Do you want another?'

Julie shook her head. 'No. I don't feel right being out and about when Joe's just been killed. I think I'll go back home.'

'I'll see you later,' said Nick.

'I'm not sure,' said Julie. 'I don't think I'll be up to it. Can you tell the boss I've had some bad news? Tell him I'll be in tomorrow night.'

'Sure,' said Nick.

He watched her as she wandered towards the stairs that led to the street. He waited until he was certain she was out of sight before picking up the telephone and dialling a number. When a familiar gruff voice answered, he said: 'It's Nick at the Blue Cat. I've just heard something you may be interested in.'

When Rosa got home after her Rivoli Bar performance that night it was to find Julie and their other housemate, Donna, sitting at the kitchen table working their way through a bottle of wine and a packet of cigarettes. Julie looked miserable.

'Aren't you supposed to be at the club?' Rosa asked her.

'I couldn't face it, not after what hapened to Joe,' said Julie. 'Putting on a happy face for the punters.'

'Won't they mind?' asked Rosa.

'I'm just in the chorus line,' said Julie. 'It's not like you, solo. If you don't turn up there's an audience and an empty piano. Me, I'm one of a dozen girls and no one's counting. Except the manager, and he's OK. I think he's got the hots for me.' She raised her glass. 'Here's to Joe.'

Rosa sat down and poured herself a glass. 'I didn't think you two were that close.'

'I didn't think so either, until your pal told me he was dead. It's the shock, him being killed. He was fun. A nice bloke.'

'It's the war,' sighed Donna. 'People you know and love dying suddenly.'

'It wasn't the war,' protested Julie. 'It was at the Ritz!'

'I lost my brother at Dunkirk,' said Donna, and she gave a heartfelt sigh of deep sadness. 'Twenty-five he was. Tom. A plumber. He had such a great future ahead of him. There was all this hoo-ha about the number of soldiers they managed to get off the beaches there, but they never rescued Tom.'

The sudden wailing tones of the air-raid siren from outside made all three women sit up.

'Bloody hell!' said Donna.

She ran to the hallway and grabbed her coat and gas mask, Rosa and Julie hurrying after her.

'Gas mask!' shouted Rosa at Julie when she saw her friend had left hers behind.

Julie ran back and snatched it from the dresser, then all three women hurried outside, locked the front door and ran towards Oxford Street and the entrance to the shelter beneath one of the large department stores. The sound of the sirens was deafening, the sirens and whistles from the patrolling air-raid wardens adding to the cacophony. Above them the broad beams of the searchlights criss-crossed as they searched the night sky for approaching German bombers, trying to pinpoint them for the crews of the enormous anti-aircraft guns surrounded by protective banks of sandbags.

The three women joined the masses of people pouring out of their houses and making for the shelter. It was going to be another sleepless night.

CHAPTER ELEVEN

Thursday 22nd August

Coburg's first call the next morning was to Rosa's house. Rosa opened the door to him, a welcoming smile on her face.

'This is unexpected,' she said. 'But a pleasure.' She opened the door wider. 'Are you staying? Donna's left for work and Julie's still in bed.'

'Sadly, no,' said Coburg. 'I wanted to check you were all right after the raid last night. Any plans to get a telephone put in? I could have called you rather than surprising you.'

'I like being surprised this way,' said Rosa. 'As for the telephone, that's down to the landlord and he doesn't want to spend the money.' She gave a nervous shudder as she said: 'We were fine, but it was a bit close for comfort. We actually felt the explosions in the shelter.'

'Where is your nearest shelter?'

'Just round the corner in Oxford Street. How near was the bombing?'

'Harrow,' said Coburg.

'That's just up the Edgware Road,' said Rosa, concerned.

'It's still a few miles away,' said Coburg. 'And it's in Middlesex.'

'You think the Luftwaffe are sticking to postal districts and county boundaries?' commented Rosa sarcastically.

'Central London still hasn't been touched,' insisted Coburg.

'So why are they bombing Harrow?'

Coburg shrugged. 'Navigational error.'

'How can you take this so calmly?' demanded Rosa.

'I'm not taking it calmly. That's why I came, because I was worried about you.' Tentatively he suggested: 'Maybe, if you're worried, you should come and stay with me?'

'They bombed Harrow last night. Who's to say they won't bomb Hampstead tonight?'

'We have shelters at the flats. Two Anderson shelters have been erected in what were the gardens at the back.'

Rosa looked scornful. 'Those things look pretty rickety to me. Just a sheet of corrugated iron.'

'Properly shaped and covered with earth,' Coburg insisted.

'The basement in Oxford Street is deeper and stronger,' countered Rosa. 'And I can get there in four minutes.' She looked at him hopefully. 'You sure you won't come in? After last night I could do with some comfort.'

Coburg pulled her to him and kissed her. 'I want nothing more, but my sergeant's waiting for me. Tonight?'

She gave a rueful grin and a sigh. 'If that's the best you can offer, it'll have to do.' She hugged him tight and kissed him, then released him. 'Off you go and be a policeman.'

* * *

Coburg and Lampson stood in the reception area at Waterloo police station and watched Sergeant Barry Moss as he studied the two pages of names. Like Coburg, fifty-year-old Moss was a veteran of the First World War where a burst of machine-gun fire tearing through his right leg had left him with a pronounced limp, meaning that most of his duties were now at the station. Moss was happy with this as he didn't have to be out patrolling in bad weather, and the police station was near enough to his home that his family could get hold of him in an emergency.

'Just two names stick out,' said Moss. 'Joe Williams and Billy Thackeray. Both as crooked as they come.'

'So, why haven't we got any record of them at the Yard?' asked Coburg.

'Too small-time,' said Moss. 'Petty offences, and as far I know they've never been convicted. Mostly they've been involved in knocking over warehouses, but on the rare occasions when they've been lifted, they've always got an alibi.'

'Who from?'

'Different people, but each time the same name seems to come into the frame. Mel McGuinness.'

Coburg smiled. 'Ah, now you're talking. Big Mel. Yes, we know him. So, you think that Williams and Thackeray are part of his outfit?'

'Small fry only,' said Moss. 'But Big Mel looks after his own.'

'What was the last thing Williams was picked up for?'

'Suspected of being part of gang that lifted a load of sugar from a warehouse, along with Thackeray,' said Moss. 'With sugar being as tightly rationed as it is, there's a big black market out there for it.'

'And they didn't go down for it?'

Moss shook his head. 'Their alibi was they were in a card game when the robbery went down, and they had these blokes who backed them up. Plus, the witness we had who'd identified Williams and Thackeray as being part of the gang – he was storeman at the warehouse which was robbed – backtracked and withdrew his statement. Said he must have been confused.'

'After a visit from Big Mel,' said Coburg.

'Exactly,' said Moss. 'Not that we could prove anything.' He pushed the two sheets of paper back to Coburg. 'And now Williams is dead.'

'He is,' confirmed Coburg.

'I guess his past finally caught up with him,' said Moss. 'So, justice of a sort prevails.'

As they left Waterloo police station and made for their car, Coburg commented: 'It looks like we're getting a bit of a picture.'

'Big Mel?' asked Lampson.

'Yes. If Williams and Thackeray are part of Big Mel's crew, that could explain why Williams might be involved in something as big as two million in money and gold.'

'I don't know, guv,' said Lampson doubtfully. 'He's got fingers in lots of pies, but most of his business is around smaller operators, and people he knows.'

'At which he makes a lot of money,' said Coburg.

'Yes, he does,' agreed Lampson. 'But this business of all that wealth still seems a bit much for him.'

'Maybe he's getting ambitious,' said Coburg.

'So, what's our next move? McGuinness?'

'No, we'll let him stew for the moment. It's my guess that as soon as we left El Torero, our friend Stavros Higgins let Big Mel know we were asking questions about Williams, so he'll know we'll be calling on him. First, we'll take a look at Joe Williams's address, and at the same time have a word with this Billy Thackeray if he's there.'

Big Mel McGuinness was sitting at his regular table in the saloon bar of the Iron Horse reading a newspaper, a cup of tea in front of him. McGuinness liked to keep a clear head when conducting business, and – for him – most of what went on in the pub was business. He was called Big Mel because big was what he certainly was: six feet six inches tall, broad-shouldered with a muscular build. In his early days McGuinness had been an amateur boxer, and a successful one. There had been talk of his turning professional, but the shrewd McGuinness had realised there was more money to be made from managing other boxers, especially if he also ran bets on the outcomes of the fights. Knowing in advance who was going to win was key to that.

The door of the bar opened, and the thin, wiry figure of Charley Barnes entered. Charley was in his forties and his skin had never quite shaken off the impoverished pallor from his early years. That, coupled with his thinning hair and his habit of wearing clothes that had seen better days, gave the impression that he was a vulnerable person, a victim ready to be mugged. Only people who didn't know Barnes ever made that error, and they usually carried the marks of their mistake ever afterwards.

Barnes sat down at the table. 'I got your message, Mel,' he said. 'Something's come up?'

McGuinness put down his newspaper and nodded. There were very few people in his business that McGuinness trusted, when you were dealing on a daily basis with people who were basically crooked the only thing you could be sure of was that they were highly likely to let you down in some way: skimming off the top, either money or goods, or selling information to a rival. McGuinness had a strict policy that anyone caught doing anything like that was severely punished before being cast out, though some still tried it on. But not Charley Barnes. McGuinness trusted Barnes with his life, and his money, both of which were of equal importance to him.

Barnes and McGuinness went right back to the time they were in prison in their early twenties. Separate offences, McGuinness for robbery and Barnes for car theft, but they'd hit it off, with both looking after each other's backs. Prison was a tough place and defending each other for the year they spent inside had forged a bond between them. McGuinness may have been the brighter of the two, but Barnes was the muscle. And when they came out, that was the way it had continued: McGuinness using his brains – and Barnes's fists and boots, along with the occasional gun or blade – to build up an organisation.

'Joe Williams is dead,' said McGuinness. 'Someone cut his throat in one of the suites of the King of Albania at the Ritz.'

Barnes frowned. 'What was Joe doing there?'

'I don't know,' said McGuinness. 'One thing's for sure, he wasn't there doing anything for me.'

'The King of Albania,' mused Barnes thoughtfully. 'The word on the street is he arrived with a stash of cash.'

McGuinness nodded. 'Two million, I hear. Most of it in gold bullion, plus foreign currency.'

'I can't see Joe going after that on his own,' said Barnes.

'Nor can I,' agreed McGuinness. 'But can you think of any other reason he'd be in this king's suite?'

'No,' admitted Barnes. 'But who killed him? The King's bodyguards?'

'If so, why didn't they get rid of the body?' asked McGuinness. 'The thing is: if Joe was working for someone else, who?'

'Maybe we should have a word with Billy Thackeray,' suggested Barnes. 'Him and Joe were very tight.'

'Yeh, good idea,' said McGuinness. 'You do that, Charley. Meantime I'm going to get someone to have a word with a little bird.'

The address for Joe Williams and Billy Thackeray was a tall, thin lodging house sub-divided into bedsits backing on to Waterloo Station. Joe's room was number 3, on the ground floor, and Thackeray's was room 7 on the second floor, the top floor of the house. As Coburg and Lampson mounted the staircase to the top landing they could feel the house vibrating from the heavy engines moving out of the train station, and even though the windows were closed the smell of coal from the trains' smoke permeated into the house. The building was shabby, no carpet on the stairs, just bare wooden boards, and the paint on the interior walls was flaking and looked as if it had been that way for some years.

There were three bedsits on the top landing, number 7 being nearest to the stairs. Coburg knocked at the door, at first lightly, but when there was no answer he banged harder, his rapping bringing the irate occupant of the next door bedsit to his door, clad in a vest and trousers, his feet bare.

'What you up to?' he demanded angrily. 'I'm on night shift and I'm having enough trouble getting to sleep as it is.'

Coburg and Lampson both produced their warrant cards and held them out to the man.

'Police,' said Coburg. 'We're looking for Billy Thackeray.'

'Huh, you and half the world!' said the man sourly. 'Well, I'll tell you the same as I told them, I ain't seen nor heard him for a few days. And usually, when he's in, he gets drunk and starts singing, and there ain't been nothing like that from him.'

'When did you last see him?' asked Coburg.

The man frowned, thinking about it. 'Three days ago,' he announced finally. 'Monday morning. I was trying to get some sleep after coming in from night shift, when he started his singing and shouting. So, I had words with him. That was the last time I saw him or heard him.'

'You say other people have been looking for him,' said Coburg. 'Who?'

'No idea,' said the man. 'Blokes, that's all I know. They came knocking on the door, just like you, loud enough to wake me up, and shouting his name, going "Open up, Billy!"' He reached inside his room and produced a stout length of wood with a ball of lead at the top. 'I showed 'em this, and they scarpered.'

'Yes, I'm sure they did,' said Coburg. 'You never asked who they were?'

'I'm not interested in who they were,' snapped the man. 'I'm only interested in getting some sleep.'

'Were any of them foreign?' asked Coburg.

'Foreign?' asked the man. 'How would I know?'

'From the way they spoke. The way they looked.'

'No. They sounded local to me. Now, can I get back to sleep?'

'Certainly,' said Coburg. 'We're sorry to have disturbed you. And thank you for your assistance.'

The man frowned suspiciously. 'You sure you're coppers?' he asked. 'You sound a bit posh. I ain't never had one talk to me like that before.'

'Scotland Yard,' said Coburg. 'They give us elocution lessons.'

'Elocution?' frowned the man again. 'Huh?'

'Learning 'ow to talk proper,' put in Lampson, deliberately emphasising his working-class London accent.

The man laughed. 'I guess you was out when they did them lessons.'

With that, he shut his door.

'Right, so it's a no show for Billy Thackeray.'

'Reckon he's done a runner, guv?'

'Possibly. Or, in view of what happened to Joe Williams, something more sinister might have happened to him if he was part of what led to Williams getting killed.' He looked at the lock, then looked towards the bedsit of the irate neighbour. 'It's a pity about our sleepy friend next door, otherwise this would be the right occasion to kick the door in. The lock doesn't look much, but I don't fancy upsetting him further.'

'No need to, guv,' said Lampson. He reached into his pocket and pulled out a key ring with some twisted bits of thin metal dangling from them, then knelt beside the lock, inserted two of the metal strips and manipulated them until they heard a slight click, at which Lampson stood up and pushed the door open.

'That's a useful skill to have,' whispered Coburg as they entered the room.

'Something I picked up when I was young,' replied Lampson, also in a whisper, putting the lockpicks back in his pocket.

'In Somers Town?'

Lampson nodded. 'An uncle.'

'You must have been a great disappointment to your family, Ted, joining the police.'

'No, they understood. And they were never criminals.'

'They just used some of the local techniques?'

'Exactly.'

'And they didn't cut you off when you joined and put on the uniform?'

'On the contrary, they were proud. Especially Mum. Someone respectable in the family.'

'Lucky you didn't have to arrest any of them.'

The pair set to work searching the property, primarily looking for letters or notes that might give a clue as to why Thackeray had vanished. All the time Coburg was expecting their search to be interrupted by the neighbour with his leaded stick, upset by the sounds of drawers and cupboards being opened, despite them working carefully. Coburg was well aware of how thin the dividing walls were in this type of property, and this was proved when he and Lampson heard the deep sound of snoring coming from next door. Lampson grinned, gave his boss the thumbs up and mouthed 'Lucky us!'

There was very little that seemed relevant or useful

in Thackeray's room, but what there was Coburg and Lampson stuffed into evidence bags to be examined in detail later. Their search finished, they retreated to the landing, where Lampson relocked the door before they headed downstairs to the ground floor, and Joe Williams's room.

Once again, Lampson did his wizardry with the lockpicks, and they began a search. It was Lampson who made the first discovery, a stash of lockpicks and skeleton keys in a drawer in the bedside cabinet.

'Well, this is interesting,' said Lampson, holding them up for Coburg to see them. 'So, Joe was a peterman. Locks and safes. Which brings us back to the two million locked up somewhere in King Zog's rooms.'

'What's more interesting is the fact they're here in his room, rather than being in his pocket when we found him. If he was in the suite to open a safe or something, he'd have had them with him.'

'Yes,' agreed Lampson thoughtfully. 'Maybe he was just casing the joint?'

'He would've still had to have his tools of the trade with him,' said Coburg.

Charley Barnes stood in the shadows of the wall around Waterloo Station and watched as Coburg and Lampson came out of the house. So, the coppers were doing their digging already. He waited until he was sure they were clear and in no danger of returning, then walked across the road and into the house. There was no use knocking on Williams's door, so he went straight up to the top floor and room 7, where he banged on the door. When there was no answer, he banged again and followed it up with a boot hard against the lock, the door springing inwards.

He stood surveying the room. With Williams dead, he wondered if anything had happened to Thackeray. Maybe he'd done a runner. If so, Barnes needed to start looking for clues as to where he might have gone.

There was the sound of a door being thrown open and then a man in a stained vest entered the room swinging a leaded stick.

'Right, you bastard—' he began.

Then he stopped when he saw who it was and hastily put the stick down.

'Mr Barnes,' he said apologetically. 'I'm sorry, I didn't realise it was you. I've just had all manner of people banging on this door while I'm trying to get some kip.'

'Were two of 'em coppers?' demanded Barnes.

'Yes, sir. They were just here.'

'What did you tell them?' asked Barnes, and even though he spoke quietly there was no mistaking the menace in his voice.

'Nothing, I swear!' burst out the man fearfully. 'I never talk to coppers!'

Barnes studied the man, then asked: 'When did you last see Billy?'

'Monday morning. Here.'

'And you ain't seen him since?'

'No. Honest. And I ain't heard him, either.'

Barnes nodded. 'Who else has been round asking for him lately?'

'Joe Williams come round looking for him on Monday.'

'Did he say why?'

The man shook his head.

'What time of day was it when Joe came round?'

'Afternoon. I'd just got me head down.'

'Anyone else?'

'Some bloke came on Tuesday afternoon.'

'Who was he?'

'I don't know. I'd never seen him before.'

'What did he look like?'

The man frowned, trying to remember. 'He looked foreign.'

'Foreign?'

'Yeh. He had an accent. Maybe Greek. Something like that.'

'What did you tell him?'

'That I hadn't seen Billy since Monday morning.'

'What did he say?'

'He started to get a bit stroppy, so I had to show him Len.' He picked up his leaded stick. 'When I did that, he left.'

Barnes nodded. 'Anyone else?'

The man shook his head.

'Right,' said Barnes. 'If you hear anything from or about Billy, you pop along to the Iron Horse and leave word for me.'

'Yes, Mr Barnes,' said the man.

'And the same goes if you hear anyone asking after him. You come and let me know.' He made for the door, the man moving aside to let him pass. Barnes pointed at the broken lock on the door. 'Shoddy workmanship,' he grunted. 'They don't make 'em like they used to.'

CHAPTER TWELVE

Julie sat in her room, smoking and thinking. Rosa was out but Donna had come home early because she only worked mornings on Thursdays. Glad of the company, Julie had once more started to express her bewilderment and her feelings about Joe, but Donna had begun to talk about her dead brother again.

I don't want to talk about your brother, I want to talk about Joe, thought Julie in angry frustration.

'I've got to go and get something sorted out upstairs,' she said, and she left Donna in the kitchen.

In her room she lay on the bed and stared at the ceiling, her mind full of thoughts about Joe. She didn't understand why she felt like this, so lost. It wasn't as if she'd been in love with him. And it was true what Donna said, people were dying all the time. It was just where he'd died, and how, that baffled her. What had he been doing at the Ritz?

She heard the *rat-a-tat* of the door knocker, then the front door opening and Donna's voice. Almost immediately there was a knock at her room, then Donna put her head round the door.

'Hey, Julie. There's two blokes at the door asking for you.'

'Who are they?'

'They didn't say.'

'What sort of blokes?'

'They look official. You know, like plain-clothes coppers. What you been up to?'

'Nothing.'

Curious, Julie headed downstairs. What would anyone official be wanting with her?

The two men, both wearing hats and overcoats, stood waiting for her. The shorter of the two had a moustache, the other was thin and miserable-looking.

'Miss Julie Stafford?' the shorter of the two asked.

'Yes.'

He produced a warrant card which he showed to her.

'We're from Special Branch. We'd like you to come with us to answer a few questions.'

'What about?'

'All we can say right now is that it concerns a matter of national importance. Would you come with us, please?'

'No,' said Julie. 'I don't know who you are, and I've done nothing wrong. If you want to talk to me you can do it here.'

The two men exchanged looks, then the shorter one said: 'I'm afraid we must insist, miss. I can assure you this is just a routine enquiry, but if you refuse to accompany us we may be forced to take you in handcuffs, and I'm sure you won't like that.'

Donna appeared, summoned by the angry tone in Julia's voice.

'What's up, Julie?' she asked.

'This is nothing to do with you, miss,' the shorter one said politely to Donna. 'If you would please leave us to our business.'

'These men claim they're from Special Branch,' said Julie, 'and they want to take me away, but they won't say why.'

'As I said, miss, it's on a matter of national security, so I'm not allowed to say more at this stage.'

Julie hesitated, then said: 'I'll go and get my coat and bag.'

'Certainly, miss,' said the short one. 'My colleague will accompany you.'

Julie's mind was in a whirl as she mounted the stairs to her room, the tall, thin, silent man close behind her. What was all this about? It could only be about Joe, the fact she'd recognised him from that photo that Rosa's policeman friend had showed her. Was this down to him? He was a copper. Had he reported her or something? Was that what this was about? If so, she needed to get a message to him to get her out of it.

The tall man waited outside her room while she gathered her coat and her handbag, but Julie noticed that although he stayed on the landing, he kept his foot against the door so that she couldn't close it. The man stood to one side as she came out of her room, then followed her back downstairs to the front door, where Donna was still standing, watching the short man suspiciously.

'Do me a favour, get hold of Rosa and tell her what's happened,' Julie said to Donna. 'Tell her to get her copper pal on to it and sort it out.'

'That won't be necessary, miss,' said the short man to Donna. 'Your friend will be returning shortly, once we've got a few things cleared up.' He pointed at a car waiting at the kerb and said to Julie: 'This way, miss.'

Coburg and Lampson pulled open the doors of the saloon bar of the Iron Horse pub in Lambeth. Within beer-glass-throwing distance of the Archbishop of Canterbury's official residence, Lambeth Palace, reflected Coburg, which said a lot about London: the highest churchman in the land cheek by jowl with one of London's most dangerous gangsters.

As Coburg and Lampson entered the pub, two men at a table between McGuinness and the door stood up. Their flattened noses and cauliflower ears were the clue to their previous occupations as prizefighters, and their current one as McGuinness's bodyguards. McGuinness gestured to the men to return to their seats and smiled at Coburg and Lampson.

'Mr Coburg. Sergeant Lampson. Long time no see. To what do I owe this unexpected visit?'

Coburg smiled. 'Oh, come on, Mr McGuinness. A man like you, who knows everything that happens on his patch?'

McGuinness smiled. 'Ah, but the Ritz isn't in my patch.'

Coburg chuckled. 'See how much easier conversation is when we don't pretend?'

McGuinness gestured at two chairs at his table and Coburg and Lampson sat down.

'What can I get you? Beer? Whisky?'

'Really, when we're on duty?' Coburg chided him. 'Tut, tut. No, just some information.'

'About what?'

'Joe Williams. One of yours, I believe.'

McGuinness shook his head. 'If you've been told that, someone is leading you astray, Chief Inspector.'

'But an acquaintance, surely. Whenever he's been lifted for anything, your name seems to come up as his rescuing angel.'

'I'm a man who dislikes injustice, Chief Inspector. When I hear of someone being wrongly accused of something, I feel it my duty to intervene.'

'And I'm sure Joe Williams was very grateful. Of course, now he's dead, the picture changes somewhat, because a lot of people want to know who killed him, and what he was doing at the Ritz to end up in a royal suite with his throat cut.'

'I can assure you, Mr Coburg, that whatever the reason he was there, it was nothing to do with me.'

'What about Billy Thackeray?'

'Who?'

Coburg gave a weary sigh. 'Please, Mr McGuinness, this conversation has been going so well, but to try and pretend you don't know Billy Thackeray, close pal of Joe Williams, living at the same address—'

'Yes, all right, the name does seem familiar, now you come to mention it,' said McGuinness. 'What about him?'

'He seems to have vanished.'

'Vanished?'

'Yes, he hasn't been seen at the house he and Joe lived in for the past few days. Do you know where he might be?'

McGuinness shook his head. 'I hardly know the bloke. Who is he exactly?'

'A waiter at El Torero. You know, the nightclub where Stavros Higgins phoned you from to let you know that the dead man at the Ritz was Joe Williams.'

For the first time, McGuinness scowled, and they saw the flash of anger in his eyes.

'Are you having my phone tapped, Inspector?' he demanded.

'Chief Inspector,' Coburg corrected him. 'And the answer is no. But I'm sure that when I report to the Intelligence services and the Foreign Office about this conversation, if it's not what I feel is satisfactory, they can arrange it.'

McGuinness studied Coburg carefully, weighing up his next words.

'Maybe the Intelligence people may not be as co-operative as you'd like, Chief Inspector,' he said finally, and his easy smile was gone now, replaced by a quiet anger at having his equanimity disturbed.

'Oh? Why's that?'

'If you're looking for who might have bumped him off, maybe you should look into his political connections. Or maybe these people you mention are already doing that.'

'What political connections?'

'By all accounts he was a member of the British Union of Fascists, before they got closed down. But then again, he wasn't, if you get my drift.'

'Let's say I don't get your drift. Either he was or he wasn't.'

'You're not very good at subtlety, are you, Mr Coburg? Take me, for example. I'm a patriot, I am. King and country first. Now I know where my loyalties lie, and it wouldn't please me to think that anyone who worked for me favoured the opposition, if you get my meaning.'

'You don't approve of the BUF.'

'No, I don't, and even though a lot of 'em have been rightfully locked up as the traitors they are, there are still quite a few out there, on the loose, stirring things up. If you know where to find 'em.'

'And Joe knew where to find them?'

'Well, he would do, being a member.'

'And he reported what they were up to? And what did you do with it? A little blackmail?'

McGuinness shook his head. 'No, no, Mr Coburg. Like I said, I'm a patriot, me. I don't take money from the likes of them scum to keep quiet. That goes against the grain.' He winked and smiled. 'If I were you, I'd have a word with some of your colleagues at Wormwood Scrubs.'

'Right, Ted, what did you make of all that?' asked Coburg as he and Lampson walked from the pub to their car.

'All that British Union of Fascists stuff?' grunted Lampson. 'And the bit about Wormwood Scrubs. That's where MI5 have moved to, ain't it?'

'They have,' replied Coburg.

'So, if he's to be believed, Joe Williams was working undercover for MI5, keeping them apprised of what the BUF and other fifth columnists are up to.'

'*If* Big Mel is to be believed,' stressed Coburg. 'Which, knowing him, is highly unlikely. The man spends so much time lying he's forgotten what the truth is. But of one thing you can be sure, he's told us about Williams, the BUF and MI5 for a reason, one which will be useful to him.'

'Divert attention away from what he's been up to?'

'Possibly. But a side of me suspects there's another reason as well, something we're not aware of yet. Though I feel we will be, once we start digging.'

'Perhaps Joe Williams was part of a team that went in to the Ritz to steal the two million and he got killed before the job went ahead.'

'But whose team? McGuinness is too sharp and too experienced to put things at risk for something that huge.'

'Maybe McGuinness was working with someone else,' mused Lampson.

'The Bell brothers?' suggested Coburg. 'They're big enough to handle two million. And Piccadilly is on their patch.'

'Yeh, but they're based north of the river,' pointed out Lampson. 'As I've said, north and south don't mix, as a rule.'

'They might when there's a fortune of that size for the taking,' said Coburg.

As Rosa walked into the Ritz she saw that the hall porter was signalling to her from his desk.

'Yes, George?'

'Miss Weeks, I've had a telephone call for you from a friend of yours. A Donna Dunn.'

'Donna? Yes, she's one of my housemates. What's happened? I can't imagine she'd phone here for me unless there was a problem.'

'She did sound upset. She asked if you could call at the house as soon as you came in.'

'Did she say why?'

'I'm afraid not. But, as I said, she did sound as if something had happened to upset her.'

'When did she phone?'

'About an hour and a half ago.'

'An hour and a half!'

'Unfortunately, I didn't know how to get hold of you,' said George apologetically.

'It's not your fault, George. I was at Chappell's selecting some new pieces of music, and I got carried away. I only came in now to practise some of them for tonight. If she phones again will you tell her I'm on my way.'

'I assume there's no telephone in your house.'

'You assume right. Luckily there's a phone box not far away from us, but it's no use if someone wants to get in touch. I'll see you later, George.'

George turned back to checking the pigeonholes behind his desk, making sure that all messages needing attention were still in their rightful places. No one but he was supposed to touch them, though one could never be sure when some interfering person, whether hotel staff or a nosy guest, might have sneaked in when his back was turned.

'Mr George!'

He turned and saw the trembling figure of one of the kitchen staff still dressed in his whites appearing from the stairs that led to the basement.

'You know the rules about appearing in the reception area wearing kitchen uniform,' George he said in tones of stern disapproval.

'Yes, Mr George, but chef sent me and told me it was urgent. Very urgent. There's a dead body in the kitchen! He wants you to get in touch with your detective friend at Scotland Yard. There's been another killing!'

CHAPTER THIRTEEN

As Coburg and Lampson entered Scotland Yard they saw the duty desk sergeant hailing them.

'More problems, Ted,' sighed Coburg.

'It might be something good,' suggested Lampson.

'In this place?' asked Coburg.

Lampson shrugged. 'Yeh, fair point.'

They reached the desk.

'Yes, Sergeant?' asked Coburg.

'The Ritz have been on for you. A Mr George. Urgent.'

'Oh? Did he say why?'

'Yes, sir. It seems there's been another murder there. Superintendent Allison has gone to look into it, but this Mr George asks if you can go there as well.'

Rosa let herself into the house, and at the sound of the door opening, Donna came hurrying down the stairs.

'Rosa! Thank God you're back!'

'Why? What's happened?'

'Two blokes came and took Julie away.'

'Why? Where to?'

'They didn't say. One of them said it was a matter of national security, but it all looked wrong to me. Julie said to tell you and for you to get your copper pal on it.'

'She must mean Edgar. He's a DCI at Scotland Yard. Yesterday he showed Julie a photograph of a man who was killed at the Ritz.'

'Joe!' exclaimed Donna. 'Remember, she was talking about him last night.' She looked at Rosa, puzzled. 'Is that why these two blokes took her away?'

'I can't think why,' said Rosa. 'Who were these blokes? Where were they from?'

'Julie said they told her they were from Special Branch. And they looked like coppers. But . . . I don't know . . . I could tell by the way Julie was not wanting to go with them and them leaning on her, that something didn't feel right.'

Julie sat in the small locked room. It wasn't a cell; she'd been in police cells before and she knew what they were like. For one thing, there was supposed to be a toilet in it. There wasn't one in this room. Yes, there was a bucket in one corner, but that was all. There wasn't even a proper bunk, just a mattress on the flagstone floor, along with three wooden chairs and a table. There was one window, partially boarded up by wooden slats nailed horizontally across it, with just enough light let in to penetrate the gloom. There was a bare light bulb dangling from the ceiling. All further evidence that wherever she was, this wasn't a police cell: in police cells the ceiling lights had protective glass impregnated with steel bars to stop them being smashed.

Whoever these people were, they weren't regular coppers. She doubted if they were even Special Branch. Certainly, the way they'd acted in the car hadn't been police-like. The short one had produced a thick blindfold which he'd insisted she had to wear. She'd tried to resist, but the tall one on her other side had simply grabbed her wrists and held them in a grip of steel while the short one slipped the band of thick material over her hair and slid it down to cover her eyes.

'Any attempts to take it off and we'll handcuff you,' she was warned.

And so she'd kept it on, and when the car stopped they'd guided her through a series of doors and down a stone corridor before they'd pushed her into this room, taken the blindfold off, and then left, locking the door behind them.

Who were they? At least they hadn't mistreated her. There'd been no grabbing or slaps, nor even any threats. There'd just been the same boring questions repeated over and over again whenever they came in, the short one doing all the questioning while the tall one just sat and watched, grim-faced. The short one seemed polite enough, didn't raise his voice, but Julie sensed there was something dangerous about him. She'd encountered men like him before, all perfectly well-behaved, then suddenly fists were flying and there would be blood.

'Tell us about Joe Williams.'

'I've already told you: I knew him. Not well. We went out a few times, that's all.'

'When did you last see him?'

'About a fortnight ago. There was a party at our house, and I asked if he wanted to come.'

'You were having a sexual relationship?'

'No.'

'Then why did you invite him?'

'We were both dancers. It was what we did. I knew there'd be other people there who were dancers, and we like to get together to swap information.'

'What sort of information?'

'Who's looking for dancers. You know, for a new show. Or if anyone's left an existing show so there's a spot free. It's a hard life being a dancer. It's not regular work or a regular payslip.'

'You were upset when you heard he'd been killed.'

'Of course I was. I liked him.'

'How did you hear about his death?'

'I've told you this time and time again.'

'Tell us again.'

'One of the girls I share the house with, Rosa Weeks, she's a singer and pianist. She came home with a friend of hers who's in the police. He showed me a photograph of Joe and said he'd been killed at the Ritz. He wanted to know if I knew who he was and what he was doing there, same as you're asking me. I told him the same as I told you: I had no idea.'

'This policeman. What's his name?'

'The same as it was before when you asked me: Detective Chief Inspector Coburg. Rosa called him Edgar, so I suppose that's his first name.'

'And you'd never seen this detective before?'

'Never. I didn't even know that Rosa knew him.'

'Why did he come to you with the photograph?'

'Like I've already told you: he showed it to Rosa, and she recognised him as being with me at the party.'

'But she didn't know him before that?'

'No. And neither of them knew his name until I told them.'

Coburg and Lampson strode into the reception hall of the Ritz and made straight for the hall porter.

'Thank God you're here,' said George in heartfelt relief. 'The superintendent is a good man, but he doesn't know the ways of the Ritz.'

'What happened?' asked Coburg. 'All I know so far is that someone else has been killed.'

'One of the kitchen staff,' said George. 'Alex Ollen. He's Swiss.' Then he gave Coburg a look as he lowered his voice and added: 'At least, that's what his papers say.'

'When did it happen?'

'His body was discovered about an hour ago, but there is talk he was killed sometime before that.'

'Where?'

'In the kitchen. That's where everyone is right now. They discovered his body when one of the staff went to a store cupboard. He'd been stabbed.'

'Thanks, George,' said Coburg.

Lampson followed him as he led the way to the stairs, then down to the kitchen area. As they neared the bottom of the staircase they could hear a battery of raised voices, some angry, some crying, some making noises of appeasement to try and calm things down.

'This is going to be chaos,' Coburg muttered to Lampson. 'A hotel kitchen's like an out-of-control lunatic asylum at the best of times. Add discovering a murder victim to it and it'll be sheer bedlam.'

They marched along the lower corridor and came upon a crowded scene: men in white jackets, some stained with food, gathered around a row that was going on between three men. Superintendent Allison was gesticulating at a man in chef's whites who was gesticulating back, while at the same time expressing himself loudly in angry French. Between them, trying to pacify both men, was a man in formal dress coat and striped trousers: the general manager. Three uniformed police officers watched from a short distance away with puzzled bemusement.

Allison spotted Coburg and immediately shouted: 'Chief Inspector! Thank God!'

At this, the general manager and the chef turned, and when they saw Coburg, they rushed over towards him, both shouting and waving their hands.

'Monsieur Coburg, I must have my kitchen back!' appealed the chef.

'I've told him we cannot do that until we've examined the body in situ,' snapped the superintendent. 'Please explain that to him. He doesn't seem to understand English.'

'I understand but I do not comprehend!' the chef raged. 'Why?'

The superintendent looked at Coburg in appeal. 'Chief Inspector, please!'

Coburg turned to face the angry chef. He launched into gentle but fluent and flowing French, accompanied by a variety of hand gestures to illustrate. The man listened, nodding, and when Coburg had finished he gave a final nod and said: '*Oui. D'accord!*' He then turned to his watching kitchen staff, barked something at them, then led them away like a general moving his troops.

The general manager turned gratefully to Coburg and took his hand in both of his.

'*Merci*, Monsieur Coburg,' he said, and bowed before he released Coburg's hand and then stood waiting ready to be of service.

'What was all that?' asked the bewildered superintendent. 'What did you say to him?'

'The short version, sir, is I assured him he could have his kitchen back within an hour if he left us to do our work. So, with respect, sir, I suggest we crack on. If you could show me the body, and where he was found, and also' – and here Coburg turned his attention to the general manager – 'if you could get hold of the person who found him so I could talk to him?'

'It will be done.' The man bowed again, and hurried off.

'This place is a madhouse,' muttered Allison unhappily, leading the way to a partly opened door where a police constable stood guard. The superintendent pulled the door open wider, and Coburg saw that it was a large cupboard, or rather a storeroom lined with shelves on which were a variety of pots, with frying pans of different sizes hanging from hooks. A large, grey-haired man was kneeling beside the doubled-up body of a man wearing kitchen whites. As the man looked up, Coburg's heart sank. Dr Alexander Stewart.

'So, you're here at last!' rasped Stewart. 'You took your time coming.'

Coburg was tempted to point out that he'd been out

doing police work, but he decided he wasn't going to start defending himself against the bullying doctor.

'What have we got?' he asked blandly.

Stewart rose to his feet and glared at Coburg. 'Eyesight failing you now, is it, Inspector?' he barked sarcastically. He gestured at the body, which looked as if it had been folded in half. 'We have the dead body of a man which has been stuffed behind some free-standing shelves so tightly that rigor has turned him into a human accordion.'

'Cause of death?' asked Coburg.

'At first sight, a knife in the back,' said Stewart. 'A long-bladed one because it's gone straight into the heart.' He pointed in the direction of the kitchen. 'I'm guessing you'll find no end of knives that fit that description out there. But then, I'm not a detective inspector.'

'*Chief* inspector,' Coburg corrected him with a weak smile.

Stewart scowled. 'As if my job isn't difficult enough, I'm having to do it in some kind of cupboard, with the door almost shut, because of the racket that's going on out there. Call this a grand hotel? You don't get this sort of behaviour in the quality hotels in Edinburgh. People there know how to behave.'

'Time of death?' asked Coburg.

Stewart scowled. 'The early hours of this morning. Some time between three o'clock and five.'

Coburg looked at him in surprise, then looked at his watch. 'Are you sure?' he asked.

'I'm not in the habit of making mistakes,' retorted Stewart indignantly.

'But that'd make it about fourteen hours ago. How can

a dead body remain undiscovered in a busy hotel kitchen for fourteen hours?'

'If you'd listened to what I said, *Chief* Inspector,' snapped Stewart, 'you'd have heard me say that the man was stuffed so tightly behind shelves that the cadaver had become seriously contorted. It appears to me that the shelves were pulled forward from the cavity wall where they stood, the dead man was pushed in while his body was still flexible, and the shelves were then pushed back in place and the pots and pans piled on top, thus hiding and securing the body in situ. But then, I'm merely a medical person, not a detective from the higher echelons of Scotland Yard.'

The short man stepped into the telephone booth, dialled a number, then inserted coins.

'Yes?' said the voice that answered.

'She doesn't know anything.'

'You're sure?'

'Yes.'

There was a pause, then the voice said: 'Very well. You know what to do with her.'

Rosa stood in the telephone box, finger poised over button A, which she pressed when the switchboard operator at Scotland Yard answered, the coins tumbling down as the connection was made.

'Hello. Can I speak to Detective Inspector Coburg, please?'

'Who's calling for him?'

'My name is Rosa Weeks. He does know me. It's very urgent.'

'Would you hold on, please, and I'll try and connect you.'

Rosa listened impatiently to a series of clicks, before the operator's voice was heard again.

'I'm sorry, madam. DCI Coburg is out at the moment, and so is his sergeant.'

'Could I leave a message? Could you ask him to make contact with Rosa Weeks? If I'm not at home I'll be at the Ritz Hotel.'

Coburg and Lampson had been given the use of one of the cloakrooms to carry out their questioning of the kitchen staff. They began with the man who'd discovered the dead body.

'I went to get some saucepans, and as I lifted them off the shelf I saw what looked like a jacket sleeve behind it, hanging down,' he said. 'I reached in and took hold of it, but I realised there was something in the sleeve. So, I took some things off some of the other shelves to see what was there, and then I saw Alex's face.' He shuddered. 'It was horrible.'

'You screamed,' said Coburg.

'I did,' the man said. 'Erik and Leno heard and came to see what was wrong. Leno went to get the chef, while me and Erik took everything off the shelves and pulled them out.'

'And you weren't aware he was there before that?'

He shook his head. 'No.'

The story was the same from everyone else they spoke to. But then, this was the day shift, most of them clocking in at half past nine that morning.

They made their way to the general manager's office. 'No one saw anything,' Coburg told him. 'We need to talk to the night shift, the ones who were here between three and five this morning. When will they be in?'

'Half past nine tonight,' said the man.

'I'll come in then and talk to them,' said Coburg. 'In the meantime, we'd like to look at what you have on the dead man. His address. Wage records. Everything. We've been told he was Swiss, is that right?'

He nodded. 'That's what his passport says.'

'Did you see his passport?'

Again, the man nodded.

'Did he have family?'

'Not in this country,' he replied.

'Where? Switzerland?'

'If he had, he never talked about them.'

Coburg and Lampson waited while the general manager went through his records and gave them the details they needed. They also took the contents of the dead man's trouser pockets, and the pockets in his outdoor jacket which was still hanging in the staff cloakroom.

'His address is in Holborn,' said Coburg, jangling two keys on a key ring. 'So that's our first port of call.'

The house where Ollen had lived was a tall, thin terraced house of four floors. It was sub-divided into bedsits, with a toilet and bathroom on every other landing. Ollen had a room on the second floor, and the first thing that struck the two policemen was how neat and tidy everything was. So often their experience in houses like this was of disorder, mess, unwashed plates and cups left on tables, clothes strewn on the floor and the furniture.

'Very neat,' commented Coburg.

'Swiss,' said Lampson. 'They've got a reputation for being tidy.'

The two men began to search through the cupboards and drawers, and in the bedside cabinet Coburg found the man's passport. He studied it for a while, then held it against the window, examining the pages with sunlight through them. He passed it to Lampson.

'I'm suspecting he wasn't really Swiss,' Coburg said.

Lampson also examined it.

'It ain't bad,' he said. 'But I think you're right.'

Coburg took it back from the sergeant and put it into an evidence bag. 'We'll get confirmation one way or another from the Swiss Embassy,' he said.

Lampson opened a drawer in the chest of drawers and took out some papers. 'This might be what some people call a clue,' he said with a grin.

Coburg joined him. There were leaflets in an unfamiliar script.

'Looks like Russian,' said Lampson.

'You understand Russian?' asked Coburg, impressed.

'Not a word,' said Lampson. 'But when I was growing up, one of my neighbours was from Russia. An old bloke. He had papers that looked a bit like this.' He looked at the papers again and frowned. 'But not the same. Similar, but different.'

'Could be Serbian?' wondered Coburg.

Lampson shrugged. 'I wouldn't know, guv. What's Serbian look like?'

'A bit like Russian, but not quite.'

Lampson lifted an envelope from the drawer, opened it and took out a letter.

'Hello, we may have something to help us,' he said. He offered the letter to Coburg, who took it and read it.

'From a woman called Anna who writes in English.'

'And very affectionate,' pointed out Lampson. 'And with her address at the top. Which is lucky. She might be able to throw some light on who he really was and why he'd upset someone enough to stab him and stuff him behind those shelves.'

'Very likely,' said Coburg. 'So, I suggest you go and have a word with her, while I take these other papers to someone I know who might be able to put us right on the language.' He held out the car keys. 'You can take the car.'

Lampson smiled happily. 'You sure, guv?'

'I am. You might have to do some searching. Me, I'm just going to the British Museum, a short stroll away.'

CHAPTER FOURTEEN

Rosa paced agitatedly around the kitchen, her eyes on the clock. Where was Edgar?

Donna appeared, her coat on.

'I've got to go to the shops,' she said. 'Have you got any news about Julie?'

Rosa shook her head. 'Twice I've left messages at Scotland Yard for Edgar. Each time they tell me he's out. At least I've left a message that if he calls and I'm not here, he'll find me at the Ritz.' Again, she looked at the clock. 'In fact, I'd better get going.'

'How's it going there?'

'So far so good. They seem to like me.'

'How could they not,' said Donna. She sighed. 'I wish I could play the piano and sing like you.'

'What's stopping you?' asked Rosa.

'Lack of talent!' replied Donna with a rueful laugh.

'Trust me, it doesn't stop some people,' said Rosa with a sigh.

Coburg knocked on the door marked 'Dr Greville Benton', one of many in the maze of corridors behind the scenes at the British Museum.

'Come!' called a voice.

Coburg opened it and walked in to find Benton stamping his foot into a metal waste bin from which smoke and flames were coming.

'My God!' said Coburg in alarm, and he rushed forward.

'No need for panic,' said Benton amiably. He withdrew his foot, lifted a soda siphon from his desk and directed a jet of water into the bin.

'There!' he said, satisfied, putting the siphon back on his desk. 'Emergency over!'

'What happened?' asked Coburg, aghast.

'A minor accident,' said Benton. 'I emptied my pipe into the bin, thinking it was out, and lo and behold there was a spark left, which, when combined with paper . . .'

'It's lucky no one raised the fire alarm,' said Coburg. 'I picked up the smell of smoke from outside and wondered where it was coming from.'

'Yes, well, they would have checked with me first before calling the fire brigade, I'm sure,' said Benton.

'You mean it's happened before?'

'Once or twice,' Benton admitted ruefully. He was a tall man, much rounded, in his early sixties with a shock of grey hair sticking out in all directions, and his jacket covered in ash. Benton was an old friend of the Coburg family and had been a tutor to both of Coburg's elder brothers to cram them through their university entrance exams. 'What can I do for you, young Edgar? Is this a social call, or police business? I'm assuming social because it's after business hours.'

'It's always a social call, Greville, but, alas, it's also to do with police business, and I know you rarely go home until long after the musuem's closed. Luckily, the security guard let me in when I showed him my Scotland Yard card.' He produced one of the leaflets they'd found in Alex Ollen's room and passed it to Benton. 'I'm hoping you can help us identify the language. We were thinking it might be Russian, or maybe Serbian,' he suggested.

'Very good,' said Benton admiringly.

'You mean we're right?'

'Close,' said Benton. 'It's Macedonian.'

Coburg smiled. 'Now that is good news.'

'Why?' asked Benton.

'Because a case we're working on has an Albanian connection. And that country borders Macedonia.'

'Are you talking about the dead body at the Ritz?' asked Benton.

'You heard about that?'

'There was a small item in *The Telegraph*. Ordinarily I wouldn't have bothered, but it mentioned King Zog, and eastern Europe is one of my areas of study.'

'Well, there's been another murder there. A kitchen hand, stabbed to death. We found this in his lodgings. He claimed to be Swiss, but there's some doubt about that. If he's Macedonian then it might tie in with the dead man in the Albanian king's suite, with those two nations sharing a border. The more we can find out about the situation with Albania and Macedonia, the better.'

'I'm sure you'll be able to find plenty from your official channels,' said Benton. 'Special Branch, the Intelligence services, the Home Office.'

'They're politicians,' said Coburg. 'They'll only tell us what they think we ought to know.'

'How much do you know about the situation in the Balkans?' asked Benton.

'That it's messy, and it's been a mess since the fall of the Ottoman Empire. Lots of strife between the different nations.'

'That about sums it up,' agreed Benton. 'The First World War broke out because of that strife. I think it was hoped that when Yugoslavia was formed after the end of that war, bringing all these different nations into one, so to speak, that the tensions in the Balkans would ease. However, the opposite was the case, with all these different nations demanding autonomy.' For the past few years the trouble has mainly between the nationalists and the communists in each separate region, although sometimes their aims coincide. For example, in 1934 the Communist International issued a proclamation calling for the recognition of Macedonia as a separate nation with its own separate language.' He pointed at the leaflet that Coburg had given him. 'This is an example of that.'

'So, it's a leaflet issued by the communists?'

'Possibly, but the fact there's no hammer and sickle insignia anywhere suggests it's a splinter organisation.'

'But it's political?'

'Oh yes.'

'So, was the killing political?'

'It's possible, but who knows? People kill one another

for all sorts of reasons. For all we know, he might have upset one of his fellow workers in the kitchen. Hotel kitchens can be very volatile places. Some of these chefs are complete madmen.'

Anna wasn't in at the address when Lampson called, but he did find out her surname: Gershon. 'I guess she's at work,' he was told by one of the other tenants of the lodging house. 'She's a waitress at the Elephant Room, it's a cafe in Piccadilly Circus.' He looked at his watch. 'They're usually open in the early evening, so she should still be there.'

But, when Lampson went to the Elephant Room, there was no sign of her.

'She's gone to stay with her family somewhere in the Midlands,' the owner told Lampson. 'Apparently they were worried about her being in London. You know, because of the bombing.'

'Did she say when she'd be back?'

The owner shook his head. 'But I told her I'd take her on again when she returned. She's good at her job. Honest. And the customers like her.'

Lampson wrote down his and Coburg's names plus the number of their extension at Scotland Yard on a piece of paper and handed it to the man.

'If she comes back, can you ask her to phone this number? And tell her it's urgent.'

The man looked at the piece of paper. 'Scotland Yard?' he said. 'Is she in trouble?'

'Not at all,' said Lampson. 'But we're hoping she'll be able to provide us with information.'

* * *

Lampson was the first back at the office at Scotland Yard, where he found a handwritten note on his desk. *Urgent. For DCI Coburg. A Miss Rosa Weeks asks him to contact her urgently. If she's not at her home she'll be at the Ritz.*

'The woman he had lunch with,' muttered Lampson. 'Wonder what the emergency is?'

The phone rang and he picked it up. 'DCI Coburg's office. Sergeant Lampson speaking.'

'Ted, it's Barry Moss,' said the sergeant from Waterloo police station. 'Is your guv'nor there?'

'Sorry, Barry. He was going to the British Museum and he's not back yet. Anything I can do?'

'Yes. We've just had a body pulled out of the Thames, and I think it might be connected to this case you're working on. The Ritz business. Any chance of you coming along to take a look at it? It's been taken to the mortuary at Charing Cross Hospital.'

'No problem, I'll be along,' said Lampson. 'I'll see you there.'

He hung up the phone just as the door opened and Coburg walked in.

'Ah, guv'nor!' said Lampson. 'Two messages.' And he handed him the one from Rosa.

'When did this come in?' asked Coburg, frowning.

'Don't know, guv. It was on the desk when I came in.'

'I wish they'd put the time on these things,' snapped Coburg unhappily. 'I keep telling them but they just ignore me. Right, Ted. I'm off again to see what Miss Weeks wants.' Then he stopped. 'You said there were two messages?'

Lampson explained about the gruesome discovery in the river.

'Man or woman?' asked Coburg.

'He didn't say, guv.'

'OK. Are you all right making your way to Charing Cross on your own? If Rosa says it's urgent, it will be. She's not the type to make a fuss, and I don't know when this message came in.'

'No problem,' said Lampson, and he passed the car keys to Coburg. 'I hope everything's all right.'

CHAPTER FIFTEEN

Rosa was in her dressing room at the Ritz, going through her music and selecting the numbers for that evening's performance, when Coburg arrived.

'Thank heavens you're here!' she exclaimed.

'I called at your house but no one was in. Your message said it's urgent.'

'It is. What did you tell your people about Julie?'

'My people?'

'The police.'

'Nothing. I haven't mentioned her name to anyone, not even to my sergeant.'

'Well, two men came to the house today and took her away. They said they were from Special Branch.'

'Where did they take her?'

'That's it, they didn't say where they were going to take her. Donna—'

'Donna?'

'My other housemate. She was at the house when they came. She was the one Julie told to get in touch with you about it.'

Coburg looked at her, puzzled. 'I don't know anything about this,' he said. 'Like I said, I never mentioned her to anyone. Did these men give their names?'

'No.'

'What about showing their identification?'

'Donna said one of them flashed a card at her, but she didn't look at it properly. She said they looked like coppers, or somebody official.' She shook her head, worried. 'I heard about the second murder here. In the kitchens.'

'Yes, that's why you couldn't get hold of me. I was here, then my sergeant and I were out and about trying to find out as much as we could about the victim.'

'Do you think it's connected with the dead man in the King's suite?'

'I'd be surprised if it isn't.'

'Connected with what's happened to Julie?'

'I don't know,' admitted Coburg.

'I'm worried,' she said.

'I'll find her,' Coburg assured her. 'I'll check out Special Branch straight away.'

'And if they haven't got her?'

'I'll keep nosing around until I find out who has.'

Back at Scotland Yard, Coburg made his way down to the basement and the rooms that housed Special Branch. It could be a funny animal, often secretive, which led many of its people to have an attitude of wariness, even when talking to other police officers. Coburg was aiming for one who he knew would be open and frank with him: Chief Inspector Albert Tenniel. They'd both come up through the ranks together, after having met as soldiers in the fields of Flanders during the First World War.

He found Tenniel's office at the far end of the basement corridor, knocked and, when he heard Tenniel's voice call out 'Enter', walked in. Tenniel was sitting at his desk, smoking a small cigar and sorting through some papers. He was a short, genial-looking man with a scar on one side of his face, the result of a German mine exploding during an advance. He was also completely bald. People said that the baldness was a side effect of the shock and trauma he'd experienced in the trenches, that before the war he'd had a full head of hair, but it was something that Coburg had never asked him about.

Tenniel's face broke into a grin as he saw who his visitor was.

'Good heavens, it's the Honourable Edgar Walter Septimus Saxe-Coburg!' he beamed. 'What brings the gentry slumming down in the lower depths?'

Coburg smiled. 'Thought I'd see how the other half lived.'

Tenniel laughed. 'You're not here as an emissary of your brother Magnus the Duke, then?'

Coburg regarded him, puzzled. 'An emissary about what?' he asked.

'My boss had a letter from him recently complaining about his chauffeur being interned. When I saw you, I wondered if he'd asked you to intercede.'

'Absolutely not,' said Coburg. 'Poor Magnus.'

'Poor Magnus?' queried Tenniel. 'Not' – he picked up a sheet of paper from his desk – 'not poor Carlo Viletti, who I assume is the chauffeur.'

'He is,' confirmed Coburg. 'And a really nice bloke, as well as being a staunch anti-fascist. He's been with Magnus for the last twenty years. He'll be lost without Carlo.'

'I still say "poor Carlo",' said Tenniel. 'I'm afraid the "Intern all Italians and Germans" rule has resulted in many of those who fled from the Nazis and Mussolini ending up behind bars here.'

'So, if you're not here to get your brother's chauffeur released, what can I do for you?'

'A young woman called Julie Stafford was picked up by Special Branch a few hours ago from her house, and no one knows what's happened to her.'

Tenniel frowned thoughtfully. 'Stafford? Doesn't ring a bell. You sure it was Special Branch?'

'That's what they told her and her housemate, who saw them. They had warrant cards with them.'

'Well, it was certainly nothing that I was involved with,' said Tenniel. 'Do you know why she was lifted?'

'I'm guessing it was something to do with a murder at the Ritz that we're investigating.'

'Oh yes. In one of King Zog's suites.'

'I hear you're keeping a watch on their money laundering activities,' said Coburg.

'Hardly money laundering,' protested Tenniel. 'They're just changing foreign currency into sterling. People do it all the time.'

'But not usually in such quantities,' observed Coburg.

'The rich are different from the rest of us,' said Tenniel

sagely. Then he grinned. 'Well, not from you and your crowd, but the rest of us.'

'My family isn't rich,' said Coburg. 'What with death duties we count as among the poorest in the land.'

'Oh, come on!' scoffed Tenniel. 'Try telling that to some charwoman in the East End with seven kids to support.'

'Yes, all right, that was an over-exaggeration,' Coburg admitted gracefully. 'It comes from listening too much to Magnus. But getting back to this young woman, Julie Stafford . . .'

'Where was she picked up from?' asked Tenniel.

Coburg gave him the address. Tenniel stood up.

'If you wait here, I'll go and have a word with some of my colleagues, see if any of them know anything about it.' He gestured at the papers on his desk. 'No peeking while I'm out. This is all highly secret.' Then he grinned as he selected two sheets of paper, which he passed to Coburg. It was on the letterhead of the Duke of Dawlish. 'Although you can have a look at this one. It's the letter I mentioned from your brother. He does know we're at war with Italy, I assume?'

'Magnus doesn't think of Carlo as the enemy,' said Coburg. 'And, to be honest, nor do I.'

'Anyway, it'll give you something to read while I'm out and keep your eyes off the other papers.'

'I promise I won't even look at them,' said Coburg. 'Scout's honour.'

'I thought you got thrown out of the Boy Scouts for conduct unbecoming,' said Tenniel.

'Yes, but it was a minor aberration,' said Coburg. 'And my word remains my bond.'

'Family motto?' asked Tenniel as he made for the door.

140

'No, that's "Don't Trust the Butler",' said Coburg.

Tenniel left, and Coburg settled down to read his brother's letter to the Minister for War. It was typical Magnus in tone, very formal, but making a lucid appeal on Carlo's behalf, citing his long years of service to the Saxe-Coburg family, his known antipathy to Mussolini and the fascists, along with his loathing of Hitler and the Nazis, and ending with a declaration that Mr Viletti was the only person who understood the machinations of the various vehicles in the Duke of Dawlish's possession, and if he was going to be able to continue to contribute to the war effort, then he could only do that with the assistance of his faithful chauffeur and mechanic, Mr Carlo Viletti. At the end of the letter someone had written in a pencilled scrawl: 'Hard luck. Tell His Dukeship to catch a bus,' which made Coburg smile.

He put the letter back on Tenniel's desk, as the door of the office opened and the man returned.

'Not us,' he announced.

'You're sure?' asked Coburg.

'I've checked with everyone who might know, and no one knows anything about it. Could it be Five or Six?'

'Why would they say they were Special Branch?'

'Easier than explaining to someone about MI5 and MI6, especially as most people have never heard of them,' said Tenniel.

Or could it be the same people who'd taken Williams's body while claiming to be from MI5, only this time pretending to be Special Branch? mused Coburg.

Lampson stood alongside Sergeant Moss, looking at the body on the slab.

'Not a pretty sight,' said Lampson.

'Beaten to death, by the look of it,' said Moss. 'And savagely.'

There was no doubt about it, the face had been battered almost beyond recognition.

Lampson nodded. 'I'd better get back to the Yard and let the guv'nor know. This is going to change things.'

After drawing a blank with Special Branch, Coburg moved on to Inspector Hibbert at MI5, then Atkinson at MI6. Both told him the same: neither of their organisations had picked up Julie Stafford, or any other young woman that day.

'Then, where is she?' wondered Coburg as he headed back to Scotland Yard. 'Who took her? And why?'

CHAPTER SIXTEEN

Coburg walked into the office and found his sergeant on the phone. Lampson hung up as he saw his boss.

'Just trying to get hold of you, guv,' he said. 'Thought I'd try the Ritz first. How'd it go with your lady friend?'

'One of her housemates seems to have been snatched. The men who took her said they were from Special Branch, but it turns out they weren't.' He sighed. 'Trouble is, there's no sign of her. What about you? How did you get on with Barry Moss and the body pulled out of the Thames?'

'It's Billy Thackeray.'

'Thackeray!'

Lampson nodded. 'The medics reckon he was killed on Monday, sometime during the day. Of course, it's difficult to pin down an accurate time with him having been in the water for four days, but it looks like he was killed before Joe Williams got done.'

'Maybe it was Williams who did it?'

'Why?'

'Thieves falling out? If they were both involved in going after the fortune at the Ritz.'

Lampson shook his head. 'This was more than just a killing. He was beaten to a pulp. But it's him all right. Billy Moss told me that Thackeray had a girlfriend, Vera. I thought I'd have a word with her, see if she can tell us anything about what Thackeray was up to. I didn't know if you wanted to have a word with her as well.'

Coburg shook his head. 'You talk to her, Ted. I'd better go and let Rosa know the bad news about her friend. I'll see you back here later.'

Rosa hurried towards the house, snatching a look at her watch as she did. She knew she was cutting it fine, that she should be at the Ritz getting ready for her performance, but she was desperate to find out if Donna had got any news about Julie. The answer came as soon as she opened the door and saw Donna at the foot of the stairs, looking upset.

'Julie's back, and she's making a run for it.'

Rosa rushed up the stairs and into her friend's room, where she saw that Julie was stuffing clothes and personal belongings into a suitcase.

Rosa hurried across the room and threw her arms around her friend, hugging her close. 'Thank God you're safe. We've been trying to find you. Edgar's out looking for you. Donna said they told you they were Special Branch.'

'They weren't Special Branch,' said Julie. 'They weren't anyone official. Trouble is, I don't know who they were or what they were up to, but I'm scared it might happen

144

again. Maybe not them, but someone else. And all because I went out with Joe a couple of times. So, I'm off.'

'Where?'

Julie shook her head. 'I'm telling no one. Last time I said anything to you I ended up being kidnapped.'

'That wasn't me!' protested Rosa. 'I asked Edgar, and he said he didn't tell anyone about you. Not your name, nothing.'

'So, how did they know about me?' demanded Julie.

'I don't know,' admitted Rosa. 'Maybe someone saw you with Joe and knew who you were.'

'You think it's a coincidence?' asked Julie, obviously still upset. 'I tell you and your copper boyfriend who the bloke in the photo is, and next thing I know I'm being blindfolded and locked up in some smelly room with just a bucket.'

'Did they hurt you?' asked Rosa tentatively.

'No,' said Julie. 'But they could have. So, I'm taking off.'

'I'm sure if you talk to Edgar, describe the men and where they took you—'

'Didn't you hear me? I was blindfolded, both when they took me to wherever it was and when they brought me home.' She shut the lid of the suitcase and pressed the catches home. 'I'm certainly not talking to your copper again and putting myself in a spot. Donna saw them. Let her tell him what they looked like.'

'But she only saw them for a minute. Please, Julie, just wait and see if I can get hold of him. Don't you want the men who took you caught?'

'I don't care. I just want to get away before they come back again.'

'Well . . . what about me and Donna?' asked Rosa.

'What about you?' asked Julie.

'Those men saw Donna. Say next time they go after her?'

Julie hesitated, then asked: 'Why would they?'

'Why did they take you?' countered Rosa.

'Because I knew Joe.'

'And both Donna and I met him, here at the house.'

Again, Julie hesitated. Then, reluctantly, she nodded. 'All right. Phone your friend. But if he's not in, I'm not hanging about.'

Rosa ran to the phone box on the corner. She dialled the number for Scotland Yard, desperately hoping Edgar would be in his office. He seemed to be out most of the time these days.

'Metropolitan Police, Scotland Yard,' said the operator.

'DCI Coburg, please,' said Rosa, and gave the extension number.

Please let him be there, she prayed silently.

There was a series of clicks, then the operator said, 'I'm afraid there's no one available in that office. Would you like to leave a message?'

Damn, thought Rosa, her heart sinking. Leave a message? To what end? Julie would be off. Still, she said: 'Yes, please. Would you ask him to contact Miss Rosa Weeks, urgently? Thank you.'

She was just walking back to the house, feeling that nothing seemed to be going right lately, when she saw the police car pull to a halt outside her house, and Coburg himself getting out.

'Edgar!' she shouted.

He turned and saw her as she ran towards him.

'I was just trying to get hold of you!'

He gave her an unhappy look. 'Yes, well, it seems—'

'Julie's back!'

He stared at her. 'What?'

'They let her go, but she says she's going away right now. That's why I was trying to get hold of you. She says she'll talk to you about what happened, but it has to be now.'

'Then let's go and talk to her before she changes her mind,' said Coburg, and he took Rosa by the arm and steered her determinedly towards her front door.

A short time later, Coburg sat with the three women at the kitchen table, listening as Julie told him what had happened: the two men, the blindfold, the empty room that wasn't a proper jail cell, their questions and the disturbing fact that they'd brought her back to the house.

'They warned me not to say anything about what had happened. Said I'd be in breach of the Official Secrets Act and I could go to prison.'

'As they weren't real officials I think we can safely say you don't need to have any fear of that,' said Coburg.

'That's all right for you to say, but I'm still scared they'll come back, real officials or not,' said Julie firmly.

'Tell me, what did they look like?' asked Coburg.

Julie looked at Donna, who shook her head. 'I didn't really notice them,' she admitted. Julie frowned, thinking, remembering.

'One was short,' said Julie. 'A bit podgy. He was the one who did all the talking. Very polite. I might have believed them if they hadn't taken me to this place that so obviously wasn't a police station or anywhere official.' And she described the room she'd been kept in.

'What about the other man?'

'The silent one. Tall. Very tall. About six feet six. And thin. Apart from that, nothing special about either of them.' Then she stopped and gave a thoughtful frown. 'Wait, the tall one had a funny ear.'

'A funny ear?'

'Yeh. Like something had chewed it at some time. A dog, maybe.' She looked at Coburg, agitated. 'Look, is that it? I don't want to hang around any longer.'

'I understand,' said Coburg. 'Shall I take you somewhere?'

'No thanks,' said Julie. She stood up. 'I'm heading for a train station, and I'll go under my own steam. The last thing I want is to be seen in a police car.'

Donna also got up. 'Let me come with you,' she offered. 'Just as far as the station.'

Julie nodded. 'Yeh. Thanks, Donna. If anyone's watching, they might think twice if there's two of us.' She gave Rosa a hug goodbye, picked up her suitcase, then waited while Donna put her coat on.

After Donna and Julie had left, Coburg and Rosa sat back down at the table.

'At least they let her go,' said Rosa.

'Yes,' said Coburg thoughtfully. 'One thing I agree with her about: they weren't official. Her description of where she was kept sounds like a storeroom. The good thing was they didn't harm her.'

'But who were they?'

'The tall one with the chewed ear sounds to me like someone who works for a local gangster, someone who Joe Williams may or may not have been working for when he was killed.'

'Who?'

Coburg shook his head. 'At the moment it's safest you don't know his name, just in case you're tempted to mention it.'

'I'm not that stupid!'

'No, but you may hear someone say it, and you might react, even without saying anything. And if anyone spots that, you could be at risk.'

'So, this man is dangerous?'

'Very.'

'But he let Julie go.'

'That's one of the peculiarities about this particular man, he has his own set of standards he prides himself on. He treats women, and others he considers to be vulnerable, with care. Unless he feels they threaten him, of course. In which case he'd have no compunction about having them disposed.'

'You know some nice people,' commented Rosa acidly.

'It goes with the territory,' said Coburg. 'My worry is, if they abducted Julie and know it was you who brought me in to show you the photo, they might be looking at you.'

'Why should they want to do that?'

'Because this character wants to find out what people knew about Joe Williams being in the suite. So, either he was behind whatever went on and he wants to make sure there's nothing to link him to it, or he wasn't involved and he wants to find out who was. Whichever it was, I'm worried in case he sends his men back here again. I don't want you to be at risk here, so I suggest you come and stay with me at my place.'

Rosa shook her head. 'No. That'd leave Donna on her own, and the two men who took Julie saw her. She's more at risk than I am.'

Coburg took her in his arms. 'I take your point, and I think I can deal with this, but maybe not till tomorrow. So, just for tonight, to make sure you're both safe, why don't you and Donna stay at my flat? Then tomorrow I'll go and see this person and warn him off.'

'You think he'll listen?'

'Oh yes,' said Coburg determinedly. 'He won't have a choice.'

Rosa nodded. 'OK,' she said. 'And thanks.'

Coburg smiled. 'You could say it's me taking advantage of the situation to get you back to my flat.'

She smiled back at him. 'Honey, I don't need persuading. So, will we do the same as before? You come to see me perform tonight and we'll go back to your place together. If so, I'll get Donna to join us there.'

'I'll be there tonight, but I'll be working,' said Coburg. 'I've got to interview the kitchen staff.'

'Oh yes, the poor guy who was killed!' She looked distressed. 'What's happening to the place?'

'Don't worry, I don't think it's some maniac bumping people off at random. I'm fairly sure the killings are connected. I'll give you my key, so you and Donna take a taxi to my place, and I'll see you there after I've finished. Hopefully, I shouldn't be too long. Is that all right?'

She nodded, then kissed him. 'Thanks, Edgar. I don't know what I'd do if you weren't here.'

He smiled at her and hugged her close. 'You'd do

the right thing, and you'd do it well. You're a strong woman, Rosa. I'm just here as your backup.'

'Time to catch up and swap notes,' Coburg told Lampson when he got back to the Yard. 'How did you get on with Thackeray's girlfriend, Vera?'

'She was out, so I'll try her again tomorrow. What about you, guv?'

'Well, the first thing is that my friend Rosa's housemate was returned home.'

Lampson frowned. 'Eh? Who by? Or maybe she wasn't snatched?'

'Oh, she was snatched all right, and I think I know who by. Two of Mel McGuinness's men. She described them to me and one of them sounds like Lofty Parks, a known associate. So, tomorrow morning we pay Mr McGuinness a visit.'

'Did they hurt her?'

'Apparently not. It seems they just asked her questions about Williams, which suggests to me that Big Mel didn't know what he was up to. Anyway, the experience frightened her enough that she's gone away.'

'Where to?'

'She didn't want to say. Friends or family, I guess. Somewhere she feels safe. The other thing is my contact at the British Museum identified the language on those papers we found at Alex Ollen's place. It's Macedonian.'

'Macedonian?' frowned Lampson. 'Where's that?'

'In the Balkans,' replied Coburg. 'Right next to Albania.'

'So, that suggests his murder is connected to what went on in the Albanian king's rooms.'

'I agree,' said Coburg. 'Two murders in the same hotel, both with Albanian links. It's too much to be a coincidence.'

'But why did he use a forged Swiss passport?'

'I get the impression that Albanian passports aren't that easy to get hold of because of what's happening in that area and questions might be asked about it, whereas a Swiss passport is accepted everywhere.'

'Do you think we're any closer to finding out who killed Williams and the kitchen hand, guv? And now Billy Thackeray?'

'Thackeray, I don't know,' admitted Coburg. 'The other two, I feel it all hinges on the money, and Albania. The problem is that brings in politics, so I'm not sure how far we'll be allowed to progress. But all we can do is keep pushing. And I'm going to dot that tonight when I talk to the Ritz's kitchen night staff and see what they can tell us about Alex Ollen.'

CHAPTER SEVENTEEN

'Good evening, George.'

The hall porter beamed in welcome as Coburg walked through the doors of the Ritz and came over to his reception desk.

'Good evening, Chief Inspector,' he said. 'I was told that you'd be returning to talk to the kitchen staff tonight, so I've arranged for the room the chefs use as their office to be made available to you.'

'With their agreement, I hope,' said Coburg. 'The last thing I want to do is upset a chef. They're notoriously short-tempered at the best of times, and within dangerous reach of sharp implements.'

'There's no danger of that. The chef is as keen as everyone else to find out who killed Alex, and why. He feels the murder disgraces his kitchen.'

'Is there any news on Count Ahmed?' asked Coburg.

George shook his head. 'Alas, no. He is still away, and no one is saying where he is. But I shall keep trying to find out.'

'Thank you, George. And now, is Miss Weeks available?'

'I believe she's in her dressing room preparing for the show.' Suddenly George spotted someone, and his face broke into a smile as he said: 'Correction. Miss Weeks is here.'

Coburg turned and saw Rosa appear from the interior of the hotel, wearing a shawl lightly over the dress she wore for her performance.

'You look lovely!' said Coburg.

'Thank you, kind sir,' said Rosa. She kissed him. 'I decided to come up and see if there was any news of you. What time you'd be arriving, that sort of thing.'

He looked at his watch. 'I'm due to meet with the night staff in half an hour so I can talk to all of them before their shift starts. My first job will be to talk to the chef before that and make sure I've a list of the staff who were here when Alex Ollen was killed.'

'It's so terrible,' she said. 'I never thought that sort of thing would happen here.'

'Oh, you'd be surprised,' said Coburg. 'Some of the best hotels hide some of the darkest secrets.' He produced his front door key and handed it to her. 'I had a spare key cut for you, in case I'm still tied up when you finish. Is Donna here?'

'She's joining me later,' said Rosa. 'Thanks for this. We'll both sleep easier tonight.' She slipped the key into her bag. 'I'll see you later.'

'Good luck tonight,' he said. 'Or, rather, break a leg I understand is the preferred wish for performers. Enjoy.'

He gave her another kiss, then made for the stairs down to the kitchen.

'Mr Coburg is a wonderful man, Miss Weeks,' said George.

Rosa smiled. 'He certainly is, George.'

She was about to return to her dressing room, when she found a tall, fleshy man dressed in a white tuxedo standing in her way, smiling at her. He had a pencil-thin moustache, thinning hair, giving the overall impression of a movie impresario. This was backed up when he opened his mouth and she heard his American accent.

'Miss Weeks. I hope you don't mind my stopping to say hi. I've seen your spot a couple of times as I'm staying here at the hotel, and I think you're sensational.'

'That's very kind of you,' said Rosa.

'And this is not from just a fan. My name's Ray Harris and I'm an executive with Swan Records in the States. I'd love to talk to you about recording with us.' He gave a wry grin and added: 'I promise you, this is not just a chat-up line.' He produced a business card and handed it to her, and she read 'Raymond Harris, Marketing Executive, Swan Records', with an address and telephone number in New York. 'I came over last summer, just before war broke out, to check out British acts and see if there were any that'd be right for the States.'

'And did you find any?'

'I did,' said Harris. 'Jack Payne, Henry Hall, Al Bowlly, Hutch Hutchinson, and now there's you.'

Rosa gave him a smile. 'Forgive me for being sceptical, Mr Harris, but I've been in this business a long time, and the number of men who've approached me to talk about possible recording contracts, or tours—'

155

Harris held up his hand to stop her.

'That's exactly how I expected you to respond, and I promise you this isn't one of those ruses. You really do have something special. In fact, when I was here a couple of nights ago I wanted to talk to you after your act finished, but I was told you'd gone off with some detective inspector. Not in trouble, I hope?'

Rosa laughed and shook her head. 'Not at all. The inspector and I are old friends, so we were catching up.'

Harris gave a smile of relief. 'That's OK, then. I worried maybe you'd been picked up for something and were languishing in a cell somewhere. With this war on there's a lot of people disappearing of late. Like this place. All the waiters have gone. And most of the barmen.'

'Italians and Germans,' said Rosa with a sigh. 'Me, I'm local.'

'Which part of England are you from?'

Rosa chuckled. 'I wouldn't let anyone from my home town hear you say that, Mr Harris. They'd be most upset.'

'Oh? And where is your home town?'

'Home city, to be exact. Edinburgh.'

'Ah, a Scot!' He frowned. 'But you don't have a Scottish accent.'

'We don't all walk around going "Och aye the noo",' she said. 'When you've spent as many years on the road as I have, gradually your original accent disappears.' She shot a look at the clock, and said: 'Actually, Mr Harris, it's been nice talking to you, but now I need to get ready. My audience will be starting to filter in.'

Harris nodded. 'No problem,' he said. 'Perhaps we could talk afterwards?'

She looked at him warily. 'That's very nice, but—'

'Business talk only, I promise,' said Harris hastily. 'Unless you're heading off with your detective inspector again? Even then, I'd be happy to talk to you with him, just to show there's no funny business in my mind. Strictly the music business.'

'Fine,' Rosa agreed.

'Great.' Harris smiled. 'It'll be a pleasure to buy you both a drink.'

'I think it'll be only me,' said Rosa. 'He's busy.'

'Let me guess. This dead guy in one of the King of Albania's suites, and now the one in the kitchen.' He gave Rosa an apologetic look. 'It's hardly a big secret. Everyone knows about it.' Then he smiled again. 'I'll wait for you at my table after you've finished your spot. Is that OK with you? All out in the open.'

'That'll be fine,' said Rosa. 'I may have a girlfriend with me. Will that be all right?'

'Fine by me. I'll see you after the show.'

Coburg sat in the small, cramped room that was the head chef's office with the night shift sous-chef, Kurt Schiller, who, according to the list of workers he'd been given, came originally from Geneva.

'You are Swiss?' asked Coburg.

'I am,' said Schiller.

'The man who was killed here, Alex Ollen, according to his papers he was Swiss.'

Schiller said nothing, just watched Coburg.

'Was he Swiss?' asked Coburg.

'If his papers say he was, then he must have been,' said Schiller.

'We have been informed that actually he was from Macedonia.'

Schiller said nothing at first, obviously weighing up how to reply, before he said: 'It is possible.'

'Did you know him well?'

'No,' said Schiller. 'The only person I would say I know is the chef.'

It was the same response he'd received from the others he'd spoken to. The denials that anyone had known Ollen was a closing of rank against authority. *Nearly everyone here has something to hide*, thought Coburg. Most of the kitchen workers were refugees of some sort, afraid of being looked into too closely, especially their papers. Many of them were political exiles doing their best to put their past behind them. At least, until the war was over. So far the men who'd been presented to him had been from Spain, Poland, France, Morocco, Norway, Belgium and now Switzerland. None from Albania or anywhere in the Balkans, if they were to be believed. But Alex Ollen had been from Macedonia, despite his claims to be from Switzerland.

'Was there anyone on the staff that he was close to?' asked Coburg. 'Someone here he spent time with outside of work?'

'If he did, I don't know about it,' said Schiller. 'I had very little to do with him. We are always too busy in the kitchen for chit-chat.'

This is getting me nowhere, thought Coburg ruefully. *I need someone who knew him as a man, not as just another worker in the kitchen.* The girl that Lampson had uncovered, the one who wrote to Ollen, that's who they needed to talk to. But say they couldn't get hold of her?

'Mr Schiller,' said Coburg gently but seriously, 'I am not here to interfere in the private lives of the people who work in the kitchens. I am not interested in who is here officially or who may have false papers. I am not here to arrest anyone for whatever their status may be. I am concerned with only one thing: finding out who killed Alex Ollen and hid his body behind the shelves in one of your storerooms. The fact that it was done that way suggests the person who did it had knowledge of this kitchen.'

As he saw that Schiller was about to protest, Coburg continued quickly: 'That does *not* mean the person who did it worked here in the kitchen. It could be someone who delivered food or anyone else who knows the layout down here. It could be a member of the hotel staff outside of the kitchen: waiters, cleaners, hospitality, anyone. Or it could be someone who's nothing to do with the hotel but knows someone who is. The point is that there have been two murders recently and I suspect they are connected, so my big concern is that the person who did it may strike again. Next time it may be another member of the kitchen staff. The next victim could be you. Until we can find out *why* this is happening, that is a possibility. The wall of silence I've encountered this evening puts everyone here in danger. You are a senior member of this team. You know the people you work with better than I can ever do.'

He passed the list of kitchen employees to Schiller. 'All I'm asking is, from your knowledge of these people, to put a cross against the names of the people who were not around at the time Alex Ollen was killed, which was between three and five o'clock this morning, or anyone you feel had no real contact with him. I won't only be asking you to do this, I shall ask everyone else on the night shift to do the same.'

'You are asking us to accuse someone,' said Schiller.

'No,' said Coburg. 'I am asking you to help eliminate people as suspects.' He handed Schiller a pen. 'Please, we're trying to save your lives.'

Rosa took her final bow, closed the lid of the piano and gathered up her music. She looked across at the entrance to the Rivoli Bar and saw Donna standing there. Donna gave her a wave, which Rosa replied to with a nod. She turned to where Raymond Harris was sitting at his table and gave him a smile, also gesturing towards Donna. Her friend looked at Rosa enquiringly as she approached.

'Who's the guy?' asked Donna.

'A record executive from America,' replied Rosa. 'He's invited me for a drink and a chat after the show, and I said I'd have my friend with me.'

Donna looked at her doubtfully. 'An American record executive?' she asked sarcastically. 'And you're buying that?'

'Absolutely not,' said Rosa. 'But you never know when it might be the truth.'

'In that case, count me out,' said Donna. 'I don't fancy playing gooseberry. I'll wait for you in reception.'

'You sure?' asked Rosa.

'Definitely,' Donna assured her. 'I have enough men who think they're important at work. I don't need to play at being the audience for one of them in my free time.' Donna worked as a typist at one of the ministries in Whitehall, and often moaned about her bosses, who were either braggarts, or touchy-feely gropers, or a combination of both.

Rosa walked across the now almost empty bar to Harris at his table.

'Your friend not joining us?' he asked.

'She's got things to do before we head home,' said Rosa, making sure he was aware that when she left, she would be going with her friend.

Harris gestured at the bottle on the table. 'I ordered wine, but if there's something else you'd prefer . . .'

'Wine will be fine, thanks,' said Rosa. As Harris poured her a glass, she said: 'I have to ask, Mr Harris—'

'Call me Ray, please,' said Harris.

'Ray. Why is an American record company interested in British acts? I'd have thought American audiences had enough musical acts of their own.'

'We have, but Swan Records have put me in charge of developing talent from Europe, initially for a European audience. And right now, with Germany, France, Italy and most of mainland Europe off limits, that means dear old Britain. Yes, we've got Crosby and Sinatra, and Glen Miller, but audiences are always keen for something new. The plan is to maybe do a compilation, samples of the best of British for the American market and see who the audience take to, but – like I say – for the moment Swan want to expand into the European market, so we're giving people their own singers and musicians.' He grinned. 'The Brits are especially patriotic at the moment.' Then he looked serious as he said: 'So, are you available to make some test pressings? Something to let the big bosses back home hear. I've got time at a studio here in London.'

'I'm here for the rest of this week and next.'

'OK, I'll see what I can arrange, if that's OK with you. But there are no promises. It all depends on the boys back home. They trust me, but it's their money.'

161

'I understand,' said Rosa.

'So, moving away from the music business, does your detective boyfriend have any ideas about the dead guy? Who he is? Who killed him?'

Rosa shrugged. 'If he has, he hasn't shared them with me. Why? Are you worried?'

'Well, you've got to admit it's not the sort of thing you expect to happen. Especially at the Ritz. I mean, if there's some kind of killer on the loose here, I'd like to know about it.'

Rosa smiled. 'I don't get the idea there's a maniac killer on the loose.'

'Is that what your pal says?' asked Harris. 'This police inspector?'

'I haven't really discussed it with him,' lied Rosa. She shot a look at the clock. 'Oh, look at the time. I have to go.'

'It's not that late,' said Harris.

'It is for me,' said Rosa apologetically. 'My friend said she wanted to talk to me tonight after I finished, which is why we're heading off together. I don't know what it's about, but I'm guessing man trouble, and she's been a good friend so I don't want to let her down.'

'I understand,' said Harris. He stood up. 'Thanks for spending the time, and I look forward to setting up a recording date.' Harris held out his hand. 'I look forward to talking again.'

Rosa collected her coat from her dressing room, and then joined Donna in reception.

'You got rid of him, then,' said Donna.

'Trust me, all the talk turned out to be about business, nothing else,' said Rosa. 'I'll get the doorman to get us a taxi and we'll head for Edgar's flat.'

'You sure this is all right, me staying with you at your boyfriend's place?' asked Donna.

'It's just for one night.'

'What happens after that?'

'We'll be fine. He's going to fix it so we can go home.'

'You sure? How can he do that?'

'Trust me, if Edgar makes a promise, it happens,' said Rosa.

Coburg drove home. On the passenger seat was his briefcase with a pile of lists of kitchen staff, each marked with crosses against some of the names. Once he'd got Schiller to agree, the others had followed suit. The head chef may be in charge, but the sous-chef was the workers' unofficial leader. How much use the information would be was debatable. Certainly, it was a time for some of them to settle personal vendettas, deliberately not putting a cross against the names of their sworn personal enemies, but a careful check of the lists would soon sort that out. There was a chance it might lead to a short list of possible suspects, but, Coburg had to admit, it wasn't much of a chance. And he still hadn't got a clue if Ollen had associates outside work; no one seemed to have known him. He'd get Lampson to try again with the vanished girlfriend, Anna.

Rosa had obviously been waiting for him because as he opened the door to his flat, she was there. He dumped his briefcase down and hugged her.

'Where's Donna?' he asked.

'Gone to bed,' said Rosa. 'She said she was tired, but I think she might have been giving us some privacy.'

Coburg grinned. 'In that case, what do you say we take advantage of such generosity?'

Once in bed, they asked each other how their evenings had been. Coburg told her his meetings with the kitchen staff had been less useful than he'd hoped.

'In short, we're no nearer to finding out who Alex Ollen really was, and why he was killed, though I suspect his death is connected with the killing of Joe Williams. How about you? Good reception?'

'Indeed,' said Rosa. 'Very flattering. Especially when I got chatted up by an American record executive who said he wants me to do some recording.'

'He wants to get you into bed,' said Coburg.

'That was my first reaction. But no, I think there's something else going on. I got the impression his purpose in talking to me was to pump me for what you knew about the murder in the suite.'

'Interesting. Did you tell him we'd discovered Joe's name?'

Rosa shook her head. 'No. And I didn't tell him about Julie, either. He seemed very keen to find out what you'd discovered, so I told him I knew nothing.'

'Maybe I'll check him out.'

'Jealous?' asked Rosa with a smile.

'Of course.' Coburg smiled back. 'But I'm also curious as to why he'd be so interested. What's his name?'

'Raymond Harris. His card said he works for Swan Records of New York. But I may be completely wrong about him. It may have been just chat on his part.'

'No, my love, you're rarely wrong when it comes to people. You are one of the best judges of character I know.'

'Which is why I'm with you,' she said, and pulled him to her.

One o'clock in the morning and Albert Gibbs shuffled along the pavement, feeling his way with his boots. When it was pitch-black like this, he had to be careful; you never knew when there might be a hole in the pavement. He was proud of being an air raid protection warden, out every night in his uniform and his tin helmet with ARP on it, making sure the rules of the blackout were tightly observed. No lights to be showing at any time during the hours of darkness so that when the Germans came to bomb the city, they wouldn't be able to identify areas of habitation. So far, they had only come on bombing raids during the day, but the authorities assured him that this was bound to change.

'And when they do come at night, Albert, it'll be people like you and me that save this country,' his commanding officer had told him. 'Not one chink of light must be allowed to escape. Any that does, arrest 'em and have 'em up in court. Fining people is the only way to make 'em stick to the rules.'

So, during the first few months of the war, Albert Gibbs had done just that, serving summonses on anyone who hadn't pulled their thick, black curtains completely closed across their windows and allowed even the merest glimmer of light to escape. He'd earned harsh words from many, but gradually it had sunk in, and he was proud that his patch was virtually guaranteed to be completely light-free during the hours of darkness. The Luftwaffe wouldn't be able to target *his* area.

And then he saw it. A light! Coming from the Four Feathers pub on the corner.

Filled with a sense of outrage, he ran towards it, shouting as he did so: 'Put that light out!' But as he got closer, he saw that it wasn't just the usual light, this was orange and red and flickering, and he realised that the door to the pub was on fire. He stared aghast as the fire took hold, flames surging up the frame and spreading to the pub window. Frantically, he took out his whistle and blew it as hard as he could, its shriek cutting through the night.

'Fire!' he shouted. 'Help! Fire! Someone call 999!'

CHAPTER EIGHTEEN

Friday 23rd August

Mel McGuinness and Charley Barnes stood looking at the wreckage of the Four Feathers. Even though he'd been phoned at two in the morning with the news, McGuinness had left it until dawn before coming. With the blackout in force he wouldn't have been able to use a torch to check on the damage. Now, in the early light of day, he saw that it was even worse than he'd feared: his pub was a twisted tangle of burnt wood. Even the roof had fallen in. All those spirits stored in the upstairs rooms, he guessed, setting light to the rafters. It was lucky the publican didn't sleep on the premises and no lives had been lost. But whoever did this didn't necessarily know there'd be no one there. And McGuinness knew it had been done deliberately; the smell of petrol still hung around the ruin. Someone had poured petrol through the letterbox, then put a lighted rag through.

'Who'd want to do this?' he asked, doing his best to control the rage he felt welling up inside him. He wanted to get hold of the person and cut their hands off before killing them as a warning to anyone else considering attacking one of his premises. And he had a few, not just his pubs: there were three nightclubs and a couple of gyms where his boxers trained.

'It's got to be the Bell brothers,' said Barnes.

'Why?'

'I don't know, but they're the only ones I can think of who'd want to do it.'

'But we've always had an arrangement. A good arrangement. Them operating north of the river, us in the south.'

'Yeh, but maybe they're getting greedy and want to move in and take over the south as well as the north. Look at what happened to Billy Thackeray. Beaten to a pulp and dumped in the river. And Joe Williams with his throat cut. Someone's after us, Mel, and the only people who'd really stand to profit from us going under are the Bell brothers. Maybe Danny and Den were doing something about these millions this king's got stashed at the Ritz and they were using Williams. He was a locksmith. And when Joe got killed there, maybe they thought it was you done it to make an example of him. You know, working for the opposition like that.'

'What happened to Joe was nothing to do with me.'

'Yeh, but they don't know that.'

McGuinness nodded thoughtfully. 'All right, set up a meet, Charley. Me with Danny and Den.'

'Neutral ground?'

'Too right. If they are behind all this I'd be a mug to walk into a place on their patch.'

Over breakfast, Coburg outlined his plan for the day to Rosa and Donna.

'As I said to Rosa, I think I've got a good idea who was behind abducting Julie, and first thing this morning I'm going to pay him a visit and warn him off trying a repeat performance on you two.'

'Think he'll listen?' asked Donna.

Coburg nodded, his face grim. 'He'll listen. Until then, you've got a key to this flat, so if you want to use this place rather than your house during the day, feel free.'

'But you're confident he'll leave us alone?'

'I am, once I've had a word with him,' said Coburg. 'So, if you feel happier, I'd leave going back home until early afternoon. Right now, I'm heading to Scotland Yard, so if you'd like me to drop you off anywhere in town . . .'

Donna shook her head. 'No, here's fine for me. I don't often get the chance to explore Hampstead.' She looked at Rosa. 'How about you?'

'Sounds good to me,' her friend replied. 'We can have a girls' day here. Or, at least, a morning.'

'In that case, I'll love you and leave you and head for work,' said Coburg.

A kiss and a hug for Rosa, a wink for Donna, and then he was gone.

As he drove to the Yard, his mind was full of Rosa, how good it was between them and how fortunate he was that she'd come back into his life. She gave him what had been missing, ever since she'd disappeared from it two years before. It wasn't just the sex, there'd been plenty of other women since, although sex with Rosa was very, very special. Different from with any other woman. No, it was their feeling of companionship. A genuine affection and caring. It had been there before, and now it was rekindled immediately, as if they'd never been apart.

I don't want to let her go again, and lose her this time, he thought. *It's too good. Too rare. Too special. We ought to make it permanent.* The realisation of what he was saying to himself gave him a shock. Marriage? He was in his forties. Most men were hitched by now, but not him.

It wasn't as if he'd deliberately avoided it. There had been plenty of women in his life, and many of them had seemed interested in making it permanent, but there'd always been something that had stopped it. The war, first. It had taken him a long time to recover from the injuries he'd suffered at Sambre–Oise. And then there was the job. Too many late nights. Too many encounters with violent death, which meant there wasn't much in the way of cheerful things to talk about. The job had also given him a slightly jaundiced view of humanity, which made him wary, suspicious; another trait that didn't go down well with prospective brides. Until Rosa had entered his life three years ago.

This is the woman for me, he'd thought soon after they'd spent time together. *She's beautiful, talented, intelligent, she laughs, she doesn't take herself seriously, and she doesn't seem to care too much if I miss a date because someone's been knifed in an alley.* But she had her own career, involving lots of touring. Although she still had her career now, still toured, this was mainly in Britain. Yet now it seemed that America might beckon in the form of Raymond Harris. If that worked and meant she had the opportunity to go Stateside, he had no right to prevent her going. But there was no way any relationship could survive that big a separation. He couldn't ask her to give it up. And he couldn't give up the job.

Damn, he thought. *We go nowhere.*

As often seemed to be the case lately, there was a scarcity of traffic on the streets. People nervous in case the bombing suddenly switched from Kent to London, along with the tight rationing of petrol, he guessed. Lampson was already in the office when he arrived.

'Morning, Ted,' he said. 'Anything new?'

'There certainly is,' replied Lampson. 'Someone torched the Four Feathers last night.'

'One of Big Mel's pubs?'

'That's right.'

Coburg frowned thoughtfully. 'First Joe Williams and Billy Thackeray killed, now Big Mel's pub attacked.'

'Think the pub torching is connected to the murders?'

'Only in as much as Williams and Thackeray worked for McGuinness, but I can't see how it's linked to King Zog's money, nor the murder of the Ritz's kitchen hand.' He shook his head. 'No, there's something else going on as well as money.'

'So, where do we start today?'

'We start by calling on Big Mel McGuinness.'

On their journey to the pub, Coburg had filled Lampson in on his intention to warn McGuinness off from threatening Rosa and Donna the way his men had done to

Julie Stafford. Lampson grinned. 'Just to add to Big Mel's troubles after losing his pub.'

McGuinness was in his usual seat at the Iron Horse when Coburg and Lampson arrived. In spite of the air of casual indifference he tried to give his visitors, Coburg could see the anger surging within the big gangster.

'Mr Coburg, I didn't expect to see you again so soon,' grunted McGuinness.

'I was planning on calling anyway,' said Coburg. 'But when I heard about the Four Feathers going up in flames, it just brought it forward.'

They sat down at McGuinness's table.

'First Joe Williams, then Billy Thackeray, now your pub.' said Coburg. 'Why is someone targeting you and your people, Mel?'

'I've told you before, Joe and Billy weren't my people. They were just blokes I helped out now and then by giving them odd jobs.'

'What sort of odd jobs?' asked Coburg.

'Occasional bar work,' said McGuinness. 'There's always times when we could do with another pair of hands here. Barrels to tap. Pints to pull.'

'Joe Williams had a set of lockpicks in his rooms,' said Coburg.

'Nothing to do with me,' said McGuinness. 'What a bloke gets up to in his own time is his affair.'

'And the Four Feathers? Who'd want to torch that?'

McGuinness shook his head. 'Who knows?' He looked inquisitively at Coburg. 'You said you were planning to call in anyway. Why?'

'Because yesterday an innocent woman was snatched

from her house and terrorised by a couple of your thugs.'

McGuinness glared angrily at Coburg, and for a moment, as the big man pushed himself out of his chair, the chief inspector tensed in readiness for an attack. Instead, McGuinness gave a scowl and sat back down.

'You're on dangerous ground with that accusation, Inspector,' he growled.

'Chief Inspector,' snapped back Coburg. 'And so are you. Two of your men picked up a Miss Julie Stafford from her home, abducted her, blindfolded her—'

'You've no proof,' grated McGuinness.

'I don't need proof,' retorted Coburg. 'I know. I've got a description of one of them and your man Lofty is very distinctive with that chewed ear of his. It was a mistake to send him.'

'I have never harmed a woman in my life,' snapped McGuinness.

'No, you just terrified her hoping she'd talk. Torture, it's called. You don't think that's harming someone?'

McGuinness bristled, and Coburg saw one of the big man's eyes twitch slightly as he fought to hold his anger in check. 'You can't come in here to my own pub and talk to me like that.'

'I can go wherever I like. I'm a Scotland Yard detective investigating a murder, and now the abduction and terrorising of an innocent woman.'

'Who said she was terrorised?'

'She did. Which is why she's fled the city in fear of her life. You and your men get a kick out of that, do you? Frightening women? Well, I'm here to warn you, McGuinness, Julie Stafford may have fled, but there are other women still in that same house, and if anything happens to them, even if someone so much as follows them, I'll have you inside so fast your feet won't touch the ground. And I'll make sure the other prisoners know why you're there. A man who gets his pleasure from threatening women.'

'I told you. I've never harmed a woman in my life!' shouted McGuinness angrily, and this time he did get to his feet and leant menacingly towards Coburg.

Coburg, in turn, edged forward so the two men were nose to nose.

'Yes, I heard you, but I'm telling you, you've been warned,' he said in firm tones. 'Stay away from that house. Stay away from those women.'

With that, Coburg headed for the door, Lampson behind him. As they reached the door it opened and Charley Barnes entered, then stopped at the sight of the two policemen. Unsmiling, Coburg nodded to Barnes in the briefest of greetings, then he and Lampson left.

Barnes came over to McGuinness. 'What did those two want?' he asked.

'Nothing I can't handle,' said McGuinness.

'Coburg looked pretty grim,' observed Barnes.

'I said, it's nothing I can't handle,' snapped McGuinness angrily.

'Yeh, all right, boss,' said Barnes. 'I just mentioned it. Anyway, I've just seen Den and Danny Bell.'

'Both of 'em?'

'You know them, boss. They're rarely apart. I reckon it's cos, deep down, they don't trust one another. Anyway, Den said to tell you he was shocked to hear about the Four Feathers.'

'Oh yeh?' scowled McGuinness. 'How did he say it?'

'He didn't grin or nothing,' said Barnes. 'It's hard to tell with Den. He lies all the time so you can't trust anything he says. Anyway, he swore it was nothing to do with them, and he said it was a good idea to meet to clear the air.'

'Those were his exact words?'

Barnes nodded.

'Where?'

'Victoria Embankment Gardens by the bandstand. Three o'clock.' Barnes looked apologetic. 'It was the nearest I could get to somewhere neutral. They didn't want to come over here.'

McGuinness nodded. 'All right. Fix up for some of our blokes to be watching, in case things turn nasty. But not to be conspicuous, so use blokes who are newish. We don't want the Bell brothers to see a crowd of faces they know on their patch, that could queer things, and the point is I want to talk to them.'

'Right, boss.'

'Oh, and get hold of Chuck and Lofty. I want a word with them.'

'What about?'

'About that little errand I sent them on.'

Barnes looked concerned. 'Did they do it all right?'

'That's what I want to find out.'

CHAPTER NINETEEN

Coburg let Lampson drive them back to the Yard. It gave him a chance to take in the air battle taking place to the south, the large German bombers, the Spitfire and Hurricanes attacking them like angry gnats, and the German planes, the Messerschmidts, hurling themselves at the RAF fighters. Coburg guessed that Hitler had believed victory would be achieved within a few days, perhaps a week at most. Yet here they were, a fortnight further on, and despite all the destruction of planes and buildings, and the number of pilot casualties, every day the young pilots were still rising up in their fighter planes from the damaged airfields, bringing down the German bombers in large numbers.

We're killing more of them than they are of ours, reflected Coburg. That was what war was about: who had the most left when the smoke cleared. The question was: how long could those boys keep going up, five or six times a day, each time flying in the face of death from the Luftwaffe bullets, knowing every time they went up that many of them would not be returning, and hoping it would not be them?

He was jolted away from the air battle by Lampson asking: 'What do you reckon's going on, guv? Williams and Thackeray killed, now Big Mel's pub torched. Gang warfare?'

'But why?' asked Coburg. 'The only gang big enough to rival Big Mel are the Bell brothers, north of the river. But why would they want to muscle in on Mel's territory?'

'Money.'

'Yes, but at what cost? Mel and the Bell brothers have got both sides of the river carved out nicely and that suits both of them. Why upset that?' He frowned. 'The puzzling thing is that Thackeray was killed the day before Williams. Why? Did Williams know Thackeray was dead when he went to the Ritz? Tell you what, Ted, you keep the car and go in search of this girlfriend of Thackeray's, Vera.'

Lampson nodded. 'They said she should be in today. What about you, guv? What are your plans?'

'I'm going to concentrate on the two killings at the Ritz. There's a new figure entered the picture I want to check on.'

'Oh?'

'Yes. An American record producer called Raymond Harris.'

'Record producer?' said Lampson. 'Anything connected with your friend, the singer?'

'She was the one who put me on to him. It seems he's very interested in how we're getting on with our investigation into the murders, and I'm curious to find out why.'

'Sounds like a chat-up line to me, guv.'

'Yes, that was my first thought, but Rosa has got a nose for this kind of thing. So, I thought I'd check him out.'

'Sure you don't want the car?'

Coburg shook his head. 'No, I can walk where I want to go. It's not far.'

'Where's that?'

'The Foreign Office. They have details of all aliens, and I'm hoping that includes visiting record executives from America.'

Sir Vincent Blessington was in his office and available when Coburg arrived at the Foreign Office.

He smiled in greeting. 'Detective Chief Inspector, a pleasure to see you again. Have there been any developments in the case?'

'Some, but nothing points to a definite answer as to who may have been responsible. The reason I'm here today is to ask if you know anything about a Raymond Harris? He's American, and I believe he's a record executive with Swan Records of New York.'

Blessington regarded Coburg warily. 'Is there any reason why we should know anything about him?' he asked.

'Well, he seems very interested in what happened at the Ritz.'

'I imagine most of the guests at the hotel are interested in that.'

Coburg nodded. 'True,' he said. 'But I didn't say he was a guest at the Ritz. He might be staying at any of the good hotels in London.'

Blessington smiled. 'Very good, Chief Inspector,' he said. 'Hoist with my own petard.'

'Not necessarily,' said Coburg. 'You may have been letting me know you're aware of him, in a subtle way.'

Blessington hesitated, then smiled again. 'Yes, there is that possibility.'

'So, you are aware of him?'

'He's a foreign national,' said Blessington. 'The Foreign Office likes to keep tabs on foreign nationals.'

'Considering there are quite a few thousand foreign nationals in the country at any one time, it's interesting you recall his name so easily.'

'Recent arrivals are always easier to bring to mind,' said Blessington blandly.

'What can you tell me about him?' asked Coburg. 'In as much as it bears on the investigation.'

Blessington looked thoughtful, obviously considering how much to tell the chief inspector. Finally, he asked: 'How much do you know about the Americans' attitude towards the war?'

'I know they've adopted a neutral position,' said Coburg.

'Yes,' said Blessington. 'The groundswell of opinion in America, especially in Washington, is that they don't want to get involved in another conflict between warring European nations. The last one cost them plenty of lives for something they felt was nothing to do with them. Once things began to look as if the same might happen again in Europe, with the rise of Hitler and the Nazis in Germany, and Mussolini and the fascists in Italy, the Americans passed a series of Neutrality Acts, the most recent last year. This stopped America going to war in support of any side if war should be declared outside of their country.

'It has to be said that these Acts were opposed by President Roosevelt, and Mr Churchill is still hoping that the American president will be able to overturn them and support the Allies' war effort. But that doesn't look likely. There is very little appetite among the politicians in Washington to get involved in another European war.

'The situation is compounded because there are elements of the American political scene who appear to actively support Hitler, and it's only the Neutrality Acts that are preventing them from giving him support in the form of weapons and access to American ports for the German U-boats.'

'But the other side of that coin is that as long as the Neutrality Acts remain in force, President Roosevelt and politicians sympathetic to us also can't help in any way,' pointed out Coburg.

Blessington nodded. 'That's right. And that includes official exchanges of information.'

'Between spies,' said Coburg. 'Their Intelligence outfits and ours.'

'Exactly,' said Blessington. 'And, unfortunately, there's little chance of those sort of communications happening because the American Ambassador to Britain, Joseph Kennedy, is not just anti-British, he's pro-German, and a supporter of Adolf Hitler.'

'Anti-British?' Coburg frowned. 'Are you sure?'

'Most definitely,' said Blessington. 'Which means no communications between British and American Intelligence through the embassy in London. But, because there are those in their government who are desperate to know what's happening behind the scenes in Europe – because, after all, it will affect America – alternative arrangements have been made.'

'Unofficial spies,' said Coburg.

'Let's just say, Americans with valid reasons for being in Britain, such as a record company executive, who sends reports back to his head office in New York or Boston.'

'Which, in turn, is passed on to someone in Washington,' finished Coburg. 'So, Raymond Harris is one of the good guys.'

'I wouldn't go that far,' said Blessington cautiously.

'How would you assess him, having worked with him?'

'Oh, I don't work with him,' said Blessington. 'That's not the role of the Foreign Office. I'm just aware of him.'

'In that case, who does work with him?' asked Coburg.

'I'd have thought you were already aware of that,' said Blessington.

Of course, realised Coburg. MI5. Inspector Hibbert.

'One other thing that might be of interest,' said Blessington. 'As is the case with many Americans, Raymond Harris is the anglicised version of his name. He changed it from Rajmond Hoxha when he started work in America.'

'Rajmond Hoxha?' Coburg was puzzled. 'What nationality is that?'

'Albanian,' said Blessington.

Chuck Watson and Lofty Parks entered the saloon bar of the Iron Horse warily, wondering why they had been summoned and what lay in store for them. They knew McGuinness well, and neither liked the grim expression on their boss's face as he surveyed them. McGuinness put down the newspaper he was reading and gestured for them to join him at his table. They sat, both with concerned expressions on their faces.

'Charley said you wanted to see us, Mr McGuinness,' said Watson, the shorter of the two.

'Yeh,' said McGuinness curtly. 'What did you do to that Stafford woman?'

'Just what you told us. Pick her up and ask her questions.'

'Did you touch her?'

Both men looked at him horrified.

'No, boss! Nothing at all! The only time we touched her was when we put the blindfold on, when we had to lead her into the factory. That was all! I swear!'

Parks nodded. 'That's true, boss. Honest.'

'You threatened her!' McGuinness accused them angrily.

'No, boss! We just asked her questions. Then we let her go, like you told us to.'

'She says you threatened her. Terrified her.'

'No! On my mother's life! All right, she may have been terrified, but that wasn't because of anything we said or did. We acted like proper coppers.'

'Better than coppers,' added Parks. 'We was perfect gentlemen.'

This time, when Lampson called at the address he'd been given for Vera Wicks, she was in. She looked to be in her early twenties, short and thin, her face's pasty skin almost hidden by her long, greasy black hair. She opened the door of the room she rented in the boarding house to Lampson and let him in after he'd shown her his warrant card. Her shoulders were slumped, and she seemed to Lampson to have been beaten down by life. Lampson knew what that was like, in Vera Wicks he recognised the same defeated posture of so many similar young women in Somers Town.

'I'm sorry to trouble you, Miss Wicks,' he said. 'But we're looking into the death of Billy Thackeray, and we've been told that you were close to him. So, first, my sympathies.'

She nodded and sighed, gesturing him to sit in the one armchair in the room. Instead, Lampson indicated that it was for her to sit there while he took the wooden kitchen chair. The room was small and poorly furnished with the cheapest possible furniture, all of it mismatched and worn. A single bed, a rickety table, the armchair and the wooden chair, with a gas ring in the hearth of what had once been a fireplace, now boarded up.

'When did you hear about his death?' asked Lampson.

'Last night,' she said. 'When I got back. I'd been visiting my mum in Poplar. My dad and brother are in the army so she needs the company. When I got back there was a message for me to get in touch with Waterloo police station.'

Sergeant Moss, thought Lampson. A good and caring copper.

'So, I went there, and the duty sergeant told me what had happened.' Suddenly she began to cry. 'I warned him!' she burst out. 'I worried something like this would happen. I warned him he was getting out of his depth.'

'Warned him about what?' asked Lampson.

'He said he was going to be rich. Really rich. He was talking about a million quid. He said we could go anywhere.'

'Did he say where the money was coming from?'

'No, but it was something he was cooking up with Joe.'

'Joe Williams?'

183

She nodded. 'Joe got killed, didn't he? In the Ritz.'

'Yes.'

'When I didn't hear from Billy and heard about what had happened to Joe, I was worried him disappearing was something to do with it.'

'When did you see Billy last?'

'Monday morning. I stayed at his place on Sunday night and he said he'd see me that night here at my place. But he never turned up. I went to his place Monday evening, but he wasn't there. I tried again on Tuesday, but there was still no sign of him.'

'Did you try calling on Joe to see if he knew where he was?'

She shook her head. 'I didn't like Joe. He was dangerous. He was leading Billy the wrong way. I told Billy that, but he just laughed. Said I didn't know Joe like he did. Said he was clever, and he needed him to get the money they were after.'

The lockpicks, thought Lampson.

'When did you hear about Joe being killed?'

'Tuesday. I went to this club he dances at to see if he knew where Billy was.'

'El Torero.'

'That's the one,' she said. 'When I heard that Joe had been killed, I got worried. That's when I decided to go to Poplar.'

'Why?'

She looked at him, surprised he should ask. 'Joe dead. Billy disappeared. I didn't know what was going on, but just in case someone decided to come looking for me to try and find out where Billy was, I didn't want to be here.'

'But you came back?'

She lowered her head. 'I had a row with my mum. She told me to get out. I had nowhere else to go, so I came back. I hoped Billy might be here. But instead . . .' Once again, she began to cry.

'Did he give any clue as to what he and Joe were planning? Anything at all?'

Vera shook her head. 'No. Just that there was a fortune to be got. A million for each of 'em, he said. Then, when I heard about the money and gold they reckon that king has stashed in his rooms at the Ritz, the same place they found Joe, and they said it was two million, well, it was obvious. I may not be clever, but I can divide two million by two and get the same figure Billy was talking about. So, it was the King's stash they was after.' She looked at Lampson, pained and upset. 'But the copper said Billy was killed on Monday. So why did Joe go to the Ritz that night?' She looked at Lampson even more intently as she asked: 'Did Joe kill Billy?'

CHAPTER TWENTY

Inspector Hibbert had a sour expression as he walked into the reception area of the MI5 section at Wormwood Scrubs from the rooms at the back.

'You again,' he grumbled as Coburg got up from the hard seat where he'd been waiting. 'What's up this time?'

'I wondered what you could tell me about Rajmond Hoxha?'

Hibbert shot a wary glance towards the receptionist who appeared to be occupied with ticking boxes on forms.

'We'll talk in my office,' he said.

Coburg followed through the door to the interior of the building and down a long, stone-walled corridor.

'Right,' he said when they were in his office. 'Who were you asking about?'

'Rajmond Hoxha, but you might know him better as Raymond Harris. He's an American record company executive. At least, that's his official position.'

'And why would I know him?'

'Because I've been informed by a very reliable source that British Intelligence are working with him.'

'Who's your source?'

'Sir Vincent Blessington at the Foreign Office.'

Hibbert scowled. 'That man talks too much.'

'He wants the murder at the Ritz solved.'

'Maybe it's best to forget it.'

'King Zog doesn't see it that way. He seems very keen to get to the bottom of it.'

'King Zog doesn't run things in this country. He's got no power.'

'But he has clout with the Foreign Office. They want to keep him sweet. Or is your concern that if we investigate Mr Harris too deeply we might find he's involved.'

'Involved?'

'He's a spy, so for my money that also means he's been trained in assassination techniques.'

'Supposition,' snorted Hibbert.

'He's also Albanian.'

'He's American,' Hibbert corrected him.

'He comes originally from Albania.'

'There are lots of Albanians in London,' countered Hibbert.

'So, are you telling me you haven't considered that he might have been involved in what happened at the Ritz? Especially now we have two murders.'

'Why are you coming to me with this?' demanded Hibbert. 'If this bloke's a foreign agent you should be talking to MI6.'

'British agents abroad are Six, foreign agents here are Five,' said Coburg. 'Also, I've met with Six twice about this case. Atkinson. I don't like him, and more importantly, he doesn't like me. He won't share any intelligence with me.'

'And you think I will?'

'You care about the security of this country. Atkinson's priority is protecting the reputation of MI6. And you at Five seem to know more about what Six are up to than they do themselves.'

Hibbert gave a grunt that seemed to confirm Coburg's opinion.

'Raymond Harris is an American citizen under the protection of the American government,' said Hibbert. 'As far as we're concerned, the fact he's residing at the Ritz is coincidental.'

'It's interesting you know he's staying at the Ritz,' commented Coburg. 'Which suggests some kind of communication between him and MI5.'

Hibbert regarded Coburg with a look of quiet exasperation.

'These are difficult times, Coburg. There's a war on, which means it's important that we maintain all levels of communication, but as far as Harris is concerned, we're at arm's length with him. There's no collusion or co-operation, if that's what you're suggesting. We know him and we know where he is. As far as we're concerned, we have the same aims, but we're not in each other's pockets. The business at the Ritz is about the money. Two million is a tempting target for anyone. But it's not an Intelligence issue. If there are politics involved, they're not the concern of MI5. That's for the Foreign Office and Six.'

'Five looks after what happens on home soil,' countered Coburg. 'Hoxha is here, on British soil.'

'And he is not a problem for us,' said Hibbert flatly. 'As far as we're concerned the murders at the Ritz are a criminal investigation, not one for Intelligence. So, it's a matter for the police. You want my advice?'

'Any advice is always welcome,' said Coburg.

'Drop the case,' said Hibbert. 'No money was stolen. A known thief was killed, and some kitchen hand. People whose deaths have much greater impact are being killed every day. There are bigger crimes being committed out there.'

'And if more people are killed linked to the deaths at the Ritz?'

Hibbert shrugged. 'Depends who they are. If anything happens to King Zog and his family, yes, of course. That has big implications. As to the rest? More low lifes and petty criminals getting bumped off? Good riddance. Makes our job a whole lot easier.'

Mel McGuinness and Charley Barnes sat on one of the benches by the bandstand at the end of Victoria Embankment Gardens. Behind them the skeletal metallic structure of the Hungerford Bridge spanned the Thames to Waterloo, as did the white-stoned Waterloo Bridge further along, past the famous obelisk of Cleopatra's Needle. McGuinness checked his watch.

'Five to three,' he said.

'They'll be here,' Barnes assured him.

McGuinness surveyed the gardens and his men stationed at irregular intervals, one on a bench not far away reading *The Sportsman* another standing by a bus stop just outside the garden, one waiting outside a telephone box, a fourth wearing a park-keeper's uniform walking around picking up litter with a spiked stick.

'I've always liked these gardens,' said McGuinness. 'I used to come here and sit and listen to the band, before north of the river got a bit dodgy. There's nothing like a good brass band.'

'Here they are,' said Barnes, tensing, his hand slipping into the pocket of his overcoat.

'Easy, Charley,' said McGuinness. 'We don't want to spook 'em before we've started.'

Reluctantly, Barnes removed his hand from his pocket, and the pistol in it, letting it rest on his lap.

Den and Danny Bell were in their late thirties, Den the older by three years. Both were short and slim, but they looked bulky today. Bulletproof vests beneath their long overcoats, McGuinness thought. The brothers were accompanied by six men who were spread out in a rough semicircle around and behind them.

'They've come tooled up,' murmured Barnes.

'Just as we have,' said McGuinness. 'I'd expect nothing less. It shows respect.'

As the brothers neared the bench where McGuinness and Barnes were waiting for them, the men protecting them stopped and fanned out, melting into the background. Barnes rose to his feet and moved to another bench a short distance away. Den acknowledged Barnes with a nod, then he and his brother sat down on the bench alongside McGuinness. When they were together the resemblance between them became more obvious. They might have been twins. Both had long, thin, pale faces, the same style of haircut, a neat back and sides, both had piercing greenish-blue eyes. The difference between them was the pencil-thin moustache that Danny sported.

'Mel, we're glad Charley reached out, cos we were going to get in touch with you,' said Den. 'This is a tragedy. A real tragedy.'

'And we can assure you that what happened to the Four Feathers was nothing to do with us,' added Danny earnestly.

'What about Billy Thackeray and Joe Williams?' demanded McGuinness.

Den held up his hands. 'Again, nothing to do with us.'

'We had nothing to do with them,' put in Danny. 'Not when they was alive, and certainly nothing to do with them dying.'

'You go to the Ritz,' said McGuinness.

'Yes, we do,' acknowledged Den. 'The food is the finest to be had in London, and as it's on our patch . . .'

'So, what was Joe Williams doing there to cause him to end up dead?' asked McGuinness.

'Mel, on our mother's life!' protested Danny. 'We didn't know he was there. How could we? We don't stay there, though we could if we wanted to. We just go there to eat now and then.'

'Which is why we're here,' said Den. 'Whatever's happened is nothing to do with us or any of our lot. We keep out of your way, and you keep out of ours. That's the way it's been, and it works for all of us because of that. There's no way we'd do anything to jeopardise that.'

'Then who did?'

'We have no idea,' insisted Den. 'We've got people asking around because we knew you'd think it might have been us and the last thing we want is to spend our time fighting a war with you. Times are hard enough as it is without courting trouble.'

'It wasn't us or any of our blokes, we can promise you that,' said Danny. 'Like I say, we're asking around, and as soon as we get anything we'll let you know straight away.'

'And if it turns out it *was* one of your blokes acting on his own?' asked McGuinness.

'If it was, and trust me, Mel, it wasn't, but if it was we'd deal with him. And we'd make sure you'd be there when we do,' said Den. 'We can't say fairer than that, can we?'

Lampson was at his desk in their office when Coburg returned to the Yard.

'Took you a bit longer than expected, guv?' said Lampson. 'Problems?'

'No, the information I got at the Foreign Office led me on to MI5 at Wormwood Scrubs.'

'You should have had the car after all,' observed Lampson.

'The walk did me good.'

'You walked to Wormwood Scrubs?' said Lampson, horrified.

'No, to the Foreign Office. I got a taxi to The Scrubs,' admitted Coburg. 'I'll tell you what I learnt in a minute. How did you get on? Did you find Billy Thackeray's girlfriend?'

'I did,' said Lampson. 'From what she told me, it looks like Williams and Thackeray were planning to steal the money from the King's suite.'

'She told you as much?'

'She said Thackeray told her that him and Joe Williams had a job on which was worth two million, and they were going to split it, a million each.'

'Yes, that seems fairly conclusive,' said Coburg. 'So, why was Thackeray killed before they made their attempt?'

'Vera reckons Joe Williams might have killed him.'

'Why? If he was going to do that surely he'd have waited until after the job was done. They would have needed both of them to handle the bullion, if not the money.' He frowned doubtfully. 'In fact, that much bullion would need more than two blokes to move it. Gold's heavy.'

'Maybe there were others involved and they were with Joe that night, and it was them who killed him.'

'Again, why? It wasn't as if there was a fight over the money; nothing was taken.'

'So this King Zog says,' pointed out Lampson. 'He could be lying.'

'Yes, he could. That's a good point,' said Coburg approvingly. 'Maybe the robbery did take place after all. Not all the bullion and cash, but some of it.'

'What are you going to do? Face the King out with it, see what he says?'

'No,' said Coburg unhappily. 'He'll just deny it. No, the person I need to talk to is his private secretary, Count Ahmed. Him, I might be able to lean on.' He picked up the phone, dialled the Ritz and asked to be put through to the hall porter.

'George,' he said genially. 'It's DCI Coburg. Is Count Ahmed back yet?'

'I'm sorry, Mr Coburg, he's not and there's no word about him. I've tried asking some of the royal staff, the junior members, but discreetly of course.'

'Of course,' said Coburg.

'I shall do my best to find out, I promise.'

'Thank you, George. I know you will.'

Coburg hung up and Lampson said: 'No joy there, then?'

'I'm afraid not,' sighed Coburg.

'So how did you get on, guv? You said you had to go to MI5.'

Coburg nodded. 'According to Sir Vincent Blessington, Raymond Harris is actually Rajmond Hoxha, born in Albania before he moved to America.'

'Bit suspicious that, using an alias,' commented Lampson.

'Not necessarily,' said Coburg. 'Many Americans have come from somewhere else, and it helps them to fit in if they anglicise their name. The interesting thing I picked up is that it seems that Harris is an undercover agent for the American government.'

'A spy?'

'Indeed. But one who's been working with British Intelligence.'

'Well, that's a relief, anyhow.'

'Yes, except it raises an interesting possibility. Spies are usually trained in all manner of subversive activities, including opening locks, theft and assassination techniques.'

'Bloody hell!' said Lampson. 'I see where you're going with this. You think he could have been involved in trying to nick the money, and he may have been the one who killed Joe Williams.' Then he frowned. 'But why would a secret agent get involved in a robbery?'

'He's Albanian,' Coburg reminded him. 'And there are those who think that the King, in liberating the money from the Albanian National Bank, was stealing it from the people of that country.'

Lampson looked at him dubiously. 'It's a bit far-fetched, guv. He'd have to have been working with other like-minded people to do that.'

'Like a kitchen hand from Macedonia?' said Coburg. 'Or others of Albanian extraction? There are quite a few of them in London at the moment.'

Lampson let out a heavy sigh. 'Well, it certainly adds a complication.' He sighed gloomily again. 'As if this case wasn't complicated enough already.'

CHAPTER TWENTY-ONE

That evening Coburg returned to the Ritz to see if there were any tables free for Rosa's performance in the Rivoli Bar, but was told very apologetically and with many sad looks from the maître d'hôtel that every one was booked. 'She is very popular, monsieur. It's not just the hotel guests coming to see her; word has been spreading even wider.'

'I understand,' said Coburg. 'Might I be permitted to stand just inside the door?'

'We don't usually permit that, but as it's you, Monsieur Coburg . . .'

There was still an hour before Rosa was due to appear, so Coburg made his way to her dressing room.

'Edgar!' She smiled happily as he tapped at her door, and then opened it at her call to enter. 'Coming to see the show again?'

'Yes, however, fortunately for you, but unfortunately

for me, every available table is booked, so the maître d' is allowing me to stand by the door.'

'That's horrible!' exclaimed Rosa.

'Not to see you,' said Coburg. 'It's worth any amount of leg cramp I may suffer. So, I thought I'd call in first and see how you're fixed for afterwards.'

Rosa sighed and shook her head. 'I really need to be at home with Donna tonight,' she said. 'Despite all your good words, she's really edgy. Did you have a word with the man you think took Julie?'

'I did,' said Coburg. 'A very firm word. But I understand how things are. Will you at least let me drive you home, get you to your door safely?'

'Yes, please,' said Rosa. 'And maybe tomorrow night, providing there's been nothing bad happening, Donna might feel able to face being in the house alone.'

There was a knock at the door, then it opened and the smiling face of Raymond Harris looked in. He was carrying a bouquet of flowers.

'Miss Weeks?' His smile wavered as he saw Coburg, then he recovered it. 'My apologies, I didn't realise you were busy.'

'Mr Harris, this is Detective Chief Inspector Edgar Coburg. Edgar, this is Raymond Harris, the record executive I was telling you about.'

'A pleasure to meet you,' said Coburg. He held out his hand.

'And to meet you too, Chief Inspector,' said Harris. 'The flowers, though, are for Miss Weeks.'

Rosa beamed. 'Why, thank you.' She took the flowers from him. 'I have a vase here that will be perfect for them. If you'll excuse me, I'll just go and get some water.'

'Allow me,' offered Harris.

'Staff only behind the scenes in the kitchen,' said Rosa. She picked up the vase and left, saying: 'I won't be a minute.'

'So, Chief Inspector, are you here to watch the show?'

'I am,' said Coburg. 'The maître d' is allowing me to hover discreetly by the door.'

'You don't have a table booked?'

Coburg shook his head. 'I didn't know how things would go today, so I didn't want to take the chance of making a booking I might not be able to keep and risk having an empty table in the audience.'

'Why don't you share mine?' offered Harris. 'I'm on my own and it will be great to have your company.'

'You sure you don't mind?' asked Coburg.

'Not at all. In fact, it will be my pleasure to share the experience of listening to her in the company of someone who also really appreciates her talent.'

'Thank you,' said Coburg. 'It will be a pleasure to accept your generous offer.'

'And far more comfortable than standing by the door,' said Harris.

Rosa returned, carrying the vase now filled with water.

'The chief inspector has agreed to be my guest this evening,' said Harris.

Rosa shot a quick look at Coburg. 'How nice. You'll both have someone to talk to in the interval.'

Harris looked at his watch. 'I guess we'd better leave you for your final preparations. Are you ready, Chief Inspector?'

Coburg nodded, and he and Harris made for the door.

Just before he left, Coburg turned and gave Rosa a wink.

Damn, thought Rosa as she looked at the now-closed door. *That man is just too damned attractive. Why did I have to fall for a policeman, for God's sake? Why not a musician, someone I'd have been able to travel with?*

I don't want to lose him again, she decided. *I don't know how we're going to make it work because I'm not going to give up doing what I love, and I know he sure isn't, but there's got to be some way.* Other people did it. She knew married couples who rarely saw one another, but who were completely together.

Married! In her head she'd spoken the M word, and it shocked her. But why not? If he asked her, she'd say *Yes. Yes.*

And if he didn't ask her?

I can't ask him, she decided. *It's not what I do. But if he doesn't . . .*

She sighed, picked up her music and made for the door. Showtime.

Mel McGuinness sat silently fuming in the rear of his Jaguar as his driver made his way through the streets of Lambeth towards Mel's large detached house. It was half past ten and travelling at night in the blackout irritated McGuinness, even though he could see the sense in it. In the first few months of the war, cars had been forbidden to use any lights at all when being driven at night. The result had been hundreds of deaths as cars ran pedestrians over or crashed. Finally the authorities relented and allowed cars to use headlights at night, providing they were kept on dip, and the headlamps were fitted with covers over the top to stop the light being seen from the sky. A twenty mile an hour speed limit was also in force during the hours of darkness. It meant that driving anywhere at night took ages.

It had been a long and unpleasant day. The meeting with the Bell brothers hadn't gone as he'd hoped. He still wasn't sure about them. Sure, they pleaded innocence, but that was what he expected from them. They weren't to be trusted. And then there was DCI Coburg, coming into his pub and slandering him the way he did. He should have punched Coburg in the face for what he'd said about terrorising the woman. McGuinness prided himself on his attitude towards women, unlike many of his contemporaries. The Bell brothers, for example, with their stables of prostitutes run by violent pimps. That's who Coburg should be directing his accusations at. Chuck and Lofty hadn't terrorised the woman, of that he was sure. They knew Mel's rules about treating women and they knew what would happen to them if they broke them. It came from the way his dad had treated his mum and sister. Brutal. Vicious. He remembered seeing them lying on the floor of the kitchen in their small, cramped terraced house, noses broken, blood everywhere, while the old man kicked and stamped on them.

McGuinness had been thirteen when he'd killed his father, smashing his head in with a coal hammer while he slept, drunk. Afterwards, he'd loaded his dad's body into a wheelbarrow and dumped it in the canal, weighed down with stones in the pockets of his jacket. He hadn't told his mum or sister what he'd done, just that the old man had been beaten to death by someone who'd got into the house, and he'd got rid of the body so there'd be no questions asked. He suspected they knew what he'd done, but they

200

agreed to let it be known locally that the old man had left suddenly, and they didn't know where he'd gone.

Again, the accusation from Coburg that he'd do anything to harm or terrify a woman filled him with rage. All right, maybe she had got frightened, but there'd been no threats made to her, he was certain of that.

'Here we are, Mr McGuinness.' Mel realised they were outside his house. He opened the car door.

'Same time tomorrow, Mr McGuinness?' the driver asked.

'As usual,' grunted Mel.

He got out, shut the car door, then headed down the short path to his front door. He stopped and looked at it, its heavy oak with brass numbers, the bay windows on ether side, and thought with satisfaction: *Not bad for a boy from the back streets.*

He was just about to put his key in the lock when he felt a presence behind him. He turned and saw a gun pointing at his head.

'What the—?' he began.

He never finished. The bullet smashed into his face and his head exploded.

CHAPTER TWENTY-TWO

Coburg drove home after dropping Rosa at her house, his head filled with thoughts of her, and also of Raymond Harris. In the car, she'd seemed amused at the idea of Coburg and Harris sharing the table. 'Was it a competition?' she asked. 'Was he sounding you out about us, seeing if he had a chance?'

'Of course,' said Coburg. 'I have no doubt at all that he admires you for your looks as much as your talent. But this evening, I think his aim was to probe me about the case, and the millions King Zog has in his suite at the hotel.'

He then told her what he'd learnt from Sir Vincent Blessington.

'Albanian?' she said, stunned.

'Only by birth. Everyone has to be born somewhere. But what's equally interesting is this business of him being a spy and acting as an intermediary between British and American Intelligence.'

'So, this business of him being a record company executive is a fake,' she said angrily.

'No, it's genuine enough. But it's also a very good cover for him moving back and forth between Britain and America.'

Coburg parked the car and walked to his flat, Rosa's question pinging around in his brain. What had he told Harris? On reflection, nothing that he was sure the man didn't know already. The questioning had been done very subtlely, innocuous comments, some about the situation in the Balkans, but there had been no direct questions, just gaps in bland talk left for Coburg to fill. Harris was good, there was no doubt about that. But there was one question that hovered in Coburg's mind: was Harris a killer? Could he have been the one who cut Joe Williams's throat? And if so, why? Were his orders to protect the King and his wealth? Or was he working for someone else? Many secret agents had more than one paymaster.

As he unlocked his door his telephone was ringing, and his first thought was that it was Rosa, that something bad had happened. He ran to the phone and snatched it up.

'Coburg.'

'Sergeant Elliott from Waterloo, sir. I'm sorry to trouble you so late, but something's turned up and there was a note in the file from Sergeant Moss that said if anything happened connected to this particular individual, for you to be advised immediately.'

'Which individual?' asked Coburg.

'Mel McGuinness, sir. He's been shot.'

'Shot?'

'Yes, sir. Dead. It happened outside his house about an hour ago. We've got his driver here telling us the story of what happened. Charley Barnes has also arrived, says he's here to represent the driver, but we think he might be useful. You know, see if he can throw any light on why this happened.'

'Keep them there. I'm on my way.'

The roads were virtually empty, everyone apparently obeying the rules of the blackout, so Coburg made good time to Waterloo despite the speed restrictions. In peacetime the reception area of a police station at nearly midnight was usually heaving with drunks, pickpockets, muggers, burglars and prostitutes. Wartime, with ARP wardens and others patrolling the streets, meant that Waterloo police station was empty except for the night duty sergeant at the desk and a couple of uniformed officers. And Charley Barnes, sitting on a wooden bench, who leapt to his feet as he saw Coburg.

'Mr Coburg!'

'In a minute, Charley. Let me have a word with the sergeant, and then with Mel's driver.'

'Matt Dorsey. He's a good bloke.'

'I'm sure he is.'

'He didn't have anything to do with it.'

'I never suggested he did.'

'I reckon I know who did.'

'I'm sure and we will talk in a minute. But first—'

'I come in of me own accord,' snapped Barnes.

'I know you did, and that's appreciated. But first I need to talk to Mr Dorsey.'

Reluctantly, Barnes sat down on the bench, but Coburg could feel the man's eyes burning into his back as he walked away. *He's angry*, thought Coburg. *No, worse than that, he's maniacal about what's happened to Big Mel.*

Coburg strode to the desk and the waiting sergeant. 'DCI Coburg,' he introduced himself. 'Sergeant Elliott?'

'That's me, sir. And thank you for coming so quickly.' He lowered his voice as he shot a look in the waiting Barnes's direction. 'He's very edgy, sir. Very edgy indeed. That's why I asked the constables to hang around, just in case he gets out of hand. I know what Charley Barnes can be like.'

'I'll deal with him after I've talked to this Matt Dorsey,' said Coburg. 'But if Barnes starts playing up, you have my backing to chuck him in a cell.'

'That won't be easy,' said Elliott warily. 'I know three of us against one sound good odds, but Barnes is barely in control when he's on edge like this. And with Big Mel being shot the way he was . . .'

Coburg nodded, then walked back to where Barnes was sitting. Once more, Barnes leapt to his feet, mouth open to start speaking, but Coburg held up his hand to stop him, then leant in so he could talk without the others hearing.

'Charley, I know you're mad about what happened, and I know that mad doesn't even cover it. But that's why I'm here, to get to the bottom of it and find out who did it. But first I need to talk to Matt Dorsey. While I'm doing that, I want you to stay here. I know it's a waste of time saying keep calm, because keeping calm isn't your style. But if you kick off while I'm busy with Dorsey, I won't talk to you because anything you say will be just anger. I need your brain thinking over what's happened, and who it might be.' As Barnes opened his mouth to respond, Coburg held up his hand to silence him momentarily. 'Not just the person you've got in your head already, but others. Think, Charley, while I'm talking to Dorsey. Then we'll talk. But kick off and us talking is gone for the night, and that won't help find Mel's killer. All right?'

Barnes stood looking at Coburg, then he swallowed and nodded.

'Good,' said Coburg. 'We have a deal. I'll see you in a minute or two.'

Coburg returned to the desk. 'We should be fine,' he said to Elliott. 'Now, take me to see Mr Dorsey.'

The sergeant gestured one of the constables to join them. 'Take DCI Coburg to interview room one.'

'You want me to stay with him?' asked the constable.

'No,' said Coburg. 'I'll be fine. You come back here.'

Coburg followed the constable to the interview room. A uniformed constable was on duty outside.

'Thank you, Constable,' said Coburg, and he let himself into the room.

Matt Dorsey was a short, wiry man with thinning red hair, wearing a jacket too large for him and which hung on him like a tent as he walked around the room agitatedly. He stopped pacing as Coburg entered.

'Hello, Mr Dorsey,' said Coburg. 'I'm Detective Chief Inspector Coburg from Scotland Yard. Please, take a seat.'

Dorsey sat on one of the two chairs at the room's only other piece of furniture, a wooden table, and Coburg took the other.

'Tell me what happened,' he said.

'Mel got shot,' said Dorsey.

'Yes, so I understand,' said Coburg. 'You drove him home, is that right?'

Dorsey nodded, his head bobbing furiously up and down, showing his nervousness.

'Was this a regular trip?'

'Every night,' said Dorsey. 'I'd pick him up from the Iron Horse. If he'd been anywhere before, he always went back to the Iron Horse for me to pick him up.'

'What time?'

'Ten o'clock. Regular as clockwork. Unless something had come up which meant he was late. In which case, I'd wait for him till he arrived.'

'Was he often late?'

Dorsey shook his head. 'No. Nine times out of ten he was there at the Iron Horse on the dot.'

'And that's what happened tonight?'

Again, Dorsey's head jerked frantically up and down, causing his thin hair to flap like a bad wig.

'It happened when you got to his home, is that right?'

'Yes.'

'Tell me what happened.'

'I pulled up outside Mr McGuinness's house like I always do and waited while he walked up the path to his front door. It's only a short path. He got to the door safe enough, so I was about to drive off and put the car away. Mr McGuinness has got a lock-up garage just a couple of streets away. You can't trust it if you leave a car unattended overnight, not even in good areas. Someone'll siphon off your petrol. Anyway, I was just driving off when I heard this bang. At first I thought it was a car backfiring, but I looked back just in case, and there was Mr McGuinness leaning against his front door and sliding down it.'

'Did you see anyone?'

'I'm coming to that. I saw a bloke, at least I think it was a bloke, but it was dark and whoever it was had a big baggy overcoat on and a hat pulled down, and he was just running round the corner of the house.'

'Did you go after him?'

'I started to, but first I wanted to check on Mr McGuinness. But he was dead. Shot in the head. Horrible, it was.'

'What did you do then?'

'Well, then I went after the shooter, but there was no sign of him. Round the side of the house there's like rough ground, and a gate into the back garden. I went into the garden but couldn't see anyone.'

'How far did you go?'

'Right down the bottom. There's a wooden fence there, and beyond that it's just small side streets.'

'Did you have a weapon with you?' asked Coburg.

'What d'you mean?' asked Dorsey uncomfortably.

'You were chasing someone who'd just shot your boss, so you knew he was armed. He could have shot you. Did you have a weapon on you to protect yourself?'

'Yeh, but it wasn't mine,' said Dorsey. 'I don't have a gun. It's illegal.'

'So, whose gun did you have?'

'Mel's. Mr McGuinness's,' said Dorsey. 'I knew he kept one in his pocket, so I took that.'

'Mel was a widower, wasn't he?'

Again, Dorsey did his frantic nodding.

'Anyone live with him?'

'No. He was all on his own. I told him once he ought to get a housekeeper, he could afford it, but he said he preferred it like it was, being on his own.'

'Was there ever any trouble any of the times you took him home?'

'Trouble?'

'Yes, anyone acting suspiciously, for example.'

Dorsey shook his head. 'No. Never anything like that. People knew who he was, and they knew the car. No one with half a brain would make trouble.'

Coburg nodded. 'All right, Mr Dorsey. I think that's all for the moment, but in the morning I'll be going to examine the crime scene and I'd like you there to walk me through what you saw.'

Dorsey nodded. 'What time?'

'Seven o'clock.'

'Seven o'clock?' said Dorsey, horrified. 'That's a bit early!'

'I want to examine the scene before it gets trampled on,' said Coburg.

Dorsey nodded again. 'No problem.'

Coburg walked Dorsey back to the reception desk.

'We can let Mr Dorsey go now, Sergeant,' he said. 'I shall be seeing him when it gets light at the crime scene. Has it been roped off?'

'Yes, sir,' said Elliot. 'The constables who attended also put up "Police: Keep Out" notices.'

'Good,' said Coburg. He held out his hand to Dorsey to shake, who took it, surprised by the action. 'I'll see you later.'

'I'll be there,' replied Dorsey.

'So will I,' said Barnes, who'd walked over to join them. 'In fact, hang on here, Matt, and you can run me home after I've talked to Mr Coburg.'

Dorsey made for a bench, as Coburg led Barnes towards the interview room.

'So, you didn't come in your car, Charley,' he said.

'No. A mate dropped me off.'

They entered the interview room and the two men sat in the same chairs Coburg and Dorsey had recently vacated. Barnes was visibly agitated, his movements jerky, but not through intimidation from being in the interview room, as Coburg guessed Barnes had plenty of experience being here.

'Right. So, who do you think killed Mel?' asked Coburg.

'The Bell brothers,' Barnes answered immediately.

'Why?'

'Because they want to take over his territory.'

'And move south of the river?' said Coburg. 'Frankly, Charley, that sounds a bit unlikely. The south is a foreign country to them, same as north of the river was for Mel, and for you.'

'They're greedy.'

'I can't see Danny and Den thinking it would be that easy to take over just by bumping Big Mel off,' said Coburg.

'Cut the head off and the rest follows, that's how they see it,' said Barnes flatly.

'Obviously, that's one line of enquiry we'll follow—'

'It's the only line of enquiry,' snapped Barnes. 'They're the only ones who benefit.'

'But just in case, let's look at other options,' said Coburg. 'Who else could be in the frame?'

Barnes fell silent, sullen, angry at Coburg doubting that the Bell brothers were behind the killing.

'There must be someone else that Mel upset enough to want to kill him,' pressed Coburg.

Reluctantly, Barnes thought. Then he said: 'There's always them fascists.'

'The fascists?'

'Yeh. Mosley's lot.'

'The British Union of Fascists?'

'Yeh. Them.'

'Why?'

'Well, he had Joe Williams inside 'em, finding out what was going on. Then he passed on what Joe picked up. It was thanks to Mel that they ended up being jailed. He was a patriot, was Mel. Someone must have found out so this was their revenge. It could have been them that done for Joe as well.'

'The BUF was closed down three months ago. Why wait till now?'

'Maybe they didn't know until just lately. After all, Joe only got killed a few days ago. And there were some pretty powerful people in it.'

'Charley, I know for a fact that the Intelligence services had been keeping their own very careful watch on the BUF for the last couple of years, and they had their own people inside the organisation. I take your point that Mel passed on what Joe picked up, but MI5 and Special

Branch would have known most of it already.'

Barnes scowled. 'Yeh, well, if you ask me, it's either the Bell brothers or it's political. There's no one else who'd have wanted Mel dead.'

CHAPTER TWENTY-THREE

Saturday 24th August

Realising he wasn't going to get any further with Barnes, Coburg ended the interview and walked with him back to the reception area where Dorsey was waiting. He watched as the two men left the station, then rejoined Sergeant Elliot.

'Can you fix for a constable to be at McGuinness's house at quarter to seven in the morning?' he said. 'I'll go there myself to go over the ground and see what daylight brings.'

'Yes, sir,' said Elliott. He looked towards the door. 'What do you reckon, sir? Who did it for Big Mel?'

'Charley Barnes seems convinced it was the Bell brothers,' replied Coburg. 'Me, I'm keeping an open mind.'

Coburg was outside McGuinness's house the next morning at a quarter to seven with a constable. He paced from the gate along the gravel path to the front door, where blood and brains still stained the wall. He checked the area around where McGuinness's body had fallen. The gravel meant there would be no visible footprints, but he hoped the grass and the bare earth path that led round the back of the house might show something. It did, but not of much use. There was a mix of different marks in the earth, but there had been a lot of trampling, most recently the boots of Matt Dorsey running after the mystery assassin, and then returning, which obscured any earlier prints.

At seven o'clock Matt Dorsey appeared, accompanied by Charley Barnes and a man Coburg recognised as McGuinness's solicitor, Pentangle Underhill. Coburg had initially doubted that Pentangle was Underhill's real first name, until he'd got someone to check with records, and discovered that was indeed the name his parents had given him. He wondered if the solicitor had ever forgiven his parents.

'Morning, Mr Coburg,' Barnes greeted him. 'You know Mr Underhill, I believe?'

Coburg nodded briefly to acknowledge the solicitor and received an equally curt but polite nod in return. Underhill was a tall man in his late fifties, his black hair streaked with grey, with a neatly trimmed greying moustache. He was always expensively and elegantly dressed, today wearing a dark pinstripe suit beneath a long camel-hair overcoat and sporting a homburg.

'Mr Dorsey, if you'll show me the route you took after you heard the shot and saw the assailant disappear,' said Coburg.

Dorsey stepped forward, as did Barnes, but Coburg stopped him, saying, 'Just Mr Dorsey.'

Barnes scowled. 'I'm here to see he's treated fair.'

'And he will be, but unless you were also here when the incident happened, I only need Mr Dorsey.'

Barnes shot a questioning look at Underhill, who shook his head. Barnes scowled again and let Dorsey join Coburg.

'You can stay here as well, Constable,' Coburg instructed the uniformed policeman. 'The fewer prints we get, the better.' He looked at Dorsey. 'Right, Mr Dorsey, repeat exactly what you did last night.'

'I was in the car and I saw Mr McGuinness fall down, just like I said to you. I saw this bloke run away down the side of the house, so I went after him.'

'Show me,' said Coburg.

Dorsey set off along the path towards the front door, Coburg following, noting the man's movements. When they got to the door, Dorsey stopped.

'I knelt down to see if Mr McGuinness was all right, and that's when I saw his head, and I knew he wasn't. He was dead.'

'And then?'

'I decided to go after the bloke.'

'Even though you knew he had a gun.'

'Mr McGuinness had always been good to me,' said Dorsey. 'I owed him that much.'

'And then you took the pistol from Mr McGuinness?'

Dorsey nodded.

'Where did he keep it?'

'In a pocket.'

'So, you took the pistol, and then what?'

'I carried on along the path . . .'

Coburg gestured for Dorsey to resume walking and followed as the man walked to the back of the house before stopping. There was a small wooden fence with a gate, which was unlatched and swinging free.

'Was this gate open last night?' asked Coburg.

'Yeh,' said Dorsey. 'So I guessed that's the way the bloke had gone, because Mr McGuinness always kept it shut. Then I went through.'

Coburg followed Dorsey into the rear garden, which was large and laid to lawn, with flower beds around the four sides.

'Mr McGuinness loved his flowers,' said Dorsey. 'Tulips, particularly, were his favourite.'

Dorsey began to walk forward across the lawn, but Coburg stopped him.

'Could you see much?' he asked.

Dorsey shook his head. 'Hardly anything. Mr McGuinness's place is all on its own, and at the back is a bit of a stream, and then just paths. There's no street lights at the back, and even if there was, they would have been off with the blackout, just like in the front.' Coburg gestured for him to start walking again and followed Dorsey until he reached the wooden fence at the end of the garden. Over the fence was a thin dribble of a stream which had various bits of rubbish in it, and paths, not often trodden by the look of it, heading away, towards the surrounding streets, Coburg assumed.

'This was as far as I went,' said Dorsey. 'I hung around for a minute, waiting to see if the bloke was hiding somewhere, but he must have gone over the fence and then off along one of the paths.'

Without falling into the stream, despite it being pitch-dark, thought Coburg. The killer knew the layout of the house and the area.

'All right, Mr Dorsey,' said Coburg. 'Is there anything

else you can think of? Anything, however small.'

'No,' said Dorsey. 'That's just how it happened.'

'So, what did you do then?'

Dorsey hesitated, then said awkwardly: 'Mr McGuinness's keys were lying next to him, so I let myself into the house and phoned.'

'Who did you phone?'

Coburg knew the answer already and wasn't surprised when Dorsey mumbled, 'Mr Barnes.'

'And what did he tell you to do?'

'He said he'd come out and sort it.'

'How did you end up at Waterloo police station?'

'Mr Barnes told me to go there and report what had happened. He said he'd be along there and see me later.'

'Thank you,' said Coburg.

He headed back to where Barnes and Underhill stood with the waiting constable, Dorsey following.

'So, after Dorsey phoned you, what did you do, Charley?' asked Coburg.

Barnes shot an angry scowl towards Dorsey, then said: 'I went to Waterloo nick to report what had happened. You know that; you saw me there.'

'I saw you when you were there. What did you do before you went to the police station? Knowing how close you and Mel were, I can't imagine you just leaving him here without checking, in case there was a chance he might be alive.'

Barnes hesitated, then nodded. 'Yeh. I came here, but he was dead, right enough. So, I left a couple of blokes to wait here with him until the law and the ambulance turned up, and my mate drove me to Waterloo nick.'

'Thank you,' said Coburg.

Coburg gestured for the constable to accompany him and he headed for his car.

'What are you gonna do about it?' shouted Barnes, angry.

'I'm going to catch whoever did it and bring them to trial,' said Coburg. 'It's what the law does.'

Coburg dropped the constable off at Waterloo police station, then continued on to Scotland Yard. Whoever had killed McGuinness had planned it carefully. He knew McGuinness's routine: the time he arrived home each night, and he knew where the paths at the bottom of McGuinness's garden led. One shot, and then gone. A professional, by the sound of it. And it seemed part of a vendetta, following on from the torching of the Four Feathers. Was the battering to death of Billy Thackeray part of the same? Coburg suspected it was. But was it all gangland related? That was the doubt nagging at him.

The door opened, and Lampson appeared, looking slightly embarrassed on seeing Coburg already at his desk.

'Good morning, sir. Sorry I'm late.'

'You're not late, Ted. I was in early today.'

'I am, though,' admitted Lampson. 'There was trouble with Terry. He went missing this morning.'

'Missing?' said Coburg, shocked.

'Yeh, but not far. He's got this obsession with tracking down spies. All this talk about fifth columnists, him and two of his mates have set themselves up as some kind of spywatchers, following people they think are suspicious. Anyway, he wasn't in his bed when I called him for breakfast this morning. It turned out he'd gone out with his mate Harry, who lives next door, to investigate the milkman because someone had said they'd heard him talking in German.'

218

'A German milkman?'

Lampson shook his head ruefully. 'A Geordie milkman, from Newcastle. He was filling in for the regular milkman who's been called up. Harry heard someone say he was talking in a foreign language and they thought it was German, and he passed it on to Terry, so this morning they were up early and following the poor bloke to see if he made contact with anyone.'

'Full of initiative,' said Coburg.

'Full of something,' growled Lampson unhappily. 'He's got an overactive imagination, that's the trouble.'

'But you found him.'

Lampson nodded. 'I did. And gave him a good talking to. And then, when I got in, Fred on the desk told me about Mel McGuinness. Is it true?'

'It is,' said Coburg. 'I got a call late last night from Waterloo. I went there and talked to Mel's driver, and also to Charley Barnes, then I visited the site early this morning.'

'Was Barnes with Mel when he got it?' asked Lampson.

'No,' said Coburg.

'So, what was he doing at Waterloo nick?'

'Looking after Mel's driver's interests.'

The phone rang and Lampson picked it up. 'DCI Coburg's office.' He listened for a moment, then said, 'Yes, sir. Right away,' before hanging up. 'That was the super,' he told Coburg. 'He wants to see you.'

'Any bets it's about Big Mel?' sighed Coburg.

'I'm not taking that one,' said Lampson. 'It's a racing certainty.'

CHAPTER TWENTY-FOUR

Superintendent Allison was at his desk, puffing at his pipe, when Coburg walked into his office.

'Mel McGuinness,' said Allison, gesturing for Coburg to sit down.

'Yes, sir,' said Coburg. 'I got the phone call telling me about it late last night. I went to Waterloo police station where his driver, the only witness, was being held. Also there was Charley Barnes.'

'McGuinness's lieutenant,' said Allison thoughtfully. 'Was he involved in any way?'

'No, sir. He said he was just there to look after the interests of McGuinness's driver.'

'No suspects?'

'Barnes says he thinks the Bell brothers were behind it. There've been a few incidents lately aimed at McGuinness's operation. His pub, the Four Feathers, was burnt to the ground the night before last. One of his operatives, Billy Thackeray, was found beaten to death a few days ago. And, of course, Joe Williams, the man found murdered at the Ritz, was one of McGuinness's men. But pretty low level.'

'Think there's any connection with the murder at the hotel? Or, rather, murders, now there's this kitchen hand as well.'

'I don't think so, sir. We've got evidence that indicates Williams and Thackeray were conspiring to steal the money and gold from the King's suite, but whether that was with McGuinness's knowledge is, I feel, unlikely. I think Williams and Thackeray were operating independently of McGuinness.'

'That wouldn't have gone down well with him,' observed Allison.

'No, sir, it wouldn't.'

'Think he found out what they were up to and had them disposed of?'

Coburg shook his head. 'No, sir. If that had been the case he wouldn't have needed to conduct his own enquiry as to how Williams ended up dead in the King's rooms at the Ritz.'

'This young woman he had abducted.' Allison nodded, then he smiled at Coburg's look of surprise. 'Yes, Chief Inspector, I do keep tabs on what's going on, even if I don't appear to.'

'I did everything by the book, sir,' said Coburg, suddenly feeling awkwardly defensive. 'And it was part of the investigation into what happened at the hotel.'

Allison gave a resigned sigh. 'I'm not reprimanding

you, Edgar. You did everything that was required and you acted properly, as I would expect a senior officer to do. And, before you ask, I am aware that the young lady entertainer was involved in the issue, and that you and she are . . . close. And no, I did not get any of this from Sergeant Lampson. He would never dream of telling me about your private life, he's far too loyal to you for that. Let's just say that I, also, have friends who go to the Ritz, and some of them are quite gossipy about who they've seen there, and with whom.'

'Yes, sir.'

'Getting back to McGuinness, if his killing isn't connected to what happened at the Ritz, what is behind it?'

'I'm not sure, sir. As I said, Charley Barnes seems to think the Bell brothers are involved.'

'If that's the case then we have to brace ourselves for a gang war, because Barnes will be after revenge.' Then he gave a thoughtful frown. 'Unless he may have been the one who did it.'

'Killed McGuinness, sir?'

'It's not unknown for a second in charge to want to be top dog. It's a familiar story throughout history. Brutus and Julius Caesar. Iago and Othello.'

'I honestly don't think that's the case here, sir,' said Coburg. 'McGuinness and Barnes were more than just business associates; they go way back. I'd say they were the closest thing to a real friend either of them had.'

'I'm sure Caesar felt the same way about Brutus.'

'That was politics and ambition, sir.'

'Gangsterism at the top level is also about politics,' countered Allison.

'True, but – and I may be wrong – I don't feel that was the case with McGuinness and Barnes.'

'So, we're back to the Bell brothers?'

'No, sir. I don't think it was them, either. Danny and Den are too calculating to risk what they have, a comfortable and profitable empire north of the river that works in conjunction with McGuinness's lot to the south.'

'So, who, then?'

'I don't know yet, sir. But we will. I believe it's someone who McGuinness has upset, who may not themselves be involved in crookery.'

'Someone outside his organisation?'

'Yes, sir.'

Allison sighed. 'That looks like an almost impossible task.'

'We'll find them, sir. Sergeant Lampson and I will be looking into McGuinness's activities and trying to narrow down a list of people who might be set on seeking revenge for something.'

'Good,' said Allison. 'Now, what about this business at the Ritz? How are you getting on with that? I'm seeing the commissioner later, and he'll be sure to ask me for an update.'

As succinctly as he could manage, Coburg brought the superintendent up to date with the investigation so far and the way that Albanians seemed to come into the picture so often. 'For example, Alex Ollen, the kitchen hand who was killed, appears to be from Macedonia, but I feel there's an Albanian connection there given the two countries share a border. And now we have this American secret agent, Raymond Harris, who turns out originally to be from Albania where he was known as Rajmond Hoxha.'

'Have you tried quizzing the Albanians at the Ritz?'

'I don't believe the King would be very receptive to us questioning his retinue,' said Coburg. 'The one person I *might* be able to get some answers from is his private secretary, Count Idjbil Ahmed, but at the moment he seems to have vanished and I'm told he's staying with people somewhere in the country.'

'And do you think he is?'

'To be honest, I don't know. But I think he's someone I might be able to talk to without causing a diplomatic crisis, which may not be the case if I tried to question the King and his family or their staff.'

Coburg's phone was ringing as he returned to his office. There was no sign of Lampson.

'DCI Coburg.'

'Edgar, it's Rosa.'

'Rosa!'

'I wondered if you were free for lunch today.'

'Always a pleasure, and I should be, unless something comes up.'

'Things always come up. Anyway, I'll be at the Ritz at one o'clock. I want to go through my music, selecting some different numbers. As it seems to be often the same people turning up, I don't want to bore them with the same routine every night.'

'They wouldn't be turning up if they were bored.'

'Maybe, but I like to give good value.'

'You always do,' said Coburg. 'I'll see you at one.'

'Unless something comes up,' said Rosa.

The door opened and Lampson came in as Coburg hung

up the phone. The sergeant nodded towards the handset.

'Something new on McGuinness?'

Coburg shook his head. 'No. I shall be lunching at the Ritz today.'

'Your lady friend?' enquired Lampson.

'Plus work,' said Coburg. 'I'm determined to track down Count Ahmed. If anything happens that you need me for, you can get hold of me there.'

'How did you get on with the super?'

'He wonders if it might have been Charley Barnes who killed McGuinness.'

'Barnes?' echoed Lampson, his voice filled with incredulity. 'What on earth makes him think that?'

'He's been reading too much in the way of classical literature,' said Coburg. 'In particular, Shakespeare. He quoted *Othello* and *Julius Caesar* at me to back up his theory.'

Lampson shook his head. 'I don't buy it,' he said. 'Barnes and McGuinness go way back.'

'That's what I told him,' said Coburg. 'The trouble is the only way to disabuse him of that idea is for us to catch the real killer.'

George was on duty at the hall porter's desk when Coburg arrived at the Ritz. It struck Coburg that George *always* seemed to be on duty, whatever the time of day.

'Good day, George, he said. 'Has Count Ahmed returned yet?'

George shook his head, then said: 'Not yet, although I've been reliably informed that he will be back tomorrow.'

'Informed by whom?'

'One of the King's entourage who wanted me to get in touch with housekeeping to make sure the Count's suite was ready for him.'

'Do you know where he's been?'

'Not officially, no,' said Coburg. Then he lowered his voice as he added: 'However, the King did make a telephone call to him yesterday, to a number somewhere in Kent, if I'm right about the dialling code. I believe that call may have been to urge the Count to return.'

'Do you remember the number the King asked for?' enquired Coburg.

George handed Coburg a small piece of paper with a telephone number on it.

'I made a note in case you should find it helpful.'

Coburg gave him a grateful smile. 'I think I'll find it very helpful indeed. Thank you, George.'

Coburg then made his way to Rosa's dressing room, where she was sorting through her sheet music.

'You made it!' she said delightedly.

Coburg smiled. 'I did indeed. I tried to arrange a table for lunch with the maître d', but he told me you'd already fixed it.'

'I did,' said Rosa. 'I was confident you'd be here.' She pushed the sheet music to one side. 'So, I suggest we grab lunch now, in case something happens to disturb it.'

I could get used to this, thought Coburg as he and Rosa sat down at the table with its white linen cloth, silver cutlery and salt and pepper pots.

'My treat, though,' said Coburg, as the menus arrived.

'No complaints from me,' said Rosa.

They both selected the soup to start, then salmon for

Coburg while Rosa once again chose the beef.

'I'm taking advantage of it while I can,' said Rosa. 'I was talking to one of the waiters who reckons it won't be long before the menu's restricted to variations on whale meat.'

Their soups arrived and as they began to eat, Rosa told Coburg: 'Just to let you know that whatever you said to your gangster chum, warning him off, seems to be working. No one came round – so far so good.'

'Actually, my "gangster chum", as you call him, was shot dead last night.'

Rosa stared at him, horrified. 'Shot?'

Coburg nodded. Rosa swallowed, then she whispered in horrified tones: 'You don't mean you . . . ?'

Coburg looked at her, angry.

'No, of course not! What sort of person do you think I am?'

'No, I'm sorry,' said Rosa apologetically, obviously flustered. 'I didn't mean . . . Yes, I did.' She looked at him, then reached out and took hold of his hand. 'It slipped out, because I know you'd protect me like no one else.'

'I don't commit murders,' said Coburg, apparently only slightly mollified. Then his tone changed, and he smiled and squeezed her hand. 'I'm sorry. I was being oversensitive. I shouldn't have been angry that you'd think I'd do something like that to take care of you. And the truth is, I would, if anyone harmed you. But in this case, I thought a warning word would be enough. Though it looks like someone else had a different attitude towards him.'

'Do you know who did it?'

'Not yet. We're working on it.'

They had just finished their soup when a waiter approached

their table and whispered to Coburg: 'Excuse me, Monsieur Coburg. There is a telephone call for you at reception.'

Coburg put down his napkin with a sigh.

'This could be my sergeant,' he said. 'In which case this might be a short lunch.'

Coburg headed for reception desk, where George handed him the receiver and confirmed his suspicions.

'It's your sergeant, Mr Coburg.'

'Thank you, George.' He put the phone to his ear. 'What news, Ted?'

'Sorry to interrupt, guv, but Den Bell's been shot dead.'

CHAPTER TWENTY-FIVE

Coburg returned to Rosa. 'As I feared, it's going to be a short lunch for me,' he said apologetically. 'But don't let me stop you.'

'Are you kidding? With food this good!' she said as their main courses arrived. Then she gave him an apologetic smile and asked: 'Sorry. What's happened?'

'Sadly, another shooting.'

She looked at him, concerned. 'Serious?'

'Very serious,' he said. 'The victim's dead.'

'I'm sorry,' she said.

'So is he, and so am I,' he said ruefully.

'Listen, I still intend to have a meal with you,' said Rosa. 'Are you free tonight?'

'Providing no one else gets killed.'

'In that case, can you pick me up after the show? I'll cook for you. Nothing to compare with what you would have had if you hadn't had to rush off like this, but I managed to get hold of some eggs and cheese. I thought an omelette would be good.'

Coburg smiled. 'You have won my heart with those very words. I'll see you later. And I'll tell George I'll settle the lunch bill, when I return to pick you up.'

Coburg and Lampson pulled up outside the Merrie Tumbler in Tudor Street, just off Fleet Street, and made their way to a small, cobbled yard at the back of the pub. Three uniformed officers, a sergeant and two constables, were standing beside a body covered with a tarpaulin. Coburg lifted one corner and saw that it was, indeed, Den Bell.

'The doctor's on his way, sir,' said the sergeant.

'Is Danny Bell around?' asked Coburg.

'He's inside, sir.'

Coburg turned to Lampson. 'I'll go and have a word with him. You stay here and make a note of whatever the doctor says when he gets here.' He turned to the uniformed sergeant and ordered: 'Sergeant, take one of your men and canvass the immediate area, seeing if you can find any possible witnesses to what happened. Although, as I suspect this is a gangland killing, I don't hold out much hope, but you never know.'

'Yes, sir,' said the sergeant. He turned to one of the constables. 'Nixon, you're with me.'

Coburg walked in through the back door of the pub and found Danny Bell and two of his henchmen sitting at a table. The rest of the pub was empty of customers, just a barman in wary attendance. Danny Bell had a whisky in front of him, his two henchmen had nothing except very grim expressions.

'Danny,' said Coburg, joining them at the table.

'Bastards!' snarled Bell. 'I won't just kill 'em, I'll rip their throats out.'

'Who?'

'Who d'you think? Whoever did it!'

'And who do you think that might have been?'

'It's got to be Charley Barnes. He's a nutter. He must've thought it was us who did Big Mel, but we didn't. I swear on my mum's life!'

'Tell me what happened.'

'I've already told the plods out there.'

'Now tell me. I'm the one who's going to find whoever did it.'

'I know who did it! Charley Barnes!'

'I'll still need to prove it in a court of law,' said Coburg. 'And for that I need evidence. So, talk to me.'

Bell scowled, but grudgingly began.

'Me and Den were sitting here, talking, and Den says he's going for a piss. The toilets are out in the back yard. He goes out, and next second there's this bang, then another. I knew at once what it was. I ran out, and there was Den, lying on the ground. The bastard must've been waiting for him.'

Outside in the yard the doctor had arrived and was examining the body of Den Bell. 'Not much to say, except the obvious,' he told Lampson. 'Two bullets in the back, both of them hitting him in the heart. A heavy calibre gun, by the look of it, though I'll know more when I get the body back to the morgue and dig around. Death would have been instantaneous. Is an ambulance on its way?'

Lampson looked at the constable, who said: 'Sergeant Tod phoned for one, sir. It should be here shortly.'

'Right. Tell the crew to take the body to Charing Cross. I've got another couple of calls to make, then I'll go there and start on him.' He replaced the tarpaulin over the body, picked up his case and headed towards the street, passing Sergeant Tod who was returning.

'Doc all done?' Tod asked Lampson.

Lampson nodded, then asked: 'Anything?'

Tod looked towards the pub to make sure he couldn't be overheard and lowered his voice as he told Lampson: 'There's a woman who lives above the greengrocers opposite the end of the yard. Mrs Black. She's an invalid and spends most of her time looking out of the window. She says she heard bangs, then saw a man come running out of the alley. He headed off along Tudor Street in the direction of the Inner Temple.'

'Description?'

Tod nodded, then said in a whisper: 'It sounds like Charley Barnes. You know, Mel McGuinness's right-hand man.'

'Have you got a picture of Barnes in the files at your nick?' asked Lampson.

Tod nodded. 'I expect every station in London's got a picture of Charley Barnes.'

'Right. Go back to the station and get the picture, then bring it back here and show her. Where's the constable who was with you?'

'PC Nixon. I left him standing guard by the street door that goes up to Mrs Black's flat to make sure no one goes up.'

'Good. Make sure he stays there until you get back. Well done, Sergeant.'

Tod hurried off, just as the ambulance arrived at the end of the yard. Lampson went into the pub where Coburg was still in conversation with Danny Bell.

'The ambulance is here,' he said. He looked at Bell. 'I thought you'd want to know.'

Bell nodded and got up, then went out to the yard, accompanied by his two silent henchmen.

'Any developments?' Coburg asked Lampson.

'Yes,' said Lampson. He gestured for Coburg to follow him out to the yard, then made for a spot away from where Danny Bell was watching the two ambulance men lift his dead brother on to a trolley.

'We've got a witness who reckons she saw a man run out of the alley right after the shooting. The description she gave sounds like Charley Barnes. Sergeant Tod has gone back to his station to get a file picture of Barnes to show her.'

'Where is this woman?' asked Coburg.

Lampson repeated the information Sergeant Tod had given him.

Coburg sighed. 'I thought it might turn out this way. Barnes has always been a loose cannon, liable to fly off the handle. It was only McGuinness holding him in check that stopped him from being worse than he was. Now, there's a serious danger of this escalating into an all-out gang war unless we stamp on it.' He gestured towards the ambulance. 'Let's go and have a word with this witness and see if she positively identifies Barnes when Sergeant Tod arrives.'

He and Lampson headed for the end of the alley,

stopping beside Danny Bell who was just turning away as the rear doors of the ambulance shut.

'We'll be in touch, Mr Bell,' said Coburg. 'As soon as we have any information. In the meantime, I'd advise against you taking any action yourself. You could be wrong.'

Bell scowled and headed back to the pub, his men trailing after him.

'He's not though, is he, guv?' murmured Lampson as they crossed the road towards the greengrocers.

'Not by the sound of it,' replied Coburg. 'But we don't want things escalating.'

They entered the doorway next to the greengrocers and mounted the narrow stairs up to the small flat. Mrs Black, a woman in her sixties, was sitting in a chair by the window.

'I saw you coming,' she said. 'You're the detectives from Scotland Yard.'

'We are,' said Coburg. 'I'm Detective Chief Inspector Coburg and this is Detective Sergeant Lampson. I know you've already described to Sergeant Tod what you saw, but I'd be grateful if you'd tell me.'

And she did. Coburg noted that from her window she had a good view of the entrance to the yard opposite. As he listened to her, and her description of the man, what puzzled him was why Barnes, if it was Barnes, had gone into the alley without any attempt to hide his face. No mask, no scarf, not even a hat pulled low, according to Mrs Black. But then, as he'd said to Lampson, Barnes had always been a loose cannon, one who seemed to think that he was invincible, that the law couldn't touch him. And, it had to be admitted, that had appeared to be the case for the past few years.

As she was telling her story to Coburg, there was the sound of footsteps on the stairs, then Sergeant Tod entered. He was carrying a manila envelope, and from it he took six police photographs which he laid on the table in front of Mrs Black.

'That's him!' she said, pointing to the two which showed Charley Barnes full face and in profile.

Tod gathered up the remaining four, which were of other known criminals who bore some resemblance to Barnes, and put them back in the envelope.

'Thank you, Mrs Black,' said Coburg. 'And well done, Sergeant. Can we leave you to take Mrs Black's statement? Sergeant Lampson and I will go and call on the gentleman concerned.'

'You gonna arrest him?' demanded Mrs Black. 'I don't want him knowing it was me who said I saw him.'

'I promise you your part in this will remain just between us,' said Coburg. 'And I'll do my best to ensure you're not involved in any trial.'

'I hope you do ensure it,' she said firmly.

CHAPTER TWENTY-SIX

Coburg elected to take one of the uniformed constables with him and Lampson. If Barnes decided to produce a pistol or put up a fight, the three of them wouldn't be able to do much. Coburg toyed with the idea of going back to the Yard and getting authority from Superintendent Allison to arm themselves, but it would take time, and Coburg wanted to bring in Barnes without delay. With the threat of a gangland war about to erupt, he wanted to put a lid firmly on it. He was taking a chance on Barnes's arrogance and self-importance. He would be defiant and sneer at them, but Coburg didn't believe he would try and kill them. That would be a hanging offence for sure, whether he had a clever barrister or not, and Barnes wasn't that stupid. At least, Coburg hoped he wasn't.

Working on the theory that a rat always ran back to its lair, Coburg guessed that Barnes would return to the Iron Horse, where he'd be busy establishing an alibi for himself. Sure enough, as Coburg, Lampson and PC Nixon entered the saloon bar, Barnes was sitting at McGuinness's usual table, obviously having taken over.

'Mr Coburg.' Barnes smiled confidently. 'This is a surprise. To what do I owe the pleasure? Do you have any news as to who killed Mel?'

'Not yet,' said Coburg amiably. 'At the moment we're also investigating another murder.'

'Oh? Who of?' asked Barnes, almost smug in his air of assumed innocence.

'Someone shot Den Bell,' said Coburg. 'We're here to ask you to assist us with our enquiries.'

'Certainly,' said Barnes. 'Ask away.'

'At Scotland Yard,' said Coburg.

Any expression of joviality vanished from Barnes's face. He shook his head.

'Forget it. You're not arresting me!'

'I agree, we're not arresting you. Unless, of course, you refuse to co-operate, in which case obstructing the police in the course of their duty is an arrestable offence, as I'm sure you know.'

'Then why are you taking me in?' asked Barnes suspiciously.

'We're not taking you in, we're asking you to help with our enquiries. We'll be talking to many people. But we'll be seeing them all at the Yard, rather than in a pub or on the street. More official. It means you're protected, everything properly recorded, especially as I'm sure you'll be exercising your right to legal representation, as would any responsible citizen.' He gestured towards the bar. 'Do you want me to call Mr Underhill, or will you?'

'I'll do it,' grunted Barnes sourly. He got up, strode to the bar and called for the telephone to be handed to him. Coburg, Lampson and PC Nixon stood and watched as he dialled.

'Mr Underhill,' he barked into the phone, adding, 'Tell him it's Charley Barnes.' There was a pause, then he said: 'Pentangle? Charley here. DCI Coburg's here at the Iron Horse. It seems someone shot Den Bell. Coburg wants me to go and answer some questions at the Yard . . . Yeh, now.' Barnes grunted his assent as he listened, then said menacingly: 'All right, but you better be there.'

With that, Barnes replaced the receiver, then turned to the three policemen with a forced smile on his face. 'Right. He'll meet us there. Shall we go?'

When they arrived back at the Yard, Coburg walked to the reception desk, followed by Barnes, with Lampson and Nixon bringing up the rear, and asked if Mr Pentangle Underhill had arrived to see him.

'No, sir,' replied the sergeant.

'In that case, will you arrange for Mr Barnes to be taken to the custody suite while we wait for him.'

'Oh no you don't!' snarled Barnes. 'I'm not gonna be locked up!'

'The custody suite isn't a cell, as you well know,' said Coburg. 'And I'd be doing you wrong if I started to question you without your lawyer present.' Then he added warningly: 'But do be on your best behaviour while you're in the custody suite. If you start throwing a strop, then it will be a cell.' To the sergeant he said: 'Let me know when

238

Mr Underhill arrives.' Finally, Coburg turned to PC Nixon. 'Thank you, Constable,' he said. 'I'll let you return to your station. And thank Sergeant Tod for me.'

With that, Coburg and Lampson headed for the stairs. All the time Coburg could feel Barnes's vengeful glare burning into his back.

'Well done, guv,' murmured Lampson. 'I thought he was gonna kick off, first at the Iron Horse and then just now.'

'He's cocky and thinks he can't be touched,' said Coburg. 'When he realises what's going on, things might change.'

Back in their office, Coburg used the phone to check the telephone number George had given him at the Ritz. The operator informed him of the location.

'Thank you,' said Coburg. He hung up, then said to Lampson: 'It seems that Count Ahmed has been staying with Lord Kirby Mainwaring at Richford Castle, near Sevenoaks in Kent.' He frowned. 'Why does that name ring a bell?'

Lampson also frowned, thinking, then he said: 'It was on a list of some sort.'

'Yes,' Coburg agreed, 'but a list of what?'

Lampson struggled to recall, then his face lit up again and he went to a filing cabinet. He opened one of the drawers and rifled through the papers inside, before triumphantly flourishing a manila file containing a thick sheaf of papers.

'I think it's this one,' he said, sitting down at his desk and starting to go through the list of names it contained. Coburg joined him, looking over his shoulder.

'Members of the British Union of Fascists,' he read.

'I'm sure I saw it here,' said Lampson, turning over the pages. Then he stopped and stabbed his forefinger at a name in the middle of the page. 'Here he is!'

'Does it say if he was locked up with the others?'

'No,' said Lampson. 'But it mentions others who were.' And he pointed to others on the list who had the word 'interned' against their entry. 'So, I'm guessing he wasn't thought to be as dangerous as the others.'

'But why would an Albanian count, a refugee from Mussolini, be spending time with a member of the British Union of Fascists?' wondered Coburg. 'And not just spending time with him, but staying at his palatial mansion?'

The phone rang and he picked it up, listened, then said: 'I'll be right down. Thank you, Sergeant.'

'Charley Barnes's mouthpiece?' asked Lampson.

'Mr Pentangle Underhill in person,' said Coburg. 'Right, let's start.'

CHAPTER TWENTY-SEVEN

Coburg and Lampson sat side by side at the table in the interview room. Opposite them sat Charley Barnes and Pentangle Underhill, and behind them two burly uniformed officers stood against the wall, ready to move in if needed. Coburg had decided it was one thing persuading Barnes to come to Scotland Yard without too much resistance, it could well turn out to be another once he realised that he was going to be kept in custody on remand. At that stage, Coburg expected Barnes's internal firework to erupt. It was fortunate that Barnes had no weapons on him. Not that Coburg had thought he would have, he'd expected that Barnes would have guessed he'd be the first person to be quizzed, and he'd have made sure to ditch his pistol once the shooting of Den Bell had been carried out.

Underhill regarded Coburg in his usual haughty manner. 'I would like to know why my client has been brought in to

Scotland Yard for questioning, Chief Inspector,' he said stiffly.

'Because earlier today a certain Dennis Bell was shot dead in the yard behind his pub, the Merrie Tumbler, in Tudor Street.'

'Wasn't me,' said Barnes. 'I was nowhere near there today, or any day. I stay clear of the Bells' territory.'

'As your client had just indicated, there is a certain known animosity between himself and the Bell brothers,' said Coburg. 'Therefore, it seemed logical to discuss the matter with him.'

'As my client has just said, he was nowhere near Tudor Street today,' said Underhill. 'Therefore, I cannot see what he can contribute to the investigation.'

'Yes, well, that contradicts a statement we had from a witness who positively identified Mr Barnes as leaving the alley connecting the rear yard of the Merrie Tumbler and walking away along Tudor Street almost immediately after the shots were fired that killed Mr Bell.'

Barnes shook his head firmly.

'Not me,' he said. 'Whoever told you that is mistaken.'

'How did this witness identify my client?' asked Underhill.

'After initially giving a description of the assailant, that matched Mr Barnes, the witness was presented with a series of official police photographs, amongst which were two of Mr Barnes. The witness identified Mr Barnes as being the person that was seen by them.'

'Who is this witness?' asked Underhill.

'For the moment we are keeping the identity of the witness a secret, until such time as we are ready to proceed with a charge being made.'

'That is in contravention of accepted legal procedure,'

said Underhill primly. 'There should be full disclosure to the defence.'

'And there will be if it comes to a trial,' said Coburg.

Barnes turned to Underhill, showing signs of agitation.

'He can't do that!' he said. 'Stopping us from knowing who this witness is.' He glared at Coburg. 'It's one of Danny Bell's boys, ain't it? This is a fit-up!'

'To allay your fears on that point, as far as we're aware the witness has no connection with the Bell family.'

'As far as you're aware,' stressed Underhill.

'My concern at the moment is to prevent this situation worsening,' said Coburg. 'As I say, we have a witness who places Mr Barnes in the rear yard of the Merrie Tumbler at the time of the shooting, which can be confirmed by Sergeant Lampson.'

Underhill looked at Lampson, who said: 'That's right.'

'And I said I wasn't there!' snapped Barnes.

'You did,' agreed Coburg pleasantly. 'But here's the problem. Danny Bell believes it was you who shot his brother, Den, in revenge for the shooting of Mel McGuinness, because you believed it was the Bell brothers who had Mel killed. The thing is, I don't think it was the Bell brothers who shot Mel.'

Barnes's eyes flared angrily. 'No?' Grim-faced, he ticked off on his fingers: 'Big Mel killed. His favourite pub torched. Billy Thackeray killed. Joe Williams killed. It's all an attack on Mel and his outfit. Who else could it be but the Bell brothers?'

'Plenty of others,' said Coburg. 'Mel hurt loads of people, you know that—'

'I must protest,' interjected Underhill angrily. 'This

is all just supposition which maligns my late client. Mr McGuinness was a businessman—'

'Mel McGuinness, with the help of your client, Mr Barnes, ran things in south London, and the Bell brothers did the same north of the river,' cut in Coburg brusquely. 'It was business, and for a long time it worked for both sides. There were the occasional disagreements which turned physical, but no one died. Until now. But it wasn't in the Bell brothers' interest to kill McGuinness and start a full-scale war, because they knew that if that happened, both sides would lose, and lose big time. But now Danny believes you killed his brother, it'll all blow up. The next logical step is for Danny to have you killed. And, after that, it's your people against the Bells, with lots of people dying.'

'Why kill me?'

'Because he thinks you killed Den, and because you were Mel's right-hand man. You're in charge now.'

'I was just Mel's business manager.'

'In the same way that Himmler is just Hitler's bookkeeper,' snorted Coburg derisively. 'I'm taking you in, Charley.'

'On what charge?' demanded Barnes, outraged.

'No charge. Protective custody.' Coburg leant forward. 'I'm keeping you alive. Out on the street you're a dead man.'

'I can look after myself,' snapped Barnes.

'I'm sure Mel and Den Bell thought the same,' said Coburg. 'I'm not going to let you and Danny Bell tear this city apart worse than it's already suffering.'

Barnes turned to Underhill. 'Are you going to say anything, or are you just gonna sit there like a dummy?' he demanded angrily. 'I'm not gonna let myself be locked

244

up. Come on, do your job. Produce a writ, or whatever it is you do. I'm walking out of here.'

'You will indeed walk out of here,' Underhill assured him firmly. He turned to Coburg. 'Chief Inspector, the law is very clear on the point of keeping people in custody without proper evidence. And I stress *evidence*, not rumour and accusations.'

Coburg rose to his feet. 'Mr Underhill, might I have a word with you outside?'

'Why?' demanded Barnes, also getting to his feet, agitated.

As the two uniformed officers moved forward, Coburg turned to Barnes.

'Please resume your seat, Mr Barnes. I just wish to discuss the possibility of a deal.'

'If there's talk of a deal, I want to be in on it,' demanded Barnes.

'No decisions will be taken without your approval,' said Coburg. 'Shall we talk, Mr Underhill?'

Underhill looked at Barnes. 'I'll see what the chief inspector has to offer, then I'll return and we can discuss it,' he said.

'In the meantime, Sergeant Lampson will be in charge during our absence,' said Coburg.

Coburg and Underhill walked out of the interview room, with Barnes shouting after them: 'No deal if it means I'm locked up!'

Outside in the corridor, Coburg stopped and said: 'Mr Underhill, Danny Bell is convinced that Charley Barnes killed his brother.'

'Yes, you've already made that clear,' said Underhill. 'However, whatever he believes, it will need to be proved in a court of law. In the meantime, there are no grounds for holding my client. You say you have a witness. Very well, produce them, otherwise I shall apply for a writ to have my client released.'

'And if he is released? I can put money on the fact that if he's out on the street, Charley Barnes will be dead within twenty-four hours. I also doubt if we'll find his body. Danny Bell is extremely upset, and that's an understatement. And if Charley Barnes dies, so do your regular payments as his legal representative. Think about that, Mr Underhill. You've done very well out of being Mel McGuinness's lawyer, and you'll do equally well representing Charley Barnes. So long as he remains alive, you can represent him when he comes to trial for the murder of Den Bell. A trial which, with all your legal interventions, could run for quite a while and be very financially rewarding for you. But with Charley dead, that's it. There's no one else in the organisation who'd authorise payments to you. So, by all means, get your writ and have Charley out on the street, and say goodbye to the generous remuneration you've enjoyed. Back to the penny-ante stuff. Defending petty criminals for low-rent money. Divorces. It'll still be a living, but not the sort you're used to. So, it's up to you. Advise your client to accept protective custody or sell that luxury car of yours.'

Underhill glared at Coburg. 'If Mr Barnes is in as much danger as you say he is, then it's your job to protect him.'

Coburg shook his head. 'Sorry, we're too busy investigating murders to nursemaid suspects. Of course, you could always advise Charley to hire some extra muscle. But tell him not to leave the country. Although, where could he go to? Europe? And you know Danny Bell as well as I do,

246

Mr Underhill. Wherever Charley goes, and however many people he hires to protect him, Danny will get him, so long as he's out on the street.'

Underhill looked warily at Coburg, then asked: 'What is it you want me to do?'

'I want you to persuade Charley to accept custody to keep him safe.'

'That won't be easy,' said Underhill awkwardly. 'He can be quite . . . volatile.'

'If he doesn't accept it, then it will be imposed on him,' said Coburg. 'With force, if necessary. But I'd rather it was done without anyone being injured.'

Underhill hesitated, then he nodded. 'Very well,' he said. 'I'll see what I can do.'

The two men returned to the interview room. Barnes sat and gave Coburg a challenging glare. 'Well?' he demanded. 'Do I walk?'

Coburg looked at Underhill, who said awkwardly: 'In the circumstances, Mr Barnes, based on what DCI Coburg has said about your life being at risk—'

'No!' shouted Barnes, and this time he leapt to his feet, then abruptly sat down as he saw the two burly officers move towards him.

'I want another solicitor!' he shouted at Coburg.

'Certainly,' said Coburg calmly. 'Just tell me their name and I'll arrange for them to come here.'

Barnes's eyes narrowed as he looked at Coburg. 'You're not going to get away with this!' he threatened. 'I know people. Important people.' He turned to Underhill. 'And when I get out, you're finished.'

'Your life is at risk,' repeated the solicitor.

'Piss off!' snapped Barnes. He held out his hands. 'Come on, then. If you're going to lock me up, do it proper. Put the cuffs on me. Cos I'm never going to have it said that Charley Barnes went to jail willingly.'

'Very well' said Coburg. 'Sergeant Lampson, please put the handcuffs on Mr Barnes. And then take him to Wandsworth for remand.'

Barnes glared at Coburg but let Lampson put the cuffs on him, scowling the whole time.

'Thank you for your co-operation, Mr Underhill,' said Coburg. 'Would you like to accompany your client to Wandsworth?'

'No!' shouted Barnes. 'I'm having nothing to do with that toerag any more.'

'I will look after your interests,' Underhill assured him. 'This is just a temporary measure.'

'You'd better see that it is,' Barnes hissed.

Coburg turned to the uniformed officers. 'Would you escort Mr Barnes outside and wait for Sergeant Lampson there? He'll be with you in a moment.'

The two officers led him out of the room, followed by Underhill, who was being glared at venomously by Barnes.

'Well, that went well, guv,' said Lampson. 'Easier than I thought it'd be. What now? I'm guessing you've got a call to make.'

'I have,' said Coburg. 'I'm going to see Danny Bell and warn him off over Charley Barnes. I want to make sure this ends now.'

'Think Charley will hang for Den Bell?'

Coburg nodded. 'But we still need to find out who killed Mel McGuinness. That's our next job.'

'Along with finding out who killed Joe Williams, Billy Thackeray, and the kitchen hand at the Ritz,' said Lampson.

'Indeed,' said Coburg. 'As I've said before, Ted, I think we're dealing with two separate cases here. The murder of Joe Williams and the kitchen hand at the Ritz are one case; the killings of Mel McGuinness and Billy Thackeray are another. The first is about the two million quid. The other is about revenge.'

'Revenge?'

'The way that Billy Thackeray was savagely beaten shows whoever did it hated him. The same thing with torching the Four Feathers and shooting McGuinness in the head. I suggest we divide things up. Once you've handed Barnes in, you set about looking into who might have wanted McGuinness and Thackeray dead. Meanwhile, after I've had a word with Danny Bell, I'll concentrate on the murders at the Ritz, especially now we've got Lord Mainwaring entering the picture.'

'Your aristocratic contacts, guv?' Lampson grinned. 'Socialising with the nobs?'

Coburg grinned back. 'It's a dirty job, Ted, but someone's got to do it. I suggest you liaise with Barry Moss at Waterloo nick. He seems to be the one who was most in touch with what McGuinness and Thackeray were up to.'

'You think it's someone they messed up?'

'I do, and more than messed up. It's someone they hurt very badly. Also, see if you can track down Ollen's girlfriend, Anna Gershon. As for me, first thing tomorrow I'm going to see if I can get hold of Count Ahmed. Let's you and I meet up tomorrow late afternoon in the office and compare notes.'

CHAPTER TWENTY-EIGHT

Coburg returned to the Merrie Tumbler as the first stage in his quest to track down Danny Bell. At first, he was surprised to find Bell still there, sitting in the bar with his two silent henchmen, an almost empty whisky glass on the table in front of him. He'd expected him to be busy ordering his men out to find Charley Barnes, but then he realised that Danny was still in a state of shock and disbelief. This was the last place he'd been with this brother and Danny couldn't bear to tear himself away, not just yet.

Bell gave Coburg a sour look as he entered and gestured for the barman to bring two more glasses over. Bell's two henchmen, Coburg noted, had soft drinks in front of them, barely touched. Keeping their heads if they were called into action.

'Can we talk?' asked Coburg.

Bell shrugged. 'Talk away,' he said airily.

'Just you and me,' said Coburg.

Bell hesitated, then said to his two waiting henchmen: 'Keep an eye on the yard outside.'

As the two men walked out, the barman appeared with two glasses of whisky which he put on the table.

'Thanks, but no thanks,' said Coburg politely. 'I'm still on duty.'

'It doesn't stop most of your copper mates,' said Bell acidly. 'Anyway, who said one of them was yours.' He picked up his glass and took a mouthful.

'I've come to tell you we've got Charley Barnes in jail,' said Coburg.

Bell studied Coburg warily. 'For killing Den?'

'On suspicion of it.'

'He did it,' said Bell grimly.

'If he did, he'll hang,' said Coburg

Bell said nothing, just glared angrily at Coburg.

'I know that's not enough for you,' Coburg continued. 'For you, this is personal. But you're going to have to live with it. My guess is that Charley thought you and Den were behind the killing of Mel McGuinness, the torching of his pub, and the killings of Billy Thackeray and Joe Williams.'

'They were nothing to do with us!' spat Bell. 'Nothing!'

'That's my opinion, too,' said Coburg. 'And I'm going to find out who was behind them. But right now, if I don't step in, there's going to be a war here. Not as bad as what the Germans are doing, but bad enough. The next logical step would be for you to take out Charley Barnes. Then someone on their side takes you out. Or maybe your wife and kids.'

251

For the first time, Bell looked unsettled at these words.

'You see what I'm getting at,' said Coburg. 'This stops now. You've both lost people—'

'McGuinness was just Charley Barnes's mate,' snarled Bell. 'Den was my *brother*.'

'I know,' said Coburg. 'And Barnes will hang for it. Now, I've been advised that the simplest thing would be to let you and Barnes's outfits carry on. Pick each other off and tear one another to bits until there's none of you left. And that will include your families, yours and Den's. With you all gone, my life becomes easier. That's what I've been told. But I know it won't, because sooner or later, and it'll be sooner in the current situation with this war going on, there'll be new people coming up. Treading on your ashes. Causing me problems. So, it stops here.' He stood up. 'I'll send your boys back in. But remember what I said.'

With that, Coburg left.

With every table in the Rivoli Bar booked for Rosa's session that evening, Coburg had to make do with standing outside to watch and listen to her, while at the same time studying the audience. He was surprised to see that Raymond Harris wasn't there. Had his interest in Rosa cooled, or had something come up?

After she'd finished her set, with two encores thrown in, Coburg drove her home.

'There's a bottle of wine on the dresser,' she said. 'Open that while I get to making dinner.'

'No sign of Donna?' asked Coburg.

'She's out with her boyfriend,' said Rosa. 'Some guy

from work she seems very smitten on. So, my guess is we'll have the house to ourselves tonight.'

'Perfect,' said Coburg.

In no time at all, Rosa had prepared a leaf salad and presented them with a cheese omelette each.

'*Voila!*' she said.

Coburg poured them each a glass of wine, and then set to work on the meal, thinking that this was such a welcome relief after the day of murder, followed by bringing in Charley Barnes.

'This is delicious!' said Coburg, forking another piece of omelette. 'In my opinion, it's better than anything the Ritz could produce!'

'It's just a simple cheese omelette,' protested Rosa.

'No, it's a *perfect* cheese omelette. The inside is soft and runny, the cheese is completely assimilated into the egg with no lumpy bits, whatever the herb is you've used is just the right amount . . .'

'It's tarragon,' said Rosa. 'I got a small jar at some place when I was on tour, and I take it with me wherever I go.'

'As I say, perfect!'

'So, we've both shown one another we can cook,' said Rosa.

'You're better than me,' said Coburg.

'Based on one omelette?' Rosa laughed. 'I don't think so.'

She topped up their glasses.

Coburg smiled. 'Such sophistication.'

'You're going to pretend it's all new to you?' asked Rosa. 'The Honourable Edgar Saxe-Coburg, son of an ancient aristocratic family, possibly related to the royal family.'

'*Possibly*,' chuckled Coburg. 'I'm fairly sure there are

plenty of people who can trace their ancestry to the royal family somewhere, given Charles II was notorious for siring children with his many mistresses.'

'But not all of them have an ancestral castle.'

'I don't, that's my brother, Magnus's. As you know, I have a modern rented flat in Hampstead.'

'The poor relation?'

'Not while I have you in my life,' said Coburg.

Rosa looked at him, then said: 'You are the sweetest man I've ever known.'

'It's a side of me that you bring out,' said Coburg. 'In fact, I've been thinking—'

Before he could elaborate on what he'd been thinking, they heard the street door open and then Donna had crashed into the kitchen, her face showing her fury.

'That bastard!' she exploded. 'That absolute bastard!'

'Who?' asked Rosa.

'Gerald,' raged Donna. 'He told me he was a widower, but it turns out his wife's alive and well and been living in Scunthorpe since the war started to look after her parents. And now she's coming back!'

Coburg looked enquiringly at Rosa, who explained: 'Gerald's Donna's boyfriend, a man at her office—'

'No longer my boyfriend!' stormed Donna. 'And not much of a man, either, after tonight. He had the nerve to tell me this while we were in bed naked! So I grabbed a vase and smashed him in the balls with it. Let's see him explain *that* injury to his wife when she comes back.' She stood, seething, then burst out: 'All men are bastards! You can't trust them! They lead you on and then you find they've cheated you!'

'Present company excepted, maybe?' asked Coburg hopefully.

Donna scowled. 'You seem OK, but so did Gerald.'

With that, she stamped out of the kitchen and they heard her tramping hard on the stairs.

'Poor Donna,' sighed Rosa. 'As long as I've known her, her life's been littered with unsuitable men.' She looked at Coburg. 'What were you about to say before Donna came in? You said you'd been thinking.'

'Yes,' said Coburg. 'But somehow—'

'I don't think you're a bastard,' said Rosa. 'As far as I know, you haven't got a wife hidden away in Scunthorpe.'

'I haven't got a wife hidden away anywhere,' said Coburg.

'Would you like one?' asked Rosa.

'Yes, I think I would,' said Coburg. 'But only if it was you.'

Rosa stared at him, open-mouthed. Then she closed her mouth and gulped.

'Are you asking me to marry you?' she asked.

'Yes,' said Coburg. 'I am. I realise, of course, I'm not much of a catch, a detective chief inspector at Scotland Yard hardly fits with the glamorous world of showbusiness that you inhabit—'

'Shut up,' she said.

'What?'

'I said shut up. Ask me again.'

'Why?'

'So I can answer. And it will be a yes, but I just want to hear you ask the question, and for you to hear me say yes properly.'

'So, Rosa, will you marry me?'

255

'Yes, Edgar,' said Rosa. 'I will.'

She picked up her wine glass and held it towards Edgar, who clinked his against hers.

'Here's to us,' he said.

'Here's to us, and a long life together,' she said. 'And I mean, *together*.'

'With you on tour all the time, and me here in London?'

'We'll work something out,' she said. She finished her wine and smiled at him. 'I think the next thing is to celebrate with some conjugal consummation.'

Coburg smiled. 'I was just thinking the same. But with fewer and more ancient words.'

'That's you old aristocratic families all over,' said Rosa, getting up and reaching for his hand. 'But tonight, quietly, no shouting. I don't think Donna could handle it.'

'I promise I'll be quiet,' said Coburg, kissing her.

Rosa grinned. 'I wasn't talking about you,' she said, as she led him out of the kitchen towards the stairs, but before they could head up them, the eerie warbling sound of the air-raid warning echoed along the street outside. They heard Donna's door open, and then she appeared, throwing on her coat.

'Bloody hell!' she moaned. 'A girl can't get a decent night's sleep in this place!'

Coburg followed Rosa and Donna as they ran, Donna in the lead, down the street towards the wide main road at the end. As they turned into Oxford Street there was an ear-shattering explosion so close to hand that the force of the blast hurled them off their feet. As Rosa hit the pavement she looked towards Donna and saw one of the huge windows had been blown out from the shopfront and was hurtling sideways directly towards her. As she watched the edge of the flying sheet of jagged glass struck her friend just below her chin, and the next second Donna's head was sliced from her body as if by a knife and hurled away to lie in the road.

CHAPTER TWENTY-NINE

'No!' screamed Rosa, and she ran to the body of her friend. Coburg ran after her, catching her by the arm.

'You can't do anything for her,' he said. 'We have to get to the shelter.'

Rosa struggled against his grip, punching at him to try and free herself, but he held on.

An ARP warden arrived beside them and shouted urgently, 'Get into the shelter!'

'My friend!' howled Rosa, gesturing to the dead body of Donna.

'She's dead,' snapped the warden. 'Get into the shelter unless you want the same to happen to you.'

Rosa sagged and almost fell, but Coburg held her up. She began to weep, her body heaving with great sobs as Coburg looked towards the warden.

'Where's the shelter?' he asked.

'Follow me,' said the warden.

Coburg, holding Rosa up, ran behind the warden until they reached a door in an alcove between the shattered windows of the store. Broken glass lay strewn across the road and pavement, and bodies lay amongst the wreckage. Although most were dead, some, Coburg saw, were moving, struggling to push themselves up.

'I need to help them,' said Coburg.

'The professionals will be on their way,' said the warden. 'The ambulances and firefighters. Let them deal with it. Get your lady friend to safety.'

Coburg looked at the distraught Rosa, who was on the point of collapse, then pushed her through the door and helped her down the three flights of concrete stairs that led to the basement. The huge open area, once filled with goods for sale, had been emptied and turned into a temporary home by local families. Mattresses, cushions and blankets made makeshift beds. Some people – obviously the regulars – had set up their own tables and chairs.

Coburg spotted a woman in uniform standing by a trolley in one corner, which had a tea urn on it. They bought two cups of tea then found a space by one wall. Coburg took off his coat, folded it up and put it on the cement floor.

There was an air of shock amongst the people here. Previously people had come down here when the air-raid warning went and had settled down for social chats. Tonight, all that had changed with the bomb going off right outside the store. Nearly everyone was covered in dust from the explosion, their clothes, hair, faces. Many were crying. Others sat in a state of shock.

Rosa tried to hold the cup of tea, but her hand was

shaking so much Coburg had to help her so she could drink.

'I c-can't stop shaking,' she stuttered.

'It affects everyone like that the first time they see someone die violently.'

'Even you?'

'Yes.' He squeezed her to him. 'The first time it happened was in the trenches during the first war. I thought I'd never stop shaking, but I had to because I was in command of a troop and I had to show the men I wasn't affected so they wouldn't be. In fact, my men were already hardened soldiers so used to the carnage that I had to keep up with them.'

'I can't believe she's dead,' whispered Rosa. 'And her head . . .' She closed her eyes and gave a whimper as the image filled her mind.

'You're moving in with me,' Coburg told her firmly but gently. 'When we leave here we'll go to your house to pick up some spare clothes and whatever you need.'

'I can't go in there,' said Rosa. 'Not yet.'

'I'll go in,' said Coburg. 'Tell me what you want me to bring. A few things just for the moment. We'll collect any larger things together later. If you can face it.' He took the cup from her and pulled her to him, wrapping his arms around her. 'You're not alone,' he whispered.

Dawn was just coming up as the all-clear sounded, and they made their way up to street level. Donna's body had been taken away, but there were still others tangled amongst the rubble from the explosion.

'Where will they have taken her?' asked Rosa. 'I have to tell her mother. We have to have her body for the funeral.'

'I'll find that out,' said Coburg.

'No,' said Rosa, moving off and heading towards where Coburg had parked the car. 'I have to do it. I have to do *something*.'

'All right,' said Coburg, following her. 'I have a list of contacts for the emergency services at home. I'll mark the ones you need to speak to. Phone them and tell them I've asked you to make contact. They're more likely to talk to you if you're making enquiries on behalf of a detective chief inspector from Scotland Yard.' As they neared her house, he added: 'I'll stay at home today. When we get home I'll phone the Yard and leave a message for my sergeant—'

'No,' said Rosa firmly. 'I need to get myself sorted out. I need to do things. Find Donna's body. Go and see her mother. Go to the Ritz to make sure everything's right for tonight.'

'You're going on tonight?' asked Coburg, surprised.

'Yes. I have to. I need to,' said Rosa. 'And then I want to find out what I can do for the war, to help.'

'You're already doing it,' said Coburg. 'You're lifting people's spirits when you perform. They need what you give them.'

'It's not enough,' said Rosa. 'All those people lying injured in the road last night. They needed medical help, not songs.'

'You're not a trained medic,' said Coburg. 'And that takes years.'

'A nurse!' said Rosa.

'Again, that takes months. By the time you're ready the war could be over.'

She shook her head. 'No, it's going on for years, just like the last one. And this one is going to be fought here, at home, not just abroad. I need to do something that helps save lives.' She turned to him, determined. 'I can drive. I'll drive an ambulance. The more ambulance drivers there are, the quicker the injured can be treated.'

'Driving an ambulance isn't the same as driving a car,' cautioned Coburg.

'I used to drive for my father's grocery shop, at first a van, then a lorry. If I can drive a lorry through the streets of Edinburgh, I can handle an ambulance. How do I apply?'

'I'll find out,' said Coburg.

'No, *I'll* find out,' she said, even firmer this time. 'This is what *I'm* doing.'

'Instead of performing?'

'I can do both,' she said. 'When I'm not appearing, I can drive an ambulance. And I can do it anywhere, so when I do a gig somewhere far away, I'm sure they'll need ambulance drivers.'

By now they'd reached her house. Rosa stopped and stood in front of it, looking at the upstairs windows with tears in her eyes.

'Tell me what you want me to get for you,' said Coburg, holding out his hand for the key she produced from her pocket.

'It's all right,' she said. 'I can do this. I need to do it on my own. Just wait here for me.'

Coburg got in the car and waited. It was fifteen minutes before she reappeared carrying a small suitcase.

'Right,' she said. 'Let's go.'

CHAPTER THIRTY

Sunday 25th August

When they got back to Coburg's flat, Coburg set to work making breakfast and, despite Rosa's insistence that she wouldn't be able to eat a thing, he was relieved to see her polish off scrambled eggs on toast.

As he'd promised, he marked his list of emergency contacts with the best ones to contact in order to locate Donna's body. 'If you have difficulties, phone me and I'll see what I can do.' He wrote down his extension at Scotland Yard. 'To save you battling with an operator. If I'm not there, my sergeant's name is Ted Lampson. He's a really nice chap, and he knows all about you.'

'All?' she asked.

'Well, what I've told him. But I think he guesses the rest.'

Coburg put the wireless on to catch the early news, but as soon as the newsreader started talking about the bombing at Oxford Street, he switched it off.

'No,' said Rosa, and she turned it back on. 'I want to hear it.'

'Reports suggest over a hundred were killed and more than three hundred injured in both the Oxford Street and Barbican bombings,' announced the newsreader. 'These marked the first time that central London has actually been bombed. 'In other news, the King and Queen—'

Rosa switched the wireless off.

'It's almost like I didn't want to believe it had actually happened until I heard it announced on the news,' she said.

Coburg washed up the breakfast things, then pulled on his jacket.

'If I'm going in, I'd better be on my way,' he said. 'But do phone me if you need me.'

She nodded.

'And I'll phone you during the day to see how you're doing,' he continued.

'I might not be here,' she said. 'I could be out, doing things.'

He nodded and took her in his arms.

'If that happens, we'll catch up later. But remember, I'm always there for you.'

The whole way on his drive to Scotland Yard that morning, Coburg couldn't stop himself from thinking about the way that Donna had died, and the impact it had had on Rosa, and therefore on him. Last night, before the air-raid warning sounded, they'd agreed to get married. Did that still stand? It was too soon to raise the subject. The last thing that Rosa needed right now was additional pressure on her. He'd leave it and see how things played out.

Lampson was already at his desk when Coburg walked into the office.

'Morning, guv,' said Lampson. 'Did you hear about Oxford Street?'

'I was there,' said Coburg. 'We got caught up in it?'

'"We"?'

'I was with my friend Rosa and her housemate Donna. Sadly, Donna was killed.'

'Killed?'

Coburg nodded. 'Rosa and I were there when it happened. Flying glass took her head off.'

'My God! You weren't harmed?'

'Blown over but physically untouched. The same with Rosa, but the sight of her friend being killed that way . . .' He gave a rueful shrug. 'It's going to be hard for her to get over. So she's staying with me for the moment. I'm telling you in case you should phone me at home and she answers, or you get a phone call from her with a message for me.'

'No problem,' said Lampson. 'Poor girl. I know there's lots being killed, but when it happens to someone you know, and right in front of your eyes . . .' He looked at Coburg quizzically. 'D'you reckon this marks a change in Hitler's tactics? So far the centre of London has been untouched. Is this the start of their next wave? Bomb London?'

'Who's to say?' said Coburg. 'I don't think even the Nazi High Command know what Hitler's next move is.' He picked up the phone and dialled the Ritz's reception desk. 'Anyway, I know what my next move is going to be.' When George answered, Coburg said: 'George, it's DCI Coburg. Is Count Ahmed back in residence?'

'Yes, Mr Coburg, he is. He's in his suite now. Do you want me to put you through to him?'

'No thank you, George. I'll be along to see him personally. If it looks like he's about to leave, could you tell him that I'm on my way and look forward to seeing him?'

'And if he should go before you get here?'

'I'll arrange for a uniformed officer to be on guard at the door of the Ritz to prevent him leaving,' said Coburg. He hung up. 'Right, now to finally nail the elusive Count Ahmed. What about you, Ted?'

'I'm off to Waterloo. Sergeant Moss is going to go through some of the cases where McGuinness's people were alleged to be involved, but nothing ever came to court. I'm hoping there might be someone who leaps out as wanting vengeance on Big Mel.'

'Good luck with that,' said Coburg. 'We'll meet up here at the end of the day and swap notes. The sooner we can lay both cases to rest, the better.'

Thirty minutes later, Coburg was sitting in an armchair in Count Ahmed's suite, facing the Count who sat on a sofa. This time, unlike Coburg's meeting with King Zog, there were no bodyguards in attendance. The Count was a small, slightly plump man, in his early fifties, dressed impeccably in a formal suit, a high starched collar on his shirt which sported a grey and blue tie with a large Windsor knot.

'Thank you very much for seeing me, Count Ahmed,' said Coburg.

'Did I have a choice?' asked Ahmed, regarding Coburg

with unfriendly eyes. 'I was informed that there was an armed police officer at the entrance to the hotel to prevent me from leaving.'

'Not armed,' corrected Coburg with a polite smile. 'And he was only there to request you stay until I arrived, if that was acceptable to you.'

'And if it was unacceptable?' demanded Ahmed.

'Then I can only apologise if there was a misunderstanding,' said Coburg. 'Certainly, no offence or disrespect was intended. I wanted to meet you after His Majesty asked me to investigate, because he was keen to find out the identity of the dead man.'

'Yes, so I understand,' said Ahmed. 'Have you?'

'We have. His name was Joe Williams, although he performed under the name of Antonio.'

'Antonio?'

'He was a tango dancer.'

The Count was silent, taking this in. Then he asked: 'What was his nationality?'

'He was English, as far as we know. Although it seems that not everything is as it appears. For example, the man who was found dead in this hotel's kitchen the other day. You may have heard about it?'

'I have been away, so I'm not up to date with recent events,' said Ahmed.

'He was a kitchen hand and he'd been stabbed to death, his body hidden behind shelves in one of the storerooms. According to his papers he was Swiss, but we now believe he may have been from Macedonia.'

'What makes you think that?'

'Evidence we found in his lodgings.' He watched

Ahmed closely as he added: 'And we understand Macedonia is closely linked to Albania.'

'What are you suggesting?' demanded the Count angrily.

'Nothing,' said Coburg. 'But I did wonder if any of your retinue may have known this man?'

The Count's expression grew even angrier. 'That is a slander!' he snapped.

'No slander intended,' said Coburg. 'Just a question.'

Count Ahmed glared at him. 'No one in the King's "retinue" – as you call it – would have had any association with this . . .' He paused, then said with a sneer: '. . . kitchen worker.' He looked at Coburg with unconcealed anger as he added: 'I think it best if you end your investigation.'

'But the King asked me—' began Coburg.

'His Majesty has changed his mind,' interrupted Ahmed abruptly. 'The dead man is no longer our concern.'

'But it is *our* concern,' said Coburg.

'The King's apartments are Albanian territory while His Majesty is in residence,' snapped Ahmed. 'You have no jurisdiction here.'

'On the contrary,' replied Coburg calmly, 'the man who died was a British citizen. The Ritz Hotel is on British soil. And we are at war, which means there are security implications.'

'What security implications?' demanded Ahmed.

'We've received information that the British Union of Fascists may be somehow involved.'

Ahmed frowned. 'I do not understand what you mean.'

'You're aware of the British Union of Fascists, I assume?' said Coburg.

'No,' responded Ahmed. 'I have never heard of them.'

'They are an association of people in this country who support Adolf Hitler and Benito Mussolini. Their leader is – or, rather, was – Sir Oswald Mosley. Currently he's been interned in prison, along with many of his followers. Interestingly, the BUF has many powerful figures among its members, including quite a few from the British aristocracy. Not all of them are in prison, but I believe they are kept under surveillance. For example, there's a certain lord with a castle in north Kent. Were you in north Kent lately, by any chance?'

Ahmed got to his feet. 'I have nothing more to say, Inspector,' he said stiffly.

Coburg nodded and rose. 'Thank you, Count Ahmed. I'm sure we will be in touch again. Please give my regards to His Majesty.'

This time, as Coburg left the suite, he noticed that, unlike at his arrival when there had been no reception committee for him, now two bodyguards had appeared at the door and were standing to attention. The two men, both sporting large moustaches, looked at Coburg with obvious distrust and suspicion as he appeared. Coburg nodded politely to them.

'Good morning, gentlemen,' he said.

They didn't respond. *Possibly I should have learnt how to say it in Albanian*, he thought as he made for the lift.

Lampson sat in Sergeant Moss's office at Waterloo police station as the man sorted through files of old cases.

'The trouble is most of the cases involving Thackeray and McGuinness are hearsay; there's not much paperwork on them because they never came to court,' he said.

'Like that one you told us about: the warehouse and the sugar robbery?'

'That's just one. I can think of others.'

'Any of them where someone was seriously hurt. Maybe killed?'

'There was one where a van driver was killed. His van was hijacked and he ran after it, grabbing the handle of the driver's door to try to pull it open, and the bloke at the wheel ran him into a lamp post to knock him off. Fractured his skull. He died two days later.'

'Who was the driver? Thackeray?'

'We never found out,' said Moss. 'The only witness statement we had was from someone who saw the van going along with the bloke hanging onto the driver's door handle, and it hitting the lamp post and him falling off into the road. Then the van roared off. We found it burnt out the next day on waste ground in Lambeth.'

'McGuinness's territory.'

'Exactly.'

'Well, that's a possibility. Who did the van belong to? And who was the driver who was killed?'

'Here it is,' said Moss, and he opened a paper file. 'Alf Watson was the van driver. He left a widow.' Moss wrote down an address on a sheet of paper. 'The van was owned by a big delivery firm. They got paid by the insurance company.' He picked up another file. 'Then there was this one: a tobacconist. He was in his shop when it got robbed by some masked men. He had a heart attack and died during it. The word on the street was that Billy Thackeray was in the frame, but we had no luck in getting evidence.' Again, he wrote down an address. 'This is the address of the shop. His widow, Mrs Porter, still runs it, along with her teenage son.'

Moss passed the paper to Lampson.

'What about the sugar robbery you were talking about? The warehouse?'

'No one was killed or even injured during it,' said Moss. Then he gave a sad sigh. 'But, by all accounts, it was the last straw for Mike Bassett, the bloke who owns the warehouse. I don't know the whole story, but I think he's had a lot to cope with lately.'

'In what way?'

'Like I say, I don't know the details, but the copper who does his beat said he's had a lot of trouble recently.'

'I'll go and see him, have a word,' said Lampson. 'You never know. Have you got his address?'

Moss took the sheet of paper back from Lampson, then began to go through the files in search of Bassett's details. As he did, he said: 'By the way, did you hear about the dreadful bombing yesterday?'

'Did I ever!' said Lampson. 'My guv'nor and his girlfriend were caught in it.'

'What were they doing in Ramsgate?' asked Moss.

Lampson looked at him, puzzled. 'No, they were in Oxford Street. What happened in Ramsgate?'

'It got flattened. As well as the people killed by the bombing, some bastard in a Messerschmidt even machine-gunned civilians in the main street.'

'Do they know who was killed?' asked Lampson, suddenly anxious. 'I've got relatives in Ramsgate. An aunt and an uncle.'

271

Moss picked up the phone. 'I'll give a bloke I know a ring. He's a sergeant at Ramsgate nick. What's their name?'

'Brewer,' said Lampson. 'George and Ada Brewer. They're both in their sixties. They live near Camden Square.'

Moss asked the operator to put a call through to Ramsgate police station, then cradled the receiver in his shoulder while he carried on looking through the files.

'Here it is,' he said. 'Mike Bassett.' He added Bassett's details to the sheet and handed it back. Lampson heard the telephone operator's voice saying something, then Moss said: 'Thanks anyway', before hanging up.

'She said there's a problem on the phone line to Ramsgate police station,' he told Lampson. 'If the bombing was as bad as I hear, I'm not surprised. I hope your uncle and aunt are all right.'

CHAPTER THIRTY-ONE

Having been stonewalled by Count Ahmed, Coburg decided to try a different tack. The connection between Ahmed and Lord Mainwaring intrigued him. What was the link between a member of Albania's royal court, known to have escaped from Mussolini's invading fascist army, and a British aristocrat, a member of the British Union of Fascists? His curiosity took him back to MI5's offices at Wormwood Scrubs and Inspector Hibbert.

'Why wasn't Lord Mainwaring interned with the rest of the BUF?' asked Coburg.

'Lord Mainwaring was not seen as a danger to national security because his support was towards Italy rather than Hitler's Germany,' replied Hibbert.

'Mussolini's still our enemy.'

'Yes, but we got the idea that it wasn't so much politics as art.'

'Art?'

'He's a collector of Italian paintings. Classical art, that is, not modern. He spent quite a bit of time in Italy before the war. His family have got an estate there, as well as the estate in Kent.'

'So, he's wealthy, then?'

'Oh yes.'

'Where's his estate in Italy?'

Hibbert checked the files. 'Just outside Brindisi,' he said.

'As I recall that's on the coast on what they term the Heel of Italy.'

'That's right.'

'Just across the strait of Otranto from Albania.'

'Right again,' said Hibbert, impressed. 'You know your geography.'

'Only some. When my brothers and I were boys we had an aunt who used to take us to Italy to improve us, and one time she took us to Taranto and the local area.'

'We had an aunt who lived in Southend and was an usherette at the local cinema, and when we went there on holiday she used to sneak us into the pictures for nothing,' said Hibbert with a slightly rueful air.

'The principle's the same,' said Coburg. 'And it's all culture. Personally, I think you had the better part of it. Laurel and Hardy beat Canaletto and that crowd every time, in my book.'

'You think this Lord Mainwaring is connected with the dead man at the Ritz?'

'Two dead men,' Coburg reminded him. 'The kitchen hand was apparently from Macedonia, which borders Albania. And Count Ahmed, King Zog's private secretary, has been a guest of Lord Mainwaring. What does that suggest?'

'But why would King Zog have anything to do with someone who's a supporter of the Italian fascists, when we were told he and his family fled Albania to escape from Mussolini's troops?' asked Hibbert.

'I don't know,' admitted Coburg. 'But maybe everything isn't as it appears to be.'

Mrs Watson, the widow of the van driver, lived in a small terraced house with an abundance of young and very noisy children, as far as Lampson could tell from the shouting coming from inside the house. She stood on the doorstep and examined Lampson's warrant card before handing it back to him.

'I won't invite you in,' she said. 'The place is a madhouse. The kids used to be quiet as mice when Alf was alive cos they knew what they'd get if they were rowdy. The back of his hand if they were lucky and the toe of his boot if they weren't. Since he's been gone they run riot.' She cast a tired look into the house. 'I can't control them. They won't listen to me. They saw me too often getting a whack from Alf, so they ain't scared of me. And fear's the only thing that keeps 'em in check.'

'You must've felt angry when you heard that Alf was dead,' said Lampson. 'Especially the way it happened, him getting killed when his van was stolen.'

'Angry?' she looked at him in disbelief. 'I saw it as my salvation. No more getting battered by him. The only trouble was the kids started playing up, but at least they don't hit me.'

'Was there anyone who might have been angry at him being killed that way?' asked Lampson.

'Are you kidding?' she scoffed. 'I'm surprised they didn't put out banners round here when they heard. Alf was a nasty bastard, too free with his fists and boots. No one liked him. Good riddance, that's what I say.'

It was at the sixth telephone number on the list Coburg had left her, the St John Ambulance Service, that Rosa got the answer she'd been seeking. After introducing herself as speaking on behalf of Detective Chief Inspector Coburg from Scotland Yard, she asked if they had collected the dead body of a young woman from the site of the bombing in Oxford Street the previous night. 'Her name was Donna Dunn, and DCI Coburg is keen to ascertain the whereabouts of her body because it affects a case he is currently working on.'

'We collected quite a few casualties from that bombing last night,' said the man. 'However we weren't able to make a proper identification of most of them. If there were bags near a particular body they would have accompanied that body, and I'm sure they will have identification inside them, ration books or the like.'

Rosa hesitated, then, forcing herself to keep any traces of emotion out of her voice, she said: 'This particular body would be noticeable because it had been decapitated by flying glass.'

'Ah, yes,' he said. 'The driver remarked on that one when he returned to base. A tragedy. Let me see, I'll just check where she was taken.' There was a pause and the sound of papers being flicked through, then he was back on the line again. 'She was taken to the mortuary at Paddington hospital.'

'Thank you,' said Rosa. Again, steeling herself against betraying her non-officialdom by letting emotion creep into her voice, she asked: 'Was all of her taken?'

'Excuse me?' the man asked, puzzled.

'Her head,' said Rosa flatly.

'Oh yes,' replied the man. 'Both head and body were taken there.'

'Thank you,' said Rosa.

With that, she put the phone down and wept.

Coburg's next port of call was to Sir Vincent Blessington at the Foreign Office.

'What can you tell me about King Zog's relationship with Italy?' he asked.

'The fact that he and his family fled just before the Italians invaded should give you a clue,' said Blessington.

'But before that. Weren't the Albanians and Mussolini allies?'

'Yes, they were, and very close. In fact, it was thanks to Italy's support that Zog was able to gain control of Albania. And then, during the economic depression of the early 1930s, Zog became so dependent on Mussolini that the Albanian National Bank was based in Rome. Unfortunately for Zog, the Albanian economy, which was always on a knife edge, virtually collapsed not long after and Albania was unable to pay the interest on the money it had borrowed from Italy to keep it afloat. The result was that Italy began to exert its dominance by taking control of the police force, as well as its major industries. The final straw for Zog was when Mussolini ordered that Italian be taught in all Albanian schools as the country's first language. Zog refused and tried to build alliances with other countries, notably France and Germany, but those attempts failed, and so Albania was forced back under the influence of Mussolini.'

'But I'm guessing that mere influence wasn't enough for Mussolini.'

'That's right. Dictators and tyrants want absolute control. Hence the invasion.'

'Which Zog saw coming and left, taking with him most of the country's money.'

Blessington nodded. 'Exactly so.'

'So why would the King's private secretary be spending time as the house guest of a British aristocrat who supports Mussolini?'

'Perhaps because two million is a large amount to dispose of easily,' said Blessington. 'To get a good price you'd need someone you can trust as an intermediary in any transaction. And Lord Mainwaring has interests in banks in different countries. Some of those interests in hostile countries are officially frozen, of course. But not all. And there are other, unofficial, channels for moving money around.'

'So, it's about the money,' said Coburg.

'Isn't it always?' said Blessington.

Rosa caught a train to Clapham High Street. She'd never been to Donna's family house before, but all three housemates had given the addresses of their families to each other 'to be contacted if anything happens'. And now it had happened. The worst news ever to be delivered. Rosa knew from things Donna had said that her father was in the army, somewhere in North Africa, and that her brother, Tom, had died at Dunkirk. Tom had been her only sibling, so Rosa was coming to tell Mrs Dunn that her only surviving child was dead. No parent should lose their child, thought Rosa, and now this poor woman has lost both of hers.

Chelsham Road was just a short walk from the railway station, and Rosa found the neat little house with bright red and purple flowers in the window box. She had met Mrs Dunn just once before, when she'd come to visit Donna soon after the three women had moved into the house off Oxford Street. She rang the bell. The door was opened, and Mrs Dunn looked out at her warily, then her face cleared and she smiled in welcome.

'Oh, it's Miss Weeks, isn't it? I met you when I came to the house. I never forget a face.'

'It is indeed, Mrs Dunn. I'm sorry to be calling on you—'

'Not at all. Please, come in.'

Rosa hesitated. Then she told herself: *You can't deliver this dreadful news on the doorstep and then just rush off.*

'Thank you,' she said,

She followed Mrs Dunn inside and was shown into the front parlour, which was immaculately clean and smelt of polish. Reserved for visitors, she decided.

'Do sit down,' said Mrs Dunn, gesturing at a comfy padded armchair. Then, as they sat, her face suddenly took on a worried expression. 'Nothing's happened, has it? I mean, if you've come looking for Donna she's not here, she's still in London.'

'No, I haven't come looking for Donna,' began Rosa awkwardly. 'I'm here because I'm afraid I've got some bad news. Donna and I were heading for the air-raid shelter in Oxford Street last night—'

At the mention of Oxford Street, Mrs Dunn suddenly went deathly pale and put her hand to her mouth.

'N-n-no,' she stammered, and she slumped back into the chair. 'Not Donna.'

'I'm afraid so,' said Rosa.

The woman suddenly bent forwards, her head in her hands, and began to cry, at first small mewing noises, and then suddenly she gave a roar of pain which became a howl. Rosa got up from the chair and went to her, putting her arms around the sobbing woman as she rocked to and fro in distress.

'I'm sorry to be the bearer of such bad news,' she said.

Mrs Dunn looked up at her. 'You were with her?'

Rosa nodded. 'She didn't feel any pain. It was very quick. Her . . . her body's at Paddington Hospital. I know you're on your own, so I'd like to help. You know, with funeral arrangements.'

Mrs Dunn shook her head. 'I can't talk about that now,' she said hoarsely, her voice almost a whisper.

'Please, let me make you some tea,' offered Rosa, getting to her feet. 'Where's the kitchen?'

'No,' said the woman. 'No. I need to be on my own. To take this in.'

'Is there anyone who can be with you?' asked Rosa.

'My sister,' said Mrs Dunn. 'She lives round the corner.'

'Do you want me to go and see her? Tell her and bring her round to you?'

'No,' said Mrs Dunn. 'That's for me to do. It's family, see.' She sat there, stunned, staring straight ahead, seeing nothing. After a silence, she finally said: 'I'd like to be alone, please. Thank you for coming, but I'd like to be alone.'

'Of course,' said Rosa. 'And I'm so sorry.'

And she let herself out of the house, leaving the devastated woman alone with her memories of her daughter and the abject misery that she was gone for ever.

Unlike Mrs Watson, the widow of Alf, the dead van driver, Mrs Angela Porter, the widow of the deceased tobacconist, still mourned her late husband, Wilf. She invited Lampson into the back room of the small shop while her teenage son, Jimmy, stayed to mind the counter. The back room seemed to double as a storeroom and also a small living room, with the stock piled in crates and boxes occupying most of the space, but one end given over to two armchairs and a small table, and even a fireplace, although there was no fire laid in the grate. On the mantlepiece above the fireplace were two framed photographs, one of Mr and Mrs Porter standing with their son between them, all three smiling at the camera. The other photograph had a black ribbon draped along the top, and showed Mr Porter, a plump man, standing proudly in front of his shop.

'He loved this place,' said Mrs Porter as she and Lampson each took a seat in one of the armchairs. 'Over twenty years we've had it. We opened it right after the last war, when Wilf came back from France. He said he never wanted to work for anyone else again, only for himself. He'd been in factories before, and he said the war had shown him just how little time we have on this earth. Loads of his comrades were killed, see. He said there was no sense in wasting the little time we have, we should do what we wanted to do with that time. And so he opened this shop.' She sighed. 'He built up a good business. People liked him. He talked to them when they came in and listened to them and their troubles. People appreciated that. He had this bad heart. I think he got it during the war, from being in them damp trenches, but he didn't let it bother him.

'I was with him here when the robbery happened. Four blokes wearing masks, and a truck outside. One of them had a gun. They came in and started shouting, and the one with the gun pointed it at me and said he'd shoot me if Wilf didn't do as he was told. I thought Wilf was going to collapse there and then, you could see the shock on his face. He had to sit down he was shaking so much.

'Then the others grabbed all our stock – tobacco, cigarettes, cigars, everything – and took it out to their van while the one with the gun stayed inside pointing his gun at me and Wilf. When it was all gone, they went, and it was no sooner they'd left the shop that Wilf collapsed. And that was it. His heart, the doctor said. But I knew it was the shock of them blokes that killed him.'

'Do you know who did the robbery?'

She shook her head. 'And I don't want to know. If I did, I'd have to face them in court, and I couldn't do that. It would be too painful.'

Lampson nodded and stood up. 'Thank you for talking to me, Mrs Porter,' he said. 'I know it must have been hard for you.'

'Is this because you're still looking into the robbery?' she asked as she led him out of the small room and back into the shop.

'No, but it may be part of a different enquiry,' said Lampson.

'Which enquiry's that?' she asked.

'The deaths of a Mr McGuinness and a Mr Thackeray.'

'Why would that be part of what happened to our shop?' she asked.

'It was just a lead that someone suggested,' said Lampson. 'But I don't think it is. Do you happen to know either of those men?'

'What were their names again?'

'McGuinness and Thackeray. They've been involved in crime in this area and we're looking into everything they might have taken part in, just to see if there's a pattern. Did you know them?'

She shook her head. 'No. We've always kept ourselves to ourselves. I'm sorry I couldn't be of more help, Sergeant.'

'No problem, Mrs Porter. Thank you for your time, and I'll wish you good day.' He gave a pleasant nod to Jimmy who was behind the counter. 'And to you, Mr Porter.'

Jimmy watched as Lampson left, and when he was sure the policeman was out of earshot, he turned to his mother.

'You know McGuinnnes and Thackeray all right,' he said accusingly. 'After Dad died, you kept pressing that copper at the station about who might have done it, and in the end he said they suspected those two blokes, Thackeray and his mate Williams and some other blokes, but they couldn't prove anything. He told you they worked for Big Mel McGuinness, which was why no one was giving them up.'

'Well? There was no need for that copper to know all that. That's our business.'

'You said you wanted them dead, and you were going to find someone to do it.'

'That was just the spur-of-the-moment talk,' said Mrs Porter. 'I didn't mean it. It may have been something I thought at the time, but I was upset. It's not something I'd ever do. And don't you forget it. I don't want you saying anything like that to anyone, understood?'

And she thrust her face close to her son's and glowered at him, her mouth tight and the look in her eyes intense.

'Understood?' she repeated, harder this time.

Jimmy gulped and nodded. 'Yes, Mum,' he said. 'Understood.'

CHAPTER THIRTY-TWO

Once again, when Lampson called at Anna Gershon's address there was no sign of her. 'She's still away,' he was told. He received the same reply at the cafe where she worked. At both places, as before, he left his telephone number at Scotland Yard.

'When you see her, can you please give her this and ask her to telephone me? We need to talk to her urgently.'

Then he made his way to the address in Norwood that Sergeant Moss had given him for Mike Bassett. There was no response to his knocking at the door.

'This is turning out to be a wasted day,' he muttered to himself.

He banged the knocker again, loudly, in case Bassett, or anyone else, was asleep, but the only reaction came from the neighbouring house, where the front door opened, and a middle-aged woman peered out.

'If you're looking for Mr Bassett, I don't think he's there.'

Lampson produced his warrant card and identified himself.

'Police?' said the woman. She shook her head sorrowfully. 'Poor man, I hope it's not more bad news. I don't think he can take any more.'

'The robbery at his warehouse, you mean?' asked Lampson.

The woman shook her head. 'No, that sort of thing people can cope with. Things happen and you deal with it. No, I mean what happened to his family.'

'You've known Mr Bassett for a while?' asked Lampson.

'Years,' she said. 'My name's Hudson. Mrs Hudson, though I'm a widow now. My Jeff died four years ago. The Bassetts were wonderful to me. Really good neighbours. I wish I could have been as good for them, but with all that happened, there wasn't much I could do.'

'What happened to his family?' asked Lampson.

'Well, first his eldest son, George, was killed at Dunkirk. At least, they presume he was killed because he was one of them who never came back, and they had a letter from the War Office telling them he had died in action. It was shortly after that that Mike's wife, Sonia, died. Heart attack, they said. Terrible it was. They'd been together for thirty years. Childhood sweethearts. Coming on top of George being killed, it sort of destroyed Mike. I'd see him, sitting in his front room, just staring out of the window, like he didn't know what was happening.'

'Poor bloke,' said Lampson.

'That wasn't the end of it,' said Mrs Hudson. 'His youngest son, Bob, joined the RAF, wanting to do his bit, but he never even got the chance. He was killed in a training accident. The plane he was in crashed, and him and the instructor with him were killed. Dreadful. I was worried he might top himself after that. First his eldest son, then his missus, and finally his youngest. All gone in the space of a few months. All he had after that was his business and then that got robbed.' She gave a sorrowful sigh. 'Strange, ain't it, how some people seem to get more than their fair share of tragedies?'

When Lampson got back to the Yard, Coburg was already in the office and looking severely unhappy.

'How did you get on with the Count?' asked Lampson.

'I didn't,' said Coburg. He filled Lampson in on his meeting with the Count, and then those with Hibbert and Blessington. 'It's been dead ends all the way. So, tomorrow I'm going to call on Lord Mainwaring and see if I can get to the bottom of the mysterious connection between him and King Zog, which I'm pretty sure will be about the money. How did you get on?'

Lampson gave an unhappy shrug and told him that he'd also experienced a frustrating bunch of dead ends. 'And I heard about Ramsgate.'

'What about Ramsgate?' asked Coburg.

'It got bombed yesterday,' said Lampson. 'By all accounts, terrible destruction. I've tried to find out how badly, but no luck. The thing is, you remember I said I've got an aunt and an uncle who live there? Well, I'd like to make sure they're safe so I can tell my mum. It's her sister.'

Coburg picked up the phone and asked the operator for a number in Whitehall.

'There's someone I know who's quite senior at the Defence Ministry,' he told Lampson as he waited for the connection to be made. 'A chap called Wesley Pithy. I don't usually play the Eton Old Boys card, but Wesley and I got on quite well when we were at school. He's a decent chap.'

Lampson watched Coburg intently as the connection was made.

'Wesley,' said Coburg. 'Edgar Coburg.'

'Edgar,' said Pithy. 'Long time no speak. To what do I owe the pleasure of this call?'

'There was a German air raid on Ramsgate yesterday,' said Coburg.

'Yes, sadly, there was,' said Pithy, his tone angry and bitter. 'So much for the Germans claiming they're only striking military targets.'

'The thing is, and normally I wouldn't ask this, but my sergeant has an uncle and an aunt in Ramsgate, and he's having difficulty getting any information on them. We're trying to find out if they were among the casualties. We understand there were quite a few.'

'A couple of hundred from what we can make out, maybe more,' said Pithy. 'The problem is no one knows exactly who may have been caught up in it. They're still lifting bits of bombed houses while they look for anybody who may, by some miracle, have survived and been buried under the rubble. Or likely, more bodies. The situation's made worse because not all the bombs the Germans dropped went off, so as the fire brigade, ARP and Civil Defence wardens dig through they're coming across unexploded bombs, so they have to stop and wait until the bomb disposal people have made them safe before they can carry on. On the plus side, when the sirens went off many of the residents made for the tunnels.'

'The tunnels?' asked Coburg.

'There's an old railway tunnel from Victorian times that runs under the town towards the harbour. The trains stopped running but a few years later the local council decided to open it again as a tourist attraction, with other tunnels linked to it. Then last year, when war was on the cards, they decided to use it as an air-raid shelter if war broke out. It's now a catacomb of linked tunnels that run for three miles, seventy feet beneath the town. But not everyone wants to go down into them.

'The authorities are doing their best to identify those who died in the raid, but it's not easy. Look, if you give me their names, I'll see what I can find out and get back to you, but it may take a day or two. Like I say, things are very confused.'

'Thanks, Wesley, I appreciate that. But in the circumstances that wouldn't be fair, I know the pressure you're all under there at the moment. I've got another avenue to explore through police channels, I'll try that.'

'Give me their names anyway, just in case I do get a chance.'

'Hang on, I'll get them,' said Coburg, looking questioningly at Lampson.

'George and Ada Brewer,' said Lampson. 'They live in Belle Vue Road near Camden Square.'

Coburg repeated the information to Pithy.

'Got that,' said Pithy. 'I'll see what I can find and get back to you.'

Coburg hung up and looked at Lampson. 'No joy there, I'm afraid,' he said. 'So tomorrow I suggest you take the car and go to Ramsgate. You'll be able to find out more there.'

'No, that wouldn't be right,' protested Lampson.

'I won't need it,' said Coburg. 'Tomorrow I'll catch the train to Sevenoaks to call on Lord Mainwaring. I can do it on my own. As to the murders of McGuinness and Thackeray, you've already got a list of possible victims who might have been looking for revenge and you can follow them up again another time.'

'But—' protested Lampson.

'It's family, Ted. And you can call it selfish on my part, but I need you alert and concentrating on the cases at hand, which you won't be if you're worrying about your uncle and aunt. So, that's an order. Go to Ramsgate. I'll need the car tonight, but I'll leave it in the parking area at the back, and the keys with the desk sergeant for you to collect. We'll meet up here the morning after tomorrow and catch up.'

'All right,' said Lampson, doing his best to appear reluctant, but in secret gratefully relieved. 'But I'll be bringing the car here tomorrow when I get back from Ramsgate. I'll put it in the yard and do the same with the keys. I don't want to take the chance of leaving it in the street in Somers Town and someone having the wheels off it.'

Paddington Hospital was busy when Rosa arrived, the reception area packed with people on the long benches, many suffering nasty facial injuries which they held handkerchiefs to while they waited to be seen. Rosa walked to the reception desk where a nurse was filling out forms.

'Excuse me,' she said.

'One moment,' said the nurse. She finished the form she was writing on and added it to a pile. 'Yes?' she asked.

'Would it be possible to talk to someone in the mortuary department?'

'What is it concerning?'

'A friend of mine was brought here last night. She was killed during the air raid in Oxford Street. The thing is, she may not have been identified so no one will know who to make contact with as her next of kin. You know, about the funeral arrangements.'

'And your name is?' asked the nurse, reaching for a pen.

'Rosa Weeks. Donna, my friend, and I shared a house.' She hesitated, then took a deep breath before saying as calmly as she could: 'Her head was cut off by flying glass. That's how I know she was brought here. The St John Ambulance people remembered her because of that.'

The nurse regarded Rosa warily. 'And how do you know she was decapitated?' she asked.

'Because I was with her when it happened,' said Rosa. 'I saw it happen.'

And she was aware that tears were starting to brim in her eyes as she saw the dreadful thing happening again, and she blinked hard to stop them rolling down her cheeks.

The nurse looked at her, sympathy on her face now. 'If you give me her details, and that of her next of kin, I'll see that the information is passed on to the right people.'

'Thank you,' said Rosa. She handed over the piece of paper on which she'd written Donna's name, their address near Oxford Street and Donna's mother's address in Clapham. She'd also added her own name and Coburg's address and telephone number. 'I'm staying with a friend at the moment,' she said. 'If you need any further information, you can get hold of me at that number. I've already let Mrs Dunn know that her daughter was killed.'

'Thank you,' said the nurse, taking the piece of paper. Then her tone softened as she added: 'I'm sorry you had to see your friend die that way,' she said. 'Please accept my condolences.'

'Thank you,' said Rosa. She was about to leave, when a thought struck her and she asked: 'One last thing. Could you tell me where I'd find the nearest base for the St John Ambulance?'

The nurse looked at her quizzically. 'May I ask why?'

'Because they were so considerate and caring when I spoke to them, I'd like to send them something.'

'Yes. Their nearest is in Praed Street, not far from the railway station. Number 163.'

'Thank you,' said Rosa. 'And you will pass on those details about my friend?'

'I promise,' said the nurse.

It was six o'clock when Coburg arrived home, carrying a parcel wrapped in newspaper. Rosa looked at him in surprise.

'That smells like fish and chips,' she said.

'It is,' he confirmed, and he put the parcel on the table and opened it to reveal two portions of battered fish and a heap of chips. 'I didn't think either of us would feel like preparing a meal tonight, and you've got a performance at half past eight. If you're still going to do it, that is.'

'I am,' said Rosa firmly.

They ate the meal straight from the newspaper with their fingers. 'It's the only way to eat it,' said Coburg. As they ate they swapped tales of their day: Rosa telling Coburg about her visit to Mrs Dunn, and then to Paddington Hospital.

'And tomorrow I'm going to the St John Ambulance station to see if they'll take me on as an ambulance driver.'

'You're still sure you want to do that?'

'Absolutely,' she said. 'As I said, I need to do something to help in this war.' She popped a chip into her mouth, then asked: 'How was your day? Are you any nearer to solving the murder at the Ritz?'

'No,' admitted Coburg. 'I feel we're nearly there, but I keep coming up against obstacles. I saw the personal secretary to King Zog today, and he virtually threw me out. Politely, of course. But there's something there that definitely rings alarm bells. So tomorrow I'm going to Sevenoaks in the hope of getting to the bottom of it.'

'Sevenoaks?' queried Rosa.

'I'll tell you more when I get back.' He hesitated, then said: 'After we've finished at the Ritz tonight, I need to leave the car at Scotland Yard, so we'll get a taxi back here.'

'You're losing the car?' she asked.

'No. I'm letting my sergeant have it so he can go to Ramsgate tomorrow.' He hesitated, wary of saying something that would bring back those awful memories of the previous night.

'Whatever it is, you can say it,' she said.

He nodded. 'Ramsgate was badly bombed yesterday. He's got relatives there and no one can get through on the phones to find out if they survived. I'm guessing the phone lines are down.'

'Was it bad?' asked Rosa.

'Very bad,' said Coburg. 'It sounds like half the town was destroyed.'

She stopped eating and suddenly shivered, tears filling her eyes.

'I'm sorry,' apologised Coburg. 'I shouldn't have mentioned it.'

'Yes, you should,' she said. 'It's war. We can't hide away from it. No matter how much we'd like to.'

CHAPTER THIRTY-THREE

Monday 26th August

The following morning Coburg woke to the smell of cooking. He pulled on his dressing gown and made his way to the kitchen, where Rosa was stirring a saucepan.

'We're out of eggs but there was porridge in the cupboard,' she told him.

'You were fantastic last night,' said Coburg, seating himself at the table.

She smiled. 'You weren't so bad yourself.' Then she left out a whoop of delight. 'God, I needed that! Sex is just the best thing!'

'I was talking about you at the Ritz,' said Coburg. 'No one in that audience would have known what you'd been through.'

'It's called being a professional,' said Rosa. 'Actors call it Doctor Theatre.' She went to him and held him tightly. 'Me, I call it having you with me.' She went back to the stove and turned the gas burner off, then looked at him with a wicked gleam in her eye. 'Fancy a repeat performance to help work up an appetite?'

Coburg caught the Underground from Hampstead to Embankment, leaving Rosa to her own task of trying to be accepted as a trainee ambulance driver by the St John Ambulance Service. They still hadn't talked more about getting married, but Rosa seemed happy with him. *Maybe I'll raise it with her tonight*, he thought. Then immediately retracted that idea; it was still very likely too soon. He'd give her space.

When he arrived at Scotland Yard, he phoned the number in Kent he'd been given. He was informed that Lord Mainwaring was unavailable, but once he'd persuaded the butler, or whoever it was who'd answered the phone, that he was indeed a detective chief inspector from Scotland Yard and that he would be coming to Kent that very day with the express purpose of speaking to Lord Mainwaring on a matter of national importance, the person answering the phone had asked if he wished to speak to Lord Mainwaring now.

'No,' said Coburg. 'But please let Lord Mainwaring know that I am on my way from London and should be at Richford Castle within the next two hours. It is vital that I talk to him.'

With that, Coburg set off for Charing Cross Station.

The train to Sevenoaks wasn't very crowded, most of the other passengers were in uniform, some soldiers but most in RAF blue-grey, heading back to their bases. Coburg had a seat by a window, and as the train left the suburbs of south London he had a close-up view of the air battle taking place. As Coburg watched, one Hurricane let fly with a burst of gunfire that tore into a Messerschmitt, which exploded in mid-air, the burning wreckage plummeting towards the ground far below. There was a flash of white, then a parachute billowed out and Coburg saw the German pilot floating down.

Everyone knew that Hitler intended to launch an invasion across the Channel from France, but first he had to smash the RAF so there'd be no danger of an air attack on his troops as they landed. That meant destroying the numerous small airfields that dotted southern England.

Every day young pilots, young men like the ones who sat and joked with one another in his railway carriage, took their Spitfires and Hurricanes up into the skies, the last line of defence against the wave after wave of Luftwaffe bombers and fighter planes. The average age of the pilots laying their lives on the line was twenty-one, and many of them would never live to be twenty-two. On one day alone, Coburg had been told that the German assault force had comprised 500 bombers and 1,300 fighter planes, with just a couple of hundred British fighters in the skies to defend against them, the young pilots going up again and again. And this continued day after day. How long could these young men go on?

And not just the young pilots. Civilians and ground crews at the airfields died as the German bombs rained down, destroying buildings, canteens, air towers and nearly everyone in them, as well as leaving massive craters in the actual fields to stop planes from taking off and landing.

If the airfields are destroyed and the RAF beaten, we'll be lost, thought Coburg. Hitler's stormtroopers would pour ashore up the beaches and spread inland. The Local Defence volunteers would do their best to halt the advance, but they were mostly elderly or invalided soldiers and they'd be no match for the might of the ruthless German military machine with their heavy weapons and superior numbers. They'd torn through Belgium and France at a terrifying speed, and now they were poised for this final assault, this final victory.

As the train pulled into Sevenoaks, Coburg got up and turned to the young men who remained in his compartment.

'We all thank you,' he said.

They looked at him in surprise as he left the train, then continued chatting to one another. He wondered how many of them would still be alive by nightfall.

There were taxis waiting outside the station. Once again, he reflected on the apparent normality of life, while above their heads and all around them were the sights and sounds of battle. Bombs and bullets, death and destruction, and people went about their daily business, albeit with a gas mask in a box dangling from their waist or their shoulder, and – in some cases – a tin helmet for those who doubled as air raid wardens.

Richford Castle was about five miles outside Sevenoaks, a mix of Norman and Tudor styles with Victorian additions. The two towers that flanked each end of the main house were certainly Victorian, a statement by a previous owner of the castle that he was a person of some high grandeur and deserved respect. Rather like his own father, thought Coburg, the previous Duke of

Dawlish. Coburg hadn't seen much of his father during his childhood. Nor his mother, come to that. He, Magnus and Charles had been brought up by a series of nannies, then sent away to boarding schools at the age of six, first to a prep school, followed by Eton.

He and his two brothers had got on well enough when at home together during the school vacations, with Magnus very much in charge, already acting the part of Lord of the Manor. This didn't bother Coburg or Charles, who were both happy for Magnus to take on this role.

Yes, he thought as the taxi drove down the long drive towards the large, ornate mansion, *I grew up in a place like this.*

When Rosa arrived at the St John Ambulance base in Praed Street, it was empty of people exccept for a harassed-looking woman in the office who was manning the phone.

'If it's urgent, I'm sorry, there's going to be a delay. Everyone's out on calls at the moment,' the woman told her.

'No, it's not an emergency,' said Rosa. 'I'd like to apply to join.'

The woman smiled. 'Great!' She took a form from her desk drawer, which she passed to Rosa. 'If you wouldn't mind filling this in. What sort of thing are you interested in? We're looking for people to help with our cadets.'

'I want to drive an ambulance.'

The woman stopped and studied Rosa. 'Can you drive?' she asked.

'Absolutely,' said Rosa. 'And I've driven lorries before, so I can handle large vehicles.'

'Any medical training?'

Rosa shook her head. 'I'm afraid not.'

'That's a pity,' said the woman.

'I've done first aid,' said Rosa.

'Qualified?'

'Well, that depends,' admitted Rosa. 'It was a course.'

'Where? Who with?'

'The Girl Guides.'

The woman looked warily at Rosa, then said: 'You need to see our manager, see what he says.'

'Yes, please. I'd like to see him. When will he be free?'

'He's out all day today, but he'll be in tomorrow.'

'Very good,' said Rosa. 'What time?'

The woman opened a large desk diary and turned a few pages before finding the current date. 'Ten o'clock?' she asked. 'He'll be in then. In the afternoon he's got a meeting of the Joint War Organisation, which will take up most of the day.'

'Ten o'clock will be fine,'said Rosa.

'What's your name?' asked the woman.

'Rosa Weeks.'

'What, like that singer who's at the Ritz?'

'Yes,' said Rosa.

'Some concidence, eh,' said the woman. 'Having the same name as her. You're not related to her, are you?'

'Actually, I am,' said Rosa.

'Oh? Well that'll interest Mr Warren. He went to see her and said she was very good.' She chuckled. 'I bet he asks you if you can get her autograph for him.'

As Rosa left, doubts began to enter her mind. So this Mr Warren had seen her at the Ritz. What would he think when she told him that she wanted to drive an ambulance? Would he dismiss her as some performer who just wanted to do something a bit different, a fly by night, not someone who was dependable? Well, if that turned out to be case, she'd have to try another avenue. The Red Cross. Or the Women's Royal Voluntary Service, though she'd been told they did mostly catering and knitting.

No, she determined, *I want to drive an ambulance and save lives.*

Lampson had intended to park by the central police station in Ramsgate, but the bombing had taken a major toll, with most of the town centre blocked where buildings had collapsed into the roadways. Water ran everywhere from broken water mains while workers tried desperately to repair the smashed pipes. Realising there was no chance of getting close to the town centre, Lampson parked the police car on the harbour road and walked. Everywhere was frantic activity, men in a variety of uniforms, some soldiers and sailors, but mostly Civil Defence and fire brigade volunteers, dragging beams from piles of smashed bricks as they searched to locate survivors or the dead. Lampson was tempted to make straight for his uncle and aunt's house, but instead he decided the best way to get co-operation was to follow the rules of protocol and introduce himself at the police station. Fortunately, he'd been given the name of Barry Moss's pal, Sergeant Peter Tremble, and he hoped that might make things easier. He knew from experience that many officers in the smaller regional forces liked nothing less than people from Scotland Yard turning up and throwing their weight about. Not that Lampson had ever thrown his weight about that way, but some did, and Lampson knew it rankled.

As it turned out, Peter Tremble was off for the day.

'So, what's Scotland Yard's interest in Ramsgate?' asked the desk sergeant, who introduced himself as Ernie Watts once Lampson had shown his warrant card.

'It's not Scotland Yard business, it's personal,' said Lampson, putting his warrant card away. He'd decided that the only way to get the locals to help him was by telling the truth and not pulling rank. 'My uncle and aunt live here. When I heard what happened my guv'nor gave me permission to come down and find out if they were all right.'

Watts regarded Lampson cautiously. 'What's their name?'

Lampson told him their name and address. Watts stood studying Lampson with a wary expression, then he called a constable over. 'Bob, take over the desk for a bit. This gentleman's from Scotland Yard and he needs help with some enquiries, so I'm taking him to Camden Square.'

'Camden Square?' said the constable. He shook his head. 'There ain't hardly anything left there.'

'That's enough, Constable,' said Watts sharply. He picked up his helmet and pulled it on. 'Right, Sergeant,' he said. 'Follow me.'

'Look, I know you're busy,' said Lampson. 'I know the way there. Like I say, I used to walk everywhere around here. I just came in to let you know I was here because that's the proper thing to do.'

'And it's appreciated,' said Watts as they left the police station. 'But right now, you won't be able to find your way around that part of town because there's not much of it

302

left. And you're gonna get stopped by the people working there and told to go away. So, having me with you prevents that happening.'

'Thank you,' said Lampson.

As they walked, Watts filled Lampson in on the air raid. Although Lampson had already been told some of it by Barry Moss, Watts's account was told with the angry, bitter tone of someone who'd experienced it.

'It happened early in the afternoon, when loads of people were around. They reckon the Germans dropped about 300 high explosive bombs on the town. We still don't know how many were killed or injured. About 2,000 houses were destroyed. The town's gas works took a direct hit, which spread the fire even further. The lifeboat station went. Most people went down the tunnels to get away from the bombing, but there were two auxiliary firemen who were cycling to work when the raid started, and the bastard who was flying escort to the bombers machine-gunned them.'

'Yes, I heard about that,' said Lampson.

'At least we got 'em back,' said Watts vengefully. 'You heard what happened on Sunday?'

'No,' said Lampson.

'Berlin. It was on the news this morning.'

'I didn't hear the news this morning, I wanted to get here. What happened?'

'Churchill ordered the RAF to bomb Berlin. I'd like to think it was in answer to what happened here, but according to the newsreader it was in retaliation for the Germans bombing the centre of London.'

'Yes, my guv'nor was caught up in that,' said Watts.

'Was he all right?'

Lampson nodded. 'But someone he knew was killed.'

Watts scowled. 'Bastard Germans,' he spat.

As they walked Lampson saw the scale of destruction in this part of town; the whole area seemed to have been obliterated.

'The Assembly Hall,' said Watts, pointing to a heap of wreckage where men were working, pulling at the rubble and wooden struts. 'Or what's left of it, which is nothing. Completely demolished.' He stopped and gestured. 'And here's Belle Vue Road.'

Lampson looked at the devastation and was filled with a deep pain that ate at his heart and right down to his stomach. Where his uncle and aunt's house had stood there was now just rubble. Like the Assembly Hall, it had vanished and been replaced by debris. As he and Watts watched, two men lifted aside a roof beam and broken floorboards, and as they tossed broken roof tiles to one side one of the men called out: 'Here's someone!'

Immediately, men working nearby came to help, joining in pulling the rubble and shattered wood to uncover what lay beneath. Lampson and Watts moved forward to join them. A foot in a heavy boot had been exposed, and gradually more of the body was revealed; then another beside it, this one a woman wearing a long woollen skirt. The men set to work even harder, ripping at the wreckage with their bare hands and tossing it aside, revealing more of the two bodies, and Lampson had to stop himself from crying out when he recognised the cardigan his uncle had always worn with the leather patches on the elbows. More and more wreckage was removed, until finally their faces were exposed.

Watts looked enquiringly at Lampson, who nodded.

'That's them,' he said hoarsely. 'That's Uncle George and Aunt Ada.'

And tears pricked at his eyes as he saw that they had died holding hands.

CHAPTER THIRTY-FOUR

The butler who opened the door looked exactly as Coburg had thought he would from talking to him on the phone: elderly with white hair, possibly in his sixties, wearing a striped waistcoat beneath a long frock coat.

'Detective Chief Inspector Coburg from Scotland Yard,' said Coburg. 'I telephoned earlier.'

'Yes, sir. If you'd come this way, His Lordship is waiting for you in the library.'

The library reminded Coburg of the one at his family home, and he wondered how many of the vast array of books on display had actually been read. Neither he nor his elder brother had been great readers, that had been the pastime of his middle brother. He wondered how Charles was managing in a prisoner of war camp without access to reading material. Or, possibly, there was sufficient reading, although Coburg imagined most of it would be in German. In which case, Charles would have no problem as he was fluent in the language. He'd been the one with the brains in the family, but also the one who seemed to be dogged by bad luck: serious childhood illnesses, injuries while playing sports, wounded during the First World War, and with a wife he'd adored who'd died of the flu epidemic of 1918 after just a few months of marriage. And yet still Charles had remained positive. He was stoicism personified, in Coburg's opinion.

The man who stood up and came forward to greet Coburg with a handshake as he entered the library was a short man about the same age as his butler. He was dressed for comfort rather than style, a worn and faded cardigan hanging loosely over a pair of baggy and faded brown corduroy trousers. He had an unkempt grey moustache, his whole image reminiscent to Coburg of the archetypical absent-minded professor.

'Chief Inspector Coburg,' he indicated for Coburg to sit in one of the library's large leather armchairs. 'A matter of national importance, your message said. I'm intrigued.'

'Thank you for seeing me, Lord Mainwaring. I'm investigating a series of murders that have taken place in London, and it has been suggested that there may be a connection with the British Union of Fascists.'

At this, Mainwaring looked decidedly unhappy. 'I really have nothing to say on the matter,' he said. 'I joined out of ignorance and because of my great fondness for Italy. It was only later that I discovered that the reasons we were given for its creation were false and that many of us had been duped. If you check with the Intelligence services you'll find that I was investigated but exonerated. I'd had no connection with the BUF for some years before it was banned by the government. So, I'm afraid you've had a long journey for nothing, Chief Inspector.'

'Not really,' said Coburg. 'The BUF was just one aspect and, I believe, a minor one, but the case I'm investigating centres on the Ritz Hotel and the retinue of King Zog of Albania. I understand that the King's personal secretary, Count Idjbil Ahmed, recently stayed with you as a house guest, and I'd like to talk to you about your relationship with him.'

To Coburg's surprise, Mainwaring stood up, his face suddenly grim. He strode to the large, ornate marble fireplace and tugged at the bell pull beside it.

'I think you need to talk to my wife,' he said.

The door opened, and the butler appeared.

'You rang, my lord?'

'Yes, Carter. Would you tell Lady Mainwaring there is someone to see her? A Detective Chief Inspector Coburg of Scotland Yard.'

With that, Lord Mainwaring strode purposefully out of the library.

Coburg got to his feet, intending to go after him, but then stopped. What was going on? Why had Mainwaring become so angry all of a sudden? And then he cursed himself for an idiot. Count Ahmed hadn't been Lord Mainwaring's house guest at all, he'd been Lady Mainwaring's.

Coburg remained standing, and soon the door opened to reveal a very handsome woman in her mid-fifties. Unlike her husband, Lady Mainwaring dressed in style. She wore a tweed suit, jacket and skirt with aplomb, especially as the tweed material was offset by a white fluted blouse and a colourful neckerchief.

'Detective Chief Inspector Coburg.' She smiled, and held out her hand for him to take. 'I understand you wish to talk to me.'

'Yes,' said Coburg. She gestured for him to sit, then took a chair herself. 'I came to talk to your husband about Count Idjbil Ahmed, the private secretary to King Zog of Albania. I believe he was staying here recently.' He paused, then added: 'Your husband suggested I talk to you.'

'Poor Kirby,' sighed Lady Leonora. 'I hope you won't be shocked by what I'm going to tell you, Chief Inspector. Particularly because I know some of your background, and in the class of society we come from, the concept of marriage can sometime be a fluid one.'

I know of your background, thought Coburg. *She also knew I was coming here today*, told by the butler, he expected, but whereas her husband had not been curious about the visit, Lady Mainwaring had obviously felt the need to make enquiries. Why? As she began to speak, Coburg realised she'd wanted to find out if he was 'one of them', one of their sort, and could be told things without fear that it would be turned into gossip. However, she still felt the need to precede with a proviso.

'What I'm going to tell you, Chief Inspector, is the frank and unvarnished truth, but I'd like your word it will not be publicised. Although the situation is common knowledge among our close friends, for my husband's sake we prefer it remain confined to that circle only.'

'So long as whatever you tell me turns out not to be material to the murders I'm investigating, you have my word, Lady Mainwaring,' said Coburg.

'The murder of the unknown man at the Ritz in Idjbil's

suite,' she said. 'Very unfortunate. But take my word, Idjbil didn't do it. He couldn't. Again, do I have your word?'

'You do.'

'Very well. I met Idjbil many years ago when I was in Italy. It was before he was a count, and before I was married to Kirby. We were young, and very much in love. We desperately wanted to get married, but my parents refused. They had other plans for me, to marry an English aristocrat. An Albanian who at that time had very little money of his own did not fit the bill for them. I defied them, of course, and insisted I would stay in Italy and marry Idjbil, but they had me brought back to England. It was all very unpleasant. But true love never dies.'

'But you married Lord Mainwaring.'

'Yes. I was told in no uncertain terms that I had no choice, and that if Idjbil entered Britain he would be arrested and then deported. There was even talk of having him killed. My father was that sort of man. So, I married Kirby. But I never forgave my parents, and I never forgot Idjbil.'

'Was Lord Mainwaring aware of your feelings for Count Ahmed?'

'Yes, but I think he thought I would grow out of it. Or, at least, that my father and his associates would keep me under control. But when my father died I decided to assert myself. I set Kirby a choice: divorce, or the freedom for me to travel to Italy and see Idjbil.'

'And he agreed?'

'His family are Catholics. The idea of divorce is anathema to them. And so, for the past many years, things have continued in a civilised fashion, with me taking

310

sojourns in Italy and Kirby entertaining himself with other companions. Of course, the current war put a stop to any idea of my travelling to Italy, but when Idjbil wrote to me and told me the King and his party were coming to England, we decided to make arrangements.'

'And Count Ahmed came here and stayed with you recently?'

'Yes.'

'And your husband?'

'He elected to stay at his club in London while Idjbil was here.' She regarded Coburg quizzically. 'I've answered your questions honestly because the fact that a chief inspector from Scotland Yard has come here to ask questions about Idjbil suggests he is in trouble, and I will do anything to help clear his name if he's suspected of anything. The dead man was found on the morning of Tuesday 20th August, is that right? Although he may have been killed the night before, the 19th.'

'That's correct,' said Coburg.

Lady Mainwaring gave a small smile.

'The 19th was our first meeting for a long time. I had a room at the Savoy. We were both there, together, all day and all night. So, Idjbil wasn't killing anyone at the Ritz. But I'm sure he could have told you all this. Why didn't you ask him where he was and what he was doing?'

'I tried, but he was reluctant to talk to me,' said Coburg.

She sighed. 'Yes, Idjbil can be very protective of my reputation. Have you talked to anyone else in the King's party?'

'The King,' said Coburg.

Lady Mainwaring smiled. 'I can't imagine he enjoyed that.'

'You know King Zog?'

'I've met him a few times in Albania, with Idjbil, before the war. He struck me as a bit of a phoney. Don't you think? Not a real royal.'

'It's not for me to say,' said Coburg carefully.

'No? But surely you're the real thing. The Honourable Edgar Saxe-Coburg, son of the Duke of Dawlish.'

'You've been doing your homework.'

'I wouldn't have been as frank with you if I hadn't checked you out. When Kirby told me he'd received a telephone call from a policeman asking to talk to him, I was intrigued. And when he told me your name, I was even more intrigued. I've met your older brother, the present Duke, a few times. He mentioned you.'

'Oh?'

'Yes, in very complimentary terms. He's proud of you. The work that you do. Your record during the First World War. You were badly injured.'

'Many were injured,' said Coburg. 'I was one of the lucky ones. I survived.'

Lady Mainwaring studied Coburg thoughtfully, then said: 'I'll talk to Idjbil. Tell him to talk to you. And to be open and honest with you. There's a lot of suspicion among the King's retinue; they believe they have enemies everywhere.'

'And do you think they have?'

'Absolutely. They wouldn't be here in London if they didn't.'

It was with a sense of foreboding that Lampson approached his parents' house, wondering how his mother would react to the news about the death of her sister and brother-in-law. Badly, he knew, but how badly? He knew his mother had problems with her heart, everyone in the family knew that. But how bad was it? Bad, like the tobacconist Mr Porter's had been; so bad that the shock of the robbery had killed him? His mother never said how bad her heart condition was, just that sometimes she got out of breath climbing the stairs. Was that a symptom?

He knocked on the door, which was opened by his dad.

'Terry's out,' he said grumpily.

Lampson nodded, then entered the house. His mother appeared from the kitchen, wiping her hands on a tea towel.

'You've got to have a word with that boy,' continued his dad, obviously upset. 'He went out with his mates and I told him to be back in time for you coming home, but he takes no notice. He's got this obsession with finding German spies.'

'I'll have another word with him,' Lampson promised. 'But I'm glad he's not here at the moment because I've got something to tell you.'

'Oh?' said his dad suspiciously. 'It's not about you and that woman whatsername.'

'Ruth? No,' said Lampson. 'It's about Uncle George and Aunt Ada in Ramsgate.'

'What about them?' asked his mother, suddenly fearful.

'Ramsgate was bombed the day before yesterday,' said Lampson.

His mother and father looked at one another, bewildered.

'No one told us,' said his father.

'It hasn't been on the wireless,' said Lampson. 'I only heard about it from a police sergeant I know.'

'When did you know?' demanded his father.

'Yesterday.'

'Yesterday!' burst out his father, angrily. 'And you never told us! Even though you were here in this house coming to pick up Terry!'

'I didn't want to say anything until I knew what had happened to them,' said Lampson. 'If anything *had* happened to them. No one could tell me anything, so I went to Ramsgate today to find out for myself.'

His parents stood stock-still, staring at him, then suddenly his mother began to cry.

'She's dead!' And she buried her face in her hands, her body shaking with sobs.

'They're both dead,' said Lampson.

'You don't know that!' said his father defiantly.

'I do,' said Lampson. 'I was one of the party of rescuers that found 'em. It was them all right.'

The painful silence was broken by the rattle of the letterbox.

'That'll be Terry,' said his father, his voice faded and broken with shock.

'Leave him to me. I'll take him,' said Lampson.

He made for the door and opened it to see Terry on the doorstep.

'Hello, Dad!' The boy grinned. 'Here, I got to show Grandad something. I found a bullet today in the street! It must've fallen from a German plane.'

And Terry produced the long metal cartridge from his pocket. He was just about to rush into the kitchen when Lampson put his hand on his son's shoulder. 'Not today, son. Show 'em tomorrow. They're busy right now.'

'Busy? Doing what?'

'I'll tell you on the way home.' He called, 'See you in the morning!' to his parents, then ushered Terry out and pulled the front door shut.

'What's going on?' asked Terry. 'Grandad and Nan are never busy.'

'I had to give them some bad news,' said Lampson as they walked. 'D'you remember your Great-Uncle George and Great-Aunt Ada?'

'Nan's sister,' said Terry. 'Yeh, course I do. They live near the seaside.'

'Ramsgate,' confirmed Lampson. 'Well, the day before yesterday the Germans bombed Ramsgate, and George and Ada were killed.'

Terry stopped and looked at his father, stunned. 'They're dead?'

'I'm afraid so,' said Lampson.

'But why did the Germans kill them? They weren't soldiers or anything. They were just . . . people.'

'Yes,' said Lampson. 'But in war it's usually the ordinary people who die. More than the soldiers and airmen and navy.'

'But why?'

'It's just the way it is, son. There's no rhyme or reason to it. People die.'

'Will we die?' asked Terry, suddenly worried.

'Not if I have anything to do with it.' said Lampson grimly. 'Anyway, it's time for tea. What do you say to pie and mash?'

CHAPTER THIRTY-FIVE

'How did you get on in Kent?' asked Rosa when they met up in the flat early that evening.

'I'm hoping it will have eased the way for me to get information from King Zog's entourage,' said Coburg. 'How about you? Did you see the St John Ambulance people?'

'I did, but the person I need to talk to is the manager, a Mr Warren.'

'You don't seem happy about it,' observed Coburg.

'I'm not. It seems he came to see me at the Ritz.'

'Well, surely that's good,' said Coburg. 'He'll be impressed that a music star wants to join up.'

'I'm not a music star,' Rosa corrected him. 'And I'm not sure it will help. In fact, the opposite. He might think I'm one of those well-meaning but useless people who think just because they can play piano in front of an audience they can do anything.'

'He'll have a different opinion when he meets you,' said Coburg. 'You'll win him over.' He looked at his watch. 'Talking of playing piano for an audience, remember I haven't got the car, so I think it'd be a good idea to make sure we get a taxi before they all get taken.'

'We could go by bus or Underground,' said Rosa.

'Taxi,' said Coburg firmly.

The Rivoli Bar was packed, word having spread that this was Rosa's last week appearing there. With every table booked, Coburg was invited to share by Lord and Lady Kerwin, old acquaintances of his family, and they spent a pleasant half-hour catching up, with the Kerwins asking after Coburg's brothers.

'We understand Charles is in a POW camp in Germany,' said Lady Kerwin.

'Yes,' said Coburg.

'So is our Steven,' she said. 'I had a letter from him the other day. Very brief – he never was a great letter-writer – but he seems to be coping.'

'Of course he is,' said Lord Kerwin. 'They say if you can survive Eton you can survive anything. It's good preparation for a term in prison.' He looked at Coburg with a quizzical smile. 'Did you find that?'

'Fortunately, I never did a term in prison,' said Coburg.

At that point Rosa appeared and took her seat at the piano, and all conversation ceased as her fingers stroked the keys and she launched into 'Georgia On My Mind'.

They were silent in the taxi on the way back to Hampstead, but it was a comfortable silence, that of close friends and lovers.

As Coburg poured drinks for them when they were in the flat, he commented that there'd been no sign of Raymond Harris at Rosa's performances the last few evenings.

'Perhaps he's lost interest in me,' suggested Rosa.

'I doubt that very much,' said Coburg. 'I just wonder what's keeping him occupied.'

CHAPTER THIRTY-SIX

Tuesday 27th August

Next morning, Coburg hugged Rosa close just before he left for Scotland Yard. 'Don't worry about this Mr Warren,' he told her. 'Just be yourself. Trust me, you'll be fine.'

'And if I'm not?' she asked.

'Try the Red Cross,' he said. 'They need ambulance drivers too.'

The car was waiting for him at Scotland Yard, as Lampson had promised. Coburg collected the keys from the desk sergeant, then went up to his office. Lampson was already in, and Coburg could tell right away that all was not well.

'Morning, Ted. How did you get on in Ramsgate?'

Lampson shook his head. 'Both dead, guv'nor. My uncle and aunt.'

'I'm sorry. Look, if you want to take some time off . . .'

Lampson shook his head. 'No, there's work to be done.

I'm better off here.' He looked deeply saddened as he said: 'It was worse getting back to Somers Town and telling my mum her sister was dead.' He looked grim and angry as he added: 'You should've seen the destruction. The whole town looks like it has been flattened. They reckon if it hadn't been for the tunnels there'd have been thousands dead. And it wasn't just Ramsgate. All the way there were signs where places had been bombed, and the damage got worse the nearer I got to the coast. They say the bombers are hitting the coastal towns more to soften things up for the invasion the Germans are planning, but I was talking to someone who reckons that what happens is the bombers turn tail when they meet up with our fighter boys over Kent and then just get rid of their bomb loads along the coast before they get to the Channel. Whyever they're doing it, they're tearing those towns apart. Thank God for the RAF, otherwise those bombers would be over London.'

'According to the Intelligence services, they'll be here soon enough,' said Coburg. 'Whether or not Hitler destroys the airfields in Kent and Sussex, London will be his next target after Berlin was bombed.'

'When do they think that'll happen?'

'It's anybody's guess,' said Coburg. 'The pessimists reckon it'll only be a matter of days or weeks.' He looked seriously at Lampson and added: 'If they're right, my advice would be to strongly consider getting your son out of the city.'

'Where to?' asked Lampson. 'Nowhere's safe, as I saw yesterday.'

'Not east,' said Coburg. 'Somewhere else. To the west. Cornwall. Devon.'

'I don't know anyone down there, and I couldn't send him to people I don't know.'

'Send him away with your parents,' suggested Coburg.

Lampson shook his head. 'They won't leave. They're too bloody stubborn.' The phone rang, and Lampson picked it up. 'DCI Coburg's office.' He looked at Coburg in surprise, then said: 'Yes, sir. Certainly, he's here.' He held out the receiver to Coburg saying: 'It's Count Ahmed.'

Surprised, Coburg took the phone. 'DCI Coburg speaking. How can I help you, Count Ahmed?'

'I believe it is I who can help you,' said Ahmed. 'I had a telephone call from someone yesterday who suggested I talk to you openly and honestly about . . . the situation. Can you come to my suite at the Ritz?'

'I can indeed,' said Coburg. 'When?'

'Shall we say in an hour?'

'An hour it is,' said Coburg. 'Thank you, Count Ahmed. This is very much appreciated.'

He hung up.

'Change of tone from the other day, by the sound of it,' commented Lampson.

Coburg smiled. 'Indeed.' He stood up and put the car keys on Lampson's desk. 'I'll walk to the Ritz. The exercise will do me good. I'll leave you with the car so you can carry on chasing up possibles as to who killed Mel McGuinness and Thackeray.'

'Will do, guv,' said Lampson. 'All the best at the Ritz.'

Chesney Warren was a small man, neatly dressed in a dark three-piece suit. He had a curling moustache, one tip of which touched a long, jagged scar across one cheek from his mouth to his ear. He gave Rosa a welcoming smile as he opened the door of his office to her knock.

'Miss Weeks, it's a pleasure to meet you. I saw you perform at the Ritz last week, and it was the most wonderful evening.'

'Thank you, Mr Warren. Your receptionist mentioned you'd been.'

'Yes, she said you were just a relative.'

'I thought I'd keep things separate,' said Rosa.

'Despite that, I still wondered if it might be the same person, and as soon as I saw you I was delighted to see it was, so I could congratulate you in person.' He gestured at the chair opposite his desk. 'Please, do sit down.'

'Thank you.'

The office was spartan: simple furniture, charts on the walls showing which people were where, along with work schedules for the coming week. The books on the shelves were mostly medical manuals and pamphlets from national and local government.

'Miss Phelps said you wanted to be an ambulance driver,' said Warren, taking his own chair.

'That's right.'

'May I ask why?'

'I want to do something to help the war effort. I used to drive lorries for my father's grocery business in Edinburgh when I was younger, so I thought it was a skill I could put to good use.'

'But why ambulances?'

Rosa hesitated, then told him: 'A friend of mine was killed the other night when Oxford Street was bombed. I was with her when it happened. There were many others lying injured and I thought: if they could be taken to hospital quickly, many of them would survive.'

Warren nodded. 'I understand.' He looked at a note. 'Miss Phelps said you'd done a first aid course.'

'A long time ago,' Rosa admitted. 'When I was in the Girl Guides.'

'What do you know about the St John Ambulance?' asked Warren.

'I know they help the sick and injured,' said Rosa.

'Indeed,' said Warren. 'During times of war, such as now, we work with the Red Cross as a Joint War Organisation, essentially doing the same kind of work, going to places where our help is needed.' He looked at her questioningly as he said: 'It is often dangerous, going out when a bombing raid is taking place. Until the Oxford Street and City raids the other night, London has escaped; but other places have not been so lucky. Plymouth was attacked last month and one of our crews was amongst the casualties. Would you be able to cope with that threat of danger?'

'Yes,' said Rosa. 'I wouldn't be here otherwise. I know what I'm letting myself in for. I want to be doing something rather than be in a shelter.'

'In that case, shall we go out to the yard where the vehicles are kept?'

'The vehicles?' asked Rosa, surprised.

'Yes. Let's see how you handle an ambulance.'

Coburg's reception at Count Ahmed's suite was in marked contrast to his previous visit. Even the bodyguards on duty at the door seemed conciliatory towards him. The Count offered him coffee. Inwardly, Coburg was wary, having once experienced coffee in Turkey which he found to be more like a thick soup and he wondered whether Albanian coffee would be similarly unpalatable, but was aware that this was a gesture of friendliness towards him and, for the purpose of getting the information he wanted, he accepted with a smile of thanks. As it turned out, the coffee was eminently acceptable, being the Ritz's own rather than imported from Albania. As he sipped it, Coburg gave a silent thank you to Lady Mainwaring; there was no doubt it was she who'd generated this sudden atmosphere of rapprochement.

'You must excuse my reservations from our previous encounter,' said Ahmed. 'I was not sure whether I was speaking to a policeman or an undercover representative of the British government.'

'Just a policeman,' said Coburg, 'trying to solve a murder. Or, rather, two murders.'

'Yes,' said Ahmed. 'You mentioned Albanians before when discussing possible suspects. I can assure you that none of His Majesty's party are in any way involved in these tragic incidents, but there may be other Albanians in London who might be.'

'Do you have names?' asked Coburg.

Ahmed shook his head. 'No. They are not people I would associate with or choose to associate with. But I think it's important that you know who these people are, as different and rival factions. Albania is riven politically. There are royalists, who support the King and his family, but there are also nationalists who have their own agenda. And most dangerously, in my opinion, there are the communists. All of these factions are enemies of the Nazis and Mussolini's fascists, but they oppose one another even more vehemently.'

'I'm guessing that the nationalists and the communists are keen to get their hands on the money His Majesty was rumoured to have brought with him.'

'I'm glad you said "rumoured",' said Ahmed.

'A rumour is enough when the figure being bandied around is said to be in the region of two million.'

'I won't go into the politics of the nationalists because it's far more complicated than just being about an Albanian identity, with the result that the nationalists themselves are divided into various factions, who all hate one another. They are too busy with this inter-group squabbling to attempt something as large as trying to steal this supposed money from the King in the Ritz. The communists, however, are another matter. They are a much smaller group, but more fanatical about their cause, which is to overthrow the royal family and align Albania with Soviet Russia. And they need something concrete to convince the Russians that they are worth supporting.'

'Something like two million in cash and gold?' said Coburg.

'Now that would be very concrete indeed,' said Ahmed with a small smile.

CHAPTER THIRTY-SEVEN

Rosa sat in the driving seat of the ambulance and tried the controls, before switching on the engine: the foot pedals, the indicators, the windscreen wipers, rotating the long handle of the gear lever to check it was in neutral.

'Just reminding myself where everything is,' she told Chesney Warren, sitting in the passenger seat next to her. 'It's some time since I last drove one of my father's lorries.'

Ten years, in fact, she ruefully admitted to herself. She remembered the difficulties she'd had with double-declutching when heading up Edinburgh's steep cobbled streets. *Please let me remember how to do it*, she prayed fervently. *I'm being given a chance.*

She turned the key in the ignition, but nothing happened except a dull clicking sound. She pulled the choke partway out, careful not to give it too much and flood the engine, and turned the key again. Again, nothing happened. This time she pulled the choke out a bit more, at the same time turning the key, and when there was a sharp cough from the engine and it barked into life, she pressed hard on the accelerator, slowly pushing the choke control down.

She sat as the vehicle vibrated with a low hum and turned to Warren.

'Where to?' she asked.

'Just round the yard for the moment,' he replied.

Rosa drove the ambulance carefully around the perimeter of the yard, taking care not to hit other vehicles and various objects as she maneouvred her way.

'Let's see you reverse,' said Warren. He pointed to a space between a car and a van parked by a brick wall. 'Over there.'

That's a bloody narrow space, thought Rosa unhappily. *I'm not even sure this will squeeze in there.*

'And I don't want to put any pressure on you,' Warren continued, 'but the van belongs to the St John Ambulance and the car is mine, so I'd appreciate it if you could be careful.'

Yes, you do want to put pressure on me, thought Rosa with a feeling of annoyance. Then she smiled to herself. *And that's quite right, too. Driving an ambulance is a high-pressure job.* She looked again at the gap between the car and the van, sizing it up, and she reminded herself of when she used to reverse her father's lorry. The first time she'd backed into a pile of crates filled with cabbages, spreading the whole lot all over his yard. He'd taken the cost out of her wages and it had taken her four weeks to repay him. She never hit anything while reversing again.

But that was then, in a lorry she'd got to know: she knew how wide it was and how long. This was different. This was an unfamiliar vehicle. She remembered her father's advice: *Always think it's wider and longer than it is. And look in your mirrors.*

She maneouvred the ambulance into position ahead of the space and checked the position of the car on her nearside and the van on the offside.

Ease it back slowly, she warned herself. *That way if you hit something it'll be a scrape rather than a write-off.*

Carefully she brought the vehicle slowly back, using a light touch on the accelerator and double-declutching between neutral and reverse to keep the ambulance in her control. She used the length of the van to judge when to bring the ambulance to a halt.

She put it into neutral, pulled on the handbrake and looked inquisitively at Warren.

'Now, let's take it out on the road,' said Warren. 'Turn right when you leave the gates, and then keep taking the first right to bring it back to the yard.'

Turn right, thought Rosa bitterly. Turning against the stream of traffic. Why not turn left?

Because it has to be done.

She took off the handbrake, slipped it into first and moved away, heading for the open gateway to the road and traffic. As she did, she thought: *Thank God for petrol rationing and a minimum amount of traffic.*

Coburg returned to the Yard thinking about what Count Ahmed had told him. The Count seemed to believe that the Albanian communists were the ones most likely to be set on liberating the money from King Zog's suite. In which case, to Coburg's mind, they'd either been working with Joe Williams, and for some reason they'd fallen out and killed him; or they were rivals who happened to be in the same place at the same time. But why was Williams' body found in the Count's suite and not the King's? Because the communists had learnt that the Count was away, and his suite was the base for them to get to the King's suite. The same was true for Williams. It had to be an accidental meeting in Ahmed's suite that had led to them killing Williams. If the communists had fallen out with Williams they'd have waited until the money had been removed before disposing of him, rather than kill him and abandon the robbery. He was just putting his thoughts down on paper, when the door opened and Lampson entered, accompanied by a short, frightened-looking young woman.

'Anna Gershon, sir, Ollen's girlfriend,' Lampson introduced her. 'I was just walking into reception when the desk sergeant called me over.'

'I got your message, but I don't like phones,' said the girl. 'So I came.'

'Please, sit down,' Coburg said to her, giving her a smile to put her at ease. 'Rest assured you're not in trouble. We just need your help with some enquiries.'

'About Alex?' And Coburg saw her lower lip tremble and tears come into her eyes.

'Would you like a cup of tea?' he asked. 'Or coffee?'

'I'd love a cup of coffee,' she said. 'I always used to drink tea before I met Alex, but he drank coffee. He used to bring it from the Ritz.'

'I'll have some sent up,' said Coburg. 'I doubt if it'll be

as good as what you're used to, it's Scotland Yard standard rather than the Ritz.'

'It'll be f-fine,' she said.

Her voice was shaky, and her nervousness was apparent in the way she twisted her hands together.

'I'll go and get the coffee,' said Lampson. 'How do you like it? Sugar? Milk?'

'Milk and two sugars,' she said.

'I'll be right back,' he said, and hurried out of the room.

'He's been looking for me,' said Anna. 'I've been away. I only got back this morning.'

'First, I'm really sorry about what happened to Alex,' said Coburg.

At the mention of his name, her tears spilled out and ran down her cheeks, and she pulled a handkerchief from her pocket to dab at her eyes.

'It was so unfair!' she said. 'He was so kind and gentle. He'd never hurt anyone.'

'How long had you known him?' asked Coburg.

'Six months. He came into the cafe where I work and ordered a coffee. I thought he looked nice. He told me later he'd passed the cafe and seen me in there, working, and he kept coming back for two weeks because he wanted to come in and talk to me, but he never came into the cafe until that day. He didn't have a lot of English, but enough to say "Please" and "Thank you" and talk about the weather. I thought he might be interested in me from the way he looked at me, but I'd never had a man look at me like that before. He told me later I was special. He made me feel special.'

'And you started going out with him?'

She nodded. 'Mostly, I went to his room to meet him

and we'd go for walks in the park. I've got a room, but the landlady doesn't like men in the rooms.'

The door opened, and Lampson returned holding a cup of coffee, which he put down on the desk in front of Anna.

'Here we are,' he said. 'It may not be the Ritz standard, but at least it's hot.'

She thanked Lampson and took a sip. 'Actually, it's not bad,' she said. 'As good as what we serve in the cafe.'

Coburg let her take another sip before asking: 'Can you think of anyone who'd want to harm Alex?'

She shook her head, then paused thoughtfully. 'There was someone who Alex seemed scared of. He came to see him a few times, and I was sure he frightened him.'

'Who was he?'

'I don't know his name. I asked Alex, but he said it was better for me not to know.' She paused, then said: 'But I saw him.'

'When? Where?'

'Once, when I called for Alex in his room. The man was there, threatening Alex, but he walked out when I arrived. Alex said he was a bad man.'

'What nationality was he? What language was he talking in?'

'The same as Alex.'

'Macedonian?'

She frowned. 'Was Alex from Macedonia? He told me at first he was Swiss, but then he said he was really Albanian.' She gave a little sigh. 'I didn't even know there was a place called Albania.'

'What did this man look like? The one who frightened Alex.'

331

Anna thought, doing her best to remember, then she said: 'He was about forty. About five foot six tall. Muscular, like he did boxing or something. He had a big moustache, thick and black like his hair. The worst thing about him was his eyes. They were always staring and angry, like he was about to attack someone. He frightened me, and I only saw him properly that once.' She gave a shudder.

Coburg took the photo of Joe Williams from his desk and showed it to her. 'Did you ever see Alex with this man?'

'No. Who is he?'

'Just someone we're interested in. It does sound like this man you mentioned may have been the one who harmed Alex.'

'I didn't say that!' she said, alarmed.

'No, I know,' said Coburg gently to calm her. 'But I'd certainly like to talk to him.'

'I don't know who he is,' she said. 'Or where he lives or works.'

'No, but there's a possibility we may know someone who can help us find out who he is.'

'Will I be in danger?' asked Anna nervously.

'No, not at all. The person I'm thinking about is one of our government people, very respectable. In his office he has pictures of people from abroad who live and work here.'

'Including Alex?' asked Anna.

'No, I'm fairly sure not,' said Coburg. 'These people are politicals. The man you describe could be one, or he may not be. But, with your help, we might be able to find out.'

Anna looked doubtful. 'I don't know,' she said uncertainly.

'You do want to help us find the person who hurt Alex?' said Coburg gently.

'Yes, of course, but if it was this man—'

'He won't know about your involvement,' said Coburg. 'That I promise you. All we'd like you to do is come with us to look at some photos and see if you can spot him among them. His picture may not even be there. We'll take you there in a car, and afterwards drive you wherever you want to go. Your home, or anywhere.'

'And no one will know?'

'No one will know,' confirmed Coburg.

Rosa followed Warren into his office, and they resumed their chairs.

'Well done,' he said. 'That was an excellent drive. I had to test you because we get an awful lot of people coming in claiming all sorts of things. We had one man who turned up saying he drove tanks in the First World War. When he hit our outside wall with the lorry as his first action, he said it was because the foot controls were different. I'm sure they are, but we couldn't trust him. You, I would trust.'

'You mean I'm in?' asked Rosa, doing her best to suppress her delight.

'Yes and no,' said Warren. 'You've passed the first test, being able to drive one of our ambulances. You've also passed the second, confidence but care. I'll need to get confirmation from head office, which will take a day or two, and then you can start your training.'

'Training?'

'Your first-aid training. Our standard is slightly higher than that for Girl Guides, but then we are often coming up against very serious situations, and although there will be fully qualified medics with you, we like all our crews to be able to work together.' He stood up and smiled as he held his hand out. 'So, welcome to the St John Ambulance Service, Miss Weeks. And thank you.'

Coburg and Lampson stood in Inspector Hibbert's office at Wormwood Scrubs, the three men watching as Anna Gershon sat at a table and went through a book of photographs. Coburg had told Hibbert of the description given to him by Anna. Hibbert had then produced a thick photograph album with page after page of head and shoulders shots of men looking at the camera, most of them with deep suspicion. There were no names on the page, just numbers.

'These are the known Albanians,' he'd told them.

'There's a lot of them,' commented Coburg.

'We started the file in the early 1930s when the first refugees started to arrive from Germany and elsewhere,' said Hibbert. 'So, there were only a few at first, but in the last couple of years it's become a bit of a flood.' As Anna turned over more pages without recognising anyone, Hibbert asked: 'You sure he's Albanian?'

'We think so,' said Coburg. 'He was heard talking to Alex Ollen in Ollen's language, and we're fairly sure Ollen was Albanian, despite claiming to be Swiss.'

'There's lots of languages similar,' said Hibbert. 'Macedonian. Slav.' He gestured at the row of photo albums. 'One for every country.'

'Ollen had documents in Macedonian in his room,' admitted Coburg.

'There you are, then,' said Hibbert.

'This is him,' said Anna suddenly.

The three men gathered round her and looked at the photograph she had her finger on. He did indeed have dangerous and vengeful eyes, thought Coburg.

'You're sure?' he asked.

She nodded and gave a little shudder. 'It's not a face I'm likely to forget.'

'No, it isn't,' Coburg agreed. He turned to Lampson. 'Sergeant, will you take Miss Gershon to wherever she wants to go, and then come back afterwards and pick me up. I just want to discuss a few things with Inspector Hibbert.'

'Certainly,' said Lampson. He smiled at Anna. 'This time you can sit in the back and think of me as your chauffeur.'

Coburg waited until Lampson and Anna had left the room, then asked Hibbert: 'Who is he?'

Hibbert noted the number beneath the file, then went to a drawer of index cards, flicking through them until he came to the one he wanted. He took out the card and read out the information: 'Anton Xhemel. Albanian, and a known communist,' said Hibbert. 'A bit of an agitator.'

'What else do you know about him? His associates?'

'To be frank, we haven't paid much attention to him, or the communists who've recently arrived. All of our efforts have gone into trying to identify fifth columnists and those who support Hitler and Mussolini.'

'Do you have an address for him?'

'Of course. And where he works.'

'Which is where?'

'He's a delivery driver for a laundry,' said Hibbert, handing Coburg the card.

Coburg read the information on the card: 'Employer: Kleen. Specialise in hospitals and commercial customers.'

'Commercial customers,' said Coburg thoughtfully. 'Hotels?'

'I expect so,' said Hibbert. 'Sheets. Uniforms. Tablecloths.'

So, that's the connection with Alex Ollen, thought Coburg. *I bet when we check we'll find out he picked up and delivered laundry to the Ritz.*

'You think he's the one who killed the kitchen hand?' asked Hibbert.

'I think there's a very high likelihood,' said Coburg, writing down Xhemel's details in his notebook. 'I'll know more once we talk to him. Can you let me have a copy of that photo? If he's not at that address, we're going to have to get a search going.'

CHAPTER THIRTY-EIGHT

The first thing Coburg did on getting back to the Yard was phone the porter at the Ritz.

'George, it's DCI Coburg. Do you know the name of the firm who does the hotel's laundry?'

'I do,' said George. 'It's a firm called Clean, although they mis-spell it as K-L-E-E-N,' he added disapprovingly.

'Thank you, George,' said Coburg. He hung up and turned to Lampson. 'It's him,' he said.

'You sure, guv?'

Coburg nodded. 'This is the way I see it. Joe Williams gets into Count Ahmed's empty suite prior to getting into the King's rooms where the money is stored. While he's there this Anton Xhemel turns up with a couple of his associates on the same mission. Or maybe they were there when Joe walked in. Whichever way it was, they killed Joe, and then had to run for it.

'Xhemel had an inside man at the Ritz giving him info, and that was Alex Ollen. But when Joe was killed, Ollen gets cold feet. This is suddenly a hanging matter and he doesn't want any part of it, so he tells Xhemel he wants out. But Xhemel doesn't trust Ollen to keep his mouth shut. He's a danger to him and his comrades. So he kills him.'

'It's a theory.'

'It is, I admit. But let's see what Xhemel has to say about it when we bring him in for questioning.'

Lampson looked thoughtful for a moment, then he said: 'Talking of theories, guv, I've got one on who did Big Mel.'

'Oh? One of Mel's victims that Barry Moss thought looked interesting?'

'Well, the ones I've talked to haven't been very promising, but there's one I haven't been able to get hold of. His name's Mike Bassett and he strikes me as the most likely candidate.'

'On what basis?'

'Do you remember Barry Moss told us about a warehouse that Joe Williams and Billy Thackeray knocked over, but they didn't even get charged?'

'The sugar,' recalled Coburg.

'That's the one,' said Lampson. 'Bassett owns the warehouse where the sugar was taken from. It was his manager who pulled back from his identification of Williams and Thackeray, and Bassett was livid about that. He wanted them both done for it. As well as McGuinness.'

'I'm sure plenty of his victims were pretty angry that they'd suffered, and McGuinness and his crew had got away with it.'

'Yes, but Bassett has suffered more than most. I think robbery at his warehouse was the last straw.'

'McGuinness and his mob had robbed him before?'

'No, I mean personal suffering. Family tragedies. I got all this from Bassett's next-door neighbour.' Lampson recounted what he'd been told by Mrs Hudson.

'And Thackeray and Williams walked away, as did McGuinness,' said Coburg thoughtfully.

'You see, guv, when the neighbour told me all this, I was remembering the sight of Billy Thackeray on the slab. He hadn't been just beaten to death, he'd been smashed over and over again, his face looked like a broken boiled egg. And I thought . . .'

Coburg looked at his sergeant admiringly.

'And you thought right! You're wasted as a sergeant, Ted. You should be an inspector.'

'I don't know about that, guv,' said Lampson awkwardly.

'Well, I do!' said Coburg.

'But we've got no proof,' said Lampson. 'Not in either case. Not with this Xhemel bloke or Bassett.'

'We've got strong enough suspicions to bring them both in for questioning,' said Coburg.

'Which one do we bring in first?'

'Both. We split it: you take some uniforms with you and bring in one, while I do the same and bring in the other. The sooner we lay this to rest, the better.'

'Right. Shall I take Bassett?' asked Lampson.

'No, I'll arrest Bassett, you take Xhemel.'

'Yeh, but Bassett's got a shooter, Xhemel's only got a knife.'

'Don't worry about me, I'll be carrying a gun,' Coburg told him. 'And I'm ordering you to book one out as well.

This Xhemel sounds like a nasty piece of work. So, do it by the book: hold the gun on him while you have him searched for weapons, and make sure the uniform who does it doesn't get between you and him.'

'I have done this before, guv,' complained Lampson.

'I know, but I want you to come back safe.'

'*You're* going up against a man armed with a shooter.'

'It'll be fine. In the last war people were lining up to shoot me, and I survived. I'll be armed, and I'll have backup. The same as you.' He copied Xhemel's address, and his place of work, on to a piece of paper and gave it to Lampson. 'Have you got the address for this Mike Bassett?'

Lampson handed it to him. 'Here, but he wasn't there when I called. I also tried his warehouse, but they say they've hardly seen him lately.'

'Well, he must be staying somewhere,' said Coburg. 'Did Sergeant Moss have any more information about him?'

Lampson shook his head. Coburg picked up the phone and put a call through to Waterloo police station.

'Sergeant Moss, it's DCI Coburg. Do you know where Mike Bassett hangs around when he's not at home or at his warehouse? I'd like a word with him, but we can't seem to track him down.'

'One of his workers at the warehouse says he seems to spend a lot at time at the cemetery,' said Moss.

Of course, thought Coburg. His dead family.

'Where were they buried? His wife and sons?'

'Only his wife and one of his sons,' said Moss. 'The one who was killed at Dunkirk, his body was never recovered. His missus and other son were laid to rest at West Norwood.'

West Norwood in Lambeth, thought Coburg. The regular cemetery for south London.

'Right, Ted, you go to the armoury and sort out weapons for both of us. I want a nice straightforward revolver, nothing where the bullets can get stuck. Also, arrange for uniformed officers to go with us. Two each, I suggest.'

'Will that be enough?' asked Lampson.

'Two will be enough for me,' said Coburg. 'I don't want to turn up with a small army, that's bound to set him off.' He stood up. 'I'd better go and tell the super what we're up to.'

'He should be pleased,' said Lampson. 'Two cases solved at once.'

'Only if we've got the right men,' said Coburg. 'At the moment, it's still supposition on both of them.'

Superintendent Allison looked up from his desk as Coburg entered his office.

'Come in, Coburg,' he said.

He's looking very unhappy, thought Coburg. *No, not just unhappy, there's simmering anger there as well. Well, whatever it is that's upset him, here's hoping my news will cheer him up.*

'There have been developments on both the murders at the Ritz, and the killing of Mel McGuinness and Billy Thackeray, sir,' he said. Briefly he outlined what they'd learnt, and their suspicions concerning both Anton Xhemel and Mike Bassett. Allison took it all in thoughtfully, but his face didn't reflect any pleasure at the news. On the contrary, he remained sombre.

'So, we're going to bring them both in for questioning. And if we're right, that'll be the four murders solved, along with Charley Barnes under lock and key for the killing of Den Bell.'

'Ah, I'm glad you mention Barnes,' said Allison, and he gave a deep and unhappy sigh.

Coburg looked at him quizzically; there was something in the superintendent's voice that suggested embarrassment, confirmed by the fact that he avoided looking at Coburg.

'We've had a complaint from the Home Office,' continued Allison.

'About what?'

'About Barnes being held in prison on remand when there's no hard evidence against him.'

'There is hard evidence. We have a witness who identified him.'

'But whose name you haven't disclosed.'

'If we disclose it at this stage, she'll be dead within twenty-four hours. You know that, sir; that's been the way that McGuinness and his crew have been able to stay out of jail, by threatening and even killing those who were ready to give evidence against them.'

'That may be so, but we have to look at the legal aspect. A very prominent Member of Parliament has raised the case of Mr Barnes with the Home Office—'

'Which Member of Parliament?' demanded Coburg angrily.

Allison hesitated, then said in an apologetic tone: 'Wister Gormley.'

Coburg stared at him, then burst into harsh laughter. 'First, he takes my car off me, now he comes to the aid of one of the most dangerous gangsters in London. As far as I'm concerned this shows he's hand in glove with Barnes and McGuinness's mob. I wonder how long he's been protecting their interests?'

'That may well be the case, Chief Inspector, but we are the law. We have to obey the rules as set down. For the moment, until you produce concrete evidence against Barnes, it looks as if we'll have to let him go.'

'He'll be dead before nightfall,' said Coburg grimly. As he said it, a new thought struck him. 'Which constituency does Gormley represent, sir? It's Westminster, isn't it?'

'Yes,' said Allison.

'North of the river,' said Coburg. 'I don't think he's working for Charley Barnes, even though Barnes may think he's acting for him. I think Gormley's doing it for Danny Bell.'

'If you're right, what do you suggest we do?' asked Allison.

'We do as our bosses say. We abide by the law. But, from now on, I'll be keeping a close eye on who Wister Gormley MP associates with.'

Lampson mounted the stairs of the lodging house where Xhemel had his room, two uniformed constables following him. Lampson held his pistol behind his back, ready to use. As he'd told the two constables, PCs Andrews and Penny, they suspected the man they were going to bring in had already killed two men. 'He uses a knife,' Lampson had told them. 'But he may also have a gun. He's dangerous, so be on your guard.'

They reached the door of Xhemel's room, and Lampson knocked at it. The door opened a crack and a moustached man looked out at them suspiciously, the same man in the photograph that Anna Gershon had picked out.

'Police,' said Lampson. 'Anton Xhemel?'

The man shook his head. 'Not here.'

'Nice try, but I've seen your photo,' said Lampson. As Xhemel began to close the door, Lampson put his boot against it and produced the pistol from behind his back. 'Step back and put your hands above your head.'

Xhemel hesitated, then did as he was ordered. Lampson pushed the door open, but waited until he was sure that Xhemel was standing with his hands in the air and that there was no one else in the room.

'Back up, nice and slow.'

Slowly Xhemel walked backwards into the room, stopping in the middle of it. Lampson and the two constables followed him in.

'Right, you'll keep your hands behind your head while the constable searches you. And if you try anything, I'll shoot you.' He nodded towards PC Penny.

The constable patted Xhemel down first, then felt inside his pockets, before stepping back.

'Nothing, sir. He hasn't got any weapons on him.'

'Good,' said Lampson, and he slipped the pistol back in his pocket, then produced a pair of handcuffs. 'Right, Mr Xhemel—'

That was as far as he got. Suddenly Xhemel produced a knife that he'd hidden inside the back collar of his shirt and he lashed out with it, the blade slicing through PC Penny's neck, sending a spray of blood. Lampson, momentarily stunned, gaped, then he moved, leaping towards Xhemel while at the same time reaching for the pistol in his pocket, but even as he was pulling the gun out Xhemel had turned on him, striking out with the knife, and Lampson felt a punch in his chest, followed by an intense pain that seemed to go through his whole body. As Xhemel pulled the blade out, Lampson saw blood gushing out from his chest, and then a terrible darkness began to close in on him and he felt himself falling . . .

CHAPTER THIRTY-NINE

His hand firmly holding the butt of the pistol in his jacket pocket, Coburg and the two constables followed the directions they'd been given at the cemetery office to the plot for the Bassett family. As they neared it, they saw the hunched figure of a man sitting on the grass next to a headstone. Keeping his distance, Coburg signalled for the constables to each move to one side and hold their positions, then he produced the pistol and held it aimed at the man.

'Mr Bassett,' he called. 'I'm Detective Chief Inspector Coburg from Scotland Yard. Please kneel and put both your hands in the air.'

The man turned and looked at Coburg, and even from a distance Coburg saw the expression of weary hopelessness on his face.

'On your knees, please, Mr Bassett. With your hands in the air,' he repeated.

Bassett shuffled into a kneeling position and raised his hands.

'The constables will approach and will search you. Do not attempt to resist them or attack them, or I will be forced to use this weapon. Do you understand?'

Bassett nodded.

'All right, go and check him out,' said Coburg. 'But keep to different sides, Edwards take his left and Johnson his right, and stay out of my line of fire.'

The constables nodded and walked warily towards Bassett, who remained kneeling on the grass. They reached him and Johnson stood back while Edwards went through his jacket pockets.

'Nothing, sir,' called Edwards. 'No weapon of any sort.'

'Stand up, please, Mr Bassett,' called Coburg. 'Keeping your hands in the air.'

Bassett rose to his feet and stood while Edwards stepped back, and Johnson took his turn to go through Bassett's trouser pockets and patting down his legs for any hidden weapons.

'Nothing, sir,' called Johnson.

Coburg took a pair of handcuffs from his pocket and approached, still holding the pistol aimed at Bassett. 'Turn around and lower your hands. Put them together behind your back.'

Bassett did as he was told. There was no resistance of any sort from him. His whole body posture was that of a man who'd given up.

Coburg handed the handcuffs to Edwards. 'Slip those on him,' he said.

Only when Bassett was securely handcuffed did Coburg put his pistol away.

'Michael Bassett, I am arresting you on suspicion of the murders of Melvyn McGuinness and William Thackeray—'

'I did it,' said Bassett, his voice sombre. 'I did both of them. And I'm glad!' As he said these last words, he suddenly seemed to come alive and he glared defiantly at Coburg.

'Mr Bassett, you don't have to say anything,' said Coburg, cautioning him, 'but anything you do say will be—'

'I did it!' repeated Bassett, almost exultant. 'They took everything, and they laughed at me!' Suddenly he dropped to the ground and turned on the grass to look at the headstone and the grave. There were three names carved on the stone but done at different times. 'When they went, all I had left was my business. My warehouse. And those bastards took that when they stole my sugar. I thought I had them because my warehouseman recognised the pair who did it: Billy Thackeray and Joe Williams. But when he got a visit from that bastard McGuinness, he backtracked, and the next thing I know, Thackeray and Williams are back out on the street.' He looked up and Coburg could see that the man was crying, tears rolling down his cheeks.

Bassett nodded towards the gravestone. 'See the names?' he said. He looked back at Coburg, a challenge giving fire to his eyes. 'Those bastards, McGuinness, Thackeray and Williams did nothing for their country, and both my boys died. And the thing that really got me was when Thackeray and Williams came round my house after they'd been released and laughed at me. Then Thackeray slapped me, hard, round the face and said: "We'll be back to your warehouse and we'll take whatever we want. And you'd better not try and stop us, or grass us to the Old Bill, or we'll carve your face into bits." And he produced this old-

348

fashioned cut-throat razor which he opened and waved it in my face, before shutting it and putting it back in his pocket.' Bassett shook his head. 'It was the last straw. I'd lost everyone I loved, but I'd decided to keep on going with the warehouse for the memory of Sonia and the boys. But Thackeray and Williams saying and doing what they did and getting away with it because they were McGuinness's men; it tainted everything. I had to get rid of them.

'Thackeray was the first. I went round his place when I knew he'd be dead drunk and helpless, because I'd been watching him. I half-carried him out to an alley where I did him with a leaded stick. Then I dumped him in the river. I went looking for Williams, but I couldn't find him. Then later I heard he'd been killed at the Ritz, so someone else had done for him. The next one was McGuinness himself. Again, I watched him, saw his routine. He was regular as clockwork. But before I did him, I wanted him to suffer. Which was why I torched one of his pubs. His pubs were precious to him, like my warehouse was to me. I wanted him to know he wasn't safe; he could be got. And then I got him. A bullet in the head.'

'Where did you get the gun?' asked Coburg.

A ghost of a smile appeared on Bassett's face. 'From Billy Thackeray's room. He had it in his bedside table.' He chuckled. 'It didn't save him, though.' Bassett pushed himself up off the grass. 'So that's the story, Inspector. You've got your man. And I'm glad I done it.' He turned towards the gravestone with the three names on it and said proudly: 'I did it, Sonia! I got them!'

As Coburg walked into the reception area of Scotland Yard with Mike Bassett and the two constables, he saw the duty sergeant gesturing him to come to the desk. Coburg knew immediately from the look on the man's face that something terrible wrong had happened.

'Take Mr Bassett to the cells,' he ordered the constables. 'I'll talk to him later.'

He hurried over to the desk.

'What is it?' he asked. 'What's happened?'

'It's Sergeant Lampson, sir. He's been stabbed. And one of the constables who was with him is dead, throat slashed.'

Coburg stared at him, then demanded urgently. 'What about Ted?'

'I don't know, sir. He was just about alive when they took him to the hospital, but he was in a very bad way. They reckon it's touch and go.'

'What about the other constable?'

'He's downstairs, sir, in the medical room, being sewn up. Superficial knife injuries, the doc says.'

'Which hospital was Ted taken to?'

'St Thomas's.'

'The constable who's being sewn up, what's his name?' he asked.

'Andrews, sir. Pete Andrews.'

Coburg nodded and headed for the medical room. PC Pete Andrews was stripped to the waist, his wounds being stitched by a nurse.

'DCI Coburg,' he said to the nurse. 'Can I talk to your patient?'

She nodded and continued with her needlework, PC Andrews wincing as she pushed it through the flesh of his hands and arms.

'What happened, Pete?' asked Coburg.

'We did all the right things, sir, by the book,' Andrews told him. 'Sergeant Lampson held his gun on him while PC Penny searched him. The suspect had his hands behind his head the whole time he was being searched, but there were no weapons on him. At least, that's what we thought, so Sergeant Lampson put his pistol away and started to take out a pair of handcuffs, when the bloke pulls a knife from inside the collar of his shirt, at the back. Before we could move he'd sliced it across Dave Penny's throat, then stabbed Sergeant Lampson. It went right into his chest. I tried to stop the prisoner, but he slashed at me and then ran. I was going to go after him, but I thought it was more important to see if I could save Sergeant Lampson.'

'You did the right thing,' said Coburg.

As Coburg headed for the door, PC Andrews called after him: 'Will Sergeant Lampson be all right, sir?'

'That's what I'm going to try and find out,' said Coburg.

CHAPTER FORTY

Coburg drove to St Thomas's Hospital, where initially he received a rather frosty reception from a staff nurse and was told that visiting hours were strictly enforced, until he produced his warrant card and identified himself as a detective chief inspector from Scotland Yard, the immediate superior of Sergeant Edward Lampson who had been admitted to the hospital with serious knife wounds sustained in an attack, which the police were investigating. At this, her attitude changed.

'I'm sorry if I seemed officious,' she apologised, 'but we have a great many people being brought in, especially from some areas of Kent where the local hospitals are being overwhelmed.'

'I undestand,' said Coburg. 'But I would be grateful if you could let me know what Sergeant Lampson's chances are.'

Her hesitation gave Coburg his answer.

'Look, I know how protocol works,' he said. 'As a detective chief inspector, we also have to stick to the rules and regulations. But if you're not allowed to tell me, I'd be grateful if you could find someone who can. Sergeant Lampson and I have worked closely together for some years. He's more than a colleague, he's a friend, and I want to know whether I'm looking for his assailant or his murderer.'

'At the moment, it's too early to say,' she told him. 'He was brought in and taken immediately to the operating theatre, where he's undergoing surgery as we speak. His injuries were very serious. I understand he could be in theatre for some time. If you'd like to leave your telephone number, I'll do my best to get someone to phone as soon as he's out of surgery.'

'Thank you,' said Coburg. He gave her his extension at Scotland Yard, and his home telephone number. 'And, if you don't mind, I'll return later, in case there's any news.'

His next visit was to Lampson's parents' house in Somers Town. Mr and Mrs Lampson were surprised, and also worried, to see Coburg, who they'd met a few times before.

'What's happened?' asked Mr Lampson as they ushered him to the parlour, the front room that was never used except for special guests.

'Is Terry around?' asked Coburg.

'Terry!' exploded Mr Lampson angrily. 'Is this about something he's been up to? He's getting out of control with that gang he hangs around with!'

'No, nothing like that,' Coburg reassured them. 'I just wanted to know if he was here.'

'No. He's out with his mates.'

'In that case, I've come to tell you there's been a . . . bad situation.'

'Ted's not dead!' gasped Mrs Lampson urgently, and she grabbed her husband's hand.

'No,' said Coburg quickly. 'No, he's not dead, but he's been injured.'

'How?' asked Mr Lampson.

'He went to bring in a man for questioning, and the man stabbed him. He's at St Thomas's hospital, being operated on right at this moment.'

'How is he?' asked Mr Lampson.

'Is he going to live?' pleaded Mrs Lampson.

Coburg hesitated, then said: 'I have to say I don't know how badly he was hurt. I wasn't with him when it happened. I only heard about it when I got back to the Yard. I've just come from the hospital and they couldn't tell me anything except the fact that he was being operated on. I've asked them to contact me as soon as he's out of surgery, and when I hear I promise I'll come and tell you what I know.'

Mrs Lampson began to cry. 'First my sister, now this!'

'St Thomas's is one of the very best hospitals in the country,' said Coburg. 'If anyone can help him recover, they can.'

The couple nodded, Mr Lampson with his arm around his wife as she struggled to stop crying.

'Thank you for coming, Chief Inspector,' said Mr Lampson.

'I'll be back as soon as I know anything.' Coburg promised them.

He left the Lampsons and made his way to Paddington and the home of PC Penny. Unlike with Mr and Mrs Lampson, he didn't know any of Penny's family, or whether the constable had been married. As it turned out he'd been single but engaged to be married. Coburg was told this by Penny's mother in between her tears as she sat on the sofa in their living room in a state of shock and then painful misery, while PC Penny's father – himself a former policeman – watched impassively. Mr Penny walked him to the front door after Coburg felt there was little more he could add.

'Thank you for coming to inform us personally, sir,' said Mr Penny. 'In the old days the best you could hope for was a visit from the station sergeant, but even that was a rarity.'

'Your son was a brave man who died doing his duty,' said Coburg. 'My calling to let you know was the very least I could do. He deserved better, and I promise you I'll track down the man who did it and bring him to justice. Once again, Mr Penny, my deepest sympathies to you and your wife, and your son's fiancée.'

On his return to Scotland Yard, the first thing Coburg did was set in motion a mass search for Anton Xhemel, making sure the photograph of the wanted man and his description was circulated to every police station. Then he telephoned Sir Vincent Blessington at the Foreign Office.

'We've identified the man who committed the murders at the Ritz,' he told him. 'He's Anton Xhemel, an Albanian. Unfortunately, when my sergeant and two constables went to his address to bring him in for questioning, he attacked them. One of the constables is dead and my sergeant was seriously injured. They're not sure if he's going to survive.'

'My God!' said Blessington. 'Is there anything I can do?'

'There may be,' said Coburg. 'Would you come with me

to see Inspector Hibbert at MI5? My hope is that if we pool our knowledge we might be able to work out where he's lying low. There's a police search on for him, but the longer it goes on, the more chance there is he'll get away. I want to bring him in now, within the next few hours.'

'Of course,' said Blessington. 'Have you spoken to Inspector Hibbert about this?'

'Not yet,' said Coburg. 'I wanted to check with you first. I'm going to call him now.'

'In that case, give me a while to make some phone calls. I was supposed to be meeting some people, so I need to rearrange that. Then I'll meet you at Hibbert's office. He's still at Wormwood Scrubs, I assume.'

'He is,' said Coburg. 'I'll call him now and will only contact you again if he's not available.'

'That's fine,' said Blessington. 'And I'm most awfully sorry about your colleagues. Trust me, we'll do everything we can to catch this man.'

Coburg's next call was to Hibbert. As soon as the MI5 inspector learnt what had happened, he, too, gave his pledge to help in the speedy capture of Xhemel.

'I was due to go to a security meeting, but that can wait. You and Blessington get over here as soon as you can, and we'll see how quickly we can nail this bastard.'

My sentiments exactly, thought Coburg determinedly. *I'm going to nail him, alive or dead.*

The mood was grim when Coburg, Blessington and Hibbert gathered in the MI5 inspector's office.

'Do they think your sergeant will pull through?' asked Hibbert.

'The hostpial staff don't know,' said Coburg. 'When I spoke to them he was still undergoing surgery. The thing is we don't know where Xhemel might go to hide. You've both had experience of the Albanian community, and those who are communists. Where might he seek refuge? Somewhere abroad?'

'No,' said Blessington. 'Mainland Europe is under Nazi control, except for the parts that are occupied by the Italians.'

'There's always Russia,' said Hibbert.

'But how would Xhemel get to Russia?' asked Blessington. 'He won't be able to get there through Nazi-occupied Europe. The only way would be by sea right up into the Arctic Circle, and unless he's very rich and can buy his way there—'

'The Soviet embassy in London,' said Hibbert. 'He'd seek refuge there.'

'They won't allow that,' said Blessington.

'Of course they will,' snorted Hibbert. 'My guess is Xhemel was trying to raise massive funds to further the communist cause in Eastern Europe. It wouldn't surprise me to discover that he had some kind of arrangement with the Soviets for transferring the money.'

'That would make sense,' said Coburg. 'It had puzzled me how he planned to move the bullion. That much gold isn't easy to transport with just a couple of helpers. If you're right, Xhemel must have had a truck parked outside with some of his Albanian communist pals, along with a Russian commissar or two. Their plan would be to take the bullion and the money to the Soviet embassy. It'd be safe there on diplomatic territory.'

'I can't accept that,' said Blessington. 'Whatever

your opinion is of the Russians, the idea that a foreign government would assist in carrying out a robbery on the soil of another nation—'

'If you look at what Nazis have done since they occupied France and Belgium, it's exactly that,' argued Hibbert.

'Yes, but those are in nations they've occupied,' insisted Blessington. 'This is altogether different. It's against the rules of international diplomacy for a foreign government—'

'Yes, yes, all right,' said Hibbert impatiently. 'How about a rogue element inside the embassy, using the place for such an action, but without the knowledge of the Soviet government?'

Blessington paused to consider this, then nodded. 'Yes, I can admit to that as a possibility. Every nation's organisations can harbour rogue elements.'

Hibbert gave Coburg a look that clearly said that his thoughts were that Blessington was either being naive or overtly diplomatic. He reached for his phone.

'Who are you calling?' asked Blessington, concerned.

'I'm arranging for some men to head for the Soviet embassy to keep watch for Xhemel. If he tries to get in they'll pick him up.'

'He may be in there already,' said Coburg grimly.

Hibbert shook his head. 'No. If he was, we'd have heard.'

Of course, thought Coburg. MI5 will have an agent inside the embassy, just like every other embassy seemed to be riddled with foreign agents.

'Get me operations!' barked Hibbert.

* * *

Coburg returned to Scotland Yard and immediately checked to see if there had been any sightings of Xhemel, but so far everyone had drawn a blank. He was hiding somewhere, and if Hibbert was right, sooner or later he'd make for the Soviet embassy. But say he didn't? Say instead he headed out of London? He wrote out an 'Alert all stations' with details of Xhemel, his physical description and the additional information about him being an Albanian communist, and requesting all forces to investigate their local Albanian or communist communities. He took this to the wireless communications room, along with an image of Xhemel and asked for it to be distributed urgently. That done, he returned to his office and telephoned Count Ahmed at the Ritz.

'Count, I have some news. There has been a development.'

'What sort of development?'

'We are now fairly sure we know the identity of the man who killed the man in your suite, and also the kitchen hand. His name is Anton Xhemel, and he's an Albanian. And, according to our intelligence, a communist.'

'Ah,' said Ahmed. 'So, my suggestion was accurate.'

'We don't know for sure, and we won't know until we can apprehend him.'

'So, you do not have him in custody?'

'No. He attacked the officers who went to bring him in for questioning and managed to escape.'

'Were the officers badly hurt?'

'Unfortunately, one was killed and another is in hospital; it's not certain if he will survive.'

There was a silence, then Ahmed said: 'My

condolences, Chief Inspector. But his violent action is surely proof of his guilt.'

'Perhaps,' said Coburg.

'Thank you for informing me,' said Ahmed. 'If there is anything I can do to help the apprehension of this person, don't hesitate to contact me.'

No sooner had he hung up than the phone rang.

'It's St Thomas's Hospital for you, Chief Inspector,' the operator told him.

'Put them through.'

This was the call he'd been dreading, the fact that the news would be bad. *Please let him be alive*, he prayed silently. *Please let him be alive.* 'Thank you for calling. How is Sergeant Lampson?'

'He's out of surgery and in recovery,' the nurse said.

Thank God! Coburg exhaled a tightly held breath.

'He's still unconscious and will be for some time,' she continued. 'His family came to the hospital, but we told them they won't be able to see him today. If he's fit enough tomorrow they might be able to see him for a few minutes, but that's not certain. If you see them, we'd be grateful if you'd reinforce that to them. The hospital is very busy and dealing with visitors takes time away from treating patients.'

'I understand,' said Coburg. 'And I'll certainly pass that on to them. From a medical perspective, what are his chances?'

'Of surviving?'

'Yes.'

'Fortunately, although the knife penetrated part of one lung, it didn't damage any other vital organs. He's also a

360

fit, healthy man, so we're holding out hope that he'll make a full recovery.'

'Thank you,' said Coburg. 'If he wakes, will you pass on my good wishes to him and tell him I'll be in tomorrow.'

'He may not be in a fit state to receive visitors tomorrow,' said the nurse.

'I'll call in anyway,' said Coburg.

He noticed that his hand was trembling as he replaced the receiver. Lampson was alive, that was all that mattered. When he left the Yard he'd make a point of calling at his parents' house and passing that on to them.

His phone rang again. This time it was the desk sergeant in reception.

'Sorry to trouble you, sir,' he said. 'There's a Commander Fleming to see you.'

Coburg paused, bewildered. Fleming? Could it be . . . ?

'Did he give his first name?' he asked.

Coburg heard the desk sergeant ask and heard the reply: 'Ian.'

'Ian, sir,' said the sergeant.

'Get a constable to bring him up.'

CHAPTER FORTY-ONE

What on earth was Ian Fleming doing here? Coburg wondered. It had to be related to the Albanian money. After all, it had been Fleming who'd helped smuggle King Zog to safety from Nazi-occupied Europe and into Britain.

There was a tap at his door, then a constable opened it and Fleming entered. It had been years since Coburg had last set eyes on him at some social event, but Fleming still had that air of authority about him. Almost regal. Tall, ruggedly handsome, his broken nose adding to the swaggering pirate image. He looked remarkably well for a man in his thirties who'd seen such action.

Coburg gestured for Fleming to sit and declined the offer of a cigarette from the man's gold-plated case.

'You still don't smoke?' asked Fleming, lighting up. 'Even in this time of death and danger?'

'I lost a lung,' said Coburg. 'I want to keep the one I have left healthy.'

'It hasn't done me any harm,' said Fleming. 'I'm still fit.'

Yes, he was, thought Coburg. He always had been.

'You asked the desk sergeant for my first name,' said Fleming. 'Was that some kind of security check to see if it really was me?'

'No, I wondered whether it was you or Peter.'

'Peter's not a commander,' said Fleming.

'But he is in Intelligence,' said Coburg.

'Is he?' asked Fleming airily. 'Our paths haven't crossed much lately.'

Unlikely, thought Coburg. Ian and Peter Fleming had always been close and supportive of each other, though there was no doubt some rivalry between them, mostly from Ian, the younger brother by a year being slightly jealous of his older sibling.

'What can I do for you?' asked Coburg.

'This character Anton Xhemel,' said Fleming. 'The one who did the killings at the Ritz.'

'We don't know that for sure,' said Coburg carefully. 'At this stage we just want to talk to him.'

'Oh, come on, Coburg,' scoffed Fleming. 'He stabbed your sergeant and killed a constable.'

'You're very well informed,' said Coburg. 'Hibbert's crowd?'

'I have contacts,' said Fleming.

'Let me guess,' said Coburg responding to a sudden insight. 'You had a call from our mutual friend Count Idjbil Ahmed.'

'The Count is very concerned about the King's safety,' acknowledged Fleming. 'This man Xhemel is an obvious enemy of the King and has shown he is ruthless in his ambitions. Count Ahmed would like him to be apprehended very quickly.'

'So would we, which is why we're doing everything we can to get hold of him.'

'The Count wonders if I can be of any assistance to you.'

'In what way "be of assistance"?' asked Coburg.

'In any way you think I can help. I know Albanians. I've heard on the grapevine about the Soviet embassy very likely being involved. I think that's correct. I warned the powers that be some time ago about the dangers the Russians posed. I wouldn't trust Joe Stalin as far as I can spit.'

'I understood you were quite a champion spitter,' said Coburg. 'Someone said to me that it was a pity that spitting wasn't part of the *Victor ludorum* at Eton or you'd have won even more times than you did.'

Fleming laughed, a genuine guffaw. 'Very good,' he chuckled. 'You, too, have been doing your homework. Is that because I was under suspicion?'

'No,' said Coburg, 'but when I discovered you were the one who brought King Zog to England, I was curious. And impressed. That was quite some achievement, getting a crowd that large out from under the noses of the Nazis and across the Channel.'

'I didn't do it all on my own. I had help.'

'Is this an official visit from MI5 or Six?' asked Coburg.

Fleming shook his head. 'If you like, it's an offer from one old Etonian to another. Particularly as you were a bit of a hero to my brother. Peter was a great admirer of yours.'

'I'd left Eton by the time you and he were there.'

364

'Yes, but your exploits were talked about. Not just at school, but during the war. That charge you led at Sambre–Oise, one of the last of the war. Peter saw it as one of the finest examples of heroism in the face of the enemy.'

'I got shot in that attack,' said Coburg. 'That's where I lost my lung.'

'But you gained a reputation.'

'For rash actions.'

'And so inspiring the Fleming brothers to deeds of derring-do as schoolboys.' Fleming smiled. 'Peter was the most daring, of course, but I did my utmost to outdo him. Which is why I was eventually asked to leave the school. So, you see, DCI Coburg, my leaving Eton was partly your fault. So, to clear your conscience—'

This time it was Coburg who laughed. 'My God, Fleming, you are absolutely outrageous. You have no shame. You take risks the whole time.'

'If I hadn't, King Zog and his retinue would not be safe in London now. Look, Coburg, I can be invaluable. I have contacts. I'm a damn good shot, and I'm not bound by the rules you and the police have to stick to.'

'Whose rules are you bound by?' asked Coburg. 'MI5? Naval Intelligence?'

In answer, Fleming smiled. *No*, thought Coburg. *He plays by his own rules.*

'Xhemel's dangerous,' said Fleming.

'You know him?'

'No, but I know the sort of fanatic he is. He's shown that by his actions.' He stood up and produced a visiting card with 'Commander I. L. Fleming' printed on it, which he passed to Coburg. 'There's a number you can reach me on if you need me. I really would like to help.'

'Thank you,' said Coburg. 'I'll bear that in mind. And that's not a platitude, I mean it. I intend to get this bastard.'

The two men shook hands, and Fleming left. Coburg slipped the visiting card in his wallet. Reckless, dangerous, yes, Fleming still was all those things Coburg had complained to Lampson about, but he also knew that if you were in a tight spot there was no one better to be with than Ian Fleming.

Coburg loooked at his watch. It was time to call on Lampson's parents; and then afterwards to see Rosa. By now she should be preparing for her evening's performance. The thought of her put a smile on his face for the first time since he and Lampson had gone to make their separate arrests earlier that day.

Stay strong, Ted, he thought silently as he left the office.

He was walking across the reception hall heading for the car park at the rear, when the duty desk sergeant hailed him. Not more bad news, he groaned inwardly.

'Yes?' he asked warily.

'We just heard about a disturbance at Wandsworth nick about an hour ago.'

'Oh?'

'Charley Barnes was coming out, being released, and there were a couple of his mob there to meet him. Suddenly a car turns up and two blokes jump out and grab hold of Barnes. One of the blokes who'd come to meet Barnes pulls out a gun and there's shooting, leaving one of Barnes's men dead and another wounded.'

'And Barnes?' asked Coburg.

'Gone. Bundled into the car and driven off.'

'Does the super know?' asked Coburg.

'Yes, sir. What shall I tell him if he comes looking for you?'

'Tell him I've gone to see Sergeant Lampson's family, and afterwards I've got people to meet. I'll talk to him tomorrow.'

With that, Coburg made for the car park.

So, Danny Bell will have his personal revenge after all, he thought.

CHAPTER FORTY-TWO

Once again, Coburg noted there was no sign of Raymond Harris at the Rivoli Bar that night. But any thoughts about him and the reason for his non-appearance vanished as soon as Rosa appeared, sat down at the piano and swung into her first number. Song after song, tune after tune flowed, each one getting a rapturous reception from the audience.

This place will miss her when she leaves at the end of the week, thought Coburg. *But I'm glad she's still going to be in London.*

'OK,' said Rosa as they drove to Hampstead after the show. 'What's wrong?'

'Wrong?' he asked. 'Nothing! You were fabulous tonight. And that's not just me saying it, didn't you hear that audience? Incredible!'

'I'm not talking about me, I'm asking about you,' said Rosa. 'There's a sadness about you tonight. Is it because the St John Ambulance want me? You're worried about me going out to incidents?'

'Absolutely not!' said Coburg. 'I think it's brilliant what you're doing. Of course I'm going to be worried every time you go out, but I'm proud of you.'

'So, what is it?'

'My sergeant, Ted Lampson, got stabbed today,' said Coburg. 'He's in hospital. He has been operated on, but it was touch and go if he'd make it. I think it still is. And a constable with him was killed by the same man who stabbed Ted.'

'My God!' breathed Rosa, horrified.

'I'm feeling guilty about it,' admitted Coburg.

'Why?'

'We had two murderers to bring in, so we split up. I thought the one he was bringing in was the least dangerous, but as it turned out my one came quietly.'

'It could have been you being stabbed,' Rosa pointed out. 'Now call me selfish, but—'

'Yes, OK,' said Coburg. 'I'm sorry, I wasn't going to tell you because I didn't want to ruin your night at the Ritz with more gory details.'

'It's your job,' said Rosa. 'It's what you do. And as we're going to get married, I'm going to have to live with it.' She reached out and patted him on the thigh. 'And because I love you, I will. Now, let's put all that away for the rest of the night and let it be just us. And tomorrow, you can go and see your sergeant in hospital, and once you've seen he's on the way to recovery, you'll feel better. Trust me.'

'I do,' said Coburg.

Once they were in Coburg's flat, it was Coburg who raised the topic of their wedding.

'I think we should fix it for sooner rather than let it drift on,' he said. 'It's wartime and it won't be long before the bombs start really raining down on us. Let's get married before that happens.'

'When do you suggest?' asked Rosa.

'Next week,' proposed Coburg.

'That soon?'

'Next week you're still in London. The week after you're off to Scotland, and who knows what will happen after that.'

'Can we get married as quickly as that?' asked Rosa. 'I thought it took weeks after the banns had been read.'

'That's for church weddings,' said Coburg. 'I'm sure we can do it if we go for a registry office, but I'll check it out.' He looked at her, concerned. 'You're sure you still feel the same about it?'

'More than ever,' she said. 'But I don't think we should rush it like that.'

He looked at her, puzzled, and worried. 'Why not?'

She reached out and put her hand on his and squeezed it.

'Honey, I've seen too many cases – especially in my business – where people rush into marriage and six months later it's all over. I don't want that for us. Yes, I believe you love me, and I sure love you. But a marriage is more than just about being in love. I want to get to know you properly first. Meet your family and your friends. I want you to meet my family too, and as they're in Scotland that's going to take time to organise.' She squeezed his hand again. 'This isn't me having second thoughts, it's me determined that this marriage isn't going to be a flash in the pan. I want it to last. OK, a bomb may finish us off in the next month, but I'm not going to use that as an excuse.'

Coburg was silent for a moment, then he smiled at her, a genuine smile of love.

'I thought I was supposed to be the sensible one and you artistes were the impetuous, take-a-risk types.'

'I am, but not with something like this. This is too important.'

He squeezed her hand. 'I am the luckiest man alive.'

CHAPTER FORTY-THREE

Wednesday 28th August

Next morning, as they left Coburg's small block of flats, three men stepped out from behind the nearest corner of the building. Each was holding a pistol pointed at Coburg and Rosa. Coburg's heart sank as he recognised Anton Xhemel. *No!* he thought. *Not now!*

Rosa looked at the men, startled, then at Coburg.

'Edgar—' she began.

'Quiet!' snapped Xhemel. 'No talking.' He scowled at Coburg. 'You know who I am?'

Coburg nodded, his mind racing. What could he do? He no longer had the pistol on him, that had been returned to the armoury. And even if he still had it, they'd shoot him and Rosa before he had a chance to use it.

'You are the detective from Scotland Yard,' said Xhemel flatly. 'Coburg.'

'Whatever you want me for, this young lady is nothing to do with anything,' said Coburg.

Xhemel gave a sarcastic smile. 'Far from it. She is our guarantee you will behave. If you do not, we will shoot her first and then you.'

Rosa looked at Coburg in alarm.

'Don't worry,' said Coburg with a confidence he did not feel. 'We'll go along with it.'

Inside, his mind was racing. Whatever Xhemel's plans for them, he assumed that keeping them alive was not part of it. The only thing he could do was pretend to go along with it, all the while looking for an opportunity to get away. Or, at least, to get Rosa away to safety.

'You will drive us in your car to the Soviet embassy,' said Xhemel. 'Your Intelligence people are watching the building, but they will not stop a police car. You will drive and the woman will sit next to you. We will be sitting in the back. Our guns will be aimed at you. Any tricks and we will shoot you both.'

'There'll be no tricks,' said Coburg.

As they walked to the police car, he wondered if he'd be able to start the engine and drive away before the three men got in, but any hope of that vanished as Xhemel's two henchmen climbed into the back first.

'In,' Xhemel ordered Coburg and Rosa curtly.

Coburg slid behind the steering wheel and Rosa got into the passenger seat next to him.

'This is a bad move,' said Coburg. 'As you say, the embassy is being watched. You'll be caught. Why not just walk away now? Make for somewhere else.'

Xhemel gave his sarcastic laugh again. 'So you can chase us? No. Drive to the embassy.'

Coburg set the vehicle in motion. The Soviet embassy occupied three adjacent terraced properties which together formed a magnificent, large white building at the junction with Bayswater Road. It was surrounded by a high fence of spiked metal poles, behind which were tall trees. Coburg assumed that Xhemel must have already made contact with someone inside the embassy so that the gates and the heavy front doors could be opened on his arrival, and he and his companions could disappear inside. And what then? Would they have already gained diplomatic immunity, preventing them from being arrested? And what would they do with Coburg and Rosa when they arrived?

They'll take us in with them, Coburg realised. They would be bargaining chips. Hostages. The embassy staff would claim that the Albanians had burst in and held them at gunpoint. The Soviets were powerless, prisoners in their own embassy, would be their defence. There was no collusion. They would warn the British authorities against trying to enter the embassy because that would risk the lives of Coburg and Rosa.

And then what? They'd keep this stalemate situation going in the hope that their ally, Nazi Germany, would invade England, and then it would be all over and Xhemel and his friends would walk free.

Or perhaps not? Coburg knew that beneath the embassy ran tunnels, some linked to adjacent buildings. Had they an escape planned?

One thing Coburg was intent on, he would do everything he could to make sure Xhemel didn't get away. But he had to make sure that Rosa was safe. At all costs, he had to make sure she didn't set foot inside the embassy, even if they managed to drag him in through its doors. Once they got her inside the risks to her became even worse.

He reached across and patted Rosa's thigh. 'We'll be all right,' he assured her.

'No talking!' grunted Xhemel.

As they drove to the embassy, Coburg considered smashing the car into something, another vehicle, but he dismissed the idea. Xhemel would shoot at once. Instead he continued to Kensington Park Gardens. There were some cars parked at the side of the street, but a space had been left clear right in front of the gates. Coburg saw that some of the parked cars had men in them, and guessed they were Hibbert's crowd keeping a close watch on the embassy, staying alert for Xhemel to appear. If he could prevent them going into the grounds, there was a chance that Hibbert's men would move in. But how would Xhemel react? He was a man with nothing to lose. The likelihood would be that he'd start shooting. Coburg assumed that Hibbert's men, unlike the regular police, would be armed.

Coburg pulled in to the kerb, hoping that his arrival would catch the attention of Hibbert's watchers. It was a police car, after all, and he hoped they might wonder why such a vehicle was calling at the embassy. After he'd stopped the car, he let the engine idle for a moment, doing his best to gain time, but there was no sign of movement from the parked cars.

I'll have to see if I can stall him once we get out of the car, he thought.

'Out!' ordered Xhemel, and he flourished his pistol at them.

Coburg took Rosa's hand and squeezed it, then they both got out of the car. Xhemel and his two comrades also exited and waited until Coburg and Rosa had set foot on the pavement before moving to join them. It was just a short distance across the pavement to the gate, which had been left open. Coburg looked beyond the gate and saw that the front door was also ajar.

They were expected.

He stopped.

'We're here,' he said over his shoulder. 'We've delivered you. Now—'

'You are playing for time!' hissed Xhemel. 'In!' And he prodded Coburg in the back with his gun to urge him forward.

This was the moment Coburg had been waiting for, for Xhemel to be up close with the gun. Immediately he struck out, knocking the gun sideways with one hand and swinging his other arm up and backwards, smashing his elbow into Xhemel's face. There was the sound of a gun going off up close, and then, out of the corner of his eye, he saw Rosa stagger and then fall. He swung round and saw one of Xhemel's men holding a gun with smoke coming from the barrel, and he threw himself at the man, but Xhemel lurched forward, his gun aimed at Coburg's head.

BANG!

Xhemel's head suddenly disappeared in an explosion of blood which sprayed into Coburg's face. There was another shot, and then the man who'd shot Rosa dropped to the ground.

'Gun down!' shouted a voice, which Coburg recognised as Fleming's.

The other man immediately dropped his gun and put his hands in the air. Coburg turned and ran towards Rosa, who was lying face down on the pavement, her clothes soaked in blood.

'No!' he howled.

He dropped to his knees and lifted her up and turned her over.

'Ow!' she said, her face twisted in pain. 'I think my arm's broken.'

He looked and saw blood where the bullet had torn through her arm.

'Bang goes my week at Ciro's,' she said, forcing a painful grin.

'The bastards!' barked an angry American voice. Coburg looked up at Raymond Harris standing next to Fleming, a gun in his hand.

Other men were appearing, running towards them from the parked cars, some armed. Coburg shot a look towards the embassy and saw the heavy wooden door close.

'Is she all right?' asked Fleming.

'Thank you, whoever you are,' muttered Rosa. 'I can talk for myself.'

And then she fainted.

CHAPTER FORTY-FOUR

Coburg walked down the ward at St Thomas's hospital to where Rosa lay in bed, her left arm in plaster from her shoulder to her wrist, and put the bunch of flowers and box of chocolates he'd brought on the bedside cabinet. He leant forward and kissed her.

'This is against the rules,' she told him. 'They're very strict about keeping to visiting hours. You'll get me into trouble.'

'I'm not a visitor,' said Coburg. 'I'm a detective chief inspector on an investigation come to talk to the victim of a crime.'

'Do you bring flowers and chocolates to all the people you have to talk to? And kiss them?'

'It's part of my special interrogation technique,' said Coburg.

'I bet you're a wow at Scotland Yard,' she said.

'How's the arm?'

'Still broken. Fortunately, I'm on some very strong painkillers, but they say it's going to be a while before I'm up and about.'

'So, no Ciro's next week?'

'Or Glasgow the week after.' She looked at him inquisitively. 'Was that really Raymond Harris in all that shooting?'

'It was,' said Coburg. 'He was there in his role as a secret agent.'

'Not secret any more,' commented Rosa.

'His name won't appear anywhere in any report,' said Coburg. 'Officially, he's still a record producer.'

'Who carries a gun.'

'I understand there are very few Americans who don't,' said Coburg.

'And that tall fellow he was with?'

'Commander Ian Fleming, Naval Intelligence. He and your producer friend were part of Hibbert's watch on the Soviet embassy.'

'I'm going to need some new clothes. Mine were ruined. I've never seen so much blood.'

'Most of it was from Xhemel and the man who shot you.' He looked down at her. 'I thought you were dead. When I saw all that blood everywhere around you . . .'

'I would have been if your pals hadn't turned up. And you would have been, too. Is it always like this for you? People trying to kill you?'

'No. Mostly it can be quite boring, usually just hanging around waiting for answers.'

'Thank heavens for that,' said Rosa. 'After this, I like

boring.' She reached out and took his hand. 'You know what I said about waiting to get married? After this, I'm thinking, the hell with it. Let's do it.'

'When?'

'The sooner the better. I mean, the captain of a ship can marry people. Is there some equivalent in hospitals?'

'Matron?' asked Coburg, and he laughed. 'Now that would be some event.' He bent down and kissed her again. 'I'll see what I can do.'

He walked away feeling happier than he'd felt in a long time. Yes, the woman he loved was stuck in a hospital bed, but she was alive and she'd recover. And the man who'd tried to kill Lampson was dead.

The men's ward was on the next floor up, and Coburg was relieved to discover that the nurse he'd previously spoken to was on duty; it saved lengthy explanations to get round the ban on visitors outside of regular visiting hours.

'Your sergeant is doing well,' she said.

He followed her along the ward to where Lampson was sitting up in bed and reading a newspaper.

'Guv'nor!' He beamed.

'Sergeant!' Coburg smiled back. 'How are you feeling?'

'Considering what happened, pretty good. They reckon I was lucky: the knife missed my vital organs. What's happened? Is there any word on Xhemel?'

'There is. He's dead. And so is one of his accomplices, with the third in custody, and he's been singing like a bird. We've got the whole story. Joe Williams interrupted them in the Count's suite as they were preparing to enter the King's suite to steal the money and bullion, and they killed him. That caused them to panic and they ran.'

'How did they plan to get it away? All that gold is some weight.'

Coburg filled him in on the Russian connection, and the involvement of the Intelligence forces in bringing the case to a close. 'Xhemel also killed Ollen to stop him talking.'

'So, it's all done and dusted,' said Lampson.

'It is.'

'What's next?'

'Next is you recover, and we'll see what else we have to deal with. In the meantime, is there anything you need? Books, magazines?'

Lampson shook his head. 'My mum and dad are bringing Terry in at visiting time. I'll let them do that, thanks, guv. It makes them feel useful.' He gave an apologetic grin. 'To be honest, I feel a bit of fraud being here. I'm hoping it won't be long before they kick me out.'

'Be careful, Ted. You had a serious injury. You could have died. Don't overdo it and try and get back before your body's ready. Do what they tell you.'

'Right, guv. I promise I'll follow orders.'

As Coburg left the ward, he reflected he hadn't told Lampson about the snatching of Charley Barnes. He'd find out soon enough, if Barnes's body turned up. Which Coburg doubted. In the meantime, there was a war to win. And a wedding to organise.

ACKNOWLEDGEMENTS

I would like to acknowledge the debt I – and all of us – owe to those who fought to defeat Nazi tyranny, with many paying the ultimate tragic price. I stress Nazi, rather than German, because – despite being born in central London in 1944 and therefore coming under siege from both V1 and V2 rockets – I think most of us who were born during the war, or immediately after, realised that the enemy were not the German or Italian people, but the extremist politicians who led those countries. I survived the war, millions didn't. I will always be grateful to those on the Home Front, as well as the armed forces fighting abroad, who kept us alive and as safe as they could, while putting themselves in danger.

JIM ELDRIDGE was born in central London towards the end of World War II, and survived attacks by V2 rockets on the Kings Cross area where he lived. In 1971 he sold his first sitcom, starring Arthur Lowe, to the BBC and had his first book commissioned. Since then he has had more than one hundred books published, with sales of over three million copies. He lives in Kent with his wife.

jimeldridge.com